THE GARGOYLE CONSPIRACY

Books by Marvin H. Albert

THE GARGOYLE CONSPIRACY

BROADSIDES AND BOARDERS

THE DIVORCE

THE GARGOYLE CONSPIRACY

Marvin H. Albert

Doubleday & Company, Inc.
Garden City, New York
1975

Library of Congress Cataloging in Publication Data

Albert, Marvin H
    The gargoyle conspiracy.

    I. Title.
PZ.A333Gar [PS3551.L26]   813'.5'4
ISBN 0-385-08562-1
Library of Congress Catalog Card Number 74–18777

To Scott Meredith

The creativity and pathology of the human mind are, after all, two sides of the same medal coined in the evolutionary mint. The first is responsible for the splendour of our cathedrals, the second for the gargoyles that decorate them to remind us that the world is full of monsters, devils and succubi. They reflect the streak of insanity which runs through the history of our species, and which indicates that somewhere along the line of its ascent to prominence something has gone wrong.

—Arthur Koestler

THE GARGOYLE CONSPIRACY

ONE

In 1973 planes flying international routes carried almost one hundred million passengers. Of these passengers, one thousand were killed. Statistically, this ratio of numbers killed to total number of air travelers represents a very small percentage. But the thousand who died perished without being aware of the comforting statistic. And it does not ease the aching emptiness left in people who loved and needed the five who were killed at Rome's Leonardo da Vinci Airport in the early spring of that year.

Afterward, no one who had been in the airport's International Terminal that morning was able to remember seeing the darkly good-looking boy who'd given Marjorie Kavanagh the box of chocolates. He didn't accompany her to the Pan American ticket counter. He stayed instead near the aisle leading to boarding control, waiting nervously while she confirmed her seat reservation and checked through her single suitcase.

She looked a little breathless when she came back to him carrying ticket, boarding pass, and passport. "I have to go in now." She was fighting back tears. "Takeoff's in fifteen minutes. They're already boarding."

Selim glanced at her boarding card. "Gate Five. That's all the way to the right in there. Better hurry." His English was a bit stiff and slow; but his vocabulary was good.

She studied Selim's face uncertainly. He wasn't smiling, but that didn't mean anything. She'd learned in the six days of living with him that he was a very serious boy; not the kind to smile easily. Even when he cracked jokes, or when he was dancing with her in the Roman discotheque where they'd met, his eyes retained a sadness that hinted at private sorrows too deep for words. It was the eyes that had gotten through her defenses, more than anything else about him.

"You *will* come to London," she asked him hesitantly, still unsure of him. "You really meant it?"

He nodded solemnly. "In two days. I promise."

Then he kissed her on the lips, softly.

And then he gave her the box of chocolates.

He stood there and watched her hurry away down the aisle. As he'd been told to, he waited until she'd gone through the passport booths and vanished inside toward the right. Then he turned away abruptly and made straight for the little bar next to the terminal post office. His legs were trembling. He had to lean against the bar to help stave off an irrational fear that he was about to fall down and draw attention to himself.

Ordering a whiskey, he gulped it and shuddered as it burned its way inside him. He was not accustomed to strong drink. But it neither warmed nor relaxed him. Squeezing the empty glass in his slim hand, Selim watched the terminal clock. When it finally reached the time when Marjorie Kavanagh's plane was supposed to take off, he forced himself to wait another few minutes.

His orders were to wait for fifteen minutes. But he was too frightened to stay there any longer. Ahmed Bel Jahra would have no way of knowing he'd done it so little earlier than ordered. Going to one of the pay phones near the postal booth, Selim dropped in a gitone, dialed the Pan American counter, and asked if the 747 to London had taken off.

Airlines are plagued by hundreds of nuisance calls of this kind every day. To check out each one for a completely truthful answer would use up too many valuable man-hours. So unless the caller becomes particularly insistent, or represents some official authority, there is a standard response. The woman who took Selim's call at the Pan Am counter was busy filling out flight tickets for a crowd of impatient tourists. She glanced at her typed list of the flight schedules for the day, and gave Selim the standard response: "Yes, that flight has already gone."

Selim hung up the phone and walked quickly out of the terminal building.

His legs threatened to buckle under him as he hurried past the buses and taxis to the parking area. After getting into his secondhand Fiat *cinquecento*, he just sat there for a while, not moving. But the urgency pulled at him: His things were still in the room he'd rented under the false name. He had to pack and get out of there.

Starting the battered little car, he drove out of the parking area into the lane leading away from the airport. But he kept thinking about what he'd just done. To ease the horror, he made himself remember everything. Ahmed Bel Jahra had told him about the necessity for doing it. He believed what Bel Jahra had said. But he could not stop himself from remembering, also, how young and trusting the girl had been.

He had to fight against a need to vomit, all the way back into Rome.

Back home in Baltimore, everyone called Marjorie Kavanagh "Midge." She was seventeen, with a cheerful, healthy face and a figure still a bit chubby with baby fat. But Selim hadn't seemed to mind that. Where he came from, he'd told her, they liked their women round and soft. "Only a masochist," he'd said with one of those rare grins, "could dig having bones sticking into him when he's in bed with a girl."

And he'd been amused by her habit of wolfing chocolates whenever she was nervous. It was because she'd told him she got frightened on planes that he'd given her the box of chocolates, to calm her during her flight to London.

Carrying it in her left hand, Midge walked quickly from the passport booths to the Number 5 Departure Gate. But when she got there she found the other passengers for her flight still crowded in front of it, not being passed through for boarding. There was going to be a delay; some kind of mechanical trouble with the plane. Immediately, Midge experienced a familiar tightening in the pit of her stomach. But that caused her to look down at her box of chocolates, and she couldn't help grinning; remembering why Selim had given it to her, for her nerves.

But she had seldom been nervous with *him*—not after that first night together. That was part of the miracle. This wasn't the first time she had had a crush on a boy; nor her first experience with sex. But she'd never actually lived with a boy before. And her feelings had never before opened up like this, into something that could not be identified by any other name but Love. Capital *L*. The real thing. Actually and at last.

That someone like Selim felt the same way *about her* was harder to accept. But he said he did; and acted like he did. . . .

The indicator above the departure counter began clicking, the white-on-black numbers revolving swiftly to announce that the Rome-London flight would be delayed for an hour and a half. Midge glanced at her watch. It was already a couple minutes past the scheduled takeoff time. She sighed and strolled to a red plastic bench, settling down to wait it out.

Other passengers shuffled past her with sullen, resigned expressions, some of them grumbling as they dispersed reluctantly to the bar or the restaurant up on the next floor. A slim, balding computer salesman from Tokyo sat down next to Midge and became absorbed in an Italian girlie magazine. A young, well-dressed Danish couple, the red-haired wife carrying their baby, sat down on a bench across from Midge. The husband got out a short curved pipe and began stuffing tobacco into the bowl. His wife gently rocked their baby on her slim lap, soothing it to sleep.

Midge Kavanagh began thinking about London, the last stage of the European vacation her father had given her as a present for graduating third in her high school class. Originally, she'd been supposed to spend a week in Paris between Rome and London. But she'd canceled out Paris to stay on in Rome with Selim. She would have done without London, too, except that Selim unexpectedly had to leave Rome later this day. A travel agency for which he apparently worked part-time was sending him to Athens for two days, and then on to London for a week.

Or so he'd claimed. She didn't think he'd become bored with her and invented the story just to get rid of her. Yet a tiny devil of doubt persisted in plucking at her. She'd be all alone in London for eight days, unless Selim really meant it about joining her there. Against her will, Midge began worrying again about whether he'd meant all the other things, too. . . .

She didn't realize what she was doing until she found the box of chocolates open in her hands. Suppressing a nervous giggle, Midge reached for one of the foil-wrapped candies. It seemed to be stuck to its indented nest in the white cardboard bottom. She had to tug to pull it out.

Tugging out any one of the chocolates tripped the firing switch of the miniature tube-detonator wired into the compressed gelignite packed in the false bottom of the box. The demolition expert from the Rasd cell in Rome had assured Ahmed Bel Jahra that there was enough explosive force in that much gelignite to blow a hole in the fuselage of a modern jet passenger plane.

In the terminal waiting room, it delivered enough to tear Midge Kavanagh into pieces of bloodied flesh and bone that were hard to identify later as ever having been any part of a human being. The explosion also destroyed the Japanese computer salesman sitting beside her, just as completely. Simultaneously, the face of the Dane sitting across from them disappeared. Later, pieces of his pipe and teeth were found embedded in the back of his skull. The baby flew out of his wife's lap and seemed to disintegrate in midair. But the mother never knew what happened to her child, because she passed out instantly from the shock of having her entire right arm and most of one leg torn off; and died without regaining consciousness twelve minutes later.

TWO

Ahmed Bel Jahra was a tall, aristocratic-looking man of thirty-four, with a lean, powerful build, finely chiseled features, and a sardonic mouth. As usual when he was in Europe, he was dressed with a casual elegance: the sandals handmade of soft expensive leather, the Levi's specially retailored for his slim hips, the blue turtleneck pullover a Cardin. But there was nothing casual now, or elegant, in his long, pale gray eyes. His face was savage as he ripped the sealed letter to pieces and burned it in the washbasin of his bathroom on the sixth floor of Rome's luxurious Hotel Hassler.

He flushed the ashes down the toilet and went back into the bedroom to stare broodingly through the tall, open windows. The enormous energy on which he operated felt trapped inside him now; frustrated and turning against itself. The letter he'd just burned had already been stamped and addressed to the American Embassy in Rome. He'd just been about to mail it when the news had come over the radio: The bomb had exploded in the airport terminal, instead of aboard the plane in flight. For Ahmed Bel Jahra, this meant disaster. A very personal disaster.

He was sick with disappointment; and rising anger against the trick fate had played on him. There was only one small bit of good luck: that he had not mailed the letter before learning the plane had not been blown up. It was bad enough as it was. He was going to seem like an incompetent, to people who were necessary to his future.

There was another penalty for his failure to destroy the plane in the air. Because the bomb had exploded in the airport terminal, there would be witnesses to tell about the girl who'd been carrying it. Police investigation of her activities in Rome might lead them to Selim Hafid. Even if this did not in turn lead them to Bel Jahra, he could not afford to lose Selim. To prevent either possibility, he had immediately sent Driss Hammou to get the boy out of Rome, to another part of Italy where he was not known and could not be traced. At this point Selim and Hammou were the only followers he could really count on.

That was a humiliating self-admission for Bel Jahra. If the jet had been destroyed in the air, along with everyone aboard it, this situation would have changed swiftly. But it had failed. *He* had failed.

Ahmed Bel Jahra stared through the windows of his room without seeing the beautiful stone waterfall of the Spanish Steps flowing down below the hotel to the narrow entrance of fashionable Via Condotti. All he could see was the bleakness of his prospects now; just when it had seemed his fortunes were at last on the rise again.

In Morocco, where Bel Jahra came from, politics are the logical continuation of civil war. Governments have always been shaky, violent overthrows frequent, punishment of failed coups bloody. Anyone involved in Moroccan affairs in any capacity, on any side, must be an agile shifter of position to survive. To shift the wrong way, or even the right way too early or late, is fatal. Bel Jahra had shifted the wrong way in August of the previous year, 1972, while Morocco's King Hassan II was spending a few weeks in France.

Though ostensibly there for a golfing vacation, King Hassan spent much of the time secretly meeting with leaders of the French government in an effort to obtain increased financial and commercial aid desperately needed by his country. The French answer was unofficial and regretful, but very firm: There would be no further aid unless Hassan fired his Minister of Defense, General Mohamed Oufkir.

Bel Jahra learned of this, and was faced with two choices, both bristling with danger. Hassan was his king. General Oufkir was his boss, and idol. If it came to a contest between the two, which would win?

Oufkir was Hassan's sinister gray eminence; the power that had maintained the King on what had been called the shakiest throne in the world. Many Moroccans scorned King Hassan as a frivolous jet-setter, whose real interests didn't extend beyond playing golf and watching Italian Westerns. They regarded Oufkir as the actual ruler of Morocco. King Hassan had received his position through inheritance and political upheavals over which he'd had no control. Oufkir had achieved his position through drive and ability: He was a brave and brilliant soldier, an adroit and cunning manipulator of subsurface politics, an efficient and coldblooded executioner.

He had been born into a fighting tradition. His father was a Berber chief who led his warriors in ambush battles that bogged down the French colonial Army in the treacherous Atlas Mountains. But by World War II the French presence in Morocco was in the process of being phased out, and Oufkir left the Dar El Beida military academy at Meknes to join the Free French forces battling Rommel in North Africa. After passing through a course in British commando tactics, Oufkir distinguished himself in fighting through Italy. When the Allied armies marched into Rome, he was the officer chosen to carry the French colors. By the time the war ended, he'd been awarded ten decorations, including the coveted Croix de Guerre. After which he proved himself again as a fighting officer in Indo-China, winning a dozen more medals and France's Legion of Honor.

Then he went back to Morocco and began proving himself as strong a politician as he was a soldier. He helped to manipulate the final independence of Morocco from France, the removal of Sultan Moulay Arafat from power, and the return from exile to the throne of Mohammed V. From the start, King Mohammed leaned heavily on Oufkir for support against rebellious factions trying to unseat him. As a reward for his success in smashing an uprising of tribes in the Rif Mountains, and subsequently chopping the right hands off one thousand other unruly Moroccans, Oufkir was made Director of National Security; in charge of the police and secret police.

But rebellion continued to seethe from every direction. When Mohammed V died in 1961, and his son, Prince Hassan, ascended to the throne, there were so many opposition factions it was difficult to name them all. There were socialists and communists intent on a different form of government; religious factions that disapproved of young Hassan as too Westernized; restless students and dissatisfied union leaders; army groups eager for a military regime; warrior chieftains resentful of restrictions from any government; and Pan-Islam factions financed from Libya which wanted Morocco to join in a holy crusade against the infidel West.

King Hassan responded to these multiple threats by making Oufkir a general and upping him to Minister of the Interior—and later to Minister of Defense—adding sweeping new powers to the ones Oufkir already had. He exercised these powers ruthlessly. His agents infiltrated dissident cells and rooted out their leaders, who were disposed of in ways that earned Oufkir a new title from his enemies: Torturer in Chief. He aborted and punished ten different attempts to assassinate King Hassan. He executed leftist plotters who attempted to blow up the King with his retinue at the National Theater in Rabat, and high army officers responsible for an armed invasion of the palace at Skhirat. And he directed operations against marauding tribes in the Atlas Mountains and Sahara Desert.

It was during this phase that Ahmed Bel Jahra drew Oufkir's notice: as a young army captain particularly effective in ferreting out guerrilla bands in the Atlas. Oufkir made inquiries, and learned that Bel Jahra was from a wealthy Casablanca family, which had sent him to France and Switzerland for most of his education. Deciding that with this background Bel Jahra was wasted in the Army, Oufkir arranged his transfer into the secret service, and sent him to France.

Based in Paris, but traveling widely through Europe in the guise of a prominent representative of the Moroccan Tourist Bureau, Bel Jahra established an excellent network of secret contacts and passed on to Oufkir all information of interest that he turned up. He was Oufkir's man; and he enjoyed thoroughly both the intrigue and the substantial expense account.

It was in 1965 that Bel Jahra figured in the murder that was later to have the effect of a delayed-action time bomb on his career. Ben Barka, the most prominent leader of the Moroccan Left, had been forced to flee to France as a result of General Oufkir's cleanup operations. But from Paris, Bel Jahra reported to Oufkir, Ben Barka began plotting a full-scale revolution. Oufkir took the threat seriously. Ben Barka was the one man who could pull it off; his name had become a rallying point for numberless dissidents of many factions. Oufkir boarded a plane and flew to France, to arrange the kidnapping of Ben Barka.

Ahmed Bel Jahra helped, through certain of his secret contacts, to dupe French policemen into snatching Ben Barka from a Paris street and turning him over. Ben Barka was never seen again. Newspapers in other countries pointed fingers of shame at France. Goaded by this, an official French investigation established what had happened—including the fact that Ben Barka had been tortured in a house outside Paris for several days before being strangled to death personally by General Oufkir.

General De Gaulle was roused to vengeful fury on learning how his own police had been used by another power. He saw to it that Oufkir, by then back in Morocco, was found guilty of murder; condemned to death if he ever again entered France.

Because Bel Jahra's part in the "Ben Barka Affair" never came to light, he was able to stay in France, where he continued his secret activities for Oufkir. In time the shock wave of the affair subsided. But it continued to reverberate silently, below the surface, waiting for its moment. That moment came in the summer of 1972, when King Hassan paid his visit to France.

By then General De Gaulle was dead. But his ministers still ran the French government. They remembered painfully the old man's fury; and felt still the stain that the affair had left on the honor of France. When King Hassan asked for increased aid, they finally grasped their vengeance: More aid would be considered—only if Oufkir was dismissed from office and stripped of all power.

Hassan did not answer this unofficial ultimatum. Whatever his thoughts, he kept them to himself. His silence and the ultimatum itself were leaked to Bel Jahra by a Gaullist undersecretary who required more than he could earn legally for the upkeep of his mistress. Bel Jahra knew that his survival depended on what he did next. He considered with care the relative strengths of King Hassan and General Oufkir. He considered also that he was certainly not the only source of information Oufkir had in France. If he did not report the matter to Oufkir, someone else probably would. Bel Jahra took the next plane to Morocco, to make the report in person.

General Oufkir heard him out behind the closed door of his private office at the Defense Ministry in Rabat. He listened impassively, the unwavering eyes masked behind the darkly tinted glasses that protected his painfully light-sensitive eyes. Oufkir was then fifty-two. His figure was still athletic. Even in the well-tailored gray business suit that almost matched the gray of his hair, his bearing was still that of a soldier and his face still that of a fasting monk. He remained silent for several moments after Bel Jahra finished, studying him through the dark lenses.

Then he asked in a cool, probing voice: "And what do you believe the King will decide to do?"

The tone told Bel Jahra he'd been right. Oufkir had already known the news he'd brought, from another source. "I don't know," Bel Jahra answered truthfully. "Whatever my opinion, I would only be guessing."

"Guess," Oufkir urged him, in the same cool tone.

Bel Jahra shifted uneasily in the leather chair across the wide, neat desk from Oufkir. "The King would be foolish to dismiss you," he said slowly, "when he needs you as much as ever for the stability of the country." Bel Jahra hesitated. "But there *is* Colonel Dlimi. . . ." Dlimi, recently in effective control of certain phases of secret police activities within the country, had performed so well he was coming to be known as "the first cop of Morocco"—and had been made senior aide-de-camp to King Hassan. "The King may believe that Colonel Dlimi is now able to take over from you effectively. That would be wrong, of course. But the King may be misled by his anxiety about French aid. It is possible."

Oufkir gave a short nod. "Misled, also, by stories that I am in a position to depose him and declare a dictatorship. In spite of my years of proven loyalty." There was a hint of something not so cool in the way Oufkir said this. A tinge of the hurt, betrayed lover. "It is more than possible. I have reason to believe it is *probable*. Now tell me, Ahmed—in your opinion, if I am dismissed, what will happen to our country?"

There was nothing in Oufkir's face but controlled waiting for an answer. Bel Jahra could not make out the expression of the eyes behind the dark lenses. But he knew that Oufkir did not like flattery; was interested only in honest appraisal. "I think, General," Bel Jahra told him finally, "that without your control our country would soon be torn apart by revolution and civil war. With so many factions struggling for power, Morocco would descend into anarchy."

"That is what *I* believe," Oufkir agreed quietly. He spread his long, strong-fingered hands flat on the table between them. "I do not intend to allow that to happen to our country, Ahmed." Having said this, Oufkir waited for a moment, giving Bel Jahra time to digest its implication. Then he said: "And now that you understand my intention, Ahmed, you may get up and leave—if you wish. I have complete faith that if you do leave, you will not reveal this conversation to anyone."

Bel Jahra remained where he was, looking across the desk at Oufkir, making no move to leave. Between Hassan and Oufkir, there was no question which had the more strength and cunning. "I am with you, General." Bel Jahra's heart was in his throat, but his voice was quite steady.

"Think carefully, Ahmed. There is an old saying: 'He who draws his sword against his prince must throw away the scabbard.' Win or lose, there will be no way to draw back from the consequences, once we have begun."

"Would I be wrong, General, to think it has *already* begun?"

General Oufkir said nothing.

"In that case," Bel Jahra said evenly, "I am already part of it. I say it again, General: I am with you."

Bel Jahra helped to arrange a number of the meetings that followed between Oufkir and certain officers of the Moroccan Army and Air Force. Officers they could be sure would join in the plot, which Oufkir code-named Operation Overflow. Everything had to be arranged swiftly—but surely. King Hassan was due back from Europe in a week. Within four days Oufkir completed planning the take-over that would be born out of the shocking violence of the opening move.

On August 16 of 1972, King Hassan's private Boeing 727 returned from Europe, after a stopover at Barcelona, where the King had lunched with Spain's Foreign Minister. Aboard the big royal jet, in addition to Hassan and the crew, were his brother Prince Moulay Abdallah, and an entourage of almost a hundred people. As the plane flew in over the coast of Morocco, four jet fighters of the Moroccan Air Force, recently purchased Northrop F5 Freedom Fighters, whipped down out of the sky and attacked it.

One of the F5s was flown by Major Kouera El Ouael, acting commander of the air force base at Kenitra. He led the fighters in a short, savage assault, smashing at the royal 727 with rockets and 20-mm machine-gun bursts that ripped open the fuselage, one wing, and much of the tail section. The 727 went into an uncontrolled dive with two of its engines failing; then managed to level off shakily on the single remaining engine. The four fighters circled down and around to finish it off.

At that point there came a near-hysterical radiophone message from the crippled, lurching wreckage of the 727 to the attacking fighters: "This is the mechanic speaking! Please stop shooting! The pilot is dead, the copilot is hit, and the King is dying! At least spare the lives of the rest of us aboard! Please let us land!"

Major Kouera was not a bloodthirsty man. With King Hassan mortally wounded, they'd achieved the objective he'd planned with Oufkir. There was no need for the rest of the hundred aboard the royal jet to die. Major Kouera led the four fighters back to Kenitra air base north of Rabat. The riddled 727 somehow managed a single-engine landing at the Rabat-Salé Airport, skidding off the runway before coming to a jolting halt.

Bel Jahra, assigned by Oufkir to observe at the airport during the execution of Operation Overflow, was stunned when he saw the first person to climb down from the wrecked 727: King Hassan II, quite unharmed. The radio message had been a trick. Bel Jahra sprinted to a phone in the reception building and called Oufkir at Army Headquarters in Rabat.

Operation Overflow had failed. But Oufkir had planned for a follow-up attempt if that happened. Bel Jahra's phone call set in motion Operation Pinkflight. Minutes later, three jet fighters zoomed down over the airport, strafing the runway and parking area, pounding the reception building with machine-gun and cannon fire. They killed eight people and wounded forty. But King Hassan fled into the pine trees bordering the airport, and was not touched.

The three fighter planes finally ran out of ammunition and winged away. Hassan got into a limousine and was driven out of the airport. According to the information Bel Jahra overheard, the King was headed for the Royal Touarga Palace inside Rabat. Bel Jahra phoned Oufkir again. Operation Pinkflight continued: Another flight of fighter planes methodically smashed at the Touarga Palace with cannons and rockets. But Bel Jahra had been misled. King Hassan was not in Rabat. He was twenty miles away, in the Skhirat summer palace—and "the first cop of Morocco," Colonel Dlimi, was already directing the swift seizure and brutal interrogation of suspects. Then Oufkir was summoned to Skhirat.

Early the next morning, General Oufkir's body was found where it had been dumped, in the driveway to his brother-in-law's home. He had been shot four times. One of the bullets had entered the back of his head and come out through his left eye. King Hassan and Colonel Dlimi announced that Oufkir had committed suicide.

After Oufkir's death, arrests and executions of the other conspirators, and suspected conspirators, came quickly. Bel Jahra, though named, was one of those who got away. He fled to Algeria, where he briefly checked into a hotel in Oran. He was deeply shaken by the disaster that had made him an exile. But his first shock was already giving way to a stubborn determination to return to his country one day and extract vengeance. To lead a coup that would *not* fail.

It was this moment, the lowest of his career, that saw the final maturity of Bel Jahra's ruthless willpower. He had made a god of Oufkir—and the god had failed him, and died. He would make no more gods of other men. He would be his own. From now on whenever he seemed to follow others, he would only be using them. His destiny was his own.

He spent his first day in Oran listening to radio broadcasts of reactions from the other Arab nations. The attempt to assassinate King Hassan was condemned by all of them. Except one: Libya hailed the plot as glorious prelude to revolution; the pilots who'd tried to shoot down the royal 727 were called "gallant eagles."

Bel Jahra left Oran and went to Libya, to have a talk with its ruler, Moamer el-Qadhafi.

The interview which Qadhafi granted him at his headquarters in Tripoli's Azizia Barracks was brief. His simple army uniform rumpled by his slumping posture in the chair behind his littered desk, he seemed to only half listen to Bel Jahra. His nerve-ravaged face was preoccupied, and his sandaled feet shuffled restlessly while his burning fanatic's eyes roamed the walls of his modest office, from the framed texts of the Koran to the shiny Bakelite map of all the Arabian countries.

Qadhafi was the same age as Bel Jahra, in his early thirties; a high-strung insomniac and a passionate Moslem possessed by crusading fervor. Austere in his personal life, he drove an old Volkswagen and retained the rank of colonel which he had held when he'd deposed King Idris and taken over Libya. But the enormous oil wealth of the country was under his absolute control. Qadhafi was pouring much of that wealth into his personal vision of a holy war to re-create a united Islamic Empire; using the presence of Israel as an irritant to goad the Arabs of many nations into co-operating toward this ultimate objective. He had levied a 3 per cent "Holy War Tax" on all Libyans. And he was paying an estimated forty million dollars each year to the most violent of the rival Arab terrorist groups, to advance his total concept.

Bel Jahra kept this total concept in mind as he began explaining what he had come for. Qadhafi was too busy with more immediate concerns to hear him out. Once he understood the drift of Bel Jahra's words, he passed him on to one of his ministers, without expressing approval or disapproval. Patiently, Bel Jahra began again.

He laid out his plans for leading a coup against King Hassan that would be patterned on Qadhafi's against King Idris. The plan was detailed and practical, with a genuine chance for success—if Colonel Qadhafi would back it heavily with arms and cash. The reward, for Qadhafi, would be a new Morocco tightly linked to Libya politically and militarily; a solid part of the united Islam Qadhafi envisioned.

Colonel Qadhafi's minister nodded abstractedly. He agreed that the plan was excellent, but pointed out that Bel Jahra had yet to prove his ability to *execute* such a plan. However, since Bel Jahra had so many secret contacts in Europe, there was a way for him to show whether he had this ability or not. It was suggested that Bel Jahra get in touch with Qadhafi's agent directing Arab guerrilla activities in Europe: a member of the Libyan Mission to the UN in Geneva, named Bashir Mawdri.

Supplied with false passports and visas, Bel Jahra flew to Switzerland to meet with Bashir Mawdri. He went with the angry knowledge that he was being used, for purposes not his own. But he determined to make it pay off. Only with Qadhafi's backing could Bel Jahra seize power in Morocco. So he would do the bidding of Qadhafi's Geneva agent, for a time. And when he sat down for another talk with the Libyan dictator, it would be as a man who had proved he knew how to execute what he planned.

At first Bashir Mawdri, the Libyan agent, had confined Bel Jahra to helping other groups. His first assignment was to assist in arranging the massacre of the Israeli Olympic team in Munich—for which Colonel Qadhafi gave the killers a triumphant parade and bestowed an extra five million dollars on the guerrilla group responsible. Bel

Jahra next played a part in two airplane hijackings and the killing of an Israeli official in London.

The assignment to blow up the Pan American passenger jet flying from Rome to London was the first operation placed totally under Bel Jahra's independent control. By then he'd acquired two aides he could utterly depend on: One was Driss Hammou, whom he knew from the past: a tough Moroccan army sergeant who'd served as one of Oufkir's bodyguards, and had fled Morocco at the same time as Bel Jahra. The other was Selim Hafid, a young Palestinian who'd attached himself to Bel Jahra during one of the hijack operations, and had come to hero-worship him. These two, Hammou and Selim, were the only assistants Bel Jahra needed, according to the plan he'd worked out, for blowing up the Rome-London flight.

There were, as stated in the letter which Bel Jahra had just burned in the bathroom, three reasons for the destruction of that flight. One was to punish the airline for flying to Israel, and as a warning to others that did so. Another was to punish the United States for interfering in Arab plans for the Middle East. The final reason was to kill four men aboard that flight: high government officials of Iran, which stood in conflict to the Arabian power play for the Persian Gulf, and aided Kurdish rebels in Iraq.

But the plan had gone awry, because of the delayed departure of the plane. It would have taken off by now, finally, to make its flight unharmed. Making the letter nothing but empty words. And leaving Bel Jahra to brood over the consequences of his failure to execute his first independent operation.

He was still gazing unseeingly through the open windows of his hotel room when Driss Hammou ben Rehamna returned.

"Selim is on his way to Genoa," Hammou reported as he shut the door behind him. His voice was soft and guttural. "The little hotel we used last time. I gave him the new papers." The old papers had identified Selim Hafid as Selim Ramouk, a Turk; the new ones gave him still another name and made him Algerian.

Bel Jahra turned from the windows and looked at Driss Hammou. He was short and squat, and very strong; with small shrewd eyes in a broad, stupid face. The history of the beni Rehamna warrior tribe was bloody even by Moroccan standards. Driss Hammou was the best of the breed: deeply courageous and utterly merciless.

"You burned Selim's old papers?" Bel Jahra asked him, and instantly regretted it.

Hammou just stared at him, hurt at the implication that he might be inefficient enough to forget such a vital detail.

"I'm sorry, Driss," Bel Jahra apologized, and patted his thick shoulder. "I have failed, and now I take my anger out on you. Forgive me."

The gentle warmth of Bel Jahra's voice brought a blush to Hammou's face. The little eyes squeezed almost shut, like those of a cat being scratched by someone it loves. "You didn't fail," he stated flatly. "It was an accident nobody could control. Things like that happen, even with the best plans. That's one thing you learn in the Army."

Bel Jahra nodded bleakly. "But this was the one time I couldn't afford an accident." Suddenly he couldn't stand the confines of the room any longer. "Take care of the packing now. We still have that Geneva plane to catch."

He left the room and took the elevator down to the ground floor. He needed a stiff drink. The upcoming meeting with the Libyan agent was not something he looked forward to. After this failure in Rome, Qadhafi's man in Geneva wasn't likely to be interested in any future plans Bel Jahra might have for another independent operation. At best, the bastard would make him sweat before letting him be part of other men's operations again. After almost a year of trying to show his only possible backer what he could do in full command, the disaster today at the airport had accomplished exactly the opposite.

Bel Jahra was crossing the hotel lobby in the direction of the lounge bar when a woman picking up a room key turned from the porter's desk, saw him, and called out in surprise: "André!"

It was undoubtedly addressed to Bel Jahra; and he had often in the past used the cover name of André Courtois, posing as a French businessman with a firm based in Morocco. But he hadn't used that name since fleeing Morocco. He stopped and stared back at her, all of him instantly wary, alerted for danger.

The expression of surprised pleasure on the woman's face changed, becoming uncertain as she saw the hostility that had tightened the lines of his aristocratic features. She was in her late twenties, her figure lean in a simple, expensively cut dress; her face too sharp-featured, but not unattractive. For a long moment he didn't know who she was. Then he remembered: Juliet Shale, an extremely up-tight English social secretary he'd met in Monaco a couple years before.

It had amused him, shortly after they'd met, to woo her to his bed and tap the enormous wealth of repressed sexuality that up-tight women so often had inside them. For Juliet Shale it had been a wildly voluptuous, unforgettable experience. Bel Jahra had forgotten about it entirely, until now. But it was an ethical rule with him never to be ungallant to a woman he'd slept with. He forced himself to relax, and smiled warmly as he strode to her, seizing her shoulders and kissing her on each cheek. Then he drew back a bit, still holding her shoulders, and used the same phrase with which he'd first greeted her two years earlier: "Allah be praised! A friendly face, just when I need one!"

She laughed, and then checked the laugh; very unsure of how to act with him. Under his gaze, color suffused her cheeks. She raised her small decisive chin in a way that made her look both defiant and vulnerable. "For a minute there, I thought you'd forgotten me."

"Don't be foolish, Julie. Of course I didn't forget you."

"But you did," she pointed out. "I never heard from you again after . . . Well, I just never heard from you again. Did I?"

"That was something that couldn't be helped, Julie. Business problems forced me to return to Morocco. I've been there ever since. Just got back to Europe this week." Bel Jahra grinned at her. "And here we meet again, before I can even hunt you down. It's fate. And it's time for us to go in the bar and celebrate."

Juliet held back nervously. "I can't just now. My boss is expecting me upstairs in his suite."

He took her arm firmly. "He can wait," he told her softly. "This is important."

His touch, and look, rekindled the remembered excitement in Juliet. She allowed herself to be led into the lounge bar. Bel Jahra selected one of the secluded curved booths, ordered a small bottle of champagne, and studied her, sitting stiffly beside him with her thin hands clenched together on the table. She still had that look of brittle, jumpy, prematurely middle-aged virginity.

You couldn't always be sure what was going on with women like this. He'd known one who'd had three children and couldn't bear to be touched by a man again. He'd known another who'd never been married and made love to him all night like a lust-starved nymphomaniac—then tried to kill herself in the morning, collapsing into shrieking hysteria when he managed to stop her. Frightening, all of them. But interesting, finding out what was really working inside them. This one had been one of the more pleasant discoveries.

"Are you still working for that movie producer?" he asked her.

"Murray?" Juliet smiled ruefully, remembering back. "No. He never did manage to finish that film. Finally vanished into limbo with the creditors panting after him. For the past year I've been social secretary to Dezso Valasi."

"To *Valasi?*"

Juliet nodded proudly. "Yes. Can you imagine?"

There had been a time, before Bel Jahra had become an army officer, that he'd wanted to be an artist. But even if he'd known absolutely nothing about art, he'd have known who Dezso Valasi was. With Picasso dead, Valasi and Chagall were the most famous artists left. A giant figure with an incredible background. Valasi now spent most of his time in a well-guarded Riviera estate that only a privileged few were allowed to visit.

"I'm impressed," Bel Jahra acknowledged.

"You should be. I must admit, *I'm* impressed myself, to find myself working for him."

"What is he doing here in Rome? I thought he always stayed at his place up in . . . where is it exactly?"

"Cap Martin. We're here to help with arrangements for an exhibition of twenty of his biggest paintings. It's a very important exhibition, or Valasi wouldn't have come with me. He doesn't travel much anymore."

Bel Jahra nodded. "He must be getting pretty old by now."

"Eighty. In two weeks. As a matter of fact, I'm flying back alone this evening, to work on the final arrangements for his eightieth birthday party. We've got so many guests coming to honor him, I can hardly keep track of them all. Including Prince Ranier and Princess Grace; *with* their children."

"It all sounds very swank."

Juliet suddenly glanced around them nervously, making sure no one was close enough to overhear. "Don't say anything to anyone about it, André. Please. It's all supposed to be very hush-hush. No previous publicity. We don't want a lot of photographers and news people hanging about outside the estate, bothering the guests as they arrive and leave."

"I understand," Bel Jahra patted her hand. "I won't breathe a word of it."

Delighted by the impression she was making on him, she leaned closer and lowered her voice: "Guess who *two* of the guests will be . . ." She paused nervously again. "This *is* confidential, you do understand that. Nobody but Valasi and I know they're coming; not even most of the people around them."

Bel Jahra's smile was indulgent. "I'm not a gossip columnist, Julie."

Her voice dropped to an excited whisper: "The American Secretary of State! *And* King Hussein of Jordan!"

For several seconds, Bel Jahra couldn't speak. Since the first attempt to crush the newborn state of Israel, Jordan had given no more than token forces to subsequent attempts, earning King Hussein the hostility of other Arab rulers—of whom the most outspoken was Colonel Qadhafi of Libya. Hussein had compounded this by brutally crushing a guerrilla attempt to take over his country. The guerrillas had extracted a measure of revenge by shooting Jordan's Premier down at the Cairo-Sheraton Hotel, during an official visit to Egypt. One of the assassins had knelt to drink the blood streaming from the victim's wounds. He'd pronounced it bitter.

But they'd missed every try against King Hussein himself. It was the same with the American Secretary of State. There'd been two plots against him that Bel Jahra knew of; probably there'd been others. None had managed to get past the planning stage.

Bel Jahra thought about the King of Jordan and the chief of America's foreign policies. In the same place, at the same time.

When he spoke again, his tone seemed casual: "It sounds like you are to be a very busy girl. But I hope you'll have *some* time to yourself. Because—fate, again—it just happens I have a great deal of business to attend to on the Riviera. If you'll give me the number at Valasi's estate, I'd like to call you and get together."

Juliet looked into the pale gray eyes and saw nothing but eagerness to be with her again.

Behind those eyes, Bel Jahra saw nothing but Qadhafi's agent in Geneva. Suddenly, he was not at all reluctant about the Geneva meeting. He had something now. Something the Libyan couldn't possibly turn down. And because of Juliet Shale, Bel Jahra was the only one in a position to execute it.

THREE

The Pan Am 747 from Rome—the one on which Marjorie Kavanagh, the Danish couple with their child, and the Japanese computer man would have been passengers—was already overhead, circling in for its landing on Runway 10R-28L, when Hunter reached Heathrow Airport after an eighteen-mile drive from London's West End.

Thin sunlight filtered through low mist as soggy as it could get without changing to rain. Hunter's large hands on the steering wheel ached as they always did in damp weather. A coal mine cave-in had broken them in a dozen places when he was sixteen. But he'd had two decades to get used to the nerve twinges radiating from his wrists to his fingertips. He was no more aware of it than a nearsighted man is of wearing glasses, as he drove into Heathrow Airport that misty afternoon.

Heathrow was built as an RAF bomber base late in World War II —so late that by the time it was ready to become operational the war had ended and there was no further military need for it. Converted into the main civil airport of Great Britain, Heathrow now sprawls across three thousand acres of Hounslow Heath, and tries desperately to cope with airplanes landing and taking off at a rate of almost 300,000 in a single year—along with some nineteen million passengers and over half a million tons of cargo. It is a still-growing complex of runways, roads, hangars, terminals, warehouses, multi-level car parks, maintenance sheds, and other buildings. It has a work force of over fifty thousand people affiliated with fifty airlines and seventeen different unions.

Part of this work force consists of over 350 members of the British Airports Authority Constabulary. But they have more than they can do handling traffic, watching out for terrorists, dealing with an average of five hundred mentally disturbed airport visitors in a given year, and trying hopelessly to stem the looting of twelve to twenty million dollars' worth of goods-in-transit during the same year. What had happened in Rome before the 747 took off for England would, at this end, be chiefly the concern of Scotland Yard's "C" Department. That would help. In Hunter's experience with the police of Europe, he'd found Scotland Yard's Special Branch men among the best to work with.

Simon Hunter was a cop. The State Department's WGCT—the newly formed Working Group to Combat Terrorism—had given him a more impressive title than that, of course, before sending him over to see what he could do in co-operation with the various security forces of Europe: Special Liaison Investigator. But it still added up to: cop.

It was what he knew he did well, and consequently got satisfaction from doing. What he'd done in the past as an investigative officer, in Europe mostly, for Army Intelligence. There is another kind of intelligence work; but Hunter had never had any interest in being in the spy business. He was good with complicated puzzles. He liked pitting his mind against them; digging into them and even dreaming them, until he chewed through to a solution. And now, after almost two years, he was working at it again.

He was a robust bear of a man, with a heavy mop of thick gray hair and a strong-boned face. And very quiet, watchful eyes; dark and deep-set. There were lines carved deep down the sides of his face, which hadn't been there two years ago. He'd been promoted to major by the time they'd learned Beth had leukemia and he'd resigned his commission. A year of "holiday" traveling with her, pretending she wasn't dying. Followed by two months of sitting with her in the hospital in London, when she could no longer travel and they could no longer pretend. And then a time of just being alone; until Chavez had pulled him into this job.

Chavez had been Hunter's superior officer in Army Intelligence. He'd said of Hunter, in recommending him to the State Department: "I won't say he's a genius, and maybe he's not even brilliant. Hell, I don't think I really know what those two words mean. But I do know this—he's a good investigator. Nothing gets past him, and if he spots a lead he can follow it further than most. He's solid and stubborn, and he's got the know-how. A pro."

What Chavez hadn't said was what he couldn't be sure of: how much almost a year and a half of watching his wife die might have taken out of him.

Hunter turned his car off the main approach road, swung around Terminal 2, and followed a series of lanes toward the south side of the airport. He parked at the end of a lane just north of Runway 10R-28L, across from the main cargo terminal. As he got out of the car, the Pan Am 747 from Rome screamed down past him and made a heavy no-bounce touchdown. He leaned against the car and watched the mammoth jet go ponderously down the runway, its engines howling in reverse to slow it down.

It stopped near the other end of the runway, turned, and began to taxi toward Terminal 3. A group of armed airport police and Special Branch marksmen were waiting for it there, just in case another attempt was made on it at this end. But there was no trouble. In five minutes the 747 was disgorging passengers and baggage.

There were 322 people on that plane, including the crew. Hunter thought about what someone had planned for them; of all those dead bodies scattered over miles of Italian countryside.

He waited for anger to stir inside him. But it didn't. His mind felt around the edges of it, but his emotions wouldn't engage. You had to deliberately numb the deeper feelings to get through fourteen months of constantly watching someone dear to you die by slow, painful degrees. It became a habit hard to break out of.

Hunter became aware that he'd unconsciously taken the three Byzantine coins from the left pocket of his jacket, and was passing them back and forth between his aching hands. He'd bought them when Beth had become interested in I Ching. Hunter didn't believe the fortune-telling aspect of it. But he appreciated the sophisticated common sense of the advice the ancient Chinese had formulated to go with it.

Dropping the coins on his right palm, he saw them all come up heads. Nine hundred years had worn them almost smooth. He hadn't been able to afford mint condition antique coins on army pay. But the outlines of Christ's haloed head were still visible on all three. He looked at them for a few seconds. That didn't do anything to him, either. Dropping them in his pocket, he got back in his car and drove to the other side of the airport, threading through the maze of lanes with the ease of long acquaintance.

He parked alongside the modern, neat-lined police station on

Heathrow's North Side. As he started for the door another car pulled up. The man who climbed out was compact and of average height, with a rugged, sleepy-eyed face. Special Branch Inspector Ivor Klar. He said, "Hello, Simon. I see they alerted you quick enough."

Hunter nodded. "They gave you the jumbo from Rome?"

"For my sins. The bag the dead girl checked through'll be brought here as soon as it comes off. If there's nothing useful in it, I'm afraid we've drawn a blank at this end."

"Nobody waiting here to meet her?"

"Not a soul. I've two men still questioning the other passengers. But it seems none of them knew her. I imagine you've had a look at the passenger list. The government figures from Iran seem the likeliest target to me. Agree?"

Hunter shrugged a shoulder. "Or the airline itself. Or a grand bloody gesture to the whole Western world. No knowing until whatever organization tried to plant the bomb issues some kind of statement of intention."

"There is that," Inspector Klar acknowledged. "But I'll lay you odds there'll be no statement on this one. Whatever their intentions, they messed up. Luckily. There's five dead. Instead of three hundred and twenty-seven."

"Anything new from the Rome end on it?" Hunter asked.

Klar shook his head. "Last I heard, they were still trying to find anyone she might've been in contact with there. I take it your people will be in touch with her parents. On the off-chance they can shed some light."

"A call was made an hour ago. By now someone'll be breaking it to them."

Inspector Klar grimaced slightly. "Glad it's not me this time. I've done it, often enough. But to me it's still the worst job in police work."

An airport constabulary car drove up. A uniformed policeman got out with a scuffed leather suitcase. "The girl's bag, Inspector. Spotted the number on the tag and snatched it off the baggage handler just as it came down."

"Good work." Klar took the suitcase and went inside the station house with Hunter. He asked the sergeant on duty at the reception desk if there'd been any calls for him; was told there'd been none. He led Hunter through a short corridor to an empty office with cream-colored plasterboard walls. Neither sat down. Hunter leaned against the wall with his hands in his pockets and his face unreadable, watching Klar place Marjorie Kavanagh's suitcase on top of the desk and open it.

The inspector began removing the contents carefully, one item at a time. Most of it was the dead girl's clothing. There were also a number of paperback guidebooks to Europe, souvenir picture books from various Roman museums, and postcards with views of Rome. Nothing was written on any of the cards. Klar leafed rapidly through each of the books without turning up anything of interest. Then he came up with a small photograph in a brand-new leather frame.

It was a picture of a plumpish teen-age girl, with a middle-aged man and woman, the three of them all dressed up and smiling into the camera. Klar removed the photo from the frame and turned it over. On the back was written, in a small, neat hand: "Mom, Me, and Dad—Graduation, 1973."

"This looks to be our Marjorie Kavanagh," Klar said quietly. "And her parents."

Hunter nodded. He let go of the coin whose smooth face he'd been thumbing, took his hands from his pockets, and reached for the picture. He looked at it in silence. The faces of Mother, Daughter, and Father smiled at him, happy and proud.

Then the anger came, surprising him. He continued to hold the photograph, studying the three smiling faces. "When you make blowups of the girl's face for Rome," he said quietly, "get me a copy."

Inspector Klar's sleepy eyes slid to him. "Not thinking of going to Rome with it yourself, by any chance?"

"Depends. On what turns up there."

"I thought you were supposed to be sticking to the diplomatic grand-planning side of it these days. Co-ordinate, suggest, and prevent . . ." There was a touch of shrewd amusement in the inspector's expression. "But once a detective, eh?"

That was part of it, of course. In addition to Heathrow, Hunter had so far checked out the new security measures being instituted at Amsterdam's Schiphol Airport, Copenhagen's Kastrup, Geneva's Cointrin, Paris-Orly, Hamburg's Fühlsbuttel, Nice's Côte d'Azur, Brussels-Zaventem, and Oslo's Fornebu. They were all doing the best they could, under the circumstances; and it had begun to feel to Hunter that he was consuming a lot of time in moving around to little purpose.

He was supposed to be investigating for the purpose of recommending improved co-operative measures for prevention of acts of terrorism. The trouble was, he didn't much believe in general crime-prevention planning. That was the cop in him. He believed the best way to prevent crimes—political or not—was to take each crime as it came, track down those who'd committed it, and eliminate them so they couldn't commit more.

He gave back the photograph. "I'd appreciate the copy, Ivor."

Hunter's tone was even and his face held no particular expression. But what was in the deep-set dark eyes caused Inspector Klar to drop whatever else he had to say. Klar put the picture to one side on the edge of the desk, and took a spiral notebook from the bottom of Marjorie Kavanagh's suitcase. He opened it, and lost some of his sleepy look. "Ah . . . *here* we are. . . ."

Written at the top of the first page with a red felt pen, in the same handwriting that was on the back of the photograph, was: "People to see in Rome—" Under that three names had been written; two male, one female, with Roman addresses. Two also had phone numbers.

"People she knew or had introductions to," Klar murmured. "*Now* Rome'll have something to work from."

He flipped the page. The next had "See in Paris—" in red, and two names with addresses. The third page was for London, also with two names and addresses. "Better and better . . ." Klar turned the third page.

The next three pages had a total of eight names with Roman addresses. A blue ball-point pen had been used to scribble these, instead of the red felt pen used on the first three pages; but the handwriting was the same.

Klar shot Hunter a look. "More for the Rome end. These she must've met while she was there."

"Some might've just been traveling through like she was," Hunter said. "They could be anywhere in Europe, or out of it, by now."

Klar nodded. "We'll trace them through Interpol, if they are."

"If you want Interpol to help, better contact 'em fast. Before this turns out to be a political thing, officially."

Because of its very nature, Interpol (International Criminal Police Organization) could not touch crimes of a political nature.

It existed for the gathering and dispersing of information among the police forces of 114 member nations. Many of these nations had opposite international interests. If Interpol involved itself in political matters, it would lose too many members to remain effective.

Klar went quickly through the rest of the spiral notebook without finding anything else of interest. Nor was there anything more that was useful in Marjorie Kavanagh's suitcase. He put everything back in it neatly, except for the notebook, which he put beside the desk phone, and the photograph, which he held out to Hunter.

"I can't leave until my men finish questioning the passengers, just in case. If you're on your way back to London, will you give this to Sergeant Rattray in my office for me. Tell him I said to get you the extra blowup of the girl's face."

"Thanks." Hunter took the picture. "I'll be at the embassy, Ivor. And later the Royal Court Hotel, on Sloane Square."

"You'll hear from me, if anything breaks." Klar sat down behind the desk and picked up the phone, asking the station switchboard operator to put through three calls for him. One to his sergeant at Special Branch in London. The second to Carabinieri Major Diego Bandini, of the Direzione Generale di Pubblico Sicurezza, in Rome. The third to the Interpol room in Scotland Yard's Criminal Investigation Department.

The Interpol NCB (National Central Bureau) for Great Britain is next door to Scotland Yard's Information Room, which receives all police calls. Fifteen minutes after receiving the phone call from Inspector Klar, the London NCB sent two messages in Morse via the special radiotelegraph network connecting it with the General Secretariat of Interpol in France.

The first message was addressed to the Criminal Records Department of the General Secretariat. It began: "XD . . . CARMO," and was followed by the list of names Klar had found in Marjorie Kavanagh's notebook. "XD" is the Interpol classification meaning "Extremely Urgent." "CARMO" is its code word for "Please send all relevant information you may possess or be able to acquire about this person, in particular about his (or her) criminal record, true identity, and criminal activities."

The second message listed the same names, and requested that any information on their present whereabouts be passed back to the NCB in London. This message was prefixed: "XD . . . IPCQ."

Which meant it was a general alert, to be relayed by the General Secretariat's central station to member nations in all of the seven Interpol zones: Central Europe, Scandanavia, the Middle East, North America, South America, Africa, and Asia-Pacific.

The central headquarters of Interpol's General Secretariat is located in the suburban town of Saint-Cloud, outside Paris. It is just off the treelined Rue Armengaud, anchored on pylons to a grassy slope overlooking the Seine. A modern concrete-and-glass building shaped like a cigar box set up on its long edge—not pretty, but as efficient-looking as a shiny computer.

The radio room of its Central Station is on the top floor, with neatly arranged radio and teleprinter equipment, plus facilities for six telegraphers to operate at the same time. There were four on duty that afternoon. The one who took the messages from London noted the XD classification, and passed it on immediately through the building's pneumatic tube system after noting the exact time on his work sheet. Three minutes later it was in the hands of Inspector Jean-Pierre Jacquoud, a short, compact police officer from Switzerland.

Like a large percentage of the 140 people working at the General Secretariat, Jacquoud had been lent to Interpol headquarters by his government for a one-year period. His small office was on the second floor, with a view across the river and the Bois de Boulogne to Paris in the distance; with a tiny Eiffel Tower poking up into a sky as misty as the one over London. Jacquoud stood by his window and examined the two messages with perpetually tired eyes in an otherwise youthful face.

He didn't have to concern himself with whether the requests touched on matters forbidden to Interpol. If they had, the London NCB would have refused to forward them.

Article 2 of the Interpol organization's constitution states its purpose succinctly: "To ensure and promote the widest possible mutual assistance between all criminal police authorities within the limits of the laws existing in the different countries."

But Article 3 says: "It is strictly forbidden for the Organization to undertake any intervention or activities of a political, military, religious, or racial character." This article is of necessity strictly adhered to, and has greatly hampered efforts to prevent the spread of unlawful acts against civil aviation—including airplane hijackings and bombings. However, Ahmed Bel Jahra had burned the letter of political intent. Interpol could proceed to operation on the assumption that the attempt to destroy the Rome-London flight was a crime of nonpolitical passion, greed, or insanity.

Inspector Jacquoud left his office and took the little red elevator down to the bottom floor, to the Criminal Records Department. There he turned over the first message, inquiring whether any of the names in Marjorie Kavanagh's notebook had criminal records. The Interpol clerks began checking the list against the million and a half file cards indexing the names of criminals all over the world —phonetically as well as alphabetically to prevent any error arising out of misspelling.

The second message, requesting information on the whereabouts of the people named in Marjorie Kavanagh's notebook, Jacquoud took back up to the radio room—with go-ahead instructions. It was a matter of two minutes for one of the operatiors to transmit it simultaneously to all fifty-four NCBs hooked into the special radio-telegraph network around the world. Jacquoud next took the message into the adjoining alcove, to be telexed to the rest of the member nations not yet directly radio-linked to Interpol's central station.

In London's Grosvenor Square the light entering the window of Hunter's temporarily assigned office at the American Embassy was already getting murky, though it was not quite evening yet. Hunter flicked on the frosted ceiling lamp. Then he pinned another white index card on the large yellow plasterboard that took up a quarter of one oak-paneled wall.

The phone on his desk rang. He swung around and snatched it up. But it was only the embassy SY, its chief security officer, wanting to discuss some new ideas he had for improving protection of distinguished visitors from Washington.

"Later, Jack," Hunter told him. "I'm in the middle of something." He hung up and turned back to the index cards he had pinned to the wall board.

On each one he'd written a question. Starting with: "Did Marjorie *know* she was carrying the bomb?" Some of the others that followed:

"If she did, how'd she figure to get off the plane before it went off?"

"If she did, how & why & where'd she get hooked into a terrorist group?"

"Which group?"

"If she *didn't* know she had it, how and why was *she* picked to plant it on?"

There were thirty-six more cards on the board, each with its question. Not bad for a start, considering how little information he had so far to work from. Hunter felt like a rusty athlete doing a preliminary warm-up before a serious reconditioning workout.

His phone rang again. This time it was Klar.

"Interpol headquarters have no criminal records on any of the names from Marjorie Kavanagh's book," the inspector told him. "And there's no word so far on any of them from any of the countries Interpol alerted. I've seen the two people here in London. Friends of the dead girl's parents. Knew she was coming, but not exactly when. And that's all they know, I'm afraid. The same for the two Paris names, according to the police there: friends of friends. Know nothing helpful."

"That's what you *don't* have," Hunter growled impatiently. "Get to what you do."

"I've just received a call from Rome direct. One of the new names there in the girl's book . . . Selim Ramouk . . . according to other people named in her book, Marjorie Kavanagh moved in with him during her last week in Rome. A quiet, serious, good-looking boy, according to the others. Dark, slender, about twenty-four or five. He's in Italy on a Turkish passport. But Turkey informs Rome that no such passport has been issued."

Hunter bit into it, and smiled wolfishly. "And now he's vanished."

"On the button, Simon. He moved out of his room within an hour of the airport explosion. No forwarding address. No trace of him, though the Rome dragnet's apparently already intense. He's disappeared."

"That all of it?"

"That's it."

"Who's in charge of this in Rome?"

"Major Diego Bandini. Carabinieri."

"Good, I know him. Thanks, Ivor." Hunter put down the phone, and thought about a dark, slender, good-looking boy in his twenties who called himself Selim Ramouk and carried false Turkish identity. Another figure partially materialized behind the boy—a shadowy image of a nameless somebody who had directed his actions.

That was the one Hunter wanted.

He started to reach for the phone again and then hesitated, looking at the appointment pad on his desk beside it. Tomorrow he had a meeting with the chief security officers of five international airlines. If he canceled that meeting, there would be trouble. The airlines were demanding protective action from the United States government. Each of them swung political weight. Hunter could not brush them aside with impunity. He was not his own master. As long as he went on meeting all the people he was supposed to, and made all the obvious correct motions, no blame would fall on him even if the practical results turned out in the long run to be minimal. But if he ignored the political obligations of his job to go off in pursuit of an independent objective of his own, and didn't achieve results big enough to compensate for acting like a maverick, he was going to get himself fired.

Hunter couldn't afford that. He needed to work, for his own self-esteem, and for the money. Almost two years of not working, and of Beth's mounting medical bills, had left him deeply in debt. Chavez recommending him to State had been a stroke of badly needed luck. If State dropped him because he failed to shape up, there'd be nothing else for him at anywhere near this level. In 1973 all the security branches of the American government were being decimated by an economy wave. The CIA had already fired six hundred of its people, with more due for the ax shortly. The Bureau of Narcotics and Dangerous Drugs was also cutting back fiercely, as it prepared to merge into the Justice Department's new Drug Enforcement Administration. So far more than forty BNDD narcs had lost their jobs. Hunter considered what that left him, if he got bounced by State: an industrial spying or security job with a European branch of one of the bigger private companies.

On the other hand, he considered what he knew of the violent rivalry within the loosely knit Arab terrorist network. Each splinter organization was fighting for a bigger share of prestige, publicity, and financial backing. The outfit that had failed to blow up the 747 was going to lose out on all counts. Unless it could make up for it by pulling off an even bigger operation, very quickly. If Hunter could uncover that operation, and destroy it, he'd come out smelling sweet enough to survive.

Hunter picked up the phone and spoke to Rina Cherney, who'd been temporarily assigned to him from the embassy secretarial pool. He told her to postpone tomorrow's meeting for two weeks; and to book him on the next plane he could catch to Rome.

FOUR

Hunter's plane was in the air on its way to Rome when Interpol's general alert to all zones turned up its first new lead in the search for Selim.

In Zone 1, which includes Denmark, Norway, Sweden, and Finland, the routine daily police check of hotel registrations in Copenhagen came across a Mrs. Joan Channon. This was one of the Rome names in Marjorie Kavanagh's notebook. Copenhagen's Interpol NCB radioed this information to the Central Station in Saint-Cloud. Inspector Jacquoud had it relayed as requested to London's Interpol office. Which in turn passed it on to Inspector Klar in Special Branch.

Klar had earlier received from Rome a brief rundown on the names in Marjorie Kavanagh's notebook, including Joan Channon. She was described as an American divorcée, working in Rome the past four years as an independent film broker. Thirty-eight years old, very pretty, quite successful in her business. Klar phoned her in Copenhagen, explained who he was and what had happened, and asked for anything she could tell him about Marjorie Kavanagh's movements and contacts in Rome.

"I'm afraid I can't tell you much of anything," Joan Channon answered. "I didn't really *know* the kid. Matter of fact I only saw her once, very briefly, after we were introduced by an artist friend. Arthur Delisio." Another name in the dead girl's book. Klar heard a sudden change in Joan Channon's voice, to a tone of awe: "My God . . . that's *fate* for you . . . my lucky star . . ."

"I'm afraid I don't follow you, Mrs. Channon."

"It just hit me, Inspector. Until about a week ago, I was booked on this morning's flight from Rome to London!"

Klar kept his tone casual: "And what changed your plans?"

"There was supposed to be a British film for sale to Italy. Then the deal fell through, and one turned up for me in Copenhagen. So I came here instead."

"I see. Mrs. Channon, do you by chance know a young man named Selim Ramouk?"

"Yes, I know Selim. Very well. Why?"

"Could you tell me who some of his friends are, in Rome or elsewhere? And what business connections he has?"

"I'm afraid not. He's not in any business, that I know of. I think he's an art student somewhere. And I don't know any of his friends. He was by himself the first time I met him, at the Bella Matta. That's a discotheque in Rome. He just came over, out of the blue, and asked me to dance. He . . . danced very well. After that . . . well, any time I saw him he was alone."

"Mrs. Channon," Klar reminded her. "I thought you said you knew him very well? Yet you don't know any of his friends or contacts; and as a matter of fact you only met him a few weeks ago."

"He's just like that—very easy to get close to quickly. Secretive about some things, but very warm, personally. Pleasant to be with. . . . Inspector, I did ask what you want to know about him for?"

"He has disappeared, Mrs. Channon. And we want to locate him. There is a suspicion he may have been involved in the attempt to smuggle the explosives aboard the plane."

"I don't believe that." Joan Channon's voice over the phone was firm. "Selim is an extremely gentle and nice boy. He's *not* a murderer."

"Did he ever talk to you about his political beliefs?"

There was a pause as the woman in Copenhagen appeared to think about it. "No. Never. Just . . . personal things. But he's definitely not your bomber, Inspector. Selim's just not like that, believe me."

"In that case, we still have to find him. So he can explain his sudden disappearance. And tell us what Marjorie Kavanagh was up to in Rome."

"Why would Selim know that?"

"They became lovers, Mrs. Channon. Didn't you know? She lived with him, for the past week."

There was another short silence at the other end of the line. Then Joan Channon said softly: "That son of a bitch. . . . So *that's* why he never came around again after I introduced him to her."

"*You* introduced them?"

"In the Bella Matta. Same place I met him a couple weeks earlier. That's the other time I saw her, that I told you about." Joan Channon gave a short, rueful laugh. "Well, what the hell. . . . It happens."

"Mrs. Channon," Inspector Klar said carefully, "it is possible this boy originally intended to use you to smuggle the explosives aboard the plane to London, and then switched to Marjorie Kavanagh after your flight plans changed. . . ."

"I still don't believe that, Inspector. Maybe he's some kind of bastard. But not that kind."

"It is still extremely important for him to be found, quickly. If he's innocent, to find that out so we can search for the real killers. If he's guilty, to prevent him and his associates from killing again. And so far we have little to go on in searching for him, except a description that would fit thousands of handsome young men. Anything you know that would help . . ."

"There's one thing," Joan Channon cut in suddenly, "that doesn't fit anyone else's description." She hesitated. "But it's not something anyone would see, usually. I mean . . ." Again the hesitation.

"Yes?" Klar urged her.

Her laugh was nervous. "Dammit, Inspector, this is embarrassing me. It *shouldn't*, I know. And it wouldn't, if you didn't sound so awfully . . . well, British."

Inspector Klar sighed. "I'm not *that* British, Mrs. Channon. My parents were immigrants from Russia."

She laughed again, more easily. "Okay. Selim's got a scar, on his left hip. A pretty big one. He said he got it in a car smashup. It's odd-looking—shaped exactly like the letter *Y*."

At the request of both London and Rome, Inspector Jacquoud sent out a new general alarm message to all seven zones from Interpol headquarters in Saint-Cloud. This one concerned Selim alone, giving his age, height, facial description—and the special mark of the Y-shaped scar on his left hip. Jacquoud headed the message: "XD . . . SOPEF . . . DUDOL."

This decoded as: "Extremely Urgent . . Please send all relevant information you may possess or be able to acquire about this person. If possible please include his photograph and fingerprints, details of any convictions. If he is wanted, please let us know whether extradition is requested and under what conditions. . . .

"If this person be found in Europe, please detain him. In any other country, please keep a watch on his movements and activities."

Hunter arrived in Rome on time to dine with Major Diego Bandini at ten-thirty that night. A normal dinner hour for a city where the three-hour afternoon siesta is religiously adhered to, and where offices that reopen at four don't close again until eight-thirty or nine. The explosion at the Leonardo da Vinci Airport, and the subsequent search for Selim, had kept Diego Bandini too busy to take the siesta that day. In spite of that he still looked quite fresh, ready to carry on for hours. He was always happiest when working hardest. It fed some mysterious source of nervous energy hidden inside his narrow figure, relaxed the fiercely intense face, injected liveliness into the gentle, melancholy eyes.

Diego Bandini was something of a wonder to his more extroverted colleagues at the Direzione Generale di Pubblico Sicurezza. Except in his official capacity he was painfully shy, especially with women. They prettier they were and the nicer they were to him, the more deeply Bandini drew into his shell. But he was a brainy, efficient, dedicated cop. Hunter had worked closely with him for almost three months on a counterfeiting case, some four years ago. He knew Bandini's wife, too: a beautiful, self-assured unsuccessful screen actress from Holland. She'd assessed and taken control of Bandini within an hour of meeting him, gotten him into her bed with understanding firmness the same night, and just as firmly married him a month later. When she was away doing one of her rare small roles in a film, there was no question about what Bandini was doing with his nonworking time: He was home alone with a good book, quite contented.

He filled Hunter in over an excellent seafood dinner served on the outside terrace of Bandini's favorite restaurant. On the other side of the low hedge bordering the terrace, automobile horns were threatening each other and unmuffled motorbikes roared defiantly as they inched through the crowd of traffic snarling its way around the Piazza del Popolo. But Diego Bandini was so used to this constant of Roman life that he automatically raised and lowered his voice with the noise level as he brought Hunter up to date on the case.

"As you assumed, the names written in red in Marjorie Kavanagh's book are contacts in Rome given her by friends in America. The ones in blue are people she met while here, through those contacts. All are agreed on one thing: that she would not knowingly have become part of a terrorist plot, political or not. Of these people, only three ever met the younger man calling himself Selim Ramouk.

"Joan Channon, as I told you, introduced Marjorie to Selim. The other two met him through Marjorie: Arthur Delisio, an American of Italian extraction who comes from the girl's neighborhood in Baltimore. And a Danish woman named Kirsten Ryberg. She runs a foreign language bookshop with Delisio behind the Via Veneto, and lives with him not far from the Piazza dei Mercanti, in Trastevere."

"They're the ones who told you Marjorie had moved in with Selim?"

Bandini nodded. "Marjorie Kavanagh was supposed to leave Rome for a week in Paris, followed by a week in London. Delisio and the Ryberg woman thought she'd gone. Until they ran into her with Selim one night in Trastevere, coming out of a theater which shows old American films. She told them she'd decided to remain in Rome for the rest of her vacation time, to be with this boy Selim."

"And she *told* them she was living with him?"

"Yes. She seemed to them very proud of it. Selim is apparently a very handsome and charming young man. She acted deeply infatuated with him. Enough to cancel her plans for Paris and London."

Hunter frowned thoughtfully at the glass of wine in his hand. "I wonder what changed her mind about going to London."

"That," Bandini told him, "is one of the many, many things we have not been able to discover so far. In fact, at this point our investigation has turned up no leads at all—except for the scar on Selim's left hip. We've been combing all of Rome. We've shaken all of our informers roughly enough so they understand we mean business. Absolutely nothing."

"Did this couple see Selim again?"

"The next night. They had dinner with him and the girl. And the answer to your next question, Simon, is no. He did not discuss politics. They learned nothing at all about him, except that he claimed to be interested in art, though they didn't find him very knowledgeable; and he told them he was from Turkey, which we now know to be untrue. Though we haven't learned where he *is* from."

Hunter eyed Bandini shrewdly. "But you've made a pretty fair *guess*. The Bella Matta discotheque, where he met Joan Channon, and later Marjorie Kavanagh—is it still a hangout for Arabs with guerrilla group expense accounts?"

"Still," Bandini acknowledged. "And also one of their contact points for traffic in drugs, in exchange for arms."

"Yet you don't close it down."

Bandini sighed and spread his hands helplessly. "Where Arabs are concerned, you know we have to tread delicately. Italy badly needs Arab oil. Every time we interfere with one of these guerrilla organizations, there are economic reprisals. Sometimes violent reprisals, as well. All we can do is keep our ears open, and occasionally have a hidden photographer take pictures of those entering and leaving the Bella Matta."

Hunter's dark eyes narrowed. Bandini shook his head. "No, Simon. We've pulled out all the pictures that were taken of young men who come near fitting Selim's description, and shown them around. But Selim just didn't happen to enter or leave the Bella Matta at any of the times our photographer was on duty."

Hunter brooded on it as he refilled their wineglasses. "What do the people who work at the discotheque have to say about him?"

"None of them admit knowing him, or who his contacts might be. We've also questioned many of the people who frequent the place. No help there, either. So you see, Simon, we really have very little to work with. Nobody knows where he's gone, who he was in touch with, or who he really is. And no photograph. We can't very well send out an order for the police to take down the pants of every good-looking young man in Italy to see if he's got the scar on his hip."

The bookshop where Diego Bandini had questioned Delisio and Kirsten Ryberg had been closed for hours. Hunter went to their home address, across the river in Trastevere. It had long been the poorest section of Rome. In recent years there'd been an influx of foreign hippies and students attracted by the low rents; and well-to-do expatriates attracted by slum buildings that could be turned back into the palaces they once were, with enough time and money.

Hunter found their address in a narrow alley smelling of garbage and cats. He had to feel his way up five flights of dark stairway to reach their apartment on the top floor. It turned out to be two small, meagerly furnished rooms; but brightened by colorful paintings of Rome. And it had the most coveted luxury in Rome: a small roof terrace with a view—this one including the dome of St. Peter's.

Arthur Delisio was a small, bald, cheerful man of about fifty. Kirsten Ryberg was perhaps five years younger, with a deliciously rounded figure and warm blue eyes. The atmosphere of relaxed contentment between the two was infectious, causing Hunter to stay with them longer than his purpose warranted.

They answered his questions as freely as they had Bandini's. And he got not one single thing more out of it than Bandini had. He hadn't really expected to; but he had to try. After half an hour he got up, thanked them, and started to leave. He was opening the door when something in the painting on the wall beside it caught his attention.

It was a watercolor of the Trevi Fountain. The signature on it was "Delisio."

Hunter took his hand from the doorknob and turned back to the man. You didn't tell Major Bandini that you're an artist."

Delisio's smile was just a tinge sad. "Because I'm not. Not a *real* artist. There was a time," he admitted, "that I thought I might be. But I didn't have enough talent, I guess. Or enough push. Now it's just my hobby, and pleasure. An *artist* is a professional who can sell his work."

"You used to," the woman reminded him.

Delisio laughed indulgently. "Sure, when I first came to Rome. You can't call doing sketches of tourists on the Spanish Steps for ten bucks apiece being a professional."

Something almost vicious flickered briefly in the depths of Hunter's eyes. "Could you do me a sketch of Selim?" he asked quietly.

Delisio frowned uncertainly. "From memory? I don't know. . . ."

"Of course you can," Kirsten Ryberg said. "Remember the one you did of my brother, after he visited us?"

"That was more of a caricature."

"It was still a perfect likeness," she insisted. "Anyone would recognize him from it. And I can help. Point out if you make the nose too big or small, things like that."

Hunter closed the door and sat down. "Try it," he told Arthur Delisio.

Switzerland's French-speaking city of Geneva has historically been the sparring ring of diplomats; the birthplace of grandiose schemes to achieve world peace and prosperity, and the burial ground for all the vain hopes. It is situated on a beautiful lake, from which the famed Jet d'Eau shoots some five hundred feet into the air and boasts of being the tallest man-made waterspout in the world. Along this lake, the Quai Woodrow Wilson leads to both the European headquarters of the United Nations and the shell of the League of Nations, that earlier collapsed endeavor to make people settle their differences with reason, instead of blood.

In 1973 the European activities of the guerrilla groups financed by Colonel Qadhafi were directed from Geneva. A young Libyan named Bashir Mawdri was the contact man there for this financing. This made him an increasingly important focal point for violent dissidents within the complex web of rival Arab guerrilla organizations.

These organizations grew out of the 1948 war, when all the surrounding Arab nations invaded Israel with the intention of wiping it off the face of the earth. The invading armies ordered the Arabs living in Israel to get out of the country temporarily—so their soldiers could kill everyone they met, without having to stop and find out what kind of Semite they were, Arab or Jew. The Arabs of Israel obediently left, confident of a quick return after the inevitable triumph of the overwhemingly superior numbers of the Arab armies.

But Israel surprised the world by beating back the attackers. The Arabs who had fled found themselves unwelcome exiles in the surrounding countries, unable to return. They were packed into ramshackle refugee camps by their fellow Arabs, and left to breed and hate. Some of this hatred was directed at the Arab nations which had misled them, and now refused to make a decent place for them out of their tremendous oil incomes. But most of the hatred was increasingly directed at Israel. Out of this hatred, and frustration, the guerrilla organizations were born.

The three largest are Fatah, the PFLP (Popular Front for the Liberation of Palestine), and Saiqa. All three are supposed to act in co-operation under the umbrella organization of PLO (Palestine Liberation Organization). But a power struggle has developed between the three, making for a growing enmity that has left them open to Qadhafi's infiltration.

Saiqa, led by Zoheir Mohsen, is based in Syria and trained by the Syrian Army, with extra backing from Iraq. By 1973 Zoheir Mohsen, though nominally chief of the over-all PLO's military department, was accusing Fatah of grabbing military funds intended for all of the groups. And there were growing rumors of plots originating in Syria and Iraq to assassinate the leader of Fatah.

The Marxist-Leninist PFLP, led by the revolutionary George Habash and supported by China, dislikes Fatah's connections with Arab monarchist and capitalist rulers. PFLP also for a long time had a mutual hatred for Libya's Qadhafi, who loathed communism because it was antireligion. This was before Libya and the Soviet Union decided their common interests were stronger than their differences over religion, and signed a pact to work together.

By 1973 the PFLP had lost control of its main splinter group: the Popular Democratic Front—now firmly in the grip of a bloodthirsty fanatic named Nayif Hawatmeh. Two smaller splinters were also going their own way: the Arab National Youth for the Liberation of Palestine, and a group called PFLP-General Command. Both of these last two had been subverted by Libyan financing and Colonel Qadhafi's vision.

The biggest and most important of the three main guerrilla organizations is the Beirut-based Fatah. Its leader is a stocky intellectual named Yasser Arafat (code name: Abu Amar), who is increasingly harassed by the inner political struggle. His military commander is Khalil Al-Wazir (code name: Abu Jihad), known, because of his shyness and quiet personal life, as "the silent man."

It was Wazir, the silent man, who thought up the name Fatah. This name has three different meanings. It is the reversed initials for Haarakat Tahrir Palastin (Movement for the Liberation of Palestine). The word "fatah" itself means "victory." In reverse it is the word "hataf," meaning "death."

Fatah's security, espionage, and intelligence service is called Rasd. By 1973 one of Fatah leader Arafat's great anxieties was the number of Rasd agents actually operating in secret for Colonel

Qadhafi. Even to the point of their kidnapping important Libyan exiles from other Arabian countries and returning them to Qadhafi's prisons.

Black September was originally the name given to Rasd's "action branch." It is this group that is entrusted with the actual carrying out of terrorist acts, for the parent organization: Fatah. Its leaders —Salah Khalef (code name: Aby Iyad), Ali Hassan Salamah (code name: Abu Hassan), and Mohammed Dawud Oudeh (code name: Abu Dawud)—are supposed to be answerable to, and loyal to, Fatah. But the Black September name has come to be adopted for any successful terrorist action. And Black September groups are increasingly financed by Colonel Qadhafi, after special indoctrination at one of Libya's four commando-training camps: Tocra, Sirte, Tarhuna, and Misurata.

The members of the Black September group that killed eleven unarmed Israeli athletes at the Munich Olympics, when freed from German custody after a threat to blow up a German airliner, flew to Libya for their triumphal parade, not to Fatah in Beirut. The Black September leader who masterminded the killing of three Western diplomats in Khartoum, because America would not release the Arab murderer of Robert Kennedy, directed the operation from Libya; and refused Fatah leader Arafat's demand that he come back to Beirut to explain this. The prepared letter which Bel Jahra had burned after the failure of his plot in Rome had been signed "Black September."

In these circumstances Colonel Qadhafi's man in Geneva, Bashir Mawdri, had become the most important contact man in Europe for "Black September" operations. His office—where the door bore his official job title of Assistant Secretary, Information Service— was in the Permanent Mission of the Libyan Arab Republic to the United Nations at 42 Rue de Lausanne. But because of the danger of bugging, meetings concerned with his real work were conducted elsewhere; a different place each time, so no one could plant listening devices in advance.

Bel Jahra waited for Bashir Mawdri at a small outdoor café facing the promenade along the lake. The place was almost ready to close for the night, and the other tables were empty. Bel Jahra sat alone at his table, nursing a tall Campari-soda and looking utterly relaxed. The dynamo of energy inside him hummed softly, contented in the knowledge it would soon be called upon. Driss Ham-

mou leaned against a railing across the promenade, a position from
which he had an unobstructed view of the approaches to the café.
His hands were deep in the pockets of the light, tan raincoat he
wore. The compact, short-barreled .38 revolver Hammou carried
was in the right pocket. Behind Hammou, the swans kept appear-
ing and disappearing, as they glided through the long streaks of
light reflected from the city across the black surface of Lake
Geneva. Beyond the lake, the Alps were like low-hanging clouds in
the night darkness.

A tall, broad-shouldered man in a brown business suit came
strolling along the promenade. He glanced at Driss Hammou, took
in Bel Jahra and the empty tables around him, and changed course,
sitting at the farthest table to Bel Jahra's right.

A moment later Bashir Mawdri appeared, followed by another
of his bodyguards. Mawdri came straight to Bel Jahra's table and
sat down without greeting him. The second bodyguard took a table
to their left. Hammou stayed where he was, watching. A tired
waiter came out to take their orders.

"Like something to drink?" Bel Jahra asked the Libyan, with
studied politeness.

"I don't drink alcohol. You know the Koran forbids it." Mawdri
ordered a tea from the waiter, who moved off to the Libyan bodyguards.

"Sometimes I forget," Bel Jahra said carelessly, and deliberately
sipped at his drink. He didn't like Bashir Mawdri, who at twenty-
five was much too smug and sure of himself. That came of being, at
such a young age, in a position to bestow power and hope upon
so many others. Which derived in turn from being the favorite
nephew of one of the "Brother-Colonels" who'd helped Colonel
Qadhafi take over Libya.

He was eyeing Bel Jahra sardonically now, as the waiter disappeared inside. "This meeting shouldn't take long. We don't actually
have much to say to each other, do we?" Mawdri's tone was bored.
"I'm sure you come armed with many explanations. But I must tell
you, I have no interest at all in hearing excuses for failure."

No anger rose inside Bel Jahra, as it had in previous meetings
with Mawdri. He leaned back in his chair and regarded the younger
man almost with affection. "Come now, Bashir, you know that the
best of plans are bound to fail, from time to time. I think *you* have
had many. Am I right? The attempts on King Hussien? All those

plots to assassinate the American Secretary of State which came to nothing? I don't imagine Qadhafi was happy with you over those."

Color rose in Mawdri's face. "The men responsible for those failures have never again been allowed an independent command. The same, I'm afraid, must now be applied to you."

Bel Jahra smiled thinly. "I don't think Colonel Qadhafi will agree with you, when he learns of the new operation I've come up with."

"It seems you don't hear me," Bashir Mawdri told him heavily. "We are just not interested in any further operations you want to manage."

"This one," Bel Jahra went on evenly, as though the other hadn't spoken, "will accomplish—at the same time and place—the deaths of both Hussein and America's Secretary of State." He enjoyed watching the shock of it hit Bashir Mawdri. Quietly, he explained about Valasi's eightieth birthday party; and what he had in mind for it.

For the first time, the smugness was gone from the Libyan's manner. The enormity of what Bel Jahra was proposing erased it; and the knowledge of how much such a proposal would appeal to his ruler. "It would be very difficult," he said uncertainly. "If it *could* be done . . ."

"It can," Bel Jahra cut in flatly. "You already see it can. There'll be security precautions and bodyguards with them at this party, of course. But not the enormous amount of protection that you get around official visits, because no one is supposed to know they're coming. It can be done. By me."

Mawdri shook his head, frowning worriedly. "*If* we were to back such an operation, you would certainly have to play a prominent part in it. That I agree. But someone else would have to be in charge of it; a man with more experience, and success, behind him."

"It can't be done without me," Bel Jahra pointed out coldly. "I'm the only one you know who can get into the Valasi estate to plan it, and get in again to enable its execution when the time comes. And I won't do either, unless I lead it, start to finish."

Mawdri chewed on that in silence to find a way around it.

Bel Jahra rose to his feet. "I have to get some sleep now. Tomorrow I intend to investigate the Valasi estate, so I know what I have to deal with and can lay out the operation detail, realistically. If you're not interested, I imagine I can find another guerrilla organization that will be. One of your rivals." He turned as though to walk away.

"Wait . . ." Mawdri snapped.

Bel Jahra turned back, smiling down at Mawdri.

"I'll be in Paris in a few days," the Libyan said, after a moment. "Contact me there, after you have investigated thoroughly, and planned it down to the last detail. If it is practical, we will proceed."

"If we do," Bel Jahra reminded him, "I command."

Bashir Mawdri slowly nodded. "Agreed."

Bel Jahra patted the young Libyan's shoulder, and strolled away to join Hammou. Bashir Mawdri watched them go off together in the direction of the Grand Quai in the old section of town. They disappeared into the night shadows by the time the waiter brought out the three orders.

Mawdri paid for all three, and got up without touching his tea. The bodyguards left their tables immediately. They converged to flank him protectively as he hurried back to the Libyan Mission, to send off a coded query to Tripoli.

It was three in the morning when the Roman taxi turned off the Via Flaminia, and entered a drab piazza hedged around by old buildings with small curved terraces at the top and tiny shops at the bottom. In the middle was a square cement island with six trees and five sagging benches, grouped around a postage stamp of grass with a wire fence around it. The taxi stopped in front of a small *pensione* sandwiched between a *trattoria* and a *macelleria*. Hunter climbed out feeling his big frame heavy with fatigue, his eyes puffy and bloodshot.

He told the driver to wait for him, and went into the *pensione*. Opening the front door rang a bell somewhere within the building. Inside the entrance foyer was a combination reception lobby and sitting room; small, dim, and empty except for several worn-out leather chairs and two tables heaped with torn copies of old newspapers and magazines. Hunter spread his tired legs and waited.

After a time, a fat, balding man in crumpled pajamas and bedroom slippers shuffled out of a dark doorway and blinked at him sleepily. "No rooms," he grumbled in Italian. "The house is full. No rooms."

"I don't want a room," Hunter told him in English. "I want Uri Ezan."

The man immediately got a very stupid look on his face "Who?" But he said it in English, and his eyes had lost some of the sleepiness as he studied Hunter suspiciously.

Hunter could understand that. He didn't know the fat man; and he did know that this house, which drew mostly Israeli tourists, also served as a contact place in Rome for the counter-terrorist activities of Mossad (Israel's "Institution for Special Tasks"). It was bugged by the Rome police and Arab agents, debugged from time to time as a gesture by Israeli specialists passing through town, and regularly rebugged.

"Uri Ezan," Hunter repeated wearily. "He owns this place. The past six months he's been running it personally. My name's Simon Hunter. He knows me. If he's asleep wake him up."

"I can't. He's not here. Out of town."

That was possible. Hunter considered trying to make contact with some other Mossad agent; but Uri was the only one he knew well. "Okay. When he gets back, tell him I'm looking for him. I'm at the Excelsior and I want to see him. Got it all?"

The fat face had dropped all pretense at stupidity. "Sure, what's to get? You say you're Simon Hunter, know Uri, want to see him, and you're staying in the Excelsior Hotel, which I wish I could afford to do."

Hunter went back out to the taxi, and had it take him to the Excelsior. As he picked up his room key from the desk, the uniformed night clerk nodded across the lobby and murmured, "A gentleman has been waiting for you."

Hunter turned and saw a clean-cut young embassy type get up from a couch, erase the sleepiness from his expression, and advance briskly across the lobby. "Mr. Hunter? Simon Hunter?" He'd obviously been briefed that Hunter was someone important from State.

Hunter got out his I.D. and flipped it open. He indicated the thick brown envelope tucked securely under the embassy man's left arm. "That for me?"

"Yes, sir. They told me to give it to you personally, not leave it for you. I've been waiting two hours." He didn't make it sound like a complaint; it was just that he wanted it known he'd done his duty.

"You did right," Hunter said, and took the envelope from him. "Now go home and get some sleep." He trudged to the elevator, went up to the sixth floor, and into his room. He snapped on the lights, sat down heavily on the bed, and pulled off his shoes. Then he ripped open the sealed envelope.

It contained dozens of photographic copies of each of the three sketches Arthur Delisio had drawn of Selim. Both he and Kirsten Ryberg had agreed these were all good likenesses. Diego Bandini had already run off his own copies, for circulation to police throughout Italy. By morning they would also be on the front pages of every Italian newspaper, going on the TV news, and getting circulated through the Interpol network. These copies which the embassy had run off for Hunter he intended to begin circulating personally tomorrow—to airline and airport security personnel, embassies and consulates, and certain carefully selected undercover agents like Uri.

Hunter finally went to sleep that night sure of one thing: Unless Selim had already left Europe, wherever he moved he was bound to get tagged within the next couple days.

FIVE

Bel Jahra stood on top of the thick wall of the ancient hill fortress
of Roquebrune. With the calculating appraisal of a conqueror, he
surveyed what lay below him: a magnificent view, reaching for
miles in either direction. Rusty-red tiled roofs, the brilliant greens
of trees and vines, vivid eruptions of multicolored flowers. All
of it tumbling down into the exquisite blue of the Mediterranean
Sea. Far to the left, Bel Jahra could see Italy. To the right, the
castle of Monaco and the skyscrapers of Monte Carlo. And directly
below him, the jut of French Riviera coast called Cap Martin,
where Dezso Valasi had his estate—and would celebrate his
eightieth birthday.

There has long been a close connection between Cap Martin
and Roquebrune, where Bel Jahra stood gazing down upon it.
Eight hundred years ago there was a convent on Cap Martin. A
dangerously vulnerable position in those days. Saracen corsairs were
raiding all the shores of the Mediterranean; sensible people built
their fortress towns farther back from the coast, on easily defended
hilltops. But the nuns of Cap Martin put their faith in God, and a
precautionary arrangement: If the Saracens did come, they were
to ring an alarm bell, summoning to their rescue the armed men
of Roquebrune, the fortress-town high above.

One night the nuns of Cap Martin decided to find out just how
much they could depend on the courage of Roquebrune. They rang
the alarm bell. The men on the hill leaped from their beds,
snatched up weapons, and scrambled down the slopes to battle the
nonexistent raiders. The nuns were pleased with the result of their

test. Their would-be rescuers were not pleased with their lost night of sleep.

Three nights later, the Saracens did come. As they swarmed from their boats onto the rugged sea cliffs of Cap Martin, the nuns awakened and rang their bell again. The men of Roquebrune woke, heard the bell, and went back to sleep, tired of being tested. The raiders slaughtered the oldest nuns, dragged the rest down to their boats for sale in the slave markets of Arabia, and set fire to the convent before sailing away. The rising flames told Roquebrune, too late, that this one had not been a false alarm.

Today, Cap Martin is one of the few places along the Riviera that has escaped being cut up by resort building developers. This is thanks to the mass of rocks rising all around its shore, making the laying down of an artificial beach impossible, and the building of boat-docking facilities impractical. So Cap Martin continues to be a secluded domain of grand nineteenth-century villas, each nestled in its large, heavily wooded estate. From his vantage point on the ancient ramparts above, Bel Jahra could just make out a part of the russet-tiled roof of Dezso Valasi's villa, peeking through the thick-clustered pines and olive groves of a walled estate encompassing the place where the sacked convent had been.

Bel Jahra experienced a keen sense of power looking down on his target from a falcon's viewpoint. But by that noon he intended to get a much closer look. He hadn't phoned Juliet Shale since flying in early that morning from Geneva. First, there'd been the matter of quickly acquiring a place to function from here. He was letting Driss Hammou rent the Roquebrune apartment he'd found for sublet, to avoid using his own false papers. That did away with the risk of Juliet Shale finding out he was masquerading under a different name and starting to wondering why.

Bel Jahra glanced at his wristwatch. By now Hammou would have signed the one-month lease at the rental office down in Monte Carlo; and have phoned Selim in Genoa to come join them here. It was time to stop surveying the coming area of operation from the heights, and get down to specifics. Time to pay a surprise call on Juliet Shale; in person, so he could look over the possibilities and problems inside Valasi's estate.

Turning from the view, Bel Jahra went down the stone steps inside the wall, through the courtyard, and out of the fortress into the small town clustered around its base. Like the fortress itself, the town clung to and burrowed into the brown rock of the hill that gave it its name. A picturesque relic of a vanished history, living now on tourist shops and tourist rentals, with a restaurant in the big cave that had once been the fortress armory. Bel Jahra descended narrow tunnel-passages that burrowed through and under the interlocked stone houses to the parking area at the bottom of the tiny village.

This was the closest that cars could manage to get into Roquebrune. Bel Jahra was opening the door of the white BMW sedan he'd rented at the airport, when Driss Hammou's car came up the hill approach road. Hammou jumped out with a folded newspaper in his thick fist and anxiety clawing his broad face.

"What's wrong?" Bel Jahra demanded. "Couldn't you get Selim on the phone?"

"I got him," Hammou answered miserably. "I told him to come here. Before I saw *this*." He unfolded the newspaper as he handed it over.

It was an Italian paper. There were two drawings of Selim on the front page. Bel Jahra recognized them as Selim instantly; before he could take in the headline over them or read what was printed under them. His face was an expressionless mask as he took the paper from Hammou's hand.

"I phoned Genoa again," Hammou said tightly as Bel Jahra read. "As soon as I saw this. But Selim was already checked out of the hotel. So he's already on his way. And he's *sure* to be recognized when he stops at the border control." Hammou considered what he knew of Italian police—and his own experience as an interrogator for the Moroccan secret police. "They'll break him like an eggshell. He'll be blabbling about *us* ten minutes after they get their hands on him!"

"Stop sounding like a hysterical old woman," Bel Jahra snapped. "You're no use at all to me that way." The coldness of the voice, and in the pale eyes, steadied Hammou down.

"He *will* inform about us," he said in a quieter, more controlled voice. "They'll think about the baby his bomb killed, and do anything they have to with him. He'll talk."

"If they get hold of him," Bel Jahra conceded evenly. He knew he was facing another disaster; but it hadn't happened yet, and he was not the kind of man to panic ahead of time. There were still possibilities, and work to be done. He felt an icy calm as he tossed the newspaper inside his car and considered what he knew about Selim; putting himself inside Selim's mind.

"He must have woken late and had breakfast in his room." Bel Jahra spoke quietly, almost to himself, "Otherwise, he would have seen his picture in the papers before you phoned. He is as interested as we are in what's going on in Rome concerning the airport explosion. He'll buy a paper when he stops for lunch, before he reaches the border. If he hasn't seen it already. . . . You didn't give him the number of the apartment phone here?"

Hammou shook his head. "It didn't occur to me that—"

"So he can't phone me when he sees these wanted pictures of him," Bel Jahra cut in, thinking it through carefully. "He'll be all alone, very frightened, no way to get in touch with me, no one else to turn to for advice or help." His pale eyes were narrowed in concentration. "So he'll keep coming. I'm his only protection, he'll feel. He'll try to get to me. But Selim is not a stupid boy. He'll leave the car, and he won't try any other transport that requires going through border police. Instead, he'll try to sneak across the border, on foot."

"And if he makes it across?" Hammou suggested uneasily. "Aren't we *still* in trouble?"

Bel Jahra nodded. "By this afternoon, his picture will be in the French newspapers, too. He'll *be* spotted, sooner or later. It could be right here. With us. Today, tomorrow, the next day." Bel Jahra's voice was matter-of-fact, but the undertone of tension was there. "We have to consider the problem one step at a time. The first problem is getting him before the police do. The first possible place is the border crossing. Selim only knows one way to slip across from Italy to France: the way he used with us the last time. . . ."

Bel Jahra fell silent, working out the logistics in his mind. Hammou watched, and waited.

After several seconds, Bel Jahra nodded. "That is our best chance," he told Hammou evenly. "The same smuggler trail we used before. Selim will try it that way, I'm sure of it. I want you on the Italian side, Hammou. As fast as you can get there. Try to stop him before he starts across. I'll be waiting at the French end, in case he gets past you."

Hammou looked into Bel Jahra's eyes. "And?" he asked softly.

Bel Jahra frowned at him. "You know the answer, Hammou.

We will soon have all the men we need. I care for the boy. But he has become too much of a danger to us, if he lives."

Hammou nodded. "I understand. Only pray it is *we* who spot him first. Not the police. . . ." He got into his car and drove away.

Bel Jahra got into his own car, and sat for a moment gripping the wheel tightly in his long, lean hands "*Insh'Allah,*" he whispered. As Allah wills it . . .

Something began knocking in the worn-out engine of Selim Hafid's little Fiat-500 as he drove into San Remo, along the northwest coast of Italy. Selim shot a frown at the temperature gauge. It registered no hotter than was to be expected, considering how fast he'd pushed the old car all the way from Genoa on the new multi-lane Autostrada. And the clutch, acceleration, and braking system were still responding normally. Yet the tiny metallic knocking continued as he turned off the highway and slowed into the heavy San Remo traffic.

Selim glanced at his wristwatch. It was two in the afternoon. No Italian automobile mechanic would be back on the job until siesta ended in another two hours. In an hour and a half Selim could be in France, even with a short stop for lunch. He decided to take the risk, and wait until he crossed the border before having the car's engine checked.

Selim maneuvered through the narrow streets in the direction of the central bus depot. There were a number of cheap little restaurants in that area. And the station news kiosk would be open even during siesta. The phone call from Driss Hammou, coming immediately after his late breakfast in his room, had made him so eager to start out that he'd forgotten to buy the morning papers before leaving Genoa. He would read them while he ate lunch, and see if they had anything new to say about the explosion in Rome's Leonardo da Vinci Airport.

Parking alongside the wide concrete mall, Selim walked across it to the bus terminal. Inside the gloom of the building he removed his sunglasses and stuck them in his breast pocket as he approached the newsstand. He was digging into his pocket for some coins when he stopped dead.

There were three newspapers hung up on the display rack over the counter. Pictures of his face stared at him from the front page of each.

Selim turned on his heel and walked away, using willpower not to run. He knew better than to buy a paper now. The nearer he got to them, the greater the danger. Anyone looking from those pictures to him would recognize him on the spot. And he didn't need to read the news story to know what it was about. There was only one reason his pictures could be in the newspapers.

Fumbling the sunglasses from his pocket, he stuck them back on his face before he'd taken five steps away from the newsstand. But he knew how pitifully inadequate that was as concealment. He felt horribly exposed to all the people brushing past; as though there were a sign pinned to his back. At any second disinterested passing glances could change to shocked stares. . . .

Lowering his head as much as he could without drawing attention, he went out of the bus station and back across the mall to his car. Getting inside it quickly, he slammed the door shut and started the motor. His ears were so stuffed with rising blood pressure he could hardly hear the resumed knocking. The pit of his stomach was burning. His mind wouldn't start working on what to do; except to scream at him that there were too many eyes around him on this city street. He needed to get someplace where he'd be utterly alone, so he could break out of this initial panic and think straight.

Praying that whatever was wrong in the engine wouldn't stall the car in the middle of traffic and draw the police, Selim drove out of the city. He went north on the Via Aurelia, following the shore road that Caesar's legions had tramped on their way to subdue Gaul and invade Britain. Halfway between San Remo and Ventimiglia, the last large town before the French border, Selim turned into another road leading away from the sea. There was much less traffic on this one. As the Fiat climbed the hills toward the interior, minutes went by without another car going in either direction.

Cutting off this hill road into a narrow dirt track, Selim followed it for half a mile before stopping. He climbed out of the car and took a long, careful look at the hill farms and sloping vineyards around him. Not a single other person was in sight, anywhere. Selim rested a hip on the car's hood and took deep, slow breaths. That was something they'd taught him at the Naher-al-Bared guerrilla-training camp in Lebanon: how to control your nerves in a crisis by first controlling your breathing.

It worked for Selim now, as it always had in the past. When

he was calm enough so that his judgment would not be affected by his nerves, he began applying his mind to the trouble he was in. If there was a way out of it, he knew he had the intelligence to find it. In fact it was his high IQ that had brought him so far from home, and landed him in this trouble.

When Selim spoke of "home" he meant Palestine—though actually he had never been there in his life. But it was the only home his emotions knew of; made real for him by the anguished, frustrated nostalgia of an older generation of Palestinian refugees.

All of Palestine had belonged to Turkey until World War I, when the British had wrested it away. Subsequently, much of it was parceled out among various Arab nations. The small part that became Israel remained under British authority until 1948. Selim's parents had lived in the northern part of Israel.

They had fled "temporarily" to Lebanon in 1948, obeying instructions from the invading Arab armies, which wanted to be able to regard all who remained as enemies to be killed. When the Arab armies failed to wipe out Israel, Selim's parents found themselves unable to return. Along with thousands like them.

None of the Arab countries wanted to absorb these refugees as new citizens. Oil had made these countries rich; but most of the wealth went into the bank accounts of their rulers and a small elite group directly under them. Very little filtered down to improve the general welfare of their countries. As a result, there were not enough jobs for their own citizens; and the refugees were unwanted competition. So they were packed into bleak, squalid refugee camps—where they were fed and clothed, not by Arab oil wealth, but by contributions from the rest of the world through UNRWA (the United Nations Relief and Works Agency). There most of them were doomed to remain as the decades merged one into another.

The bitter nostalgia of these confined exiles was worsened by what they learned of developments in the land they had left and lost: Arabs who had not fled from Israel were soon enjoying there the greatest prosperity they had ever known. The tribes of Bedouins who had actually fought alongside the Israelis, against the invading armies that contained their traditional blood-enemies, had been made Israeli citizens. And the Israelis were soon turning their part of the arid, barren land known as Palestine into orange groves and well-irrigated farms. The refugees in the Arab camps contemplated what they had lost in fleeing, and festered with anger.

Selim had been born in the Lebanese refugee camp of Ain el Hilweh in 1950, and grown up absorbing this anger through his pores. His father had reinforced it, reminding him every day of what had been lost, and teaching him that he was born to extract vengeance for it. Hatred for Israel became as natural a part of him as eating and breathing.

But because Selim quickly proved to be an unusually bright boy, his father made sure he learned other things as well. There were only two possible ways out of the misery of the refugee camps: the destruction of Israel, or education. Educational facilities in the camp were as meager as everything else. Selim's father made up for this as best he could. He'd learned English from British troops stationed near his old village. This he taught to Selim. And he found men in the camp who knew other languages, and enjoyed relieving their boredom by giving lessons to a bright boy. By the time he was fourteen, Selim was able to speak excellent English, plus a good deal of Italian and some French.

Knowing the languages, he'd inevitably longed for a chance to visit the countries, and escape the crushing boredom of the refugee camp. His first chance for escape and new excitement presented itself when he was fifteen, in the form of a recruiter from the Fatah guerrilla organization. Selim had seized the opportunity.

He'd been sent first to the guerrilla-training camp at Naher-al-Bared, where he'd been taught how to handle revolvers, grenades, and explosives. He'd learned so well and quickly there that he'd been sent on to Fatah's Syrian field headquarters at Dera, for advanced training in demolition and sabotage techniques. Again, he'd proved himself an exceptionally apt pupil—and been forwarded to an Egyptian officers' training school some miles from Cairo, in the desert camp of Haimat Az-Zaitun.

He'd been halfway through this school's intensive course on commando tactics when an agent from Rasd, the guerrilla intelligence network, came to see him. He'd learned of Selim's command of European languages, and felt that Selim would be wasting this special knowledge by confining himself to guerrilla activities in the Middle East. He would be much more valuable with the terrorist organizations operating in Europe. The lure was there, and Selim seized on it eagerly.

But before going to Europe, Selim found himself being passed on by the Rasd agent to a special indocrination course at Tocra, the largest of the Libyan guerrilla-training camps. It was there that Selim learned for the first time the attitude of Colonel Qadhafi toward Israel and the Palestinian refugee problem. The Libyans didn't want an end to either, as long as they served their purpose. They wanted Israel and the angry refugees to continue, as a beneficial irritant. Like grains of sand caught inside an oyster, irritating it into producing a pearl. The pearl Qadhafi envisioned would be a new Pan-Islamic empire.

Selim had been turned off by the concept; by its cynical use of the refugee's misery as a means to its own ends. But because he still wanted very much to see Europe, he'd kept his attitude pretty much to himself. And eventually he'd been sent to Switzerland, where the contact man from the Libyan Mission in Geneva, Bashir Mawdri, had assigned him to Ahmed Bel Jahra.

From the start, Selim was attracted by Bel Jahra's determination and honesty. After feeling Selim out a bit, Bel Jahra had confessed that he, too, was not at all interested in Qadhafi's Pan-Islam schemes. His sole interest, he'd told Selim frankly, was to be able to return to his own country through a revolution, and create a new Moroccan government. Just as Selim's only interest lay in destroying Israel and getting the Palestinians out of the Arab refugee camps. But practicality required Bel Jahra—and Selim—to co-operate with the Libyans for a time in order to get the backing they needed for what they themselves desired.

Selim began by admiring Bel Jahra's honesty and being drawn to his similar motivations. Before long he'd come to regard Bel Jahra as the one man he could look up to, follow—and trust.

It was to Bel Jahra that his thoughts turned now, in the hills northeast of San Remo, as he sought a way out of his sudden danger. No great mental effort was required of him to realize that if his pictures were on the front pages of Italy's newspapers, no place in Europe was any longer safe for him. He had to get out somehow; back to the Middle East. But there was no way he could himself make even the preliminary contacts for getting smuggled out, without the risk of someone recognizing him and calling the police. His only refuge lay in Bel Jahra, who could make the necessary arrangements for him; and hide him somewhere until they were completed.

He couldn't reach Bel Jahra by car, train, or bus. Any legal way of crossing into France meant being looked at closely by first the Italian border guards, and then again by the French. They would have his pictures tacked up inside their frontier stations. He was certain to be recognized, and seized. Even if he could find a way to disguise himself, his picture was in the false passport he'd have to show them at both posts.

That left only one way: sneaking across the border on foot, by way of the smuggler's route he'd once followed with Bel Jahra and Hammou.

Selim got back into his little car and drew a map from the door pocket. The way to the smuggler's route, from the Italian side of the border, lay near the tiny hill village of Mortola Superiore. But Selim didn't want to leave his car anywhere close to the village. There was always the danger some cop would spot it as belonging to him. Since he had bought the Fiat with false papers long abandoned, Selim couldn't figure out *how* they could possibly know it was his. But then, neither could he understand how his pictures had come to be on the front pages of the newspapers. And anything he couldn't be absolutely sure about, he could take no chances with.

Using the map, he worked out a way of reaching a spot some distance below Mortola Superiore, without driving through Ventimiglia. Selim put the map on the seat beside him, drove back out of the dirt lane, and followed a series of narrow hill roads in a northern direction. When he was three miles from the French border, Selim turned the Fiat-500 into a tangle of wild bushes off the road, and abandoned it.

From that point he could look almost straight down a fall of cliffs to the sun-dappled sea—and the flat modern roof of the lowest border control post, at Ponte San Ludovic, above the stony beach. The road he'd been driving along continued on to the older and higher border post of Ponte San Luigi, hidden from him by a massive shoulder of mountain rock. There was a third one even higher, Selim knew: on the mountain slope above Grimaldi Superiore. At this one there was a powerful telescope keeping watch on marine traffic in the sea along the coast. And another regularly scanning the wooded gullies and rugged cliffs which have been used by generations of Italian and French smugglers to cross the border illegally. Because of that telescope, and the roving border patrols on both sides. Selim had already decided not to make his try until dark. It was a dangerous decision, and he knew it.

The smuggler routes in this area begin at various points above Grimaldi Superiore, and wind up in the neighborhood of the Grange St. Paul on the French side. In the mountainous no-man's-land between, the routes climb and descend and climb again via steep, obscure footpaths at heights varying from several hundred to two thousand feet, with hundreds of unexpected changes in direction all along the way. These abrupt shifts in direction occur where the paths reach the tops of cliffs that fall away sheer to jaggedly upthrusting rocks hundreds of feet below.

Over the generations, hundreds of people trying to slip across without detailed knowledge of the routes have fallen to their deaths. During World War II so many refugees unwittingly walked straight off the top of one massive cliff in the dark that it came to be officially marked on French maps as *Le Pas de La Mort*—the Step of Death. In the past twenty years scores more have died trying to sneak across without an experienced smuggler-guide.

But it had been a professional tobacco smuggler who'd led Bel Jahra, Hammou, and Selim across the last time. And Selim was sure he could remember the way well enough to make it on his own; even in the dark, if he was extremely careful. It was less of a risk than chancing being spotted while crossing in daylight.

Selim began to climb on foot, using a steep trail twisting its way up the slopes between the hill villages of Mortola (310 inhabitants) and Grimaldi (115 inhabitants). It was going to be a long climb to the higher and even smaller village of Mortola Superiore. A hunger pang squeezed Selim's stomach as he thought of the food to be had in these villages. He hadn't had anything to eat since the single roll with his morning coffee. But he was going to have to stay hungry. He couldn't risk getting near anyone who might have just seen his pictures in a newspaper.

He was almost grateful when his legs began to ache from the stiff climbing. At least it diverted his mind from the hunger; and the climb meant less time that he'd have to hide near the border and wait for dusk, with nothing else to think about. He knew the hunger was going to get much worse before he reached Bel Jahra. Once across the border into France, it still would not be safe to take any form of public transportation. That meant hiking it, all the way from the border to Roquebrune; a matter of an additional four hours. It couldn't be helped. There was no other way.

Selim detoured onto a steeper slope as he passed the isolated, walled little cemetery of Mortola, dominated by its onion-domed Russian tomb; a reminder of how many foreigners from all over the world have come to these sun-blessed hills to die. Beside the cemetery entrance, carved on stone in English, are the words:

> The days and months are passing away;
> The years do not wait for us.

Confucian Analects, Book XVI

Selim passed without noticing it. He was concentrating on the climb—and the security waiting for him at the end of it, when he finally got to Ahmed Bel Jahra.

SIX

Menton is the last French town along the Riviera coast before it reaches the Italian frontier. Bel Jahra parked his rented car beside the covered market, across the Quai de Monléon from the Old Port, and strode through the Place aux Herbes to a sporting-goods shop. When he came out he was carrying a knapsack, into which he had stuffed his other purchases: a long insulated camping jacket, rubber-soled hiking boots, a thermos, a canteen, and a geologist's hammer.

Getting back in the car and putting the filled knapsack on the seat beside him, Bel Jahra drove on by way of the Quai Bonaparte past the memorial to Queen Victoria, who had led British vacationers in flocking to enjoy Menton's exceptionally mild winters. This route took him along the shore road of Garavan, a residential-vacation suburb of Menton that now stretches to the border. A quarter of a mile before the border, Bel Jahra made another stop: at a promenade café above the new marina. He asked the proprietor to make him five sandwiches, fill his thermos with coffee and his canteen with mineral water.

While he waited for his order to be taken care of, Bel Jahra stood in the warm afternoon sunlight and gazed up in the direction of the Grange St. Paul, the French end of the smuggler's trail he was sure Selim would try to use. Directly above the promenade, the pastel villas of Garavan dotted gently rising foothills among a profusion of pines, palms, and fruit trees. In this early part of the spring, the sweet scent of orange blossoms mingled with the ever-present tang of lemons and sea. Bel Jahra breathed deeply of this spicy mixture as he looked above Garavan to the woods and farm terraces clinging to the more sharply rising mountain slopes. And above that to where cliffs of sheer rock rose massively into the sky.

On the ridge of one cliff, a row of umbrella pines showed against the golden-blue transparency of the sky. They were very tiny at that distance, but Bel Jahra could count them. There were six trees in that row. Beyond them, unseen behind the high ridge, was the place he intended to wait for Selim.

The five sandwiches were presented to him in paper wrapping, along with the filled thermos and canteen. He paid, left a generous tip, and got back in the car. Turning off the shore road that led to the border station, he drove up through Garavan via the narrowly winding Chemin Vallaya. This took him onto the Route de Garavan Supérieur. Shifting into second gear, Bel Jahra began negotiating the steep hairpin bends by which this road climbs the mountain slopes rising from the foothills. High above Garavan and the sea, one of these bends enters a stony gorge between harsh, near-vertical walls. Enormous concrete pylons march across the gorge, bearing the weight of an elevated superhighway that disappears into a mountain tunnel, to join up with the Autostrada on the Italian side. At this point the road Bel Jahra was using turns in the opposite direction from the border.

Bel Jahra drove off the road. His tires churned up clouds of dust as he gunned the car up a dirt track cutting between the pylons, under the shadow of the elevated highway. He parked where the track ended, at the base of a gigantic pile of boulders. Taking off his shoes and dropping them on the car floor, he got the hiking boots from the knapsack and put them on. Packing the sandwiches, canteen, and thermos in the knapsack, he hung it on his shoulders and began climbing on foot, carrying the geologist's hammer in his hand.

He climbed steadily, drawing pleasure from using the physical power of his lean figure, his legs untiring and his breathing remaining even all the way. He hauled himself over projecting limestone formations and worked around rockfalls, sometimes having to detour away from the border, but always to get higher and swing back. In less than an hour he was up on the ridge with the six umbrella pines.

Hiking through the level forest behind the ridge, he was soon climbing again, following a shallow ravine that cut up a barren slope between fallen boulders held in place only by their ponderous weight. He was moving roughly parallel to the frontier now, with the brown cliffs and dark blue peaks of the Italian mountains looming to his right, beyond tangles of forest and mazes of rock. Bel Jahra stopped from time to time, stooping and using the hammer to break open a rock, occasionally putting a piece in his knapsack after examining it. Then he rose and moved on.

He was aware that border guards on both sides could be looking him over, through field glasses. This was no danger, in itself; as long as he didn't seem to be attempting to cross. The border guards knew most of the regular smugglers by sight; which was the reason the professionals usually crossed when it was dark. Someone unknown to the guards would never be bothered, unless he acted in a suspicious manner. There was nothing unusual about hikers climbing these wild trails above the overmanicured Riviera. And many of them came looking for interesting pieces of rock, or hunting fossils hidden inside them.

Bel Jahra was hunkered down, breaking a chunk of rock in half, when a three-man French border patrol appeared following a ridge to his right. Each of the three carried an FN automatic rifle slung on his shoulder. Bel Jahra raised an arm and waved. One of them waved back. Bel Jahra examined the two pieces of rock, tossed one piece away, and put the other in his knapsack. When he rose from his crouch, the patrol was gone from sight, down the other side of the ridge. Bel Jahra climbed to the path the patrol had been using, and followed it in the opposite direction. It curved along another ridge, then dipped down into a wide, heavily wooded ravine.

Leaving the path, Bel Jahra forced his way through dense bushes to a hump of gray concrete projecting about ten inches above the ground between two stunted olive trees gnarled with age and contorted by mountain winds. The concrete hump was almost hidden by an overgrowth of vines and brush. If Bel Jahra hadn't known it was there, he'd have passed on the trail without spotting it. There was a hole sunk about five feet deep into the ground behind the projection. This hole was walled with concrete, reinforced by rusty iron rods like the projection itself. Bel Jahra forced himself down into the hole, breaking the vines and weeds choking it.

By crouching a bit inside the hole, he could peer toward the path through a narrow slit in the curved jut of reinforced concrete sticking above the ground. The shelter had been built by the French in World War II; intended for a single observer who could watch from it for enemy movements coming across the border, while remaining invisible himself. If the enemy movement along the path consisted of no more than three or four troopers, the observer could cut them down from this shelter, while it protected him from their return fire.

But once down inside the observation pillbox, Bel Jahra found it wouldn't do; not for his purpose. If Selim diverted from the path once he came over the border, he could go through this area by a route that couldn't be seen from this position. Too many trees and high bushes had grown around it since the war. And the observation slit further confined his scope of vision.

Climbing out of the half-pillbox, Bel Jahra returned to the path and crossed it, climbing the less wooded slope rising in the other direction. On the crest two hundred feet up the slope was a long, low stone building abandoned ever since it had been bombarded during the war. Most of the roof was gone. In spite of the thickness of the stone walls, gaping openings had been smashed through them in several places, revealing the vaults inside where grain had once been stored.

Bel Jahra was aware that he could be observed on this slope. But there was nothing too unusual about hikers sometimes camping in the abandoned building; even overnight. He stepped through an opening in the near wall. Inside, the stone-and-dirt floor was completely carpeted by thick wild grasses. The late afternoon sun came through the gaping roof and shone in his face. He narrowed his eyes against the glare and hooked through a large hole in the opposite wall. Beyond it, he had a wide view of the trees and boulders along the border area through which Selim must appear —when and if he came.

Unstrapping the knapsack from his shoulders, Bel Jahra sat down in the grass. He leaned his back against the inside of the near wall, facing the view framed by the hole in the opposite wall. If Selim did come, it might not be for hours—or not until some time in the night. Perhaps not even till early the next morning. Bel Jahra was prepared for that. If the waiting stretched through the night, he had the insulated camping jacket to keep him warm, and the coffee to keep him awake.

Taking the canteen out of his knapsack, he drank two mouthfuls of water, and unwrapped one of the sandwiches. He began to eat it as he settled into the waiting with steely patience, his pale eyes staying on the area through which Selim must come on his way down from Italy.

Mortola Superiore is an Italian village overhanging a gorge that forms, from below the village down to the sea, a natural boundary between Italy and France. It is a meager village: one very old church, one recently built rustic-style *taverna,* and eleven small houses whose ages range between the two. But in the past ten years it has begun getting sightseers, drawn by the historic interest of the church, and by the magnificent view, from the heights of the *taverna*'s dining terrace, of the sea and the hilly coastline of the French Riviera undulating away to the left far below.

This was not the view that interested Driss Hammou. He sat stolidly at the edge of the terrace, as he had ever since finishing his meal of omelet and rolls, keeping watch on the view in the opposite direction. There, to the right below the perched village, the gorge widened into a rugged but more negotiable valley.

On the other side of this heavily wooded valley, mountain slopes rose abruptly, reaching high toward green peaks and stone ridges that belonged to France. It was through this area that Selim had once traversed the smuggler route with Hammou and Bel Jahra. It was the way into this area that Hammou had been watching all afternoon.

On the slopes several hundred feet below Mortola Superiore were the roofless, bomb-blasted ruins of an even smaller village. A white goat grazed among the trees that had grown out of the ruins. The ruins still had a name: Ciotti. But that name no longer stood for a living town. Its six stone buildings had been so smashed that no one had returned to it after the war—except for one old woman, who still lived all alone among the ruins and washed laundry for Mortola Superiore. Among the overgrown footpaths between Ciotti and a four-house village called Gina lay the beginning of the smuggler trail.

Hammou had not taken his attention off this point for hours. Had not moved at all; except to eat his lunch and drink the two cups of strong coffee he'd taken since. Sunset now touched the mountain peaks. The shadows of dusk were gathering in the valley. The bottom was already concealed in purplish murk. It would soon be night. But there was still no sign of Selim.

Either Selim was waiting for dark, Hammou decided, or he'd already gone through before Hammou had taken up his vigil here.

There was a third possibility: that Bel Jahra was wrong, and Selim was not coming this way at all. Hammou had a high regard for Bel Jahra's logical mind; but hedged with a good sergeant's understanding that even the best officer can make a mistake . . .

The white goat turned suddenly and scampered out of the ruins of Ciotti. Hammou's shrewd eyes became slitted as he leaned forward against the terrace rail, concentrating on the blasted village below. A figure appeared out of deep shadow inside the gaping remains of a stone house, small in the distance; and then vanished into a patch of tree shade.

Without diverting his attention from that point, Hammou dug a small pair of opera glasses from his pocket and brought them to his eyes. He adjusted the focus to bring the ruins up sharply through the magnification. The figure emerged just below the ruins, and dodged downward into a clump of bushes, angling to bypass the four clustered houses of Gina.

The figure was Selim Hafid.

A relieved smile softened the brutality of Hammou's broad face as he lowered the opera glasses. He stuck them back in his pocket as he rose to start down after his quarry.

Then he froze in position, the smile fading. Two uniformed and armed Italian frontier cops were coming up out of the gorge, into the valley. From the way they were moving, it didn't seem likely they'd spotted Selim. But their line of movement was bringing them between the point where Selim had vanished, and the place from which Hammou watched. Hammou couldn't start down now without the two-man patrol seeing him, and stopping him to ask questions. The valley below was too close to the border.

Hammou sagged back down in his chair and continued to watch, dully. The patrol reached Gina, and began climbing up through the Ciotti ruins toward Mortola Superiore. Selim didn't show himself again; but he'd soon be too far in the opposite direction for Hammou to catch up. It would be totally dark down there in half an hour; and just as dark up on the opposite slopes and cliffs an hour after that. Hammou knew he didn't remember that smuggler route well enough to follow all of its treacherous twists in the dark.

If that boy *could*—it would be up to Bel Jahra, on the other side.

Selim reached the other side of the valley as night closed in around him. Just before total darkness hid it, he found the start of the narrow trail that snaked up the first cliff, exactly where he'd remembered it being. He was less than a third of the way up when he ceased being able to see anything at all; not his legs, not the trail under his feet, not even the cliff wall beside him.

Placing both hands flat against the rising wall, he climbed the rest of the way by feel alone, one short cautious step at a time. When he finally got to the top, utter blackness prevented him from making out the next leg of the trail. Sitting down on the ground, Selim waited for the moon to brighten and show him the way. Not moving relieved his fear of the heights for the moment. But he began shivering in the creeping cold of the night; and the intensity of his hunger increased.

When the moonlight finally pierced the blackness, giving silvery shadowed shapes to the trees and contortions of rock beyond the top of the cliff, it revealed that he had been wise to wait. In front of him was an open, level stretch that would have taken him in four steps over a ledge to a fall of perhaps fifty feet into a pit of dark. Beside this treacherous stretch, but diverging to the right after two steps, was the trail Selim remembered, marked at erratic intervals by flattened stones sunk in the ground.

This path took Selim into dense underbrush, with the land underfoot rising unevenly. Selim stopped from time to time, carefully studying the slopes and ragged crests rising around him. He had always been able to depend on his memory. It served him now. The moonlit outline of a flat-topped hill appeared off to his left, up between two steep diverging slopes. He grinned and turned toward it, using it as a homing guide point.

It served as long as the ground continued to rise. But then the land sloped down into a tangle of forest, and the landmark was lost to his sight. Worse, he was in total darkness again under the trees, and could no longer see the path. He was reduced to groping his way, arms outstretched to keep from walking into a tree, feeling with his feet one cautious step at a time for the stones that had been sunk in the earth to hold the path. Finally he sank to his knees and crawled, feeling for the way with his hands on the ground ahead of him.

This served against a greater danger than merely losing the trail. According to Selim's recollection, somewhere directly ahead the path made a sharp twist along the edge of a cliff top.

He had been crawling for perhaps six minutes when his groping hand felt nothing beneath it. Stopping instantly, Selim stretched out flat on the ground and snaked forward three more inches. His exploring hands went over an edge and felt sheer descending stone.

Staying flat-down, Selim shifted direction and began warily snaking to the left, his right hand feeling the way along the edge of the cliff top beside him. Then, at last, the trees began to thin out. Moonlight once more showed him the way—and the flat hill up ahead.

An hour later he was circling its base by way of a crumbling ledge. When he got around it to the other side, he could see a massive cliff looming ahead. Beyond that cliff lay France.

The way to the cliff took Selim up along a narrow ridge that climbed irregularly, and changed direction slightly every step of the way. With a drop on either side that could break a leg or neck. It became necessary, as Selim climbed the spine of the ridge, to test each step before resting his full weight on it. Where higher slopes blocked out the moonlight, he could not be certain of each twist in the ridge under him. In places he could help himself along by grabbing exposed roots and projections of rock. In others he could depend on nothing but extreme caution, slowness, and the failing strength of his legs.

It was the weariness of his nerves and muscles that made him pause. He looked up to see how much farther there was to go. And saw three shadowy figures appear on the upper end of the ridge.

Shock froze him for several seconds. There was moonlight up there. It glinted off a rifle barrel carried by one of the figures. Selim had no doubt about what they were: a night border patrol. They were swallowed in blackness as they started down in his direction.

He turned and started back to find cover. They couldn't have seen him yet; but if he remained on the narrow ridge they would walk right into him. In his terror, he moved too quickly. A large stone gave way under the weight of his left foot, tearing out of the ground and rattling down the slope below. Selim fought to catch his balance, and could not. He fell on steeply sloping ground and rolled downward out of control.

His hip rammed against the trunk of a tree, sending a jolt of agony through him, but stopping his rolling fall. Clenching his teeth against the ebbing pain, he stayed exactly the way the tree had stopped him, listening. There was no sound above for several moments. And then there was: boots, crunching down the slope toward him. They had heard his fall.

Selim got his knees under him and crawled around the tree, getting it between him and his pursuers. Farther below him lay a tangle of forest. He rose to his feet and headed for it in a low crouch. Crashing into a clump of bushes, he forced his way through into the concealing shadows of the forest. He kept moving away from the slope, shifting direction several times, groping from tree to tree, deeper into the forest.

The trees ended suddenly, and he stepped off a ledge into thin air before he realized it. He fell straight down, but luck was with him. The fall ended after about ten feet, and he landed on a mound of soft earth. Shaken but not hurt, Selim got to his knees and felt a thick tangle of thorn bushes in front of him. He crawled under them and went flat and still, waiting.

Minutes passed before he heard movement in the forest he'd come through. Boots crunched dry twigs, coming closer as the patrol searched for him. Selim lay frozen under the bushes, his heart thudding against the ground as the bootsteps reached the top of the ledge he'd fallen from.

The sound made by the hunters ceased, for a moment. Then resumed, moving to the right along the top of the ledge. Selim told himself it was too dark for the patrol to see any marks left where he'd gone over the ledge. But he stayed utterly motionless, scarcely breathing as he waited. The sounds died out, and then came again as the patrol returned along the ledge above. The boots went on past the point where Selim had fallen, not pausing, going off to hunt in the other direction. Finally, the sounds of their going faded away. There was only the night silence in Selim's ears.

Still Selim didn't move. Not until almost an hour had gone by without the patrol returning did he crawl out from under the thorn bushes. He stood up, and studied the cliff he'd fallen over. It was only about ten feet high, but it was sheer rock with no visible toeholds. Selim stood on his toes and reached up as far as he could. His fingers couldn't reach the top. He began moving along the rock face, feeling for projections he could use to climb back up into the forest overhead.

There were none. Before long the wall of rock bent sharply in the other direction, taking Selim away from the forest—and the way to the path up the slope. When he finally reached a break in the rock wall, he pushed through and found himself going in still another direction. He made himself stop. The convolutions of land rising all around him were too deeply shadowed for him to explore. He was getting too far from the one trail he knew. He was lost; and he would become more lost if he kept moving in a blind attempt to find another route.

There was only one sensible thing left to do: stay where he was, close enough to the smuggler trail so he would have a chance of finding a way back to it with the first light of dawn. That was going to make for an uncomfortable and frightening wait, through the rest of the long night. But there was no choice. Selim forced himself to accept that.

By this time the Italian border had given up the search for Selim, and was continuing down toward its control post. On the way, the three members of the patrol made an educated guess about Selim's probable route. The border guards on both sides in this area know the ways across as well as the smugglers, being, like the smugglers, local boys. They have no hatred of the local breed of smugglers. Trying to catch them is regarded in the nature of a sporting game. If caught, these smugglers face nothing worse than a stiff fine, since they're seldom carrying anything more dangerous than cigarettes or liquor. Smuggling of narcotics and illegal worker-immigrants from North Africa is usually handled by nonlocal groups, using vehicles with hidden compartments or vessels capable of making a transfer beyond sight of the coast.

The Italian patrol assumed Selim was a local smuggler. On reaching the frontier post at Ponte San Luigi, one of its men strolled fifty yards to the French station, and passed on the information with a challenging grin. A French border guard then got on the phone, and told the officer in control of patrols about the general area in which Selim would probably arrive on French soil.

Meanwhile, Selim had settled on the ground to wait out the rest of the night. The luminous dial of his watch showed twenty minutes before midnight. Bringing his knees against his chest and hugging them for warmth, he dozed off.

He woke suddenly, with a spasm of fright. But there were no alarming sounds around him, and his fear gradually subsided. Though it was still pitch dark, it seemed to Selim that he had slept for a long time. When he peered at his watch, however, he saw it was only midnight.

He was miserably cold and hungry. And now that the tension of escaping the patrol had passed he was also painfully aware of the many scratches and bruises he'd acquired during his flight through the woods. He tried to find oblivion by falling back to sleep. But a small, sharp edge of the terror that had wakened him wouldn't go away; and wouldn't let him sleep again.

At midnight in Rome, Hunter was leaving the Parioli apartment of James Ferguson, an aging newspaperman who covered the Italian scene for a London daily. That was well known; he'd been doing it for two decades. What was not well known, except to a few, was that for the same length of time James Ferguson had also been reporting on the Italian scene for MI6, now renamed DI6 but still in the same line of work: British intelligence abroad.

Ferguson had recently been handed an additional *sub rosa* chore: passing on to London's drably functional Tintagel House any information that might eventually prove of use to Britain's Illegal Immigration Intelligence Unit. In this last function, Ferguson was exceptionally conversant with the movements of alien groups through Italy. In all his functions, his contacts in the Italian underworld were numerous. Hunter left copies of Selim's pictures with him, having extracted an agreement that Ferguson would show them to certain contacts.

If any of them turned out to know the boy—or, even more important, knew who was running him—Hunter would be informed. Should Hunter have left Rome, Ferguson would pass on the information via Inspector Klar in London.

Two blocks from Ferguson's apartment Hunter found a taxi, and had it take him to the Excelsior. He went inside and checked at the message desk. There was no message for him from Uri, so the Mossad agent still wasn't back in Rome. Nothing from Diego Bandini, so there was still no trace of Selim or new lead to him. Nothing from Inspector Klar, so no further developments had turned up in London or through Interpol. And no messages from any of the people Hunter had contacted through this long day, ending with Ferguson.

The only message was a long-distance call from Chavez in Washington, requesting that Hunter call him back. Hunter didn't wonder how Chavez had learned so soon that he was in Rome. State had spies watching spies watching spies. The tone within the department was set by the lengthy report all career employees had to make out each year, giving a critical estimate of the quality of work done by their fellow employees.

Hunter glanced at his watch and estimated the time difference. It would be 6 P.M. in Washington. Chavez would still be in his office. Regularly working late was one of the reasons he'd risen so high in the Army; and Chavez was still an army man, though on temporary loan to State's WGCT. Hunter didn't think Chavez was worried yet about what he was up to. It was too soon for that. Chavez just liked to be kept up to date on the activities of the men responsible to him: Hunter in Europe, and men like Hunter in South America, the Far East, the Middle East, and Africa.

Hunter folded the message in half and stuck it in his pocket. He had a prepared explanation for what he was doing: a practical test of co-operation between the security forces of Europe in an actual situation. But he didn't relish trying that con on Chavez. Chavez's rise in a snobbish outfit like the U. S. Army, starting as a private whose parents had been Mexican fruit pickers, said something about his abilities. He was not a man you could con easily; and not at all for very long.

An entire day had gone by since the pictures of Selim had begun circulating; and Selim remained uncaught and unseen. It didn't create a very hopeful mood for Hunter, as he went up to his room and began making out the account of his expenses since leaving London.

Each expense had to be explained; Chavez was a stickler for that, having superiors of his own to account to. Hunter put down the over-all explanation he'd decided on: checking liaison effectiveness between various police and security agencies of Europe. That was true enough, as far as it went. But if there was no specific result forthcoming very soon, Chavez would smell a rat.

Hunter stopped working on the expense account and thought seriously about Chavez's message to call him. He knew that he could not afford to louse up on this job, and lose it. And the make-or-break of this job was: results.

The probable reason for Selim not being spotted yet would be that he'd found a very good hole to hide in. If so, he'd have to come out sooner or later—and get tagged.

But the other possible explanation, that Selim might already have left Europe, would leave Hunter with nothing but a complete dead end.

Hunter decided, finally, to give it one more day. If nothing solid turned up out of the Selim lead by then, he'd have to drop it and get back to work. The State Department's version of work.

Heavy morning mists still shrouded the mountain slopes on the French side of the frontier when Selim came down through the wooded pass leading toward the Grange St. Paul. He moved quickly, and avoided unobscured places where the heat of the rising sun had already soaked up the mist. Minutes before, he had spotted a two-man patrol circling behind him with their weapons in their hands. Selim was sure they'd glimpsed him in turn, before he had dodged into a ground-clinging cloud.

He had managed to lose them in the patches of mist; but he was aware of them up there behind him, searching. It was frighteningly unexpected; as though they'd been waiting for him.

Staying as much as possible in the concealing fog as he continued to work his way down, Selim came to the main footpath. Below, the fog had lifted completely. Selim could see clearly the blasted building of the Grange. He could also see another two-man patrol, coming up quickly and purposefully along the path in his direction.

Like the ones somewhere behind Selim, these two held their automatic weapons ready, not slung on their shoulders as they would be during a normal patrol. Selim dodged off the path, into the cover of the dense woods on the other side of it. When he was deep in the cover, where they could not possibly see him, he moved downward again as quietly as possible.

A hand shot out from behind a thick scrub oak. Strong lean fingers closed on Selim's arm. Selim twisted and almost screamed before he saw who it was. With a sob of relief, he threw his arms around Bel Jahra.

"Come . . ." Bel Jahra whispered. The weariness that lined

his face was not in his voice, nor in his movements as he led Selim farther down through the woods. Selim followed his savior without question, sticking as close as he could.

They reached the curved concrete guard projecting up from the observation hole. Bel Jahra stopped beside it, turning to peer in the direction of the path. Through the dense foliage he and Selim could make out the distinct figures of the two-man patrol from below stopping as they met the patrol coming down from above. Their voices were audible, though not their words. They would realize now that Selim must be somewhere very close, off the trail. They were certain to spread out to search the woods carefully.

Bel Jahra lowered himself into the concrete-lined hole in the ground, crouching. He drew a small pistol from his pocket, aimed it through the observation slit, and fired two shots in the direction of the partially glimpsed figures on the path.

Selim, still crouched on the ground above the shelter, stared down at Bel Jahra incredulously. In the same instant, four automatic FN rifles let go with a sputtering barrage that echoed thunderously along the surrounding mountain slopes. Hails of bullets slashed the foliage, whipping blindly back and forth across the place the pistol shots had come from. Several thudded into the observation projection, knocking out small chunks of cement. One bullet ripped into Selim's side. He sprawled on the ground, still staring down into the hole at Bel Jahra, his face contorted with pain and confusion.

Bel Jahra took careful aim with the small pistol, and sent a third bullet smashing through Selim's left eye into his brain.

The four border patrolmen, by now scattered to cover along the path, assumed it was another shot in their direction. Again, answering volleys of automatic fire slashed through the woods. Bel Jahra stayed hunched down in the protection of the shelter as bullets slammed off the curved observation hump and hissed over his head. The barrage went on for about ten seconds, and then slackened off. The echo of a final burst reverberated along the slopes. Then there was silence again. The border patrolmen were waiting to see if there'd be further pistol shots fired their way, or if they'd hit their man.

Bel Jahra wiped his fingerprints off the pistol and slipped it into Selim's dead hand, closing the limp fingers around it. Then he hauled himself out of the hole in a low crouch, and snaked away from it quietly for fifty yards. He became motionless as stone under a heavy tangle of juniper bush.

Ten minutes later the four border patrolmen entered the woods, spreading out from the path and advancing cautiously. Bel Jahra lay absolutely still and listened to their boots crushing low bushes; and their voices, when they found Selim.

As Bel Jahra had anticipated, they searched no further. Only one man had been spotted crossing the border—and there he lay, with a pistol in his hand. They had to assume that Selim was the one who had fired it at them, and that their answering fire had killed him. Closer examination by experts would reveal a different story. But that would be later. In half an hour the four border guards were gone, carrying Selim's body down with them toward their command post.

Bel Jahra stayed where he was for another fifteen minutes. Then he rose from the junipers and left the woods in the opposite direction from the path. He followed a wide circle to get back to the abandoned building, because he could be observed from a distance once he got near it. Picking up his knapsack, he hung it on his shoulders and started down toward the place where he'd left his car the previous afternoon.

From time to time, he stopped and crouched to break open a rock with his geologist's hammer. Twice, he selected a piece and put it in his knapsack before continuing downward.

SEVEN

About the time that Bel Jahra reached his car and drove back toward Roquebrune, Uri Ezan was wakened by a heavy fist pounding on his locked door. For a moment, Uri didn't remember where he was. He leaped naked off the bed snatching the snubnosed .38 Colt revolver from under his pillow.

Then he realized it was Roman sunlight filtering through the slats of the closed shutters; and that he was back in his own apartment, in his own Roman *pensione*. And in Rome the police don't pound on your door. They like to ring politely, and then watch the surprise on your face when you open up and find yourself looking at their shiny buttons, somber eyes, and nasty little guns.

By the time Uri slipped the .38 back out of sight under the pillow, he had stopped quivering. He padded naked to the door and opened the tiny peephole. The fat face of Dov Tobias, who ran the *pensione* for Uri, grinned at him through the hole, showing crooked, discolored teeth. His pounding had been Israeli-style practical joking.

Uri released the security lock and let him in. "That is not funny," he told him.

Unperturbed, Dov handed him a little paper bag. "I brought you a cornetto for breakfast."

Uri took it into the kitchenette and started a small kettle of water on the boil. Dov followed him and said, "I didn't know you came back last night, until Ossie just told me. You could have woke me."

"I was tired," Uri growled. "What do you want?"

"There's an American looking for you. Says his name is Simon Hunter. Says he's staying at the Excelsior. Says you know him."

"Okay. Fine, Now go away."

Dov looked hurt as he went. He could remember when Uri had not been so irritable all the time. When he was alone, Uri dumped Nescafé into the big red cup from Catania and looked bleakly at the kettle, waiting for it to steam.

He had a long muscular torso, short hiker's legs, and pitch-black eyes in a very dark, hawk-nosed face of a desert Bedouin. He was a Yemenite Jew. His family had been exiles in the southern tip of Arabia since biblical times, but had returned to the Promised Land five generations ago. Uri had been born in Jerusalem, spoke seven languages including two Arabian dialects, and had been a Mossad agent abroad ever since he'd recovered from being gut-shot in the '48 war. His high point had been Buenos Aires, in 1960. His low point, Munich in 1972.

In 1960 he'd been part of the secret commando team sent to capture Adolf Eichmann, who had efficiently managed the ship-ment of millions of Jews to Hitler's death camps. Eichmann had been declared a war criminal after the fall of the Third Reich, and gone into hiding in Argentina. Uri could still remember the tense excitement of the night they'd grabbed Eichmann outside his house in the Buenos Aires suburb; of the days and nights of dodging Argentine police and Nazi underground agents hunting them and their captive; and of finally managing to slip Eichmann aboard a plane taking off over the Atlantic a hairbreadth ahead of their pursuers.

Uri had been promoted for his part in bringing Adolf Eich-mann to trial; and promoted twice more in the years that fol-lowed. Then had come 1972, and the armed killer-squad of Black September slipping into the Munich Olympic Games. And the Israeli athletes who had died in the resulting carnage, with no means of defending themselves.

Uri had been sent to Munich a month ahead with other security men, to make sure such a thing could not happen. For failing to detect the plot in time, and prevent it, he had been demoted. He was not the only one; but he had quit the service in a fury, and retired to the Roman *pensione* he'd bought with his life's savings during duty there several years before.

Mossad hadn't let him completely retire, of course. He had too much valuable experience. It was still needed from time to time. They began coming to him with assignments. In spite of his anger, he never refused any of them. But he had no delusions about his future. There would be no more promotions. He was getting old, and the assignments would soon come less frequently. Eventually he would be nothing but what his cover claimed him to be: a foreign owner of a Roman *pensione*.

It wouldn't be a bad life. There was no one dependent on him anymore. His two ex-wives were both married to men with more reasonable professions. His children were old enough to be independent now: the girl in the Army, the boy working his own small farm north of Safad. Uri could wind up his days reading all the books he'd never had enough time for before, or drinking tea in the warm Roman sun with old friends passing through.

But Munich still rankled.

Uri poured boiling water into the big red cup, mixed it with the Nescafé, dunked in the cornetto, and took a bite. Chewing, he left the coffee to cool, going into the other room to put on his best suit for the Excelsior Hotel. It was several years since he'd last seen Hunter. Uri wondered what he was doing in Rome.

Hunter woke slowly with the gentle weight of warm sun on his face. Keeping his eyelids closed, he turned his head away from the light shafts streaming through the partially opened slats of the window shutters. The sounds of Rome lethargically surging to life outside had an oddly lulling effect. Hunter almost dozed back to sleep when the phone on the bedside table rang.

His first thought was Chavez, and his eyes snapped open. Propping himself up on one elbow, he reached out and lifted the receiver.

It was Uri Ezan: "I'm down in the lobby. They won't give your room number."

Hunter gave it to him, hung up, and swung himself off the too-soft bed. Crossing the thick carpeting, he threw open the shutters, eyes narrowing against the morning sun glare as he took in the length of the Via Veneto below. The tables in front of Doney's and the Café de Paris across the street were empty. The crowds that had been there last night searching for la dolce vita were sleeping off their disillusion with the prices of anything sweet or soft they'd managed to find. Hunter went back to the phone and asked room service to send up coffee and buttered rolls. Unlocking his door, he went in the bathroom to shower.

Uri came in while he was toweling himself dry. He stood in the bathroom doorway while Hunter shaved and told him why he was in Rome.

"The explosion *was* the work of an Arab outfit," Uri said when Hunter had finished. "*Which* one, we haven't turned up even a hint. So it has to be a very new combination we haven't penetrated."

"Try to find out. I *want* them."

"We're already trying." Uri smiled slightly. "So we find ourselves on the same side at last, eh? I remember when you called us fanatics."

"You are. So's your opposition. Neither side is willing to even consider any merit in the other's position. To try to find a compromise."

"You know what Arabs are like. If we softened our position, they'd take it for a show of weakness."

"Some of them may figure the same about you. You're both Semites. Too proud and too suspicious. And a plague on both your houses."

"At least *we* don't blow up passenger planes full of people who have no connection with the problem."

Hunter nodded. "That's why I come to you, instead of them." He went in the other room to dress. "Have a look at the pictures on the dresser. They're Selim Ramouk, the kid we're looking for."

Uri went for a look at the pictures, and nodded. "I saw the papers. I don't know him. I see so many pictures of possible terrorists, I can't remember all of them. But I'll circulate these with our people." He stuck copies in his pocket. "We've got a boy watching the airport up at Nice. Kosso Shamir. Very young, but a memory like a computer. If he ever saw pictures of this Selim, he'll remember where. And I'll get word to you, wherever you are."

The room service waiter came at that point, and set the tray on a table beside the windows. Hunter and Uri sat down and shared the coffee and rolls while they discussed various means for getting some inkling of which outfit was running Selim. It was two hours before they ran out of ideas and Uri got up to leave.

The phone rang. It was Major Diego Bandini. "They've found him," he told Hunter over the phone. "The boy, Selim. But he's dead."

Bandini filled Hunter in on Selim's attempt to slip across the border between Mortola Superiore and Menton; and the French border patrols that had cornered him in the hills. "They thought at first it was their shots that killed him. But it develops he was killed with the pistol he was holding. Of course, it might be that he decided to commit suicide when he realized he was trapped."

"That's one possibility," Hunter granted. "The other is that somebody decided Selim had become a handicap after his pictures showed up in the papers."

"Agreed. Though there is no proof, either way. Only one thing is certain: This dead boy *is* our Selim. The pictures fit him, and he has the Y-shaped scar on his hip."

"Thanks, Diego." Hunter's face had gotten a withdrawn, remote expression. "I appreciate your letting me know so fast."

"And *I* will appreciate, if you let me know just as promptly, what you discover as a result of it."

"Depend on it." Hunter hung up and told Uri what had happened.

"I wonder," Uri mused, "why he was trying to get out of Italy in that direction. There are easier ways."

"Exactly my thought." Hunter's eyes got a dull shine to them. "And he was using a smuggler route to get across. That means he knew about it, from before. Which means, in turn, he's had or still has some kind of connection up there."

"We have some pretty good people in that area," Uri told him. "Along the Riviera." He wrote a phone number on a slip of paper and put it on the dresser. "Call this, in Nice, if you want help."

"I've got a contact of my own up there," Hunter said quietly. "Somebody who knows the area better than your people."

He picked up the phone again and asked the travel desk in the lobby to book him on the plane leaving in an hour and a half for Nice.

From Nice in the direction of Italy, the Riviera's lowest corniche follows the sinuous coastline for twenty-five kilometers before reaching Monaco. Just beyond Monaco it cuts between the heights of Roquebrune and the promontory of Cap Martin, which juts into the sea between the Bay of Roquebrune and the Gulf of

Peace. Bel Jahra drove out onto the cape itself by way of the Avenue Sir Winston Churchill, flanked by low pine-forested hills, ancient olive groves, and shrub-veiled gardens. Far out on the cape he turned into the Avenue Douine. Between the deepest curves of this road and the harsh, tightly bending shore are Cap Martin's most secluded estates.

Dezso Valasi's estate was hidden from the road by a high stone wall. The narrow entrance gate was set between brick columns bearing gilded statues of a dragon and an angel. The parking area was outside; a long graveled strip between the wall and the road.

Bel Jahra put his car between an old Citroën *deux chevaux* and a dusty British-built Ford Capri. There was a foretaste of summer in the hot sunlight as he walked back toward the gate. The still air was heavy with the cloyingly sweet scent of datura growing along the shady base of the wall. Finding the wrought-iron gate locked, Bel Jahra pulled the chain of an old copper bell hanging below the dragon. The clanging sound brought a grizzled, heavy-set man in overalls from a stone gatehouse inside. He scowled through the iron grillwork with a peasant's habitual suspicion.

Bel Jahra asked for Juliet Shale. He gave his name as André Courtois. He had to spell it before the other understood it. The man spoke into an intercom phone on the wall of the gatehouse, and then went on watching Bel Jahra until Juliet came hurrying into sight along a shrub-bordered path inside.

She looked surprised, delighted, and nervous; all three at the same time. "Good Lord," she said shakily as she unlocked the gate, "when you say you may be coming, you really *mean* what you say." She opened the gate and stepped out, not asking him in. Her nervousness was caused by the fact that her employer didn't like uninvited visitors; even when he was away. But it was undermined by her pleasure in seeing Bal Jahra again, so soon. "Why didn't you phone? We could have arranged to meet somewhere, this evening."

"This evening I have a business meeting in Nice. From that, unfortunately, I'll probably have to go immediately to Paris, for several days or a week."

She fought not to let the disappointment show. "Oh. So you're just passing through."

Bel Jahra laughed softly. "I'll be back. You don't know it, but we're already neighbors. I've just rented an apartment practically looking down on you. In Roquebrune. It seems I'm going to be here at least six months. Possibly a year."

The heady promise in that made it impossible for her to speak for a moment.

"I suppose," he went on, "I could have waited till I got back from Paris to get in touch with you. But . . ." He shrugged, and smiled down at her. "I just wanted to see you." He glanced at his watch, pointedly. "I've got about an hour. Then I have to start for Nice, to make arrangements for the meeting."

For a moment he thought he was going to have to ask her to invite him inside. But then she broke through her anxiety about Valasi's disapproval. "Well, I can't leave now. I'm snowed under with things to do here. So . . . I can't ask you into the house. Valasi doesn't like guests he doesn't know about. But I can show you around the grounds, if you'd like."

"I thought Valasi would still be in Rome."

"He is. But he still wouldn't like my taking someone in the house without his permission."

Bel Jahra didn't push it. Once they were inside the estate there would be a simple way to get her to take him into the house; without his interest in the layout of the interior being obvious. "It doesn't matter," he told her easily.

She led him inside, casting a defiant glance at the gateman though he hadn't said anything nor changed expression.

Bel Jahra grinned as they followed the path. "That's quite a tough guard Valasi's hired for the place," he commented casually.

"He *is* tough," Juliet agreed, "but not hired. He's one of Valasi's nephews, brought out of the old country. He's got *six* of his family living on the property. Gardeners, cook, housekeeper. All tough Hungarian peasant stock. Better guards than money could pay for."

Bel Jahra knew that on the one night he was interested in, there'd be more guards around than Valasi's family. Security men sent by the company insuring the estate, as a precaution against the robberies Riviera parties are prone to. Bodyguards accompanying the more important notables. The ones who'd come with King Hussein and the American Secretary of State would be the best professionals. But not too many of them; because their attendance at Valasi's party would be unofficial, and unannounced. . . .

Bel Jahra noted everything they passed as he followed Juliet, picking out the likeliest points for guards to station themselves. Juliet turned along a path that opened into a wide lawn with spaced flower beds and huge cactus plants that rose almost as high as the house behind them. It was a fairly compact, cream-colored villa with a red-tiled roof.

Bel Jahra frowned slightly. "It doesn't look big enough to hold that party you were telling me about in Rome."

Juliet laughed. "Inside, it would be absolutely impossible. We're going to have the party outside."

So there was no need, after all, for him to check the interior layout of the house.

"Here . . ." Juliet took his hand tentatively. "I'll show you."

He laced his fingers with hers, firmly; and watched the color mount in her face as she led him around the house. Behind it there was a large, blue-tiled terrace; and a vast manicured lawn sloping gently down to close-spaced trees in the direction of the sea.

"I'm having the main pavilion set up there on the terrace and alongside it," Juliet told him, pointing. "The tables there . . . with enough braziers for warmth . . . tenting stretched overhead there, in case it rains . . . the works . . ."

Bel Jahra's eyes and mind were busy with distances, likely guard points, and covered approaches.

"We'll have a smaller pavilion out on the lawn over here," Juliet was continuing, proud of the thoroughness of her arrangements. "For the children. There'll be at least twelve of those. Valasi's six grandchildren, and the rest coming with guests. I've arranged for a puppet show, to keep the kids out of the grown-ups' hair."

That, Bel Jahra decided, would probably be the key to getting his people out of here alive, after they'd finished with their killings. All those children made for enough hostages to get them past any number of armed guards. Even professionals wouldn't take the risk of firing under those conditions. And if the guards tried bluffing it out, it would only take the killing of one child before their eyes to make them back off.

That still left the problem of getting his people in. "Who do you have catering this party?" he asked Juliet casually. "I know an excellent firm in Monte Carlo I used once."

"I've already got the best on the Côte d'Azur," she told him flatly. "I always stick with them. Giovanetti's, in Nice."

Bel Jahra registered the name. "You couldn't do better," he agreed. But that was only one possible way in. There had to be others set up. He wouldn't leave anything to chance. This time, nothing must go wrong at the last minute. Besides, he had to assume the catering staff might be searched at some point for concealed weapons.

He looked toward the trees that concealed the sea. "The property goes all the way to the shore?"

Juliet nodded. "There are some ruins of an old abbey in there, near the top of the cliff, where Valasi likes to paint. The atmosphere is conducive, and it gives him solitude. Like to see it?"

"Very much."

They went down the slope of the lawn by way of a flagstoned pathway. At the bottom they entered a curving tunnel neatly cut through dense, high bushes whose foliage intertwined a few inches above their heads. Emerging from this living tunnel, they threaded through a labyrinth of hedges six feet tall, working in the direction of the sea.

All of which would provide absolute cover for an approach to the lawn and terrace where the party was to be held.

Where the hedge maze ended, mossy stone steps led down between twin lines of dark cypresses to a miniature bridge arching over a deep footpath. The ruins were on the other side. There wasn't much left. A large curving remnant of a low Romanesque tower; the stones from its upper structure half-hidden in the tall weeds around its base. A detached length of refectory wall, containing a broken but still gracefully pointed early-Gothic window. The stub of a marble column, with sections of other columns partially buried in the ground around it. The crumbling remains of one corner of a cloister, connected to the collapsed vault of a chapter house, and a doorway with a still-intact ogee arch that had led into the nave of a long-vanished church.

Juliet followed Bel Jahra as he wandered through these ruins, stopping to take in a striped awning stretched at a height of seven feet inside the half-curve of the tower.

"This is where he works," she told him. "The awning is for shade, so the sunlight won't distort his color judgment."

Bel Jahra turned his back on the crumbling tower, and took in the view of sea and sky. Far to the left, across the Gulf of Peace and Bay of Garavan, were the curving shore and rising hills of Italy. He could even make out the high slope, on the French side of the frontier, where he had killed Selim.

Closer, to his left in the remains of the cloister corner, fallen masonry partly covered a hole in the ground. He strolled to it and glanced down. The hole had led into the abbey crypt. The opening was small, the stone stairway leading down collapsed, and the darkly shadowed cavity underneath seemed partially choked with fallen stones and earth. Thick weeds grew up out of it.

But there might be just enough space left under there to serve. Bel Jahra fixed it in his mind, and walked out of the ruins to the edge of the sea cliff.

Below, the surf sloshed in and out under a jumble of huge rocks so shattered and clawed by ages of raging seas that they looked like ripped, petrified gray sponges. With thousands of long, jaggedly sharp edges. It wasn't a very long way down to them: perhaps a hundred feet, no more. But the cliff that began beneath Bel Jahra's feet fell straight down all the way. It would require an expert climber to mange it. . . .

"Come away from here . . ." Juliet was saying nervously behind him. "I can't stand getting that close to the edge. Or seeing anybody else do it."

Bel Jahra turned from the edge. His mind was busy with the various possibilities of cliff, ruins, garden layouts, pavilion positions, puppet show, children of guests, security men, catering staff —and timing. And the need to get an invitation for himself to Valasi's party. That would have to come from Juliet. And first she must be bound to him utterly, by her uncertain emotional needs.

He strolled past her, back among the ruins, looking in the direction of the house. It could not be seen from here. He sat down on a mound of grass and looked to Juliet, waiting. After a moment, she came over and carefully sat down beside him, folding her thin hands tightly, without being aware of it, against her lower belly. "Do you have cigarettes?" she asked nervously. "I left mine in the house."

He put his arms around her and lay back in the grass; not forcing her but letting his weight pull her with him.

"No!" Her voice was choked and her face suddenly savage. "Not *here.*"

His left hand closed around the back of her neck, gripping her mercilessly. His other hand seized her loins. She gasped, and then flung herself against him with a fierce broken sob.

It reminded Bel Jahra strangely of what Selim had done on seeing him up there, minutes before he'd died.

EIGHT

When Hunter's plane landed at the Côte d'Azur Airport that afternoon, the sun was still hot along the Riviera, but the air was no longer still. A tramontane was blowing; the wind from Italy that usually brought rain. So far only a few ragged clouds scudded across an otherwise golden sky. But a profusion of whitecaps already chopped the cobalt surface of the sea along the edge of the airport's main landing strip.

Hunter rented a new Renault in the terminal and drove into Nice and through it, along the aging glamour of the shoreline's Promenade des Anglais. Swinging around the long, narrow harbor, he took the Moyenne Corniche up into the hills east of Nice. At the Col de Villefranche he turned down the Avenue of Golden Sunshine. Above to his left loomed the peaks of the pre-Alps. Below to his right the foothills descended by easy stages, past colorfully painted houses and terraced gardens, to the old port of Villefranche-sur-Mer. Hunter pulled off the road in front of a small wooden gate with a rusty tin mailbox bearing the name "Olivier Lamarck."

Lamarck's house was below the level of the road. Only the orange tiles of the roof showed. Hunter opened the wooden gate and went down stone steps to a narrow walk that bent sharply to the left, between the rocky wall of the hillside and the washed-out pink of the house wall. The house was on three levels down the slope. The top level held the living-dining room, kitchenette, and sleeping alcove for guests. Hunter had slept in it four years ago, while working with Lamarck on the case of an AWOL GI charged with raping a girl in Marseilles. The room below was the main bedroom and bath. The bottom level was a "cave," holding wine bins, gardening tools and mud-caked shoes, and toilet; with a shower on the patio outside it.

The two lower rooms were built into the living rock of the slope, with small holes in the walls for the mountain to "breathe." A newcomer to the area some years ago, who had scorned local superstitions about mountains that lived and breathed, had built a solid stone house without these holes. Gradually, inexorably, the mountain slope had shoved against the walls until they had finally collapsed. Olivier Lamarck stuck with local tradition.

He had bought the place in installments over two decades as a Brigade Criminelle inspector—and then commissioner—for the Police Judiciaire of Nice, before reaching retirement age three years ago. His wife had helped with her extra earnings as a customs clerk, but had been killed by a drunken driver on the Avenue Malmaison the year before Lamarck's retirement.

Hunter found no one on the first terrace, where red and yellow roses climbed the slope wall and arched over on trellises to create squares of shade. The door to the top room was open, but no one was inside. Hunter went down steps to the second terrace, with its row of lemon and pepper trees. This was empty also. But directly below Hunter, on the small patio beside the shower outside the cave, a woman was sunbathing in a bright green bikini.

She was stretched out face down on a blue canvas beach chair. Hunter remained where he was, gazing down at her. Above, a Vespa boomed briefly along the unseen road. Otherwise the peaceful quiet of the hills was disturbed only by the twitter of birds and the rustle of the growing wind through the trees. The patio where she lay was protected from the wind, and from any prying eyes on surrounding terraces, by screens of fig trees, eucalyptus, and great flowering bushes.

Her outstretched left hand was in a patch of shade. The rest of her lay squarely in the hot sun. She had unhooked the bikini bra, and its thin straps lay beside the flattened bulge of her breasts. Suntain oil glistened on her ripe flesh. A rivulet of sweat moved down the groove of her backbone, leaving a wet trail from between her shoulder blades to the faintly dimpled indentation in the small of her back, where the smooth rise of the buttocks began.

She was freckled all over, the freckles showing pinkly in her deepening tan. Her hair was a gingery red.

Hunter started down the steps to her. "Odile?"

She turned her head and squinted at him. The bone structure of her freckled face was too strong for her to be called pretty; but the dark green eyes were beautiful, and the long mouth delicately curved. She was Lamarck's daughter; about thirty, according to Hunter's recollection. "Simon Hunter . . ." she said after a moment. "My God, it's been a long time. Four years?"

She raised herself on an elbow, seemingly unaware of how much this exposed of her full breasts. She looked him over appraisingly, in that special direct way of Frenchwomen for whom sexual equality enhances femininity. "You have changed," she told Hunter. "You never used to look so grim."

He smiled and shrugged. "I'm getting older. Is Olivier around?"

"He's down at the harbor, playing chess. I've got to do the shopping down there in a few minutes. We can go together." She was still studying his face. "I was sorry to hear about your wife, Simon."

Hunter nodded, and changed the subject: "You're here on holiday?"

"No, I moved in with Olivier a year ago. I've been getting free-lance work from some of the photographers in Nice."

He remembered that Odile and her husband had been running a photo-retouching firm in Paris. "What happened? Decide you preferred the sun of the South to the profits of the big city?"

"I did. Not my husband. We divorced. Not for that reason."

Hunter remembered something else. "The last I heard, you were pregnant."

"I had a miscarriage." She said it matter-of-factly, without self-pity.

It was Hunter's turn to say he was sorry. "But you'll find yourself another husband when you're ready. You never had any trouble getting men, as I recall. And there's no reason you can't still have children."

"Oh, I intend to." She paused, appraising him again. "The same applies to you, Simon."

The faint clean smell of her perspiring, sun-heated flesh mingled with the fragrance of ripening fruit and blooming flowers. Hunter shook his head. "I'm getting too old for another try at that."

Odile cocked her head, smiling faintly. "That's the second time you told me how old you are, so I guess you're making a point. If you're too old for me, should you be looking at my figure the way you are?"

Amusement twitched Hunter's mouth. "You always were a fresh little thing."

She sighed ruefully. "I know . . . *Merde,* I've *got* to stop teasing. Olivier says that's why I can't hold a man. I'm not respectful enough of their egos."

Hunter laughed, and his face relaxed in a way that revealed a surprisingly strong sensuality. A sensuality that had always been deeply part of him, and that he had had to repress much too long.

Odile lay face down again after a moment, and asked him to hook the back of her bikini bra. Her skin was slickly smooth under his fingers, leaving them wet. She sat up and suddenly shivered as cool shadow enveloped the patio. They both looked up. A large dark cloud was moving overhead, blocking the sun. More dark clouds, in solid low banks, were coming over the mountains from Italy.

"Going to get one of your spring storms," Hunter said.

Odile nodded, her curly red hair bobbing. "And soon. A big one. Be ready to go in a minute." She picked a towel off the bricks of the patio and patted herself dry as she ran up the steps to get dressed.

The slim elegance of Olivier Lamarck's figure, and the taut bony structure of his long face, gave him the appearance of being too young to be retired. He still had all his hair, though most of it was white. His deep tan hid the network of wrinkles in his face, unless you looked closely. And the caustic humor in the eyes made you forget the wrinkles.

The table where he sat playing chess was under the awning of a waterfront bistro on the Quai Admiral Courbet, near the ocher-yellow arcade of the Villefranche Customs House. The bistro belonged to the plump little man he was playing with: Bernard Minelli, a Corsican who'd retired from a career as a petty mobster after getting his right arm shattered by a police bullet during a night chase in the Panier quarter of Marseilles twelve years earlier.

The ruined arm was still useless, and Minelli made his chess moves with his left hand. It was Olivier Lamarck who had shot him, but Minelli never mentioned this, out of delicate regard for Lamarck's feeling of guilt. Lamarck did feel guilty about it, whenever he looked at that arm. But it didn't prevent him from wanting to destroy the other man again, on the battleground of the chessboard. Chess was the only outlet left, for the latent aggression that lurked beneath Lamarck's elegant appearance and intelligent mind.

"Chess is its own world of war," he had once expounded after beating Hunter two games out of three. "Vicious, unrelenting, malicious. The combat quite serious. But it is still an old-fashioned gentleman's war, of course. That is one of the appeals. Not today's kind of war. The victorious general smiles modestly when it is over, and graciously invites his beaten opponent to lunch. The general who has been humiliated by defeat accepts with polite thanks, and eats with his stomach burning for revenge. Only soldiers are killed; no civilians. And after lunch the generals can set up new soldiers and begin another battle."

Olivier Lamarck always played with a fierce lust to win. When he now made the small pawn move, which left Minelli no alternative to being checkmated in the next three moves, Lamarck leaned back in his chair and smiled in triumph.

Minelli studied the position, sighed, and knocked over his king with a flick of his thumb. "I resign, you bastard. Do I get a revenge game?"

Lamarck was about to say yes when he saw Hunter's rented Renault pull into the quay. Odile got out with Hunter, kissed him on the cheek, waved to her father, and climbed up into the shadows under the arches of the Rue Obscure. Hunter stayed by the car, waiting.

"Another time," Lamarck told Minelli, pushing back his wicker chair. "Another old friend waits for me."

Minelli nodded and raised a hand in farewell as Lamarck walked away. His left hand. His right lay in his lap; pale, withered, useless.

Lamarck strode jauntily to Hunter and shook his hand firmly, studying him much as his daughter had done. "So . . . how does it go with you?"

"It goes. And you?"

"Retirement begins to be a bore. Try to die before yours. What are you working on?"

The first drops of rain struck their faces as Hunter told him. They climbed inside the car. The rain stopped seconds later. But the sky had completely clouded over and the sea was slate gray, with the waves piling higher and smashing fountains of spray off the rocks along the jetty. The bones in Hunter's hands and fingers, broken and badly mended so long ago, began to ache harshly. Without realizing he did it, Hunter gripped the steering wheel tightly with both hands to ease their throbbing.

Lamarck was considering what Hunter had told him, enjoying digging his mind into work again; even another man's work. "I agree," he said deliberately, "that if this boy Selim knew a way across the border, he probably learned it from a local smuggler at some time. One of the professional small fry around Menton, I'd say. I know a number of them, of course. But they would never tell me anything connected with their work. I don't blame them. A *flic* is still a *flic,* even retired."

"But you know someone they *would* talk to."

Lamarck got a stubby pipe from his pocket and thumbed tobacco into the bowl while he considered. Someone like Bernard Minelli wouldn't do; he'd been too long out of the local heat, and had never operated at that level. As Lamarck lit his pipe, Hunter watched two fishermen drag their nets across the quay so they wouldn't be washed away in the coming storm. Lamarck took a couple long puffs on the pipe and said, "Right now, I would say your best contact would be a fellow American. George Shansky. Used to work for your CIA.

Hunter remembered the man. "Shansky the Spook"—a tricky, cocksure intelligence agent who'd been operating in France a long time. They'd met twice, and Hunter hadn't much cared for him. But then, he never cared for any of the people involved in the dirty-tricks side of espionage. They thought along devious lines that irritated him. "When'd he get fired?" he asked Lamarck.

"Some months ago. Your government seems to be having an economy wave. Shansky's cover in France was blown long ago, and he didn't want to be assigned elsewhere because of an expensive mistress he was keeping in Nice. Who left him as soon as she realized he was out of funds. I understand he's deeply in debt: the mistress, gambling, and alimony payments to an ex-wife in America."

Lamarck took the pipe from his teeth and shook his head in

wonder. "It has always amazed me, the opinion your courts have of the inability of women to earn their own living, and the obligation of former husbands to go on supporting them as though they were helpless children. At any rate, Shansky is desperate; and beginning to get involved with people engaged in desperate enterprises. I'm afraid he will be in very hot soup soon. But in the meantime, he knows the sort of people you can make your connection through."

"Where is he staying?"

"He has a room with a family outside Monte Carlo." Lamarck gave Hunter the address. "If he is not there, they will probably know where to find him. He's looking for work, and he owes them rent."

"Thanks, Olivier. Want me to drop you at your house?"

"No, there's time for another chess game before dinner. My friend's nephew can drive me, if it is raining too hard by then." Lamarck started to climb from the car. Then he paused and looked at Hunter again. "Simon, if this business of yours happens to heat up in this area, perhaps I can be of help to you. Because you will get little or no *official* help. Not if Arabs are involved. Not in France."

"I know the situation." Hunter's tone was heavy with cynicism. "Your country's hard up for oil, and your government's trying its damnedest to take a hand in Mideast power politics. So everybody's supposed to look the other way when terrorists are around."

"Exactly. Most of our cops don't like it. But what can they do, against official policy? They had the point driven home to them recently, with that bomb-car case."

Hunter had heard of it: Three Arabs had been caught redhanded, with a car full of explosives and plans for killing a number of people in Paris. Nabbing them had been a brilliant piece of detective work. The detectives who'd accomplished it had then had their knuckles rapped, for being overzealous. And the three terrorists had been promptly let out of jail and out of France. To return, probably, under other passports.

This official stance led to odd unofficial alliances: There were members of the French secret service (SDECE, known in the trade as the Swimming Pool) actually co-operating with the activities of Arab guerrilla organizations. On the other hand there were French narcotics agents, who didn't like Arab involvement in dope smuggling—and airport security men who didn't like innocent passengers being terrorized or killed—secretly passing information back and forth with Israeli agents.

"If it does heat up around here," Hunter told Lamarck, "I'm going to take help wherever I can get it. So you'll hear from me."

"Good. I could use some retirement from retirement." There was appeal in Lamarck's thin smile. And nostalgia. "At the least you can use me as a contact center. I've gotten a phone in the house since you were last there."

Hunter nodded, and watched the slim figure stride back toward the waterfront bistro. Turning the car, Hunter drove from the quay. As he passed behind the Welcome Hotel, Odile appeared out of the Place du Marche carrying a large wicker basket loaded with groceries. Hunter picked her up and took her back up the hills.

In front of her father's house she got out of the car and stood beside it, looking at him. "Will we be seeing you again soon?"

"I'm not sure yet. Depends on developments."

Her dark green eyes were steady on his face. "I would like to see you again," she told him firmly, without a smile. "I would like it very much." She walked around the car and down the steps to the house without looking back.

Hunter drove on toward Monte Carlo. The rain started again, in earnest this time, before he was halfway there.

George L. Shansky (he always stressed the middle initial) was down in the harbor of Monaco, having a daydreaming stroll past the yachts moored there, when the rain caught him. He climbed swiftly up the long flights of steps from the breakwater; drawing a certain amount of pride out of the fact that he could still do that without puffing. Reaching the opulence of Monte Carlo's casino complex on the cliff, he ducked into the ornate Hôtel de Paris.

Crossing the turn-of-the-century luxury of the great plush lobby, Shansky the Spook looked a bit seedy in contrast. It was the breaking down of his aggressive self-assurance that did it, more than anything else. His clothes were all right, and his long, lanky figure still had a tough resilience. But he seemed prematurely aged, and it was not just the receding hairline. It was the slump of his wide shoulders, the defeat in his face, the haunted bitterness in the eyes.

Going into the bar, he settled at a corner table and ordered a *capucino* from the smartly dressed barman. Considering his meager supply of borrowed francs, the gouging price here was an enormous extravagance. It was the only one he still allowed himself occasionally: pretending he could still afford to lounge in a well-padded chair surrounded by the jet-set ambience of the bar's rich green walls and carpeting, the dark woods and burnished leather and shiny brass studs. For three and a half French francs, *servis compris*, it was a much-needed investment in fantasy.

By the time the barman brought his order, the rain outside had become a steady downpour. Shansky dropped two sugar cubes in his *capucino*, lit a crooked little Toscanelli cigar, and gazed idly through the floor-to-ceiling windows.

The windows in one wall gave a view of cars splashing around the curving street, palm trees bending before the sharpening wind, and the sea below flat and almost black under a solid overcast. No pleasure yachts out on that patch of Mediterranean now; the storm warnings had brought them all in. Only a couple commercial fishing boats, fighting their way back toward the shore.

Through the windows in the other wall he could see the ugly modern buildings obliterating the charm of the old town, the orange cranes making more modern monsters up on the hills, and the aging baroque dignity of the Casino and Opera House across the street. The hotel doorman's blue-and-lavender uniform was getting drenched as he kept his huge black umbrella over the heads of guests he was ferrying across from the casino.

Shansky was having his first hot sip from the cup when he spotted Maurice Hammelring coming out of the casino across the street. Hammelring hesitated under the canopy, hatless and with no raincoat, his old dark business suit still fitting his small figure well. Finally he put both hands on his head to protect his ten-year-old toupee from the pelting rain, and marched across toward the hotel. His dignity wouldn't let him run.

He vanished from Shansky's view for about thirty seconds. Then he reappeared in the tall entrance of the bar. He paused, took off his glasses, and cleaned raindrops from the thick lenses with a spotlessly white but unironed handkerchief. He put them on again with a flourish, looked around, and beamed when he saw Shansky. Maurice Hammelring's smile brought an unexpected sweetness to the harsh lines of his aging Prussian face.

He came straight to Shansky's table and sat down. His expression became businesslike as he lit up a cigar. Like Shansky's, it was

a Toscanelli. They were very cheap across the border in Ventimiglia: a box of four for a hundred Italian lire.

"I saw you come up the steps from the harbor," Hammelring said,
eyeing Shansky slyly through the cigar smoke between them.
"Thinking of renting a boat for a weekend of sailing—like in the
old days?"

Shansky shrugged a thick shoulder, the bitterness spreading
from the eyes and tightening the ends of his wide mouth. "They
don't charge for dreaming. Not yet. I guess they'll get around to it."

Hammelring glanced around to make sure no one was within
hearing. "Perhaps," he told Shansky softly, "the time has come to
make the dreams a reality. This is a remarkable coincidence. At
the very moment that I saw you coming up the steps, I was speaking with a certain person who needs someone of your talents."

Shansky drew a slow breath, and something unpleasant came into
his expression. Hammelring said hastily: "Don't worry, G.L., *he*
didn't see you. He was facing the opposite way. And of course, I
didn't mention you by name. I wouldn't let anyone know about . . .
your talents. Not before obtaining your agreement to meet with
him. I am not an amateur, remember."

Maurice Hammelring had been a thief. A fairly successful thief;
it was on what lawyers had left him of his past profits that he now
scraped by, as if he had a meager pension. He had stolen a few
large bundles. But he had also spent too much time in prisons. He
couldn't stand the thought of going into another one; so the courage
to be a thief was gone. Now he supplemented his dwindling savings
by charging a percentage fee for acting as a middleman.

Shansky sipped more of his *capucino*. "Who's the guy? And *what*
is he?"

"He told me to call him Serge. I don't imagine that is his name. I
don't know anything about him except that a reliable man gave
him my name. He sounds like a Ukrainian. I do know he has
money; he is not just talking."

The corners of Shansky's wide mouth drew down. "The OUN?"
The Organization of Ukrainian Nationalists was a well-financed
group of fanatic anti-Soviet exiles.

Hammelring raised and lowered his narrow shoulders. "Possibly,"
he admitted. "Even probably." His voice dropped another notch.
"He is ready to pay two thousand pounds, in British sterling."

Shansky lowered his cup very slowly. After a second he asked: "What's the job?"

"Moving someone."

"Who? And from where to where? Iron Curtain job?"

Hammelring did his shrug again. "He wouldn't tell me any details. But he says it would be an easy job. Short and simple."

"For two thousand sterling? Don't make me laugh."

"Eighteen hundred," Hammelring corrected him crisply. "I already have my ten per cent commission on the job."

Shansky looked at him with dull malice. "Suppose I don't take it?"

"Then I have to give back the commission."

Shansky's smile was thin. "*Would* you?"

"Of course. I promised." Hammelring hesitated. "And he is not the sort of man it would be intelligent to cheat."

"That makes the picture very clear," Shansky said dryly.

"I could have this client here in a minute or two. Will you wait for us?"

"No. Forget it."

Hammelring looked elaborately puzzled. "But why? The money is very good."

"Too good. For any kind of reasonably safe job. And not enough to pay me for taking a really big risk."

"You have done much more dangerous things, in the past."

"In the past, I was a hell of a lot younger."

"That Yugoslav thing was only two years ago."

"Yes. I was two years younger then."

Hammelring's expression was admiring. "That was really something, G.L. Something wild. The excitement you must have felt, I envy that. And the exultation, pulling it off."

Shansky made the mistake of remembering. Genuinely remembering.

"Yeah," he said, "it was pretty hairy."

He picked up his cup, and had to put it down. His hand was trembling. The old glands, in there working again.

Hammelring was watching him with shrewd eyes. "Don't you sometimes want to feel that again? Suppose I can get my client to raise the amount he's offering? Even double it, perhaps. *Four thousand?*"

Shansky didn't say anything.

Hammelring leaned across the table and touched his arm. "Will you wait, while I check it out with him?"

Shansky hesitated. Then, with deep self-anger, he said: "All right."

"Good." Hammelring stood up, shook his head at the barman who'd begun hovering politely, and marched out of the bar.

Shansky finished his *capucino* and relit his cigar. That was another thing about Toscanellis, in addition to being cheap and evil-smelling: They drew badly, and went out every time you stopped dragging on them for a few seconds. Which had the compensation of making them last longer.

He felt tired. It wasn't physical; he knew he was basically in as good shape as ever. It was more a weariness of the soul. Shansky hoped the Ukrainian would not go along with doubling the offer. That would be just too much money to refuse. Shansky did not want to lose his life on some crazy suicide stunt against the Russians, for people he did not respect and a cuase he didn't believe in. But neither did he want to go on living like an impoverished rat.

A fatalistic certainty that Hammelring's client would agree to the four thousand scared hell out of Shansky. People talked a lot of crap about how great it was to be a tough old pro. Crap was what it was. In Shansky's line, you hit your peak young. After that, it got a little harder each year than it had been the last. You could still do it; but you began to operate on your memory of how you'd done it in the past; instead of on concentrated drive and perfect reflexes. That was what could get you killed where a younger man would survive.

Shansky was crushing the small stub of his cigar in the gray-blue plastic ashtray when another man came into the bar and looked around. A big man with a shock of gray hair and a hard, alert face. It took a moment for Shansky to remember who he was. And another moment to recall the name. By then Hunter had seen him and was coming over.

Hunter stopped at the table. "'Lo, Shansky. Long time."

Shansky nodded. "Long time is right, Hunter." He gestured at the chair Hammelring had vacated. "Take the load off."

Hunter asked the barman for a calvados as he sat down. Shansky said, casually but quickly: "I was looking forward to a calva myself. But I forgot to bring enough dough with me."

Hunter called after the barman to make it two. Shansky looked at him curiously. "What're you doing 'round here? Still Army?"

Hunter shook his head. "I'm working for a new State Department agency. WGCT."

"Heard about it. Thought it was just another talk show."

Hunter told him about his job, and then about the explosion at Rome's airport—and about Selim. The bitter, beaten look on Shansky's face changed as his mind automatically absorbed the details and began working on them, trying different combinations.

The barman brought over their drinks. Shansky took a long swallow and half closed his eyes in pleasure. "I do know some of the boys over in Menton who handle the little smuggling jobs," he acknowledged carefully. "And I'd like to help you out on something like this. But I'm pretty busy right now."

"I heard the CIA dropped you."

Shansky flushed. "I'm working on some private deals. That'll net a helluva lot more than the U.S. of A. was paying me."

Hunter leaned back easily in his padded chair, unimpressed. "I'll pay you fifty bucks for helping me make the contacts. A hundred if I turn out to be right, and we find a smuggler who remembers Selim. If it turns out I'm also right about the other thing—that Selim trying to slip over the border here means whoever was running him is planning something in *this* area—there'll be more work for you. Forty dollars a day, and expenses."

"That," Shansky said with flat anger, "is not a hell of a lot of money."

"That's what I can pay you," Hunter told him evenly.

Shansky leaned both forearms on the table and clenched his fists, looking at them and thinking it over miserably. Fifty bucks certain. A hundred possibly. And maybe forty a day for a short while after that. It was a long cry from the two and maybe four thousand *pounds* Hammelring's client would come across with. But he also had to consider the fact that this job didn't sound like anything likely to get him killed. . . .

When he raised his head, he saw Maurice Hammelring hesitating in the bar's entrance, looking uncertainly at Hunter's back. Shansky's expression didn't change. He only raised his index finger slightly from the table, and moved it back and forth once. Negative. Hammelring shrugged, assuming Hunter had outbid him with some job, and went away.

Shansky looked into Hunter's eyes, all pretense gone. "How about making it *fifty* a day?" His voice broke a little. "Please? I really need it bad."

Hunter considered how Shansky's name was going to look on his expense sheet. Chavez would recall the name. And Chavez had his own aversion to espionage types. But then Hunter looked across the table, and saw what had become of the old Shansky the Spook. A possible portent of his own future, if he loused up this job.

"Okay," he said finally. "Fifty. If there's work for you."

Shansky drew a long breath, and let it out slow. "Deal." He glanced at the darkening storm outside. "But we won't find anybody till this breaks. Figure on tomorrow morning." He drained the rest of his drink, and gasped. "Can your swindle sheet handle another of these? And then maybe you could buy us dinner in someplace halfway decent? I'll tell you the truth, Hunter—it's been awhile since I've have a really good meal."

Hunter nodded, and ordered him another.

Only a few miles away, up in Roquebrune, the same storm was darkening the fading daylight entering the living room of Bel Jahra's newly rented apartment. He spoke sharply to Driss Hammou, without looking up from the careful sketches he'd drawn on three sheets of paper spread on the table before him. Hammou turned on a lamp beside the table, and went over to light another lamp. Then he continued to watch what Bel Jahra was doing in respectful silence.

Bel Jahra added several small details he remembered to the sketches he'd made of Valasi's estate down on Cap Martin. When he was finally certain that he had forgotten nothing that he had observed there, he moved these sketches aside and drew over three fresh sheets of paper.

On the first he wrote: "*Situation.*" This he placed to one side with the sketches. At the top of the second sheet he wrote: "*Mission*"; and on the third: "*Execution.*"

Bel Jahra had prepared many briefings during his military career. He employed the techniques automatically, assembling them methodically in correct order. Situation, Mission, and Execution are the three cardinal pivots of any military operation. All three grow out of accurate reconnaissance.

The first phase of Bel Jahra's basic reconnaissance had been achieved that day at the Valasi estate; through keen observation of the area of operations and oblique questioning of Juliet Shale. The second phase had been accomplished after leaving the estate, and before returning to the Roquebrune apartment: For three hours he had nursed soft drinks in a café on the Rue Gounod in Nice, watching the entrance of the Giovanetti Catering Service across the street. During that period two employees of the catering service, and a waiter who obtained jobs through it, had come separately into the café. Bel Jahra had managed to strike up conversations with the waiter and one of the employees. Over drinks he'd bought them, he had extracted each fact he needed to know in order to infiltrate a guerrilla team as part of the Valasi party's catering staff.

Now Bel Jahra was applying the information derived from these two periods of reconnaissance. On the sheet of paper headed "Mission" he drew a rectangle. He didn't know, yet, the *exact* spot where the main table would be set during Valasi's eightieth birthday party. But Juliet Shale had told him who'd be seated around it.

Bel Jahra drew small circles around the shape of the table, one circle for each: Dezso Valasi, his son and daughter-in-law, the Prince and Princess of Monaco, and an elderly couple who had saved Valasi's life during the war when they'd been members of the French underground. Plus King Hussein. And the American Secretary of State. These last two would have with them, certainly, armed professional bodyguards.

Bel Jahra put aside, for the moment, this page marked "Mission." He now concentrated on the one headed "Execution." On this he labored longest.

First he worked out an over-all plan for infiltration, assassination, and escape. Then, with other sheets of paper, he made two detailed breakdowns of this plan: The first was a breakdown of each step in the execution. The second was a breakdown of separate tasks required during the execution; and the kind of man each task demanded. This second breakdown arrived at a minimum of seven basic tasks: one each for himself, Driss Hammou, and a commando team of five specialized guerrillas.

Two of the tasks in the breakdown involved close-range rapid fire with .45 caliber Colt revolvers. Automatic .45s had a number of distinct advantages over revolvers. But they had one disadvantage Bel Jahra could not afford to chance: Automatics can jam at the crucial moment. Therefore, Bel Jahra chose revolvers. He was an expert marksman with a revolver. One of the members of the five-man guerrilla team would have to be equally expert.

Two of the guerrillas would have to have proven skill with sub-machine guns. Both submachine guns, Bel Jahra decided, should be Czech VZ-58s. These were lightweight and accurate at close quarters, almost jam-proof, delivered a tremendously fast rate of fire, and with the butts removed would be easily concealed until the moment of use.

One guerrilla must be a demolition specialist. Almost anyone can prime and throw a grenade. But it takes an expert to judge exactly where to throw it, and get the detonation timing down to the split second. All explosives are tricky, and chancy. A man sitting next to an exploding barrel of TNT has been known to survive, while people a hundred yards away were killed by the blast. Grenades, in particular, have uncertain burst patterns. But the newly developed grenades supplied by the Arabian PFLP to three members of the Japanese Rengo Sekigun group, for the Lod operation less than a year before, overcame most of these problems. This grenade functions in two quickly succeeding stages: The first detonation releases the shrapnel from the mother pack. On release, these flying pieces of shrapnel explode themselves, with devastating effect. At Lod the main burst/secondary burst sequence had blown people's heads, arms, and legs off; and ripped an eight-year-old girl into three separate parts. These were the explosives Bel Jahra decided on; and they required someone who knew how to use them.

The fifth guerrilla would have to be, like Driss Hammou, capable of killing a child without an instant's hesitation.

When Bel Jahra finished his breakdown of "Execution," it came to seven pages. Having worked this out, the details were imbedded in his brain and the pages no longer necessary. He tore them up and gave them to Hammou for burning. Then he returned his attention to the sheet headed "Mission."

The two mission targets would be among the ten seated around the main table. These ten were represented by the ten small circles he had drawn around the rectangle. Two or three bodyguards must be expected to remain somewhere close behind each of the two main targets. But Bel Jahra could not be certain exactly where these bodyguards would be, until he found out which of the small circles represented the two targets. This, he was fairly sure, could not be pinpointed definitely until the last minute before execution.

Of one thing, however, he was certain from his breakdown of the execution plan: There was absolutely no way the two intended targets at that table could be assassinated alone. Certainly not quickly enough to prevent the bodyguards from flinging themselves in the line of fire, and firing back. It would have to be a total job, accomplished all at the same time: with massive gunfire and grenade explosions wiping out everybody at the main table almost simultaneously.

One by one, Bel Jahra crossed out each of the ten circles he had drawn around the table.

NINE

It continued to rain steadily until an hour before sunset. Then it slackened off but the wind grew stronger, beginning to break up the solid cloud cover. Streaks of harsh sunlight broke through and slashed the gray sea with gold, white, and bright green. The wind force kept mounting relentlessly, churning the surface of the sea, whipping trees, smashing great waves against the Monaco breakwater and over it. Out on the sea big cargo and passenger vessels fought to keep away from the shore. Along the coast, water rose across roads, blocking all traffic. Even trains began delaying departures as news of tracks ten inches under water was telegraphed along the stations.

Shansky had been right: Their smuggler hunt would have to wait until the next day. Hunter bought him the good meal he'd promised, and took a room for the night in the small Hôtel Louvre. By the time he prepared for bed the wind had eased; but the rain was coming down full force again. Hunter slept badly, unconsciously rigid against the pain radiating from his hands. He was still asleep when the rain changed to an abrupt hailstorm that destroyed half the flowers along the Riviera in the thirty seconds it lasted. It was shortly after that that the wind shifted direction completely. The tramontane faded, and the mistral came sweeping down from the Rhone Valley, scattering and chasing the clouds.

By dawn it was all over. The sky was spotlessly clean and the rising sun began its job of soaking up the night's accumulation of moisture. Hunter breakfasted early with Shansky in the hotel dining room with a hot glare streaming through the windows. By the time they set out in the Renault, the road was already dry. Hunter drove out of Monte Carlo toward Menton along the tortuous, cliff-hanging lower corniche. Shortly after they passed the *Point Noir* sign—whose big black spot marked a bend where more than five road deaths had occurred in the past two years—a white BMW sedan swept by them going the other way.

The driver was Ahmed Bel Jahra, on his way to the airport to take a plane for Paris, and another meeting with Bashir Mawdri.

The occupants of both cars continued on in their opposite directions, unaware of each other—as though fate were mocking them, and biding its time.

For Hunter, most of that day turned out to be a severe test of his patience; with absolutely nothing to do but wait. On reaching Menton early in the morning, Shansky went alone to show the pictures of Selim to a tobacco-and-brandy smuggler he knew. The man didn't recognize the boy in the pictures. But he agreed to show them around to other local smugglers. For one hundred francs; plus two hundred more if he located one who remembered Selim. Hunter and Shansky settled down to wait at a bistro terrace on the promenade above the stony beach of Garavan, Menton's seaside suburb.

At three in the afternoon, they were still waiting. Occasionally one of them took a stroll, to loosen up his legs—in the direction of the frontier post astride the coastal highway, or toward the Casbah-like town of Menton clinging to its hill rising out of the sea. But always one of them remained on the bistro terrace under the big umbrella shading their little round table.

They had had lunch there, and then later coffees, and now they sat nursing beers—two silently waiting men surrounded by vivid colors: the red, orange, yellow, green, and blue of the umbrellas and plastic chairs. The colors of the Riviera; basic, with few subtleties. Shansky seemed the more nervous of the two as the hours stretched by. But that was only because Hunter was better at keeping his frustration private. He sat listening without expression to the gentle surge of water among the rocks below, gazing at the boats out on the rippled surface of this last little French bay before the curving arm of land that was the beginning of Italy.

There were quite a number of boats: rubber rafts, sailboats, motorboats. Here and there, farther out, some large yachts. And occasionally a big ship, creeping along the distant, barely defined horizon line where sea met sky. Closer, just below the promenade next to the breakwater rocks, about a dozen sunbathers were stretched out on towels spread across the small stones.

Hunter's eyes, narrowed against the sunlight, took all of this in while his mind tried not to dwell on the fact that if the smuggler notion didn't pan out, he was at a dead end here. He was used to it, of course. Following leads which kept dead-ending was the essence of police work. Local or international, that was the basic job; always hoping that sooner or later one of the leads would not be a dead-ender. But waiting was the hardest part. Especially when the lead you were waiting on was the last one in your bag.

A rotund man in an old floppy straw hat had appeared on the beach to the left of the sunbathers, carrying a fishing rod and basket. He made his way slowly across the stones toward the surf. Shansky's index finger tapped Hunter's hand.

A small muscle flexed in Hunter's cheek. Otherwise his expression did not change. He got two hundred-franc notes from his pocket and slid them to Shansky, who folded them into a small wad concealed in his hand as he stood up and left the bistro terrace.

Hunter fished a cigarette from the nearly empty pack on the table and lit it. Through the smoke, he continued to gaze idly at the beach and bay. Shansky was strolling slowly down across the beach, head down, squatting occasionally to shift through the stones looking for seashells. Anyone from the area could have told him there weren't many left to be found, anymore.

The fourth time Shansky squatted down, he was close behind the fisherman, who had cast his line from the water's edge and appeared not to notice Shansky's presence. Hunter could not detect any exchange of words between them; neither did he spot the two hundred francs being transferred. Shansky the Spook might have come a long way down from what he once had been, but he hadn't lost certain of the old acquired skills. Rising, he continued his fruitless shell search farther along the beach before climbing the next set of steps and strolling back to the bistro terrace.

He looked different as he reached the table. Younger, suddenly; the sullen hang-dog look gone and the shoulders no longer sagging. Shansky was at a stage in his life when even very small triumphs in his old line of work had an exhilarating effect. He grinned down at Hunter. "Got it, pal. He found a guy who knew your boy Selim. He'll meet us up in the cemetery."

Hunter let his breath out slow, and stood up. "Let's go."

They drove up the Chemin Vallaya and followed the sweeping curves of Garavan Boulevard away from the border to the Old Cemetery. Surrounded by a high stone wall and set atop a hill, it perched above Menton's crooked, rising passageways like an ancient fortress. Shansky followed Hunter up the steps and in through the partially opened rusty iron gates.

Inside, the Old Cemetery was crowded with crumbling monuments, ancient trees, and the silence of the dead. Most of the tombs and gravestones were moss-covered and eroded with age; many were weed-overgrown ruins. There was a new cemetery a short distance away; but when anyone said "the cemetery," they meant this one. The only person in sight was an old, heavyset man wearing comfortable bedroom slippers, stained overalls, and the red bandanna around his neck that Shansky had been told to expect. He had the weathered skin of a farmer, which was probably what he was. None of the petty local smugglers considered it their profession. Smuggling was for them merely a way to make some extra money, in their spare time.

He was seated on a fallen, eroded tombstone, and he eyed Hunter thoughtfully as he came over and sat beside him. Then he glanced to Shansky, who had leaned against a wind-contorted olive trunk, and was watching with his hands in his pockets.

"I'm the one with the money," Hunter told the old smuggler.

The eyes returned to him. "How much?" The way he asked it sounded more like curiosity than the start of a bargaining session.

Hunter gave him a hundred-franc note. Roughly twenty dollars. "This is for nothing. How much more you get depends on how useful the information is to me. I'll be fair."

The old smuggler shook his head. "I don't like to do business that way. I always work for a flat fee, fixed in advance. Give me another hundred francs, and I'll tell you anything I can. I won't hold anything back. I have no reason to. My friend told me that you—or the other man there—would not allow anything I say to reach the *flics* and hurt me." He laughed suddenly. "It doesn't matter anyway. What could you prove? I would only deny everything."

Hunter put another hundred on the man's thick leg. Between them on the surface of the eroded gravestone, he could just make out the faint outlines of: "Died—1853. . . ."

The old man took Selim's pictures from a pocket and studied them. "I remember this boy. I never knew his name. Or the names of the other two. But I remember them, well enough. It was only a year ago."

"A year ago—you took this boy, and two other men, over the border?"

"Yes." The old man frowned a little, thinking. "I don't think there is any more I can tell you. They wanted to cross without being seen. They didn't tell me why. I took them. They paid me. I never saw them again. I know nothing about them." He frowned again. "I can tell you what the other two looked like, if that will be of interest."

"It is. Tell me."

"One was short and wide. Very strong. Ugly face. Stupid-looking, though I don't think he is stupid. The face of a man who cuts throats. A butcher of people; but that is only my opinion, you understand. He said nothing to indicate it. But I would not like to have an argument with a man like that."

"Age? Hair? Eyes?"

"About thirty, perhaps a bit older. Brown hair, I think. I'm not sure. I don't remember the color of the eyes."

"Any scars?"

"No. . . . Oh yes, his face was pitted badly. Smallpox scars. Little ones. Many."

Hunter questioned him point by point, but got nothing further of descriptive value. "And the other man?"

"He was the leader of the three of them. That much was obvious. A gentleman. Tall. Handsome . . . except his eyes were too pale. I remember that. Pale eyes, in a thin face. But handsome. Tall and slim, but strong. He was the one who contacted me. And paid me. Even if he hadn't, I would say he was the leader. A leader sort of man, you understand."

Hunter wasn't able to get any further description of the tall leader. Even the age seemed to be uncertain; though he was not old. "They never used each other's names when they were talking near you? Think a minute."

"They never talked," the old smuggler said flatly. "Not at all, the whole time. Only the leader talked—to me. When he contacted me, and when he paid me; part before we started out, and the rest after we got to the other side."

Hunter was silent for a bit, thinking it over. His eyes had a withdrawn look. His mouth got sullen as he contemplated the emerging figure of what had been until now merely an imagined shadow directing Selim's actions.

After a while, he asked quietly: "How did this man make contact with you?"

Mademoiselle Laure was a shrunken, bright-eyed little woman of eighty-five living alone in a fading yellow Spanish-style villa set among neatly tended lemon groves on a long slope above Garavan Boulevard. Her house was taken care of, her lemon trees tended, and her groceries brought daily, by a local family to whom she had promised the property when she died. But she had many other daily visitors; local people who came to listen respectfully to anything she had to say. She never turned on a light in her house; rising with the sun and going to sleep when it set, and filling most of the time between with reading. She had never married; had never been known to even go with a man.

Her villa was filled with books; mostly histories, political comment, and religious works. Mademoiselle Laure was a believing Catholic who had opened late to the challenge of new ideas. All the fiction in her house were the classics; she couldn't get interested in novels written after World I.

The daughter of French aristocracy, Mademoiselle Laure had barely learned to read and write before balking against her tutors and running off to ride her horses over the family estates in Brittany, or to play with her goats around the family's vacation property where she now lived. She hadn't read anything but an occasional newspaper headline until she was forty. It was at fifty that she had suddenly begun swallowing books at an astounding rate; lost in a totally new world of printed pages. At seventy she had begun to teach herself ancient Greek, to get back to the sources. She was currently reading all of Plato in the original.

Mademoiselle Laure had a way of asking her local visitors penetrating questions, and listening attentively to the answers; ready to pounce on a meaningless or patently wrong opinion. It made them rethink even some thoughts that had been part of them since childhood. Her price for shaking up their mental processes involved presents of chocolates, cakes, and feed for her twenty caged birds. And staying with her until she tired of their company and told them to go away.

It was Mademoiselle Laure who had put the man Hunter wanted to know about in touch with Mario, the old farmer-smuggler. Her tiny shriveled figure reclining on a tattered chaise longue, surrounded by piles of books and birds singing in their cages, she regarded Hunter and Shansky with bright interest as she told them about it.

"I don't even know the gentleman's name," she said in a crisp, thin little voice. "But he is a gentleman. Definitely. Though a bit too handsome for his own good. Or for the good of certain foolish women, I think." There was mild disapproval in her tone; but also an understanding that all people were flawed, by original sin.

"I don't know about the other two men you say went with him to Mario. I never saw them, or even knew of their existence."

"But the one you do know," Hunter probed carefully, "you apparently knew well enough to send to a local smuggler. Yet you say you don't even know his name?"

"I didn't send him to Mario," Mademoiselle Laure corrected him precisely. "I told a lady I know about Mario. Helena Reggiani. *She* sent the gentleman to see him. As a matter of fact, I only saw this gentleman once in my life, briefly. That was more than two years ago, when he came to fetch Helena, who was paying me a visit. He hardly spoke to me, he was so anxious to go away with her."

Hunter kept his eyes on her small wrinkled face, concentrating on picking the tiny bits of information out of all she was saying. "It was *one* year ago you sent him to the smuggler, through this Helena Reggiani."

Mademoiselle Laure nodded. "He was apparently with her again, though I didn't see him. Tell me, please, what is your interest in this gentleman?" There was no wariness in her question; only interest.

Hunter was surprised to find himself telling her the truth: "A bomb was exploded in the airport outside Rome a few days ago. It killed five people. Four adults and a baby. I have reason to believe this man we're talking about was responsible."

"I see. Thank you for explaining. I don't like puzzles."

"You don't seem surprised to learn he may be a multiple murderer."

"No. *Every* person has ultimate evil in him. Only by understanding that can we fight against evil, in ourselves. And punish it, in others. You do believe in punishment, Mr. Hunter?"

"Yes."

"I'm glad to hear it. So many people these days do not. They think it better to forgive and forget. They don't understand the meaning of the words 'To err is human, to forgive divine.' This means that only God has the power to forgive. Men must punish misdeeds, for the sake of civilization. That is simple justice, and morality. And a man who transgresses must *be* punished, for the sake of his own soul."

She suddenly darted a look at Shansky. "You think I am a very foolish old woman, but you don't say so. You have opinions, yet you let your friend here do all the talking. Why is that?"

"He's the boss," Shansky told her sourly. "I'm only an employee."

"Is that why you are such an unhappy man?"

Shansky looked embarrassed. "Does it show that much?"

"Oh yes," Mademoiselle Laure told him firmly. "You pity yourself. Pity is a destructive force. You should cure yourself of it." She turned back to Hunter with a surprisingly gay laugh, like a mischievous little girl. "I am confusing you both. I ramble on, while you desperately try to make sense of it. Now I promise to behave. Ask me questions."

Hunter smiled. "You could start by explaining who Helena Reggiani is."

"Helena is a lovely Sicilian widow. Truly lovely. And a noblewoman. I own a cottage on Cap Ferrat. For the past three winters she has rented it, through my estate agent in Monaco. She came to see me when she first thought of renting the cottage, and we found we enjoy talking together. Since then, she always visits me from time to time, when she is on the Riviera.

"I believe the gentleman you seek has been one of her lovers for quite some time. Helena has unfortunately had a number of them, over the seven years since her husband died. Her husband left her more money than is good for an emotionally unstable woman with her good looks. She quite fails to understand the harm she does, to herself *and* the men, through these immoral relationships. I tried to explain that if she would only cut her hair shorter, and dress more modestly, men would not constantly be thinking she wants to attract them. But Helena only laughed, and said she *wants* to attract them. So sad, for such a lovely and otherwise intelligent woman."

Hunter gently brought her back to the point: "Why did she say her boyfriend wanted to contact a local smuggler?"

"She told me he wanted to write an article about refugee smuggling during the war. I believe he is a journalist. For a North African news syndicate."

Hunter added this, for what it was worth, to his image of the man he was after.

Shansky spoke up unexpectedly: "For such a religious-type lady, Mademoiselle, it's funny you should know smugglers." He smiled crookedly. "They *are* criminals, you know."

She nodded. "Yes, but in such a small way. Everyone around here knows who they are. The ones like Mario especially, who helped so many desperate refugees in the war, including many who could not pay. I'm sure that God will consider that, and forgive Mario's little misdeeds with cigarettes and liquor."

Hunter, convinced that she knew nothing more of any use concerning Selim's chief, asked her about someone who was certain to know more: "Would your estate agent have an address where I can find Helena Reggiani at this time of year?"

"*I* know where she is. She still keeps her late husband's estate, in Sicily. I received a lovely picture postcard from her, only two weeks ago. She's staying there now, in Taormina. Would you like me to get you her address?"

"Please. And the address of your estate agent, in Monaco."

Mademoiselle Laure reached out a shriveled hand and Hunter helped her rise from the chaise. She walked with slow, careful steps out of the room, and returned with the two addresses on a slip of paper. Hunter pocketed it and thanked her.

She shook hands with both of them in parting. "It was a most enjoyable visit. Quite interesting. And Mr. Shansky, you look so much better, now that you are smiling. You should do it more often."

Shansky laughed. "I'm trying. It's just that I'm out of practice."

They left her and went down a series of stone stairways between the lemon groves, to the Renault parked on the narrow road below Mademoiselle Laure's property.

"That's some little old lady," Shansky said as they got in the car. "Next stop, Sicily?"

Hunter nodded, feeling the repressed excitement inside him. The search was heating up; he could feel it. A new lead, a solid one this time; with no dead end in sight.

"*I* go to Sicily," he told Shansky. "You stay here. Nose around Cap Ferrat. Find out if anybody there knows our man from the times he stayed with Helena Reggiani. Start with the estate agent in Monaco." He got out his wallet, took fifty dollars from it, and gave it to Shansky. "That pays off the rest of what I owe you for finding the man who showed Selim the smuggler route. I'll arrange in the consulate in Nice to start getting you the fifty a day we agreed on, as long as I need you."

Shansky pocketed the money, after looking at it a moment.

"So . . . it looks like I'm working regular again."

"That's how it looks," Hunter agreed, and started the car.

Shansky leaned back in the seat beside him, his eyes half closing. "It feels good," he said softly.

At the consulate in Nice, Hunter made the necessary arrangements to get his growing expenses forwarded to him there from Washington. He also sent a message with the request, partially explaining to Chavez what he was doing; and promising to phone with the rest of it the following day.

Then he made a series of phone calls. The first was to Olivier Lamarck, asking him to dig around the area and see if he could find anyone who knew Helena Reggiani—and who might also know her tall, handsome boyfriend who claimed to be a North African journalist. The second call was to London, where Inspector Ivor Klar told him there'd been a total absence of further developments on the case. The last call was to Major Diego Bandini, in Rome, requesting information on a wealthy Sicilian widow named Helena Reggiani.

"I've got to come through Rome, anyway," he told Bandini over the phone. "To get a plane to Sicily. The next one out of here lands me in Rome at seven this evening. Will you see what you can dig up on her by then? I'll call you when I get into the airport there."

Diego Bandini did better than wait for Hunter's call. He met him at Leonardo da Vinci Airport, as he came off the plane from

Nice. "I get bored with my fellow carabinieri around me all the time," he explained. "It is good to get out and see a fresh face, once in a while."

"My fresh face is pretty tired right now, Diego. What've you got for me?"

"Over drinks, my friend. The next shuttle to Sicily doesn't go for an hour. I already made sure they keep a seat for you." Bandini led Hunter to the VIP lounge. They settled into the comfortably upholstered chairs, ordered Americanos, and then Bandini told what he had found out concerning Helena Reggiani:

"She is well known—and well connected—here in Rome. The answer to the first question you have *not* asked yet is no. Helena Reggiani has never had any known contacts with terrorists, revolutionaries—or political types of any variety. Her late husband was Luigi Antonio Reggiani, part of an extremely old, distinguished, and disgustingly rich family. Officers of the church, Army, and government for generations. Luigi Antonio was the other sort that distinguished old families generate: a playboy. I say this advisedly. He was seventy when he married his Helena; and still a playboy. He died as most Italian men would like to: in the bed of a beautiful woman who was not his wife. Leaving his wife, who has the youth to enjoy it, considerable wealth.

"She is Swiss. Before her marriage, she had considerable success as a fashion model, and as an orament of the international jet set. She attempted a movie career in Rome, at which she did not have success. Though a beautiful woman, she was no actress. In Rome this is usually no handicap. But it seems to have worried her, this lack of talent she discovered, and she quit. Whereupon she married Luigi Antonio Reggiani.

"Her main male interests, before him, seem to have been other wealthy older men. Since the death of the one she married, I understand her interest has changed to pretty younger men. Quite naturally. In addition to the estate her husband left her in Taormina, she owns a Parioli apartment here in Rome, and another apartment in London. She apparently flits from one place to another, leading an utterly useless but entirely blameless life, morality aside. And that, my dear friend, is all there is to tell about Helena Reggiani. I think I have earned that *you* pay for our drinks. You agree?"

Hunter ordered them refills, and tried to work out exactly how the man he was after might fit into this total picture Bandini had given him.

He still had fifteen minutes' waiting time when Bandini left him. He used it to make calls to Uri, Ferguson, and others in Rome he'd given Selim's picture to. None of them had turned up any sort of lead to the man under whose control Selim had acted.

On the flight to Sicily, Hunter reviewed what he did have: a woman who should be able to tell him a great deal about the man he was after; and strong indications that this man was now up to something new around the area of the French Riviera. Point by point, Hunter systematically went down the facts that took him to this conclusion:

The man he was after was known to have spent some time in the Riviera area, presumably knew it well, and definitely knew the smuggler trail Selim had used.

Three reasons made it improbable that Selim had killed himself with the gun found in his hand. First, he had been well hidden when the firing of that gun revealed his position. There was no reason for him to deliberately let the patrols know where he was and provoke their answering fire. Second, Hunter could not recall a case of a suicide in which the victim had shot himself in the eye. The gunshot suicides he knew of had shot themselves in the ear, temple, mouth, or heart.

Third, and most important, Selim had had little to fear if he was arrested—even if it could be proved that he was the bomb-killer of the four adults and baby at Leonardo de Vinci. Perhaps he would have been knocked around a bit by some angry cops; but not after their superiors got on to it. As for being sentenced to prison for the mass murder, at the most Selim would have had to serve less than a year for the crime. European countries were never severe with captured Arab terrorists—because of fear of retaliation, and pressure from the big oil interests. Arab terrorists who were caught in Europe, after committing murders or planning to, could expect to be allowed to leave the country quietly, *perhaps* after having served a few months in jail. The *longest* period any of them had ever been held in prison was *eight months.* To avoid a maximum of eight months in prison, Selim would have tried to escape from Europe; but certainly would not have committed suicide.

So—someone else had killed Selim. The most likely reason: to prevent him from being caught by the police and revealing the identity of the man who controlled him. But not because that controller feared punishment for the airport deaths he was already responsible for. He wouldn't murder a fellow terrorist merely to avoid a barely possible maximum of a few months in jail.

That left only one reason for killing Selim: to prevent Selim revealing the next operation planned by that man. The fact that Selim was on his way into the Riviera area when he died indicated that was the area of the next operation. So did the fact that the man who'd killed Selim had *known* Selim was coming there; and was in that area himself, in a position to get to Selim before the police.

Hunter deliberately poked some large holes in this general line of reasoning. In spite of the holes, the direction it led to still held up for him. The Riviera. Hunter felt it; he could practically smell it.

When his plane landed in Catania, he decided he was getting too tired to drive up to Taormina in the dark and immediately deal with Helena Reggiani, until his wits were resharpened with some rest. Checking into a Catania hotel, he ate dinner in its dining room and went to bed early, after leaving word with the desk to have a rental car ready for him early in the morning.

Two hours later Hunter suddenly came wide awake, shocked out of sleep by a dream that tied his insides into cramped knots. It was a simple memory dream: He was back in the hospital room, smiling and joking and playing the cheerful clown, to ease the last weeks of his wife, dying visibly before his eyes. . . .

Climbing off the bed, Hunter made his way into the dark hotel bathroom and savagely sloshed cold water on his face. Then he pushed open the bedroom shutters and stood at the window sucking in cool night air—while he forced the agony of the dream into another channel: cold, purposeful hatred of the nameless man he was tracking down.

That man—Ahmed Bel Jahra—was at that same time of the night in Paris demonstrating exactly how he intended to execute his plan, to Bashir Mawdri and a much older man named Jamal al-Omared.

TEN

The Avenue Hoche begins at the Place de l'Étoile and ends at the lovely Parc Monceau, which forms a green center for one of the most aristocratic little neighborhoods of Paris. The big nineteenth-century houses along the Rue Murillo face the park, which gained fame in 1797 as the site of the first parachute jump (from a balloon some three thousand feet in the air) in history. Less than a century later the Parc Monceau acquired another kind of fame when so many people were slaughtered in it during the Commune uprising of 1871 that all the grass was stained red with blood for a week. Nowadays the houses on the Rue Murillo, each with its private garden, belong to people with the most solid kinds of wealth: banking wealth, land wealth, industrial wealth, oil wealth.

Jamal al-Omared, in whose home across from the Parc Monceau Bel Jahra revealed his operational plans that night, was both oil wealth and banking wealth. He was one of the top board members of the Union des Banques Arabes et Françaises, a financial conglomeration of the huge Crédit Lyonnais banking organization with twenty-four Arabian banks. He was also a senior representative in Europe for the combined oil interests of the United Arab Emirates, which, in conjunction with the other three biggest oil countries on the Arabian side of the Persian Gulf, anticipate reserves of one hundred billion dollars by the end of the decade.

Much more private was al-Omared's financial interest, and influence, in the Popular Front for the Liberation of the Occupied Arabian Gulf. This solidly backed guerrilla organization aims to conquer Oman and Iran, and bring them under the control of the

Arab power complex. In addition, for the past two years, al-Omared had been giving considerable support to Colonel Qadhafi's use of terrorism to create a newly united Islam.

At sixty-five, al-Omared carried his enormous power, and responsibility, with regal calm. Bel Jahra noted how quiet Bashir Mawdri became once they entered the house on the Parc Monceau, deferring to their older and vastly more important host. Though al-Omared had lived for two decades in Paris, and wore a sensible dark French business suit, he still moved like a Persian Gulf sheikh as he conducted them into his ground-floor library and shut the heavy door.

The big windows in the wall facing into his private garden were curtained against prying eyes. Though the likelihood of anyone getting close enough to the house to spy on them was remote, considering the efficiency of al-Omared's staff of prowling armed guards. Three tall lamps burned, gleaming on the warm deep brown of the Hungarian-parquet floor where it was not covered by the rich Bukhara carpet. The room was exceptionally tall, with a narrow balcony running around three dark-paneled sides to hold an upper level of bookcases. Under the balcony in the wall opposite the windows, small logs crackled in a fireplace framed by mother-of-pearl Chinese mosaics.

Bel Jahra spread his sketches out on a long Louis XV desk once al-Omared had settled himself in the high-backed Voltaire armchair behind it. Bashir Mawdri took a side chair as Bel Jahra began to explain what the sketches represented. He spoke for over an hour, detailing step by step how he intended to manage the double assassination, and then the escape of himself and his commando group. He explained how many men he would need for this group, exactly what kind of men, and what each one would have to do. Plus his other needs: the money, the weapons, the explosives . . . and a boat.

Al-Omared listened throughout in silence, giving Bel Jahra his entire attention and thinking over every point.

"The infiltration of the party," Bel Jahra explained, "will be achieved in three ways. I will enter by invitation." He was certain of this, though he had not pushed Juliet Shale for it yet; nor for certain points of information he still needed. He did not want to show too much interest in the party, until Juliet was certain that his *first* interest was in her. "Driss Hammou will enter with the arms, using the boat. I will detail that shortly. The best way to infiltrate the five commandos assisting us will be as members of the catering staff. This will allow them to get very close to the targets before arousing suspicion."

Bashir Mawdri looked dubious. "How do you intend to do that? I know that ever since all those jewel robberies at various Riviera parties, the companies insuring those estates insist on having security guards at the parties these days. And strict security checks of everyone catering the parties. Various documents are needed; I don't know exactly what these are but—"

"I do know," Bel Jahra cut in, quietly but firmly. "Each commando we infiltrate will need certain basic papers I'm sure can be manufactured in Libya: A *carte de séjour et résidence*. A *carte de travail*. And of course passports and visas. All of these should identify our men as coming from either Portugal or Spain. These nationals have a reputation for reliability and honesty with catering firms."

Mawdri nodded. "Our government printing plant in Tripoli can turn all of these out, so perfectly that no one can detect that they are false."

"The last document our men need will be more difficult," Bel Jahra stated. "This is a bond guarantee for each man, supplied by the company which insures Valasi's estate against fire and theft. Without such a document from the insurance company, they cannot be part of the catering staff at the party. They will have to show these bond guarantees to the chief security man at the party before being allowed to enter the estate. Unfortunately, there is a code number on this document, which is altered at certain intervals and is known to the insurance company's security men."

Bel Jahra paused, looking at al-Omared and waiting.

Al-Omared nodded slightly. "I can perhaps obtain these documents for you. Which insurance firm handles the Valasi estate?"

"This I do not know, as yet," Bel Jahra told him. "I also don't know the name of the chief security man the insurance company will assign to the party. But I *will* know both, by the next time we meet."

"Won't it still be difficult," al-Omared asked him, "to get the catering firm to accept these men for Valasi's party? These firms tend to select the staff needed from a pool of men they have come to depend on. I'm sure the staff for Valasi's affair will already have been selected."

"That is the problem," Bel Jahra agreed. "But I have a solution for it." He explained it in detail, one step at a time:

On the night of the party, the five commandos would be waiting, dressed in uniforms from the company which supplied the Giovanetti Catering Service. These would be obtained by Hammou, who was already checking it out through Mawdri's agent in Nice. Five members of the catering staff would be seized and killed as they were on their way to the Valasi estate. This would leave the catering staff five men short.

When the head of the catering staff at the Valasi party was going crazy because of their nonarrival, there would be a phone call to the Valasi estate. The call would be made by the secretary of the director of the Giovanetti Catering Service. Bel Jahra had learned who she was, from the employee he had questioned in the café across the street. She would have a knife at her throat, to insure that she said what she was told to; and would be killed immediately after making the call. She would ask for the head caterer by name. She would explain that the missing five had been in a car accident; and tell him that five last-minute replacements had been found, and were on their way.

He would be too relieved, and harried, at that point, to be over-interested in whether he had ever worked with these five before. She would ask him to pass her on to the chief security man at the party (again, by name). To him she would also explain the situation, and give him the five names listed on their false papers.

The five commandos would arrive, dressed properly, and possessing the documents—including the all-important insurance bond —which would allow them to enter the estate.

Al-Omared nodded, thinking it over carefully. But Bashir Mawdri remained worried: "And suppose, in spite of all this, we can't manage to infiltrate these five men, for some reason. Unexpected obstacles can always crop up at the last moment. Then all these preparations would be for nothing."

"No. I was coming to that." Bel Jahra spoke evenly, without looking Mawdri's way. It was al-Omared he had to convince this night. "I will need a *second* commando group. The same number as the first. The same kind of men. Trained to do exactly the same tasks, man for man. This insures that if one group cannot get in, the other can—by another way. And perform the same functions."

He detailed the other way, carefully. And added: "That is one reason for the sort of boat I have asked for. But it will be required in either case. To get the weapons and explosives into the estate beforehand. And to get us out, after the execution. Remember, we have to not only escape from the estate, but out of Europe. Completely."

When he had finished outlining his plan for this final phase, he had told them everything he could. His mouth was dry and his head suddenly began to ache, behind the eyes. Mawdri started to speak, and then changed his mind, looking inquiringly to their host.

Al-Omared remained silent for several minutes, his eyes nearly closed and his hands folded on his lap.

When his eyes finally opened, they rested unblinkingly on Bel Jahra's tensed, waiting face. "It is obvious from what you have said," al-Omared began quietly, "that you fully understand that Hussein and the American cannot be assassinated unless you simultaneously kill all the other people at their table, and around it. I believe you have the courage to do this, without any fatal hesitation."

Bel Jahra nodded. "There is no other way."

"Concerning the escape afterward, of you and the members of your commando group—it will be extremely difficult. I do not think you can manage it—unless some of the children you take hostage are killed to impress the remaining guards with your seriousness. Are you just as prepared for *that* eventuality?"

"One child *must* be killed," Bel Jahra told al-Omared. "Immediately. For the shock value. So they will understand our determination, and not endanger more lives. This is essential." His tone was regretful, but unwavering. "I do not want to kill *more* than one. But if they force it, by refusing to believe my warning, it will be on their heads, not mine. And then I *will* carry out the threat."

Al-Omared studied him with eyes that had read the inner weaknesses of many men in their time. At last he said: "I believe you." He turned to Bashir Mawdri. "Inform your superiors that I give my support to this project. I think you should arrange tomorrow for Ahmed Bel Jahra to be flown to Libya, to begin putting his plan into practical movement. The time is already short. I leave such details as choosing the right men, and boat, to him and your people."

Bel Jahra felt a slight dizziness from the release of tension. Suddenly, he was one very long step closer to his ultimate goal. And he knew that goal could be achieved. Qadhafi had done it in Libya. Bel Jahra was certain he could stage an equally successful coup in Morocco—with the backing of Libya, and al-Omared.

Only part of his mind heard Mawdri saying, "We have no shortage of the sort of men he'll need, already trained and ready in our indoctrination camps. As to the boat, I already have exactly what is needed. It was used to smuggle arms into Germany, through Hamburg, three months ago. Now it is in the Mediterranean, playing at being a pleasure yacht, and entirely clean of suspicion."

"As I said," al-Omared told him, "I leave such details to the two of you." He rose from his armchair. Mawdri started to get up, but al-Omared motioned him to remain seated. "We have other matters to discuss this night. I will see Ahmed out, and be back."

Bel Jahra refolded his sketches and slipped them in his pocket as he followed his host out of the library and down a wide corridor toward the entrance door. A tall guard with a revolver holstered under his unbuttoned jacket unlocked the door for them. He followed them out and moved discreetly to one side as al-Omared plucked Bel Jahra's sleeve, detaining him in the hedge-screened garden. The hedges were high enough to block the view of the Parc Monceau on the other side of Rue Murillo. In turn, the hedges hid the lower windows of al-Omared's house from the park.

"I have a strong feeling about you, Ahmed," al-Omared told him now that they were alone. "I feel strength, purpose, and intelligence in you. You will succeed in this project. With enough luck. One must always consider chance."

"I do always take that into consideration. Without luck, nothing can succeed."

"And if you succeed in this project," al-Omared went on as though Bel Jahra hadn't spoken, "you will have fully proved yourself. I will then see to it that you have Libyan backing for your own project in Morocco—and my support as well."

The abrupt openness of it took Bel Jahra by surprise. After a moment he said simply and honestly: "That is my dream."

"It will be a reality—again, with luck. When you succeed in Morocco, I hope that you will not forget those of us who made it possible. I hope you will not forget—that you depended upon the co-operation of other Arabs for your success."

"I won't forget," Bel Jahra assured him.

"I hope not," al-Omared repeated firmly. "Islam lost its former glory because Arabs did forget their first loyalty—to each other." His fingers closed on Bel Jahra's arm, and he led him to the right, along a narrow garden walk. At the end of it were three large birdcages on a marble platform, with glass around them to protect the sleeping birds inside from the cool night air of the Paris spring.

"Do you know what breed of birds these are?" al-Omared asked Bel Jahra.

Bel Jahra peered into the cages, without genuine interest. "They look like pigeons—or doves. I don't know much about birds. I've never had time for hobbies."

"These are pigeons. A special kind. *Homing* pigeons. Did you know that we Arabs were the first to use homing pigeons for military purposes?"

Bel Jahra shook his head. "No, I didn't know."

"The first the barbarian Westerners ever knew of such birds occurred when the Normans invaded Sicily. I'm sure you know our Arab history. You know how we conquered Sicily and held it. By the time the Normans came against us, in the eleventh century, we had complete control of the whole island. And through its harbors, of most of the Mediterranean."

Bel Jahra nodded, not liking being lectured to; but enjoying the feeling of intimacy with a man of al-Omared's vast influence.

"When the Normans came," al-Omared went on quietly, "an Arab army was sent from Palermo to battle them. Our army lost the battle. It was wiped out. When they looted our baggage trains, the Normans found a cage of homing pigeons. One of the few Arab survivors explained what the birds were; and that they had been intended to carry news of an Arab victory to the Emir in Palermo. The Normans had a grisly sense of humor. They released the homing pigeons to fly back to Palermo, with bloodstained rags torn from the clothes of our dead tied to their feet.

"*That* was the beginning of our loss of Sicily, of the Mediterranean—and finally of most of our empire. And do you know *why* we lost? Because there were three emirs controlling different parts of Sicily; and instead of co-operating with each other in the face of the common infidel enemy, they went on fighting against each other. Arabs did not stand firmly together, and Islam was lost."

There was deep emotion in al-Omared's voice, unquestionably from the heart. He put his hand on Bel Jahra's shoulder and looked closely at his shadowed face. "That must not be allowed to happen the next time," he said heavily. "And there *will* be a next time. *That* is what this is all about."

The trip from the Parc Monceau to Montmartre takes one up the highest hill in Paris, but a long way down in status. Favored by the best view of central Paris below, Montmartre was once the haunt of some of the best Impressionist and modern painters. Today it has a distinctly split personality: the garish honky-tonk glitter of the Pigalle tourist traps; and above that the climbing streets and pleasant little squares of an essentially lower-middle-class residential neighborhood, most of the buildings cut into smallish apartments for people of modest income. Some of the buildings have been kept or renovated as private homes for people with money. But not the kind of money represented by the houses on the Parc Monceau.

Bel Jahra registered the difference as his taxi turned out of Place Blanche and took him up the climbing Rue Lepic, lined with meat and vegetable markets whose corrugated iron shutters were locked tight against the night. But the contrast did not cause Bel Jahra to envy Jamal al-Omared. Money had little importance for Bel Jahra, except as a useful tool. Political power was what he was after; and that could be grasped even from a slum, with the right hook in your fist.

Bel Jahra got out of the taxi at the corner of Rue Duratin. It was two in the morning. The surrounding buildings were dark and silent. Bel Jahra entered a narrow, four-story house several buildings from the corner. He pressed the timer-button that lit a bulb on each of the small landings, and swiftly climbed the worn wooden stairways smelling faintly of rot, and garbage in the small cans in front of each door. At the top landing he selected a key from several in his pocket, and slid it in the lock of one of the two facing doors. As he opened the door, the landing bulb flicked out, plunging him in blackness.

He shut the door quietly and relocked it from inside. Making his way unerringly across the darkness of the apartment's small living room, Bel Jahra turned on a table lamp beside the secondhand sofa. The room was cheaply furnished but comfortable-looking; with few frills. There was an open kitchenette, a door to a bathroom, another to the bedroom.

Bel Jahra took a look in the bedroom. She was there; her slim figure sprawled under the bedcover, the mass of dark red hair spread out on the pillow around her absurdly childish face. Anticipated pleasure tautened the lean lines of Bel Jahra's face. But first there was a call to make. Softly closing the door to the bedroom, he went to the phone on the living-room table and dialed the code number for the Côte d'Azur, then the number of the apartment he'd rented in Roquebrune. As he waited, he gazed through the window, down into the night-shadowed cemetery where Nijinsky, Berlioz, Heine, and the Lady of the Camellias were buried.

Driss Hammou answered on the second ring. Bel Jahra gave him the good news without wasted words: "We're going ahead with it. They're backing us." There was a harsh sound of relief at the other end. "I'll fly to see Mawdri's people," Bel Jahra went on, automatically careful about revealing anything specific over a phone connection that could be tapped. "It may take several days. Begin checking your contacts in Nice while I'm gone."

"I'll get on it in the morning," Hammou promised. "Our late friend's picture is in the newspapers again. But there is suspicion he may not have killed himself. But there's no proof, either way. They're only guessing."

Everything was as it should be. "Anything else?" Bel Jahra asked.

"The girl called. Your English friend. I told her I was your cousin, visiting here a few days. She sounded upset that you were already gone."

Bel Jahra hung up and got a small address book from his jacket pocket. Juliet Shale had her own separate phone line to her room, so calls to her would not disturb the rest of the Valasi household. Bel Jahra found the number and dialed it.

She picked up on the first ring, her voice thick with sleep: "Yes . . . Juliet Shale here . . . what . . ."

Bel Jahra cut in quietly: "It's me, Julie. Sorry to wake you."

Sleepiness fled from her voice "André? That's all right . . . I don't mind. Are you back?"

"Afraid not. Still in Paris. Just finished a very long and late business conference, and I got this crazy desire to call you. Just to say good night."

"What time is it? Oh, my God, after two. . . ." Juliet giggled into the phone. "You *are* crazy. Will you be back soon?"

"I can't, for a few days." Because he knew what her answer would be, Bel Jahra added eagerly: "Look, Julie—why don't you fly up here? I've got a place. We can be together; fly back south together when my work here is finished."

"I *can't*, dammit. Valasi comes back tomorrow. I have to pick him up at the airport. And then I have all the preparations for his birthday party." She sighed, almost angrily. "I *wish* I could come there, but . . . I'm sorry."

"I am, too. But I *will* be back in just a few days. I hope all these party arrangements aren't going to keep us from getting together?"

"I'll manage to get free and see you," she swore. "For at least a few hours. Somehow."

"Good." Bel Jahra smiled to himself and added softly: "I miss you." And immediately hung up.

Still smiling, he went back to the bedroom door and opened it. He went in, leaving the living-room lamp on. It cast just enough light into the bedroom. He liked to watch the changes in a woman's face when he made love to her. Again, Bel Jahra gazed with taut anticipated pleasure at the girl sleeping in the middle of the wide bed.

Her name was Rosalynde. She was eighteen and somehow managed to still look fifteen, in spite of the life she'd led since she'd really been fifteen. Mostly, she had been a whore. Bel Jahra didn't mind that. There was one kind of sexual excitement to be had with insecure women like Juliet Shale; quite another kind with a vicious, tough-minded little bitch of Rosalynde's experience.

He studied her pretty, snub-nosed face while he undressed. Asleep, she looked so innocent, almost angelic. He was sure she had other men, when he was away. He didn't mind that, either. It added a special quirk to the relationship. When he was in Paris she was his alone; all his. He owned her. Like a toy, slightly soiled but delightful. A toy well worth the modest rent for this apartment and the small allowance he gave her. A toy with as much power over his emotions, in bed, as he had over so many older women.

Arranging his discarded clothes neatly, Bel Jahra slid under the covers beside her. His hands reached for her warmed flesh, fondling with growing roughness. The girl stirred, turning toward him automatically. Her eyes slitted open sleepily. Still not fully awake, she grinned wickedly—and lazily wrapped her slim young nakedness around him. Her fingers and tongue began their work, tauntingly at first, and then savagely. And once more he drowned in the deliciousness of her knowing sexuality.

The heady Sicilian sunlight, and the spectacular wild beauty of Taormina's setting on its mountain slope above the sea, have made it a favored winter resort for two thousand years. Helena Reggiani's palazzo was on a wooded hill above the ancient amphitheater built for the entertainment of vacationers when Sicily was a Greek colony, and enlarged when it became a Roman province. The palazzo, constructed by the Reggiani family in the seventeenth century, spread out through three wings containing dozens of large, high-ceilinged marble rooms. Generations of gardeners had fashioned the grounds around it, sculpting the high bushes and hedges into a variety of ingenious shapes. The Olympic-size swimming pool was new, installed by the late Luigi Antonio Reggiani to relieve the boredom of his young wife when they stayed here.

Seated beside the pool in minimal shorts and a silk blouse, Helena Reggiani still looked like a young fashion model, though Hunter guessed her age as late thirties. Her long tanned legs were beautifully curved. Straight golden hair framed a lovely face with exquisite bone structure. Hunter could understand why old Reggiani had thought her worth all his family fortune. The wide-set eyes held a capacity for tenderness. The heavy curve of breast against silk promised warmth and security; a cushion against hard reality.

But tight lines at the corners of chewed lips hinted at a price to be paid, in nervous tension.

Hunter sensed in her a disillusion with her way of life; a growing boredom with what her beauty had won for her. But he was surprised to find it impossible not to like her. She was bright, unpretentious, with a dry sense of humor about herself and her wealthy widowhood. He had quickly made his own judgment, and pretty much leveled with her. It had already gotten him a name, for the man he was after: Ahmed Bel Jahra.

"But I'm pretty sure you're going to find out you've been wasting your time looking for *him*," she told Hunter. "He's just not the kind of man to get involved in something like that. He's not a political type. At least, I never heard him express any interest in any sort of politics. Let alone the sort that kills people."

"What *is* he interested in?"

Helena Reggiani smiled wryly. "Sex. Do I embarrass you, Hunter? You're the quiet, withdrawn type it's hard to tell with."

He shook his head, keeping his eyes on her.

"Well, I think I'm embarrassing myself." She picked up a pair of sunglasses from her lap and put them on. "Anyway, you asked me and that's the answer. He was a very good lover. *Very* good."

"You say that in the past tense. How long's it been over?"

She looked away from him, across the wide pool to the sculptured garden on the other side. "Almost a year. I haven't seen him since about a week after that time you were interested in. When I put him in touch with that smuggler in Menton. I've heard from him though, a few times. The last time about a month ago. From Rome."

She saw the look on Hunter's face and frowned slightly. "That makes your hunch a little stronger, doesn't it? I still say you're after the wrong man. He didn't sound like a man in the middle of something that frightening. He sounded on the phone as though the only thing on his mind was the same old thing: getting together with me again. And I gave him the same answer: No."

"Why?"

"Because I think he wants to marry me. For my money." She looked at Hunter, and laughed. "Isn't that a wildly funny way to wind up? All my life I've at least known what a man was interested in when he was nice to me. Now, for the past seven years, when a man makes a pass at me I have to wonder if it's for my money. It's driving me absolutely paranoid."

She laughed again, but there was little amusement in it. And then she shrugged, causing the swelling curves of her breasts to move pleasantly under the silk of her blouse. She watched the effect on Hunter's face. "Anyway, Ahmed turned out to be a fairly coldhearted son of a bitch, once he's too sure of a woman. And I don't like my emotions played with, for someone else's amusement."

Hunter wondered what it was that had triggered that reaction. But that wasn't what he'd come to Sicily to find out about. "Bel Jahra sounds Arabic. Where's he from?"

"Morocco."

"You're sure?"

She shrugged again; and watched him again. "That's where I met him, four years ago. In Rabat. He picked me up, in the Hilton bar. And . . . well, I told you, he's an excellent lover. After that —it turned out he lived most of the time in Paris, because of his work. So we saw a lot of each other. I'd go stay in his apartment in Paris, sometimes. Other times he'd visit me here, or on Cap Ferrat."

Hunter drew a slow breath. It felt very close. "Where does he —or did he—work in Paris?"

"Somewhere around the Champs-Élysées. The Moroccan Tourist Bureau. His job was to visit its different offices in Europe, to see what could be done to up the number of tourists to his country. That's why he could move around so much."

"Ever visit him in one of those offices? In Paris, or anywhere else?"

Helena Reggiani shook her head. "No reason to. I don't even know exactly where it was."

"But you do know the address of his Paris apartment."

"Thirty-four Rue Mouffetard," she told him promptly. "Top floor. That's right off Place Contrescarpe, over on the Left Bank. But he doesn't live there anymore. He told me he'd moved out, the last time I saw him, a year ago."

Hunter considered the profusion of leads she had just given him. Many of them were probably false; but he was certain *she* thought they were true. "Let's get down to that time—a year ago.

He asked you to find him a smuggler who knew a way to get over the border illegally. Why?"

"I'm not sure. I did ask him. He just laughed and said he intended to steal some paintings and smuggle them across. Which meant it was none of my business. And I don't usually pry into other people's business. So I saw Mademoiselle Laure, and got a smuggler for Ahmed. As far as I knew, until now, he never used him."

Hunter described Selim, and the other man who'd been with Bel Jahra when the smuggler showed them the way across.

She shook her head. "I never met either of those men. As a matter of fact, I never met *any* friend of Ahmed's."

"Never? Think about it a minute."

"I'm sure. I got the feeling Ahmed didn't *have* friends. Male friends. I'm sure he had women, but he'd see to it I didn't meet them."

Hunter mentally crossed his fingers as he asked the next one: "You wouldn't happen to have a picture of Bel Jahra around, for old time's sake?"

Her smile this time almost erased the tension lines at the corners of her mouth. "No. I'm not given to that kind of sentimentality. I never did have one. I either have a man with me, or I don't. A picture is no substitute."

Hunter questioned her a bit longer, but there was no more information to be had from her. As it was, he had more than enough to get working on. Hunter thanked Helena Reggiani for her openness as he rose from his pool chair.

She stood up quickly, looking oddly disappointed. "It's almost lunchtime. Why don't you stay and have lunch here?"

"Can't. I've got to get on the next plane out. I'll grab lunch at the airport."

Still looking disappointed, Helena Reggiani went with him around her sprawling palazzo to the drive. His rented car was parked beside a gray Bentley and a black Mercedes.

She watched him slide in behind the wheel. "Well, it was nice practicing my English on you. I'm going to my London place in a few days. Ever get to London?"

He nodded. "Now and then."

"Maybe I'll look you up." She was chewing her lips again. "Or maybe you'll look me up. I'm in the book. You never know."

As he reached the bend in the long drive, where it turned toward the gates leading out of the Reggiani estate, Hunter glanced at his rear-view mirror. She was still standing there beside her Bentley and Mercedes, watching him go.

He made the drive back to Catania as fast as he could, in approved Sicilian daredevil manner. The only Sicilian trick he didn't pull was their favorite: passing on tight cliff-hanging curves where the question of whether you'd smash head on into a truck coming around the curve the other way became a kind of Russian roulette. When he got to the airport he had an hour to wait before the next plane to Rome.

He used the time to place a call to Rome. Not to Bandini, because there was so far no proof that Ahmed Bel Jahra—if that really was his name—had done anything criminal. And what Hunter wanted to find out from the Moroccan Embassy could turn delicate, politically. Hunter called the American Embassy's chief SY, Ben Grahame. He'd known him as long as Grahame had been handling embassy security, some ten years. Well enough to explain frankly why he wanted to know if anybody at the Moroccan Embassy had ever heard of, or could dig up information on, an Ahmed Bel Jahra. Grahame promised to have an answer waiting for him by the time he arrived.

Three hours later Hunter was on his way by cab from Leonardo da Vinci into Rome. He had the driver swing around through Via Boncompagni and drop him behind the American Embassy. Hunter went past the trickling grotto fountain and in the second back door to the left. He went up the wide stairs inside and tried the side door of Ben Grahame's office.

It wasn't locked. But the man behind the desk inside, under the large wall map of Rome, wasn't Grahame. It was Chavez.

"Grahame is still out doing your legwork," Chavez informed Hunter caustically. He shoved back Grahame's black leather chair and stood up. "Let's go to Harry's Bar. I need a drink before I start listening to you."

ELEVEN

It was the wrong time of the day for the sleekly modern bar's usual well-heeled clientele. So they had the place pretty much to themselves. A corner booth, with the low-backed padded booths on either side empty.

Chavez downed a third of his tall rye and soda before launching his opening volley: "I didn't come to Europe just to see you. But you're *one* of the reasons. So I made calls when I hit London, found out you left Rome for Sicily and had to come back this way. So I got here an hour before you. That took some doing, Hunter."

He hadn't raised his voice, and he didn't look angry. Just concerned; which was a bad sign with him. It was strange to see Chavez in civilian clothes. He still held himself like the career soldier he'd been since seventeen; as though he had a ramrod up his ass. He was shorter than Hunter, but wider; a barrel of solid bone and muscle. He had flat features that seemed cut from durable sandstone. His hazel eyes watched Hunter steadily as he talked.

"I am on my way to Istanbul, Bombay, Singapore, Manila, and Tokyo. I got to check out the situation in each of those places, and be back in Washington in exactly five days. But I'm using up some of that valuable time with you. Because you didn't call me, and I like to be informed, in case you forgot about that. So what're you up to, Hunter? And don't give me the same line that's on your expenses. About making a practical check of international co-operation through one case."

"It's the truth," Hunter told him flatly. You couldn't give away any points with Chavez. The milder he looked and sounded, the faster he'd eat you up.

"Bullshit." Chavez still sounded controlled and reasonable. But the hazel eyes were like bullets. "You're playing detective on a case of your own. At the department's expense. While those airline reps complain about you canceling their meeting with you."

"It's not canceled. Only postponed. There *is* a difference."

"Swell," Chavez drawled. The sarcasm leaked through a little. "They still don't like it. That makes the department not like it. And *I* get it shoved up my nose. And what the hell's this latest thing—putting Shansky on *our* expenses. Even the shits over at CIA don't have any use for the Spook anymore."

"I do," Hunter said coldly. "He's in the right spot at the right time."

Chavez finished off the second third of his drink, working to hold his formidable temper down. Some people thought it was amusing the way Chavez was always struggling with his temper. Nobody who had been around when he lost it ever thought it was funny again. "To do what?" Chavez asked. "That's really a very simple question, Hunter. Answer it without the frills. Okay?"

Hunter told him the whole thing, step by step. He didn't try to explain *why* he was doing it anymore. Chavez could put facts together for himself; better than most. It was up to him to decide if he thought what Hunter was doing was justified.

Chavez was silent a long time after Hunter finished, the sharp mind behind that sandstone face chewing over each point Hunter had made. Hunter waited to get blasted, and got surprised:

"It just may turn out," Chavez mused, "that what you're doing is the answer to what's needed against these terrorists that hit and run in a different place each time: somebody doing what you're doing—running back and forth keeping everybody at different ends of a situation in touch. Able to put together a lot quicker the pieces the security people at each of those ends are picking up. . . ."

Chavez fell silent again, for a long moment. "*But*, it's not what they hired you to do. And you know as well as I, that when you go off on your own initiative, instead of following orders—the only way you can justify it is with *results*. If you don't get results, you won't exactly have proved your point. And then you'll be in trouble, for not playing it safe and sticking to what they think they hired you to do."

Hunter's mouth got stubborn, and his eyes stayed steady on Chavez's. "I'm sure this man Bel Jahra is responsible for the bomb at Leonardo da Vinci. I'm sure he's working out something else now, that could be just as bad or worse. And I'm getting on top of it. I know it in my head, and I can feel it in my guts. Something's there, and I can stop it if I keep after it." Hunter put both fists on the table and forced it out: "If you yank me off it now, I quit. I'm *that* sure."

Chavez looked mildly surprised. "I wouldn't yank you off. You've *got* to stick with it, now. Too many people know parts of what you've been doing; and soon they'll want to know why. So, sure you stick with it—but you'd damn well better pull something out of it. If you come up empty, you've had it. You get the picture."

"Uh-huh." Hunter's voice was cool, his face stiff. "You're saying there's no backing off and if I don't come through with something, you'll fire me. I don't much like that."

"I didn't mean it as a threat." The voice became exceedingly gentle, the worst sign of all with Chavez. "I'll protect you with the department—but only as much as I can without hurting my own career. If my men get in trouble following orders, *I* take all the responsibility for it. But you're not following orders; mine or the department's. It may turn out you're doing exactly the right thing. But if it turns out wrong, *I* won't take getting clobbered for your mistake. Got it?"

Some of the stiffness went out of Hunter's face. "Sure, Standard Operating Procedure."

"Yep. If you foul up, it'll be *your* ass. Not mine."

Hunter nodded. "Understood."

"Fine. Then there's no problem." Chavez drained the rest of his drink and stood up. "Put this on your next swindle sheet. I've got a plane to catch." He paused, looking down at Hunter, the hard hazel eyes softening, just a little. "All overseas branches of the department're still under orders to extend you full co-operation. Until the shit hits the fan. Just try to make sure it doesn't."

"Thank you, sir."

Chavez smiled frostily. "Good luck, soldier." He turned smartly and walked out as though he were marching a battalion across a parade ground.

Ben Grahame was in his office when Hunter got back there. He had two items waiting on his desk for Hunter.

"His picture," Grahame said with self-satisfaction. "And a complete dossier on him. And his name *is* Ahmed Bel Jahra. Did I do good, Daddy?"

"*Real* good." It was as much as Hunter could have hoped for. He remained standing before Grahame's desk, picking up the full-face head-and-shoulders photograph of Bel Jahra. The shadowy figure he was pursuing suddenly became a real person.

"I got to admit it was easy," Grahame told him. "My opposite number at the Moroccan Embassy was pleased to co-operate. Seems your boy there took part in a plot to kill their King. They're not exactly after him themselves, as long as he's out of their country. He wasn't that big. But they'd be kinda happy to see him in *somebody's* jail. And don't worry. I didn't tell 'em what kind of trouble you figure he's in."

In the photo, Bel Jahra was wearing an officer's uniform of the Moroccan Royal Army. The face looked out of the picture at Hunter: lean, handsome, aristocratic, unsmiling. Hunter concentrated on memorizing it.

"That picture was taken five years ago," Grahame said. "So figure he looks that much older now." He tapped the dossier. "Prepared by the Moroccan secret police. In French, but I guess you can handle that."

Hunter nodded. He put down the picture and flipped through the dossier. It seemed to be a thorough rundown on Bel Jahra's life, career, and habits, up to and including his involvement in the attempt to assassinate King Hassan. Appended to it was a final page, with a detailed formal description of Bel Jahra, plus his fingerprints. Hunter began to experience the malicious sensation of breathing down Bel Jahra's neck.

He tore off the last page and handed it with the photo to Grahame. "I need a lot of copies of both of these. Enough to circulate to all branches of the State Department, plus ten for me. In small, so I can carry them around."

"You're getting to owe me a lot of favors, pal." Grahame took the photo and description page out of the office with him. Hunter sat down and began a careful reading of Bel Jahra's dossier. It gave him a fairly complete picture of the man. It also gave him certain facts that could be put together: Bel Jahra had been using the tourist business as a cover for his activities as a secret service agent. He had a network of contacts around Europe, and a working knowledge of Europe. And the last item in the dossier was a report that Bel Jahra had met with Libya's Colonel Qadhafi, after fleeing from Morocco and before vanishing in the direction of Europe.

Just as important, Hunter got the *feel* of the man from the dossier: what sort of character he had, what he'd be likely to do under differing circumstances. The dossier gave Hunter the feeling of a man with strength, cool nerves, courage, intelligence, quick wits— and ruthless ambition.

There were a number of things the dossier didn't give Hunter. It didn't tell him where Bel Jahra was. It didn't give him anything criminal that he could use to persuade any police force outside Morocco to seek to detain Bel Jahra for. And it didn't tell him what Bel Jahra was up to now.

One more negative point: Bel Jahra was definitely political. That meant no further help from Interpol. If Hunter hid that fact in getting the police of any country to use Interpol for him, the police of that country would soon find themselves in trouble with the entire Interpol organization. And they'd pass the word about the man who got them in that kind of trouble. After which no law agency anywhere would ever give Hunter co-operation again.

So he would have to explain to Diego Bandini; and to any other law officer or official security man to whom he gave copies of Bel Jahra's picture, prints, and I.D. Hunter began making a mental list of others through whom he intended to circulate the Bel Jahra items: Uri Ezan, Ferguson, and all the other sub-rosa characters he'd contacted earlier here in Rome. Then to a variety of connections along the Riviera, which Hunter still felt had to be the general area of Bel Jahra's next operation.

Using Grahame's phone, Hunter checked on the last night plane from Rome to Nice, and booked himself on it. Then he called Olivier Lamarck's number on the Riviera. It was Odile who answered. Her father was out somewhere trying to track down any information that might be of use to Hunter. So far without success. Shansky, who had checked in with Lamarck a couple times, wasn't managing to turn up anything either.

Hunter had expected that. None of them had had anything solid to work from. Until now. He asked Odile to have Shansky meet him when he landed at Nice.

He had decided to send Shansky on ahead to Paris, to begin the job of tracing Bel Jahra backward from his years there. Starting from the neighborhood of the apartment Bel Jahra used to have in Paris; the address supplied by Helena Reggiani.

The dragnet would then be closing in from three crucial points: Paris, where Bel Jahra had operated from in the past; Rome, where he had failed in his last operation; the Riviera, where he was probably planning his next one.

Now that they had his name and picture, traces of Bel Jahra were almost certain to be found somewhere between those three points.

The biggest and best equipped Black September guerrilla-indoctrination camp in Libya is just outside Tocra, a hundred kilometers east of Benghazi. It is in a stretch of coastal desert between the sea and the main Benghazi-Tobruk highway, overlooking the Mediterranean and with the arid Barqah Plateau rising to the south. The camp's training area reaches to the water's edge, including a length of beach cordoned off with multiple-stranded barbed-wire fences. It has facilities for five thousand guerrilla trainees and instructors.

Bel Jahra was flown there from Tripoli in one of the Libyan Air Force's new French Mirage jet fighters. The Mirage made short work of crossing the Great Sirte Gulf, and put down on the long military landing strip beyond Tocra. A jeep and driver were waiting there to take Bel Jahra to the camp. Obviously everyone had been briefed about him by phone from Tripoli. Including the officer waiting for him just inside the gates to the camp.

He was a captain in the Syrian Army Engineering Corps, he explained as he began showing Bel Jahra around the camp. He was in charge of a sabotage-instruction team the Syrian Army had seconded to the Tocra camp. Instructions from Tripoli were for him to help Bel Jahra pick the guerrillas for the two commando units he wanted; and then to supervise, under Bel Jahra's direction, the specific training of these men in the job they would have to do.

The camp the Syrian captain led Bel Jahra through was bleakly functional: tents and long barracks, scattered across an expanse of dusty desert baking in the harsh heat of the sun. There were hordes of young trainees in movement everywhere Bel Jahra looked, being put through the basic-training obstacle courses and lining up for their turns at the practice firing ranges. They ranged in age from about twelve years old to thirty; mostly male but with several female groups training separately. Most were dressed basically alike: checkered burnous, loose Chinese-style jacket, dungaree slacks, canvas shoes with rubber-tire soles. The air was filled with blown sand, the acrid fumes of burned gunpowder, and the continual crashing of machine guns and small arms from the practice ranges.

The Syrian led Bel Jahra to the top of a huge boulder and gestured downward. Along the stretch of beach fenced with barbed wire, tiny figures swarmed in through the surf from anchored rowboats, holding weapons above their heads. As each figure hurled itself behind cover on the beach, an instructor there sent it back out to the boats to charge ashore all over again. Some distance to their left along the beach, other figures in scuba outfits slipped in and out of the water with sealed plastic bags.

"Instruction in amphibious commando landing tactics," the Syrian explained. "They have to learn to do the same things at night, too."

Muffled explosions sounded behind them. Bel Jahra turned and saw clouds of smoke and dust rising from a deep, wide ravine on the south side of the camp.

"That's where our trainees learn about detonating explosives. All sorts. Dynamite, grenades, plastic, and homemade bombs. This also, under night conditions as well. Before passing the course, each trainee must make his own bomb, and prove he can activate it in the dark. If he kills himself while detonating it, he automatically fails to pass the test."

The Syrian officer grinned to show he was joking, revealing two rows of clean false teeth under his virile moustache. Bel Jahra noted the jagged scar along his lower lip. He'd seen enough like it, during his own army service, to know the Syrian had lost his teeth as a result of getting a rifle butt smashed against his mouth.

"I think I've had enough of the guided tour," Bel Jahra told him. "Suppose we get down to work now."

"Of course." The Syrian led him off the boulder, settled down in a patch of shade at its base, and got out a notebook and ballpoint. He made notes as Bel Jahra sat on the ground beside him and detailed what he needed: two commando teams, each trained to do exactly the same things. Except for a single difference: One of the men in the team that might have to be infiltrated by boat would have to have extensive experience in rock-climbing techniques.

Each team was to consist of five men. Bel Jahra outlined in detail the job required of each; and the weapons and explosives each must practice using properly, in simulated rehearsals of the real operation Bel Jahra had planned.

The backup commando group would be taken across the Mediterranean in a Libyan fishing vessel—to be used if needed. The other group would be flown much earlier to France (though Bel Jahra did not tell the Syrian the country's name) by regular commercial airliners, each man carrying false papers and using a different route. The actual weapons and explosives to be used in the operation were now being readied in Tripoli, to be ferried north by the fishing boat and transferred at sea to the yacht Bashir Mawdri had waiting somewhere on the Riviera. When the time came, these weapons would be put in the hands of Bel Jahra's commandos. Here at the Tocra camp, they must rehearse the operation with exactly the same kinds of weapons. Bel Jahra was emphatic on this point.

"We usually do that," the Syrian told him. "Don't worry about it."

"I do worry about it," Bel Jahra said pointedly. "*I* am the one in command of this operation. I have to be absolutely certain you understand every detail I've given you. If you fail to, on some small point, you will be sorry afterward. But *I* will be dead. Do you understand my concern, Captain?"

The Syrian looked at his eyes, and had to stop himself from flinching. He said quietly: "Yes, sir."

By dark Bel Jahra was satisfied that the sabotage officer had every detail engrained in him. They went together to the officer's mess hall, a simple building of unpainted cinder block, with a roof of noninsulated iron sheeting. The interior was an oven, still holding all the heat of the desert day. Bel Jahra's clothes were drenched with perspiration as they sat at one of the plank tables and he was introduced to the other officers around it.

No real names were used. Only code names, for Bel Jahra as well. His Syrian liaison officer ate quickly, and left before the others. When he returned half an hour later, Bel Jahra was waiting outside, leaning against the wall and smoking a cigarette.

The Syrian took him to a barracks building at the west end of the camp. They went inside, to a large room at the rear, lit by a kerosene lamp resting on a large unpainted table. There was no other furniture in the room. Ten young guerrillas were waiting there for them; five grouped to one side of the table, five on the other side. The youngest looked about nineteen. The oldest was perhaps twenty-five.

The Syrian officer closed the door and introduced Bel Jahra to them, detailing the previous practical experience and recent training of each one. Bel Jahra quietly questioned each man in turn, listening attentively to the answers he got, studying each man's face. It took a great deal of time. But when he was finished, Bel Jahra was satisfied that the Syrian had chosen his two commando teams well. The men were diverse types, from different countries: Palestine, Lebanon, Syria, Iraq, Egypt, Saudi Arabia, and various of the small Arab Persian Gulf states. But each was strong, intelligent, superbly trained, and had already taken part in at least one actual guerrilla operation. And each was fanatically eager to be part of another one.

Bel Jahra anticipated at least a full day, and perhaps two, of personally briefing them on the operation before turning the rest of it over to the Syrian sabotage officer and returning to France. He took out his sketches, spread them on the table, and got started.

Though he hammered into his guerrillas every detail of the Valasi estate on Cap Martin, he didn't tell them what or where it was. Nor did he tell them the names of the two specific targets among all the people they must kill around the main Valasi birthday table.

This was a standard precaution for all of the guerrilla operations. To make sure none of the team inadvertently exposed the target and area to someone connected with an enemy spy; or gave the operation away under torture if caught before it could be carried out.

Bel Jahra did not intend to tell these men whom they were to kill, nor where they were to carry out the killing, until the time came: at the last possible moment before they put his plan into execution.

TWELVE

Up on the open second-floor terrace of the Côte d'Azur Airport, a young man named Kosso Shamir sat by the rail over his fifth tea of the evening, this time with a piece of what the terminal menu listed as English Cake. At any rate it was filling. The sun had set an hour ago, and by now his wife would have finished eating her dinner in their room in Nice. All there'd be by the time Kosso called it a night here, and went home, would be some cold cuts. That was one reason he hated taking the late shift. But he had to trade shifts half the time with the other man assigned to this job.

Kosso took a sip of the rapidly cooling tea, made a face, and looked down at the runways and apron between the terminal and the sea. The last plane from Rome had just landed and stopped. But the passenger stairway being pushed out on rollers wasn't in place yet. The soft music from the silvery loudspeaker over the terrace window cut off, and a female voice announced, in French and then English, the imminent departure of the TWA flight to Madrid. Kosso leaned against the rail and gave his concentrated attention to the departing passengers filing out to the left below, streaming toward the waiting TWA 747. He recognized none of them. Which meant, unquestionably, that he had never been shown a photograph of any of them.

Kosso Shamir was an innocuous-looking boy of twenty; skinny, dark, homely, already married one year and expecting to be a father in two months. Nothing very unusual. But he possessed one unique talent, and it was because of that talent that he was on the terrace of the Côte d'Azur Airport.

He had a fantastic memory for faces. A freak thing he'd been born with. One of his officers in the Israeli paratroops had found out about it. A week later Kosso had found himself out of the paratroops, sitting in a Mossad operational library at the Defense Ministry in Jerusalem, looking through one album after another filled with photos of Arab terrorists and suspected terrorists. When they were finally convinced that Kosso really could perform the astounding feat of remembering every face he'd seen in those albums, he was sworn in as a Mossad agent and shipped off to the Riviera.

The Côte d'Azur Airport is one of the major entrance points to Europe, for people flying in from North Africa and the Middle East. And as a leftover from the days when the French had ruled large parts of North Africa, the cities along the southern coast of France are full of Arabs—and Arab activity. Kosso's assignment was just to sit on that terrace for a major part of every day, his mind stocked with a rogues' gallery of hundreds of terrorist faces, reporting to his control if he spotted any one of them arriving or departing.

The last of the passengers for Madrid and points west were climbing into the 747. Passengers debarking from the Rome plane were now walking toward the terminal. Kosso switched his attention to this line, watching it file to the right below the terrace, following the "Arrivée & Transit" sign. There were no known Arab terrorists in this line, either. But there *was* a face Kosso knew: Simon Hunter. He'd met him three weeks earlier when Hunter had been down here checking out security arrangements in the airport.

Kosso stuffed the last of the English Cake in his mouth, got up on legs that were numbed from hours of sitting, and went inside and down the stairs. Hunter was conferring with Shansky to one side of the waiting room. Kosso hesitated a bit, until it seemed they had finished whatever they were saying to each other, and then walked over. "Hello, Mr. Hunter. Remember me?"

Hunter looked at him, shook his extended hand, made sure there was still no one within hearing, and made the introductions: "Kosso Shamir . . . George L. Shansky. You can talk in front of each other. Kosso works for Mossad," he told Shansky. And to Kosso: "Mr. Shansky is working for me."

Kosso nodded politely at Shansky, and told Hunter: "Uri Ezan sent word from Rome, Mr. Hunter. You got a picture for me?"

Hunter got a three-by-four photo of Bel Jahra from his pocket.

Plus a folded sheet with Bel Jahra's vital statistics and fingerprints. "Know this man?"

Kosso studied the face of Bel Jahra, and shook his head. "I've never seen his picture."

"You have now. Remember it. And pass it on to your people here. I want them to circulate it. I can be reached in this area through an Olivier Lamarck." Hunter gave the phone number.

Kosso got out a notebook and pencil, grinning sheepishly. "I'm not so good with numbers."

Hunter repeated it and Kosso wrote it down. The loudspeakers began a first-departure announcement for a Sabena flight to Paris and Brussels. Kosso stuck notebook, photo, and info sheet in his pocket and shook their hands respectfully. "Got to get back to work now. Nice meeting you, Mr. Shansky."

Shansky watched him hurry away, up the steps. "Funny kid."

Hunter was glancing at his watch. "That's the last flight to Paris tonight. If there's still a seat, I want you on it." He told Shansky the address Helena Reggiani had given him of Bel Jahra's last known apartment in Paris. "Dig around the area, see what you can find on him, using the picture I just gave you."

Shansky grimaced. "For Christ's sake, Hunter, I got stuff I need that I'd have to go home and pick up first. Toothbrush, razor, change of shirts. . . ."

Hunter already had his credit card out and was heading for the Sabena counter. "You can buy a few things when you get to Paris. Call Lamarck and leave word which hotel you book in when you get there."

"I don't even have enough dough left," Shansky protested as he followed Hunter. "I had some little debts to pay with the hundred, and you haven't come up with a penny more yet."

Hunter gave him thirty dollars. "This'll hold you till tomorrow. Check in with Max Stevens at the embassy in the morning. I called from Rome. He'll have your first five days' worth of fifties waiting for you."

"Hunter," Shansky said fervently, "I think I'm gonna learn to like you."

When Hunter got there shortly before midnight, Olivier Lamarck had his chessboard set up on the dining table in the main room of his house, and was using a book on the Fischer-Spassky world championship match to replay some of the games.

"I don't think Bobby Fischer is as good as he thinks he is," Lamarck said as Hunter stepped inside and shut the latticed door. "I just beat him two games." Without changing tone he added: "Odile isn't here. She has a date in Monte Carlo with a flashy young Italian whose mother just gave him a Rolls-Royce for a birthday present. A *Rolls-Royce*—my God!"

"I came to see *you*, not your daughter."

"In a way, I'm a bit sorry to hear that. She's single, you are single, and I like you both. It's a natural thought."

Hunter regarded the old cop with a certain wry affection. "When a man turns matchmaker it's usually a sign of senility, you know."

"I am not getting younger, that is certain. I would like to see grandchildren."

"Nothing wrong with them riding around in a Rolls," Hunter pointed out. And then: "Had a call from Shansky yet?"

"A few minutes ago. From Paris. He said to tell you he's at the Hôtel Julien. On the Quai de la Tournelle. I understand we now have a face and name?"

Hunter produced one of his photographs of Bel Jahra and put it down beside some chessmen Lamarck had killed. "Here's our man. The name's Ahmed Bel Jahra. He's a Moroccan, but I think he's working with the terrorist movement for the Libyans now."

Hunter sat down across the table from Lamarck. "I'd like to tell you everything I've got so far. What I *think* I've got. What I've done so far; and what I plan to do. I want to hear what you think. I want to hear myself, using you as my sounding board."

Lamarck picked up his stubby pipe and began reaming it out with a small penknife. "Go ahead."

Hunter told him all he had gathered, from other people and from the Moroccan secret service dossier. In the middle of it, Odile came in.

Lamarck asked her with thin sarcasm: "How was the Rolls-Royce?"

"He's a very sweet boy. And quite bright." She went to the kitchenette and put on a kettle to boil. Hunter heard her moving around there behind him as he went on bringing her father up to date on the investigation. In a few minutes she put two cups of coffee on the table for them, and went into the bathroom.

When she came out she was wearing a white terry-cloth bathrobe. "I'm going to sleep now." She kissed her father good night; and then kissed Hunter, in the same way.

"I won't stay much longer," he told her.

"You don't have to hurry. Your voices won't disturb me. When I'm ready to sleep, I sleep. I'm a healthy animal." She went into the sleeping alcove and pulled across the Chinese screen to shade the narrow bed from the light of the main room.

Hunter lowered his voice and finished filling Lamarck in on the steps he had taken, and intended to take.

Lamarck considered it all as he studied Bel Jahra's picture. "Good face. Strong, intelligent. They have a new photocopy machine down in the Customs House. I'll have them run off copies of this for me. It won't cost you much. But I'll have to circulate them on a strictly personal-favor basis. As we discussed before, there can't be any official co-operation on this. Now that it is deffinitely an Arab affair.

Hunter told him the sort of people he'd already given Bel Jahra's picture to, between the time he'd left the airport and come here. And those he intended to contact before his night was finished.

Lamarck nodded, frowning a bit. "That is all very well, Simon, but I think you are concentrating too much on this area, prematurely. I agree there are strong indications this man's next operation may be in this area. But the same indications could merely mean he had a rendezvous set for this area—before going on to operate elsewhere. I think you should concentrate more on Paris, for the moment."

"Shansky's already there. And I'm flying up in the morning."

"Good. Because apparently this Bel Jahra was only transient in Rome; and the same in this area. But he *lived* in Paris, in a neighborhood I know well. The Mouff, they call it. Working-class, most of the people who live there. And many students with very little money—including a large percentage of students from Arab countries. It is a cozy neighborhood. People know each other and talk to each other. They'll remember him there, no matter how secretive he was. They'll have observed him, day by day. And discussed him, in the little neighborhood bistros. That is your best place to find a lead to him."

"Agreed. Unless and until something new turns up here." Hunter talked with Lamarck a bit longer before getting up to leave. As he went out, he looked at the Chinese screen. He wondered if Odile was really asleep behind it, or if she had been lying there awake, listening to their voices.

The nightclub was in the Rue Halevy, halfway between the Nice beach and Place Grimaldi. It was small, intimate, dimly lit; and closing for the night when Hunter came in. The club was owned by a German believed to be a retired Hamburg gangster. He was seldom around. The place was run by his wife, Frau Irmgard Stiller. It was to her Hunter gave the picture of Bel Jahra, and explained what he was after.

She was a short, round woman in her late forties, with straight pitch-black hair, blue eyes, and a manner that radiated sex. She was also the most effective agent on the Riviera for the Bundesnachrichtendienst—West Germany's Federal Intelligence Service. Her promise to check around for him was contingent on *his* promise of co-operation, when it came her turn to need a favor. As he'd told Lamarck, he was taking help wherever he could get it.

The Negresco in Nice is the queen of Riviera hotels. Between the American Civil War and World War I it was the Côte d'Azur home-away-from-home for Europe's nobility, and often its royalty. Most notably from England and Imperial Russia. There was a time when you couldn't get a room if you didn't have a title.

Titles no longer have that exclusive kind of leverage. Between the world wars cash took over. But the Negresco, just a bit faded and just a bit modernized around a few edges, remains the grand old lady of the Promenade des Anglais. You still get the impression, as you cross the lobby and approach the beauty of her domed ballroom, that the next person you see is likely to be a king; or at least a lovely duchess in a turn-of-the-century gown. This impression drops away when you enter the large bar to the right. It is a handsome room; but the clientele is definitely credit-card twentieth-century.

Hunter moved to the darkly varnished bar and ordered a double scotch, with water on the side. Then he turned, leaning against the bar, and glanced around. Most of the tables were taken by affluent business types from various parts of the globe having a last nightcap. There was a man Hunter knew at a small table in one corner: Frank Lucci.

Lucci was the most elegantly dressed man in the room. But there was still that vicious gutter-hunger in his darkly tanned simian face. It was said that he was the most prosperous pimp on the Riviera, in addtion to being a fence; both with percentage payments to the Unione Corse for permission to operate. The blonde sitting with him was also elegant; with a spectacular figure and provocative young face. Lucci handled only the choicest merchandise; and the costliest.

The men along the bar and at the other tables couldn't keep their eyes from straying repeatedly in her direction. Hunter sipped his scotch and let his own eyes stray that way. Lucci caught it and looked Hunter over, sizing up the quality of his clothes and the sucker-potential in his expression. He got up and came over to the bar beside Hunter, telling the barman to give him a dish of peanuts. His accent, in French, was still New Jersey.

Hunter glanced again in the direction of the blonde Lucci had left. She gave him a small smile. Lucci leaned toward Hunter and whispered, "Interested?" Hunter gave him an annoyed look, finished his drink, and told the barman to charge it to his room. He put his key on the bar so the number could be copied on the bill. Then he picked up the key and walked out.

His room was on the third floor; a small room, without a view of the sea. But neatly furnished, with a few small touches of the old opulence. He was drawing the heavy brocade curtains when there was a knock on his door. Hunter called: "It's not locked."

Frank Lucci stepped in, shut the door, and leaned his back against it. Hunter gave him Bel Jahra's photo and vital statistics, filling him in on what it was about. "I'm interested in anybody who knows this guy. Especially anybody who's seen him recently. And anything you can turn up for me about something new brewing in one of the Arab communities, here or in Marseilles."

"Okay. If I hear anything I'll get in touch. I hear you're using Olivier Lamarck as your letter box."

Hunter was not surprised. Frank Lucci had been undercover for the BNDD in the South of France for six years. Undercover narcs survived by knowing what was going on around them.

"I'll spread the picture, and the request, with the French narcs, too," Lucci told him. "Tomorrow. Right now I got to get back to work." He started to leave, and then turned back and grinned at Hunter. "Sure you're not interested? She *is* available. And I *am* in that business, too, you know. For real."

"Uh-huh. But your prices are too high for me."

"The better to feed my four kids with. See you." Lucci flipped a hand in farewell and was gone.

Hunter undressed, showered, got six hours' sleep, and took the morning plane to Paris.

It was noon when the taxi from Orly delivered Hunter at the Hôtel Julien on the Left Bank's Quai de la Tournelle. The hotel was a plain, unlovely, narrow building six stories tall; much like the other sooty brick buildings between which it was sandwiched. There was only a single star on the rusting sign beside the door. But the windows that faced the Seine had one of the loveliest views in Paris: the trees and bookstalls along the quay, the splendid architecture of the Île Saint-Louis rising in the middle of the river, the magnificent bastion of Notre-Dame Cathedral of the Île de la Cité.

The lobby inside was large enough for about five people to stand up in. An old woman in an apron behind the short counter told him Shansky was in Room 16 and hadn't come down yet. Hunter climbed four flights of newly carpeted stairs and knocked at 16. There was a muffled grumbling sound inside. Hunter knocked again. More seconds went by before Shansky opened the door, naked except for a towel around his waist, blinking sleepily at Hunter.

"Christ, I hate to get waked up like that."

Hunter stepped in and shut the door. "It's twelve o'clock."

"I had a long, long night." Shansky picked up the phone beside the bed and asked for a large coffee with cream and an apple tart. Then he trudged into a tiny bathroom to splash water on his face.

The bedroom was simply furnished, but very clean and twice the size of the one Hunter had had at the Negresco. He looked through the narrow window at the barges gliding past on the river, and decided he liked Shansky's choice of hotels. Besides, it was only a short walk to the address where Bel Jahra had lived.

Shansky came out of the bathroom toweling his face and dripping hair. His body was surprisingly muscular, with only a little softness beginning around the waist and hips. "I prowled the whole goddamn Mouff neighborhood last night," he told Hunter as he began to dress. "I didn't get much. But at least I found out what's not there to be gotten. Which is a start. Bel Jahra rented his apartment from a French couple who live in the apartment below. They own both, live in one on the rent from the other. Nice retired people. I had a talk with them. They don't know anything about Bel Jahra except the same phony story he gave your Helena Reggiani; about working for the Morocco tourist people. He rented the place four years, wasn't there a lot, never talked to them about anything except the weather. Left a year ago, and they don't know where he went. Not even if he shifted to another place here in Paris, or left town for good."

"What about visitors?"

Shansky paused in the act of tying his shoelaces. "I'll get to it, without prompting if you don't mind. I *did* ask all the right questions. I'm not an amateur, remember."

Hunter took another look at Shansky. The man was changing. Or reverting. The old sureness was there; but without so much of the old arrogance. "My apologies," Hunter drawled. "You're enjoying yourself, aren't you."

"I like working. And getting paid for it." Shanksy finished with his laces as the door opened without a knock. The old woman in the apron came in with the coffee and tart on a small beer tray. She set it on the table next to the bed, smiled at the two men prettily, and went out. Shansky gestured Hunter to a sagging but comfortable wing chair, sat on the edge of his bed, and dunked his apple tart in the hot creamy coffee.

"Okay. Visitors." Shanksy spoke between mouthfuls. "They don't remember him ever having any men drop by. So wherever he did his undercover business, it wasn't there. Girls, now and then. But the only one steady sounds like Helena Reggiani. That's all they know about our Bel Jahra. And nobody else in the building, or any of the other houses around it, knows anything more about him than that. Not where he worked, not where he went, not any men he had contact with, not the names of any of his women friends. Like it?"

Hunter studied him shrewdly. "I think you got something. You're saving it for the punch line."

Shanksy chuckled. "Yeah, but it's not *much* of a punch line." He swallowed the last of the tart, and washed it down with a long sip of coffee. "I hit all the bars, bistros, and restaurants in the vicinity, naturally. There's a bar on Place Contrescarpe—the Irlandais. Bel Jahra used to go there for his coffee, a lot of mornings.

"One morning, about two years ago, Bel Jahra got into a fight with another Arab. Slapped him pretty hard, right there in the bar. A guy who it seems knew Bel Jahra pretty good, and didn't like him. The barman I talked to doesn't know what the argument was about. He works nights, and the fight was in the morning. He was only told about it, by the day man. *He's* the one that was there, maybe knows what the fight was about, and probably knows who the other Arab was. He apparently still lives somewhere in the neighborhood; but he's another strictly morning customer. Also, the night guy I talked to figures the day man'll know other things about Bel Jahra, being as how he saw more of him."

"Simple way to find out," Hunter said, and got out of the chair. "He'll be on duty now."

"Right." Shansky finished off his coffee and stood up. Let's go."

Hunter shook his head. "No sense both of us doing the same job. We'll find out more, faster, if we split up and go at it from two different angles."

Shansky eyed him warily. "With you taking the angle *I* spent all night getting us?"

Hunter smiled. "I'm a cop, remember? I can probably follow your lead further than you could."

"And what does that leave me?"

"You're a spook. And we know now that Bel Jahra was also a spook. Operating most of the time in or from this city. For a number of years. Wouldn't you say that in all that time, some *other* spooks might've tumbled to what he really was behind the tourist cover?"

"That is a thought," Shansky acknowledged after a moment's consideration. He considered it a bit more, and brightened. "I know an awful lot of people in the business here. I'll check 'em out. If any of 'em did catch on that Bel Jahra was Moroccan secret service, back in those days, they'd've begun keeping tabs on him from time to time. Could give a contact he's still in touch with."

"That's the idea. And when you drop into the embassy today to pick up your dough, tell them I want an extension number and secretary to answer it. So we have a place to leave word for each other."

They went down the steps to the tiny lobby. Hunter learned from the manageress that there was a room on the floor above Shansky available, registered for it, and they went outside.

"Good luck, George L."

Shansky grinned crookedly. "You too, baby." He strode off along the quay looking for a cab.

Hunter turned away from the Seine and climbed through a rabbit warren of little streets toward Place Contrescarpe.

THIRTEEN

Place Contrescarpe is the heart of the Mouff neighborhood; a small-ish square with four trees and five bars—a big noisy one for night owls and sightseers, and four small, quieter ones for the people who live and work in the area.

The Irlandais was a small, quiet one; at least by day. The day barman's name was Jean-Claude; tall and good-natured, with the strength of a bull and the profile of an old-fashioned movie star. He pushed Bel Jahra's picture back to Hunter and nodded. "Ahmed. . . . Sure, he used to come in a lot, for breakfast. At different times, so I always figured he didn't have a regular job he had to get to. Or else he had a night job. Sometimes he didn't come in until noon."

"Always alone? Or with other people?"

"With a girl, sometimes. There was one he used to bring in with him pretty often—a real beauty." Jean-Claude's description fitted Helena Reggiani. "But then I guess he began to want them younger, like some guys do when they worry they're getting older. The last month, before he stopped coming around, he came in a lot with a girl that couldn't be more than sixteen. Pretty, but way too young for him. I don't like to see that. Guys getting middle-aged sleeping with kids."

"How do you know he was sleeping with her?"

"They had breakfast together." Jean-Claude shrugged. "That means they got up together. Anyway, you get so in this job you can tell, just by how a guy and girl act around each other that early in the day. Lazy-smiling, you know? Remembering how it was at night; reminding each other with their eyes, how they did it."

Hunter decided that Jean-Claude was a pretty fair observer. "Is she from around here?"

"Never saw her, except with Ahmed."

"Remember her name?"

Jean-Claude thought for a while. "I don't think so."

Hunter put that aside for the moment. "The night man here says you told him about a fight Bel Jahra had in here with another Arab."

"Bel Jahra . . . that's Ahmed's last name? I never knew it."

"The fight," Hunter pressed.

Jean-Claude shook his head with an easy-going smile. "It wasn't a real *fight*. But this one morning Madj—that's the other guy's name—he walked in, saw Ahmed, and started yelling at him. Until Ahmed got up and slapped him. Hard enough to knock him down."

"That all? The other Arab didn't hit back?"

"No." Jean-Claude's frown was puzzled. "And that was strange. Because Madj is bigger than Ahmed. I think stronger, too. I expected him to get up and start swinging. And Ahmed was waiting for it, too. But he didn't. He just stayed there on the floor, looking sore—but staying down. When Ahmed finally saw Madj wasn't going to get up, he paid for both their coffees and walked out. Not another word. And Madj didn't get up until he was gone."

Hunter added another small piece to his feeling about the kind of man he was after. "What were they arguing about?"

Jean-Claude shrugged. "They were talking Arabic of some kind. You'd have to ask Madj."

Hunter slid off the barstool. "Where do I find him?"

"He used to work in the first bakery you come to on the left, down here on Rue Mouffetard. They'll know."

Hunter pushed Bel Jahra's photograph back across the bar to Jean-Claude. "Maybe you'll remember something else about him. Or his young girl friend. Think about it." He left the bar and turned the corner on Rue Mouffetard, going into the first bakery on the left. He didn't really expect finding Madj to be that easy, and it wasn't.

The owner of the bakery didn't know where Madj was working now, or had moved to on leaving the neighborhood. But he was able to give Hunter three essential facts about Madj: his last name was Harana; he was from Morocco; he had a Sécurité Sociale number, which Hunter copied down.

The fact that Madj Harana had this number meant that he was not "working black"—but was registered as required by law for employee medical insurance and family benefits. Which in turn meant that he was not in France illegally, and so would be registered as a foreign resident with the police. He would have to have a *carte de séjour*, which would be lifted if he failed to give notification of any change of address within eight days. Hunter went farther down the street to a *tabac*, and phoned Inspector Moreau, at the Préfecture de Police on the Île de la Cité.

Having a contact like Moreau was basic in any country of Europe. Without such a contact, tracing even a registered person could take days of wading through red tape and civil servants burdened with other work that took precedence. Hunter gave him the name and number of Madj Harana—and while he was at it, of Ahmed Bel Jahra, on the off-chance there was something recent on him, too. Inspector Moreau asked for half an hour.

Hunter lunched in the *tabac* on a sandwich and beer, and called back in thirty-five minutes. Inspector Moreau was ready for him. He had obtained Madj Harana's new address from the Renseignments Généraux, which was in charge of all foreign residents in Paris, and his present place of employment from the Sécurité Sociale. On Bel Jahra, however, there was nothing more recent than a year ago, when he'd left his Rue Mouffetard address and his cover job at the Moroccan Tourist Bureau. Hunter was not surprised. He thanked Inspector Moreau, promised to send him the usual bottle of his favorite expensive cognac, and went looking for Madj Harana.

The search continued to prove frustrating. The bakery where Madj now worked was just off the Place Stalingrad, on the edge of the heavily Arab working section above the Boulevard de la Chapelle. But it turned out Madj worked there from four in the morning until twelve noon, and was gone for the day.

The place where Madj Harana lived was in the heart of the most crowded Arab area of Paris, between the Métro Barbes Rochechouart and Rue de la Goutte d'Or. A neighborhood almost totally without women; packed with men working temporarily in Paris to support their families back in Morocco and Algeria. The house in which Madj lived was not as depressing as the Goutte d'Or, where men slept twelve to a room in three shifts, and stood patiently in line for hours outside certain houses, waiting their turn at the few aged prostitutes inside. But it was squalid enough. And Madj was not home.

Hunter prowled the area asking questions, and did not find him. At 5 P.M. he called the American Embassy. Shansky had been there, picked up his pay, and arranged the extension phone for Hunter. A woman picked up in the middle of the first ring: "Good afternoon, Mr. Hunter's office."

"This is Simon Hunter," he told her.

"Oh. Hello, Mr. Hunter. I just got assigned to you. I'm Janice Hardinger."

"Has George Shansky called in with any message for me?"

"No, sir. No messages at all for you."

Hunter thanked her and returned to Madj Harana's address. He was still not in. Hunter resumed his prowl of the area. At 8 P.M. he had an excellent couscous dinner in a local Algerian restaurant. At 10:30 he found a man who said that Madj had a girl friend "somewhere in Paris" and was probably getting his daily sleep at her place. Hunter went wearily home to the Hôtel Julien.

Shansky was already falling asleep when Hunter got there. Opening the door and crawling back in bed, he took a long swallow from a bottle of rye as he listened to Hunter's frustrating day.

"I did better'n you," he told Hunter drowsily. "Bel Jahra was definitely under observation by *somebody* at the agency. I've got *twelve* different spooks checking around to find out *who*. Maybe I'll know by tomorrow, sometime."

With that, Shansky fell asleep, with Hunter standing there looking at him. Hunter tucked him in, took a long swallow from Shansky's bottle of rye, and climbed the stairs to get his own sleep. One day down the drain.

The next day things started to break a bit, for both of them. But not through Madj Harana.

Hunter got to the bakery off Place Stalingrad at nine in the morning just as Madj Harana was coming out for a lunch break. Madj Harana was tall and wide as a truck, with a fierce black beard and kind black eyes. There was a bistro on the next corner, with the two little tables outside empty. Hunter asked if he could buy them both a drink there.

Madj stayed where he was, planted on the sidewalk in front of the bakery, studying Hunter suspiciously. "What do you want to know about Ahmed Bel Jahra for?"

"I understand he slapped you," Hunter said harshly, and rubbed it in: "In public, before other people."

Among Arabs, that was enough to start a feud that could wipe out whole families. But Madj just scowled, shrugged, and said: "So what? That is between him and me. And it doesn't make me a stool pigeon."

"And I'm not a French *flic.*"

"So what are you? And why do you ask me questions?"

Hunter had to be careful with this one. "I'm an American detective," he said slowly, feeling his way and watching Madj's eyes. "An American girl was killed recently in Italy. We think Bel Jahra killed her. So we're looking for him."

Madj thought it over, and nodded, "Okay. I'll have a drink with you."

They ordered *pastis* and sat at one of the outside tables, with the morning crowds swarming around them. "I don't know about Ahmed killing any girl," Madj said heavily. "But I do know he's a bad man. A bastard."

"You know him long enough to say that?"

Madj shook his head. "I don't *know* him. Just who he is. *What* he is—secret police." Madj hawked and spat contemptuously on the pavement, narrowly missing the shoe of the passerby.

Hunter made it emphatic: "You knew that? For a fact?"

"Sure."

"Who told you he was secret police?"

Madj shrugged. "I'm from Morocco. He's from Morocco. Only I'm a socialist. So I had to get out. Because the secret police were after me. Everybody there knew Ahmed was one of them. In Paris he was claiming he's in the tourist business. But I knew the truth."

"Why did he slap you?"

The face of the huge Arab darkened with the memory of that slap. "Do you *know* who Ben Barka was?"

Hunter nodded. "A socialist leader, in your country."

"*The* leader. A man who tried to help poor people. He really cared. And they chased him out of Morocco. Like they chased me. Only they followed *him*, and killed him."

Tears sprang in Madj's eyes. He wiped them angrily. "Do you know *who* killed this beautiful man?"

"Your secret police."

"Yes. Them. So when I walked in the bar one day, and saw Ahmed Bel Jahra—who was one of them—I lost control of myself. I called him names. The worst names and curses I could think of."

He stopped abruptly. Hunter nudged him: "And he slapped you down."

Madj Harana nodded slowly, embarrassed, saying nothing.

Hunter nudged harder: "Why didn't you get up and hit him back? Were you afraid of him?"

Madj said slowly: "There are people who have something about them . . . that causes fear in other men. It is hard to put words to, what it is. But *he* has this thing. Yes. I was afraid of him."

There was no more. Madj Harana had no idea where Bel Jahra was now, nor did he know anyone Bel Jahra had been in contact with in France. Another of the dead ends. Hunter went back to square one: Place Contrescarpe.

Jean-Claude was pleased to see Hunter come into the Irlandais. "I did remember something," he announced with a grin, like someone who had suddenly found the solution to a difficult crossword puzzle. "Two things."

Hunter gave him full attention.

"First thing, that young girl Ahmed used to come in with—she had long dark red hair. That help?"

"It could turn out to," Hunter said deliberately. "The other thing?"

"There's an American girl I know who lives just down on Rue Monge. Nancy Fine. Nice girl. Friendly. She was in here one morning when Ahmed was at a table outside with his young red-head. Nancy and the redhead said hello to each other. Like they met before." Jean-Claude grinned again, showing strong white teeth. "So *Nancy* should be able to tell you something about her."

"What's her address?"

"I don't remember the number. I was only to her place once, when she invited me to a party there. But it's easy to find. Go down to Place Monge and turn right. There's a little Algerian sandwich shop before you reach the next corner. She lives above it."

It wasn't a likely time to find her home, if she had a job. "Do you know where she works?" Hunter asked.

Jean-Claude shook his handsome head. "No idea. I know she teaches English. But I don't know where."

Hunter had no trouble finding her address, walking to the right along Rue Monge from the *place*. The Algerian sandwich shop was no more than an open cubbyhole in the ground floor of an old apartment building. A wooden counter dividing the hole from the sidewalk was piled high with huge sandwiches of heavy rolls filled with a mixture of tuna, olives, peppers, lettuce, and oil. A small, elderly man wearing a red fez sat dejectedly on a stool inside. There was a door next to his place. Inside, Hunter found the name "Nancy Fine" on one of the mailboxes, and cimbed two flights to knock at her door.

The lack of response didn't surprise him. He went back down to the Algerian sandwich maker. "I'm looking for an American girl named Nancy Fine who lives in this building. Do you know her?"

The man perked up a bit, glad to have someone to talk to in his loneliness. "The tall American girl? Sure, I see her all the time." He lost some of his perk. "She never buys sandwiches from me. Never."

"Do you know where she works?"

"No." The Algerian shrugged. "But I guess she works. Somewhere. She is never around during the day. Except weekends."

"During the week, when does she come back?"

The Algerian thought for a while, and shrugged again. "Five. Sometimes six. Sometimes later."

Hunter thanked him and crossed the street to a corner *tabac*. Going to the phone in the rear, he called the American Embassy, and got Janice Hardinger, his temporary secretary. He told her what he wanted:

"I've got a job for you. Check on an American girl named Nancy Fine who lives here in Paris. Got the name?"

"Yes, sir. Nancy Fine."

"She apparently teaches English. I want to know where. Get Mort Crown in the SY office to help you with it. I'll call back soon."

He recrossed the street and began checking out the other apartments in Nancy Fine's building. There were people home in only two of them. They knew the American girl only to say hello to; didn't know where she worked. It was past noon when Hunter came out of the building. He looked at the flies crawling over the Algerian's sandwiches, and crossed to the *tabac* for a beer and ham sandwich. When he finished, he called his extension at the American Embassy.

"We have a Nancy Fine registered as an American citizen resident abroad here," his secretary informed him. She gave him the home address he already had. "She was teaching for six months at the International School, but I called and she no longer works there. They don't know where she works now. Mort Crown called all the schools in Paris that would hire an American to teach English. She isn't at any of them. So we haven't had much luck yet, I'm afraid."

"Any messages from Shansky?"

"No, sir. No messages."

Hunter hung up, and made another call to Inspector Moreau. Twenty minutes later Moreau informed him that Nancy Fine's last registered place of work was the International School where Hunter already knew she no longer worked.

Which meant that she was now probably "working black"; for employers who didn't want to register her and have to pay the extra amount required on top of her wages, for her benefits and insurance with the Sécurité Sociale. Hunter prepared himself for a long day's wait.

He went out into the thin spring sunshine of Paris. At this point Nancy Fine was his only lead to a nameless young girl with dark red hair who *might* have some kind of lead to Bel Jahra. And an entire afternoon stretched ahead of him before Nancy Fine was likely to return home. Hunter began to use up that afternoon prowling the neighborhood of the Mouff.

Often he entered a local shop or bistro to show his picture of Bel Jahra. Occasionally one of the people of the area remembered the face. But none had any information of use to him. Hunter kept walking the neighborhood; up one short street, down another.

He didn't allow impatience to begin tampering with his nervous system. This was police work as he knew it. Dogged, determined tracking, from one possible informant to another. Searching, following, waiting. That never changed, no matter what kind of case it was, and Hunter was used to doing it. He was like an experienced alley cat, persistently prowling a known rat area, knowing that eventually one of them was bound to show itself. And that when it did, he'd be ready to pounce. He only hoped that it wouldn't be too late by the time that happened.

Hunter did some thinking as he prowled. But most of it wasn't conscious, methodical thought. Much of that afternoon was spent merely walking the streets of the Mouff, letting his mind dream on everything he saw in passing: two grimy *clochards* slumping in the doorway of a demolished building passing wine bottle back and forth, women shoppers with their wicker baskets and plastic bags, passing faces, walls, roofs, chimneys . . . all the things that Bel Jahra had seen daily when he'd lived in this neighborhood. Hunter moved through it absorbing the feel of the streets and buildings and people and air—and the feel of Ahmed Bel Jahra moving through all of it as he was now. Gradually and deliberately, Hunter was entering the mind of Bel Jahra.

At three in the afternoon, Hunter made another call to his extension at the embassy. But there was nothing further on Nancy Fine—and still no message from Shansky. Hunter wondered how the former espionage agent was faring, as he resumed his prowl of the Mouff.

It had taken Shansky hours of trekking from one of his old CIA colleagues to another, this day, before he'd finally turned up an agent who'd at one time had Bel Jahra assigned to him for O.O. —Occasional Observation. But Shansky wasn't tired. He felt great. He had money in his pocket and he was working.

It had been the loss of the job, more than the sudden lack of funds, that had been such a shocker to his self-respect. He hadn't realized until that had happened how completely his ego depended on his work. That was one big difference, as Shansky saw it, between men and women. His wife hadn't been that broken up about losing her position as his wife. A woman stayed a woman, no matter what. But a man was his profession. Without it he was nothing. Nothing.

Shansky had been working steadily at the same profession since World War II, when he'd left college for the Army at twenty, and been made an OSS agent in Italy and then France. After the war they'd dissolved the OSS and created CIA, and he'd been one of the agents to make the shift. All those years with "the Company," as its agents called it—and suddenly he was dropped, for economy reasons. Suddenly he was too much of a burden on the taxpayers of America. So they'd made him a nothing—until Hunter hired him. How long that would last, Shansky didn't let himself think about.

The future scared him. But right now he was working. And working well.

Walter Fischman was a slightly plumpish man of average height, with a neat little goatee and a round bald head. He wore old-fashioned-looking glasses on his mild and pleasant face. His cover business was in a small, elegant office building on the Rue de Berri, across the street from the Hungarian Legation. The sign on the frosted outer door said: "Fla. Estates Enterprises." Fischman was ostensibly in Paris for the purpose of selling land in Florida to French real estate brokers. But there was no secretary in his small outer office. And the only business equipment in his inner office were the three items on his desk: a pad for noting times, dates, and names; a pair of binoculars; and a Nikon-FTN camera with a 200 mm. lens and tele-converter. Walter Fischman's present assignment was observing everyone who went in and out of the Hungarian Legation across the street.

"I was really sorry to hear you'd been dropped," he told Shansky with genuine sympathy. "I'm glad you got another job so fast."

Shansky believed the sympathy; Fischman was thinking of how shaky his own job was at the moment.

"Man," Fischman went on unhappily, "do you know how many *other* guys been phased out since you were? We had ten in one day here in Paris last week. *Ten.*"

"Could be you next," Shansky pointed out blandly.

"Don't I know it. And I know the chances against lucking out like you've done. From CIA to State—that's falling out of a beehive into a tub of honey."

Shansky had refrained from explaining how unofficial and temporary his present job was. "If you get bounced, look me up at the State Department. I'll help you there, if I can."

"That's really decent of you, George L. I won't forget it."

"About Bel Jahra . . ." Shansky said firmly, shoving him back to the subject.

"There's just not much to tell you. I had him on O.O. for about a year, after we found out he was here working for Oufkir's secret service. I didn't find out much, because I wasn't trying that hard. Wasn't supposed to. Just routine keeping tabs on him, now and then. I made some of his Moroccan contacts. Even started to bend one of 'em. But they're all gone now. Disappeared when Bel Jahra did; after Oufkir got hit in the head. We heard he took part in Oufkir's coup attempt. But nothing definite."

"You don't know *anybody* still here in France that he used to be in touch with?"

"Nobody. Sorry."

Shansky regarded the agent with sudden distaste. "You watched a whole year, and you can't come up with a single lead to him?"

Fischman shrugged. "Like I said, I'm sorry. I also said I wasn't tagging him that much. Just time to time."

"If that's all the help you can give me," Shansky told him coldly, "don't expect too much from me when you come hunting a job at State."

"Don't be such a hard-ass, George L. Let me think awhile. . . ."

Shansky was silent, sitting very straight in his chair as he waited.

Finally, Fischman said slowly: "There is a guy—used to work for the Company. Quit awhile back, to beat being fired. He's another lucky one; had something ready to fall back on. Ralph Borio."

"I know him," Shansky snapped. "What about him?"

"Well, he knew I was doing O.O. on Bel Jahra. Last time I saw Borio, he told me he saw Bel Jahra here in Paris, about four months ago. Said he was with some young girl. And Borio had a girl with him that knew her . . . I think."

Shansky got up. "Borio still got the same dump?"

"The loft, yeah."

"Thanks for the help, Walt." Shansky headed for the door.

"Maybe I *will* be contacting you," the agent called after him.

"Just ask for me at the State Department," Shansky said, and went out to find Ralph Borio.

Hunter was nursing a *citron pressé* at a red table outside the *tabac* on Rue Monge when a tall girl in faded jeans turned into the doorway beside the sandwich place across the street. He glanced at his watch. It was twenty minutes past six in the evening. He looked up toward Nancy Fine's third-floor window. After a few minutes the girl appeared inside there, opening the window to let in fresh air. Hunter left money for his drink, crossed the street, and went in and up the stairs.

She opened the door at his knock and looked at him with weary lack of curiosity. "What is it?" she asked in French. Close up she looked older; perhaps thirty. But tiredness and dejection might account for that.

"I'm from the State Department," Hunter told her.

Before he could tell her anything else, she groaned: "Oh, Christ —I *knew* I'd get in trouble forgetting to notify them about my change of job."

"You're not in any trouble with me," Hunter reassured her. "I'm after information about someone you might know, that's all. If you're Nancy Fine."

"That's me. Well . . . come in. I've got a date, and I've got to take a bath, but if it won't take long . . ."

"It won't," he assured her. The room inside was long and narrow, crowded with a bed, dining table, chairs, bureau. A door to a small bathroom, another to a smaller kitchen. Nancy Fine was not doing so well in Paris. "Had a hard time looking for you. Called all the schools in Paris."

"I'm giving private lessons now. Just finished three hours with two kids whose parents want them to learn English—much against their will. Talk about *American* kids being brats . . ." She shuddered, and got a half-empty bottle of wine from the top of the bureau. "Like a drink?"

Hunter shook his head. She poured some in a glass and drank it down, savoring it. "That is one of the good things about living in Paris. Less than a buck for a bottle of *good* wine. The bad thing is I just can't seem to earn enough money to get by on." She glanced at her wristwatch. "Look, I really have to get started with that bath. Who was it you wanted to know about?"

He told her. And watched her frown, thinking back. "Long dark red hair," he repeated. "And young; about sixteen, according to Jean-Claude."

"Oh, I remember her. It's her name I'm trying to remember."

"Known her long?"

"Only met her once before that time in the Irlandais." Nancy Fine poured more wine in her glass and sipped it. "I had this great camera my father gave me, and I thought maybe I could make some extra money with photography. I used the girl you're talking about as a model once. Because she was so pretty, and I thought she'd look good in photographs. I wanted to show people what I could do with a camera, maybe get somebody interested."

She snapped her fingers suddenly. "I remember—her name's Rosalynde."

"And her last name?"

Nancy Fine shrugged. "It never came up, so I don't know."

"Who introduced you to her?"

"Nobody. I saw her having a coffee at one of the bars along the Champs-Élysées, one day when I had the camera. I asked her if I could take some pictures of her. Just for fun; I didn't have any money to pay her. She didn't mind; kind of liked the idea I thought she was so pretty. So I took the pictures and went on my way. Only other time I saw her was that once at the Irlandais."

Hunter began to have that heavy feeling of another dead end coming up. "You don't know the man she was with?" He showed her Bel Jahra's picture.

She shook her head. "I didn't even notice him."

One last hope: "Do you still have those pictures you took of her?"

"Sorry, no. I finally had to sell the camera, to pay my rent. I threw out all the pictures after that. You're not getting what you wanted from me, are you?"

Hunter's smile was bleak. "Afraid not."

"She's German. I know that because she told me. Her English was better than her French, but with a funny accent, so I asked her where she was from. Does *that* help?"

"I don't know," Hunter admitted. "But it's better than nothing."

Actually, it wasn't much better. But Hunter had to be satisfied with it, because that was all there was.

Ralph Borio was tall and skinny, with a pale, intense face. He lived in a single huge room with a skylight at the top of a high old building in the Marais, two blocks from the Place des Vosges. He acknowledged that he was one of the fortunate ones, as he handed Shansky a brandy and poured one for himself.

Borio had been twenty-three when the CIA had stationed him in Paris. Because he had worked his way through college playing a guitar, it was natural to use that as his cover here: pretending to be a struggling young musician. But the pretense had become a reality in the three years since. Two years ago he'd become part of a Paris rock-music group. The group did so well that Borio found himself spending more time playing his guitar, for good money, than he was giving to his CIA work. Finally, he'd had to choose between them, and the CIA found itself contributing a new star to the French musical scene.

"As it turns out," he told Shansky over their brandies, "I quit just in time. With what's happened since, I'd've been fired around now."

The brandy was the best. Shanksy felt it warm his guts as he took in Borio's expensive Irish-knit pullover. He couldn't repress a certain envy—for the luck, the talent, the youth. "And your rock group's doing okay, I hear."

"Better than okay," Borio grinned. "Right now we've got more good paying dates than we can handle."

"Swell," Shansky said, and told him what he was after.

Borio lost some of his grin. "I don't want to talk about anything that might wind up hitting the fan and getting me in trouble. I want to keep that old business behind me, George L."

Shansky nodded understandingly. "You mean if the French found out you were a CIA agent here, they might kick your ass the hell out of the country. Just when you're doing so well here."

"That's what worries me," Borio admitted anxiously.

Shansky smiled pleasantly. "In that case, you'd better tell me what I want to know."

Borio stared at him. "You wouldn't spill on me."

Shansky said gently: "Yes I would."

"You bastard. We were friends."

"No we weren't, Ralph. We just worked for the same outfit. My only loyalty's to the people I work for. Right now I'm working for a guy who is trying to find Bel Jahra. So *give.*"

"You bastard," Borio repeated. But then he smiled, a bit sadly. "What the hell, I guess I can't be that mad at you. *I* did things like this to people, when I was in that lousy job."

"Now it's lousy. Then it paid your bread. We're wasting time, Ralph. You saw Bel Jahra about four months ago. Here in Paris. With a girl. And you were with a girl who knew her."

Borio grimaced. "*She's* what I'm worried about. The girl I was with. If it got out, what I used her for when I was with the Company . . ."

"It won't go past me," Shansky promised. "I've got enough bodies of my own to hide."

Borio downed the rest of his brandy and poured a refill. He didn't offer to refill Shansky's. "Okay . . . it was in the Drouant on

Place Gaillon. We were just going in to have dinner. Bel Jahra was coming out, with this very pretty, and *very* young, redhead. Vicki, the girl I was with, knew her. They grabbed each other and kissed each other; told each other they were both doing fine. And that was *it*. Bel Jahra went his way with the redhead, and we went inside the Drouant to eat. End of story."

"Not quite," Shansky growled. "You know better than that. Tell me about this Vicki, first."

Borio heaved a trapped sigh. "Victoria Smythe. Twenty-four, gorgeous, the most beautiful black hair you ever saw, and stacked. She's an English whore. I picked her up here in Paris, and started using her for the Company, on foreign diplomats. A swallow. You know the form."

Shansky nodded. "Swallow" is espionage argot for a girl used for sexual blackmail. "Dump her in their beds, get 'em doing kinky tricks with her, then squeeze them."

"Uh-huh. Vicki was a natural at it. Shame the Company had to lose her. A Jap wouldn't stand still for it; started yelling she was a spy trying to force info from him. They had to ship her out in a hurry."

"What'd she say about the girl Bel Jahra was with?"

"Nothing." Shansky looked skeptical and Borio shrugged. "I didn't ask her. The Company wasn't interested in Bel Jahra anymore, and I sure wasn't. I was already set to quit the next week. All *I* was interested in was getting a piece of Vicki for myself that night. Before they assigned her to somebody else."

"She didn't say *anything* about the girl with Bel Jahra, on her own?"

"Just that she was older than she looked. That's *all*."

"Where do I find this Victoria Smythe?"

Borio shook his head. "I don't know. Doubt if the Company knows either, anymore. They lost interest in her fast, after she got exposed —if you'll pardon the pun. I *guess* she's back in London, plying the same old trade."

Hunter made the call to Ivor Klar in London from the office he'd been assigned on the top floor at the American Embassy on the Avenue Gabriel. Shansky stood at the windows, watching the lights going on in the evening dusk across the vast Place de la Concorde.

Hunter was informed by the switchboard at Scotland Yard that

Inspector Klar had gone off duty for the night. Hunter got him at his home number. He explained about Victoria Smythe, and what he hoped might be found out through her, if she could be located.

"I can't do anything about finding her tonight," Klar told him. "We have guests for dinner. I'll see what I can do tomorrow."

"Fair enough. Eat well, Ivor." Hunter hung up the phone and leaned back in his padded swivel chair. He swung his legs up on the desk and looked blankly at the ends of his shoes as he reviewed what they had.

Shansky, still gazing out toward the Place de la Concorde, said absently: "You know what Madame Roland said just before the people that used to be her fellow revolutionaries guillotined her down there? She said: 'Liberty! How many crimes are committed in thy name!' Interesting thought for the day."

"Thank you very much," Hunter said dryly, and methodically continued to go down his mental list. At this point they had:

A young girl Bel Jahra had been seeing a lot, as close as four months ago.

Who *might* be able to provide a further lead to Bel Jahra, if she could be found.

About this girl they knew: she had long, dark red hair. Unless she'd cut it short. Or dyed it another color. Or both. She was probably German. She looked sixteen but might be older. Her name was Rosalynde. No last name.

Which meager collection of vital statistics made her virtually impossible to locate.

Unless an English hooker named Victoria Smythe could be found, and came through with a few more facts.

It did not seem, at the time, to add up to very much of a return for two full days' work put in by two skilled men.

The lights of Tripoli fell away abruptly below the plane as its great jet engines hurled it steeply into the night sky. Bel Jahra looked down at the dark coastline of Libya through his passenger window on the right of the aisle, as the plane banked around and flew east. Next stop: Cyprus. He would sleep there, and fly on next day to Athens, before proceeding to Nice. As a precautionary rule, Bel Jahra always tried to avoid entering Europe directly from an Arab country.

Bel Jahra unbuckled his seat belt as the sign flicked off. He tilted back his seat and closed his eyes, thinking of all he had accomplished. His two commando teams were fully briefed for the operation. They—and the necessary explosives and weapons—would start on their way to France by various destinations tomorrow.

He thought ahead to what tomorrow held for him. First, the Riviera, and Juliet Shale. To keep her warmed up, and insure his invitation to Valasi's birthday party. Then, late the next evening: Paris. He would not meet with al-Omared until the following morning. That would leave him one full night to enjoy, perhaps for the last time, the unique pleasures of a girl named Rosalynde.

FOURTEEN

"The Dirty Squad" is the name given by the London underworld to a department of Scotland Yard officially known as the Obscene Publications Squad. The nickname was originally intended to be derogatory. But its picturesque accuracy proved irresistible. Now even the police use it, among themselves. Detective Sergeant Neale Slater, a large, handsome, and placid plainclothes policeman of thirty, had been a member of the Dirty Squad for three and a half years. He knew "the dirt trade" inside out, and was on familiar terms with most of the people engaged in it. When one of the copies of Inspector Ivor Klar's request was routinely passed on to him by his own chief inspector, Sergeant Slater knew exactly where to go to find Victoria Smythe.

London's densely populated Soho section has a vaguely exotic flavor contributed by its foreigners from the Mediterranean area. Its short, narrow streets contain some of the best restaurants and grocery stores in the city, in addition to the main business offices of England's largest film companies. They also contain the makeshift studios of less reputable film companies, plus a high concentration of pornographic bookshops, strip clubs, and little rooms used for working purposes by a large percentage of London's fourteen thousand prostitutes. Sergeant Slater made his way purposefully from Piccadilly Circus through Soho to Greek Street, and turned into a sleazy brick alley that dead-ends halfway inside the block between Bateman and Compton.

One of the alley doorways had a number of soiled white cards tacked on the wall beside it. On one card was neatly typed: "Riding Academy & Leather Goods for Gents—Ilsa Stern, Proprietress."

Printed on another in pencil was: "French Lessons by Marie." A third had only the name "Olga" scrawled with bright red lipstick. Each had a room number, and there were six others like them. Sergeant Slater went in, climbed to the top floor, and opened a door that had no number on it.

Inside was a large square room with a big window covered with black paint. A stocky middle-aged woman with a camera was snapping pictures of two naked girls on a wide bed. One was a tall, slender blonde, brandishing a riding whip as she knelt astride the other: a pretty and richly curved girl with a mass of lustrous black hair, whose wrists were handcuffed to the old-fashioned brass bedstead. Their pose was illuminated for the camera by a powerful strobe light held by a ferret-faced adolescent boy. He turned in surprise when Sergeant Slater entered, swinging the strobe away from the girls on the bed just as the camera clicked.

"Goddammit!" the photographer snarled, and glared at Sergeant Slater. "If you had any manners, Neale, you'd know you're supposed to *knock* before opening people's doors. You just spoiled a shot."

"You *could* try locking it, Ryan," Slater told her calmly, and looked to the black-haired girl on the bed. "Got a minute, Vicki?" It wasn't really a question, though he asked it politely.

Before she could answer, the photographer snapped: "I hope you *mean* a minute. I have to finish shooting the rest of this roll, *and* develop it, before one o'clock."

"Shut up, Ryan," Slater told her serenely, and strolled toward the bed. The boy leaned against the wall watching him nervously. The blond girl sighed impatiently and climbed off the bed, putting on a soiled bathrobe.

Victoria Smythe slipped out of the handcuffs and sat up on the bed, primly covering her pubic area with one hand and her bosom with the other arm. "What's the problem, Sergeant?"

"No problem at all, unless you don't tell me what I want to know. *Then* I might make you some problems, with the Street Offences Act."

She sneered at him. "Are you kidding? You know I haven't been a prosty since I got married. He didn't like it, so I quit."

Slater looked bemused. "But he doesn't mind *this?*"

"Why should he?"

He let it go. "Vickie, you know a girl named Rosalynde? You ran into her in Paris about four months ago. Young German girl, very pretty, dark red hair?"

"Sure," Victoria Smythe said promptly. "Rosalynde Hagen."

"Lovely. What d'you know about her?"

"Not very much. I know she came to England from Germany to be an *au pair* girl. But she got bored pretty quick with taking care of some family's housework and kids. Wanted a bit of fun and money, you know how it is with girls on their own. Only she was so dumb at first, she didn't even *know* about the Street Offences Act. Got herself arrested soliciting men right out in the open. Down here on Shaftsbury."

"So we have a record on her," Slater interjected.

"Just that one time. After that she got smarter—a bit. Took a room on Frith Street, put a card outside. Same building I was using, at the time. So she was okay with the law then—but she still didn't know the score about paying protection to the boys that handle Frith Street. You know."

Slater nodded, his face suddenly unpleasant. "Harry Bond and his gang. Bad lot."

"They're no *so* bad. I mean, when Harry talked to Rosalynde, and she wouldn't go along, he didn't rough her up or anything right off. Instead he asked me to just wise her up about how things are done here. *That's h*ow I got to know her. I explained she couldn't work unless she paid them half. Or she'd get herself beat up some night. And if she still didn't get reasonable they'd cut her face with a razor. That *really* frightened her."

"So she paid?"

"Uh-uh. Not her. Stubborn little thing, Rosalynde. She told me she wasn't going to give away half of what *she* earned, to anybody. Said it wasn't like that on the Continent. So—she packed it up and went back there to work."

"As a whore?"

Victoria Smythe shrugged her smooth shoulders. "She certainly didn't know any other way to make a decent living."

"I understand *you* went to the Continent for a time, too."

"Because of *her*, in a way. I got to thinking about what she'd said: not having to pay all that protection money to work over there. So finally I went and tried it. I did quite well for myself, too. Until I . . . got in a spot of trouble and had to come back."

"But you saw her in Paris."

"Only once. By accident. I didn't even know that was where she was. Until one night I was going to a restaurant with a friend of mine. And there she was, coming out. We said hello, and all that. And I haven't seen her since."

"Know the man she was with?"

"No."

"Where was she living in Paris?"

"I don't know that, either."

"Know what part of Germany she's from?"

"Düsseldorf."

It was one in the afternoon when Inspector Klar phoned this information to Hunter in Paris. Hunter immediately began a methodical check on every normal source of possible information on Rosalynde Hagen's whereabouts, if she was still in France. At the same time, Shansky got in touch with an old contact at the Direction de la Surveillance du Territoire, the French equivalent of America's FBI and England's DI5, and induced the DST agent to make an unofficial investigation through the counter-espionage records.

By three o'clock that afternoon, they had collected a frustrating quantity of negative information. Shansky's contact learned there was no DST record on Rosalynde Hagen. Concerning Ahmed Bel Jahra, the DST files revealed the same old story: Bel Jahra had left France a year ago and had never returned; at least not under his own name. Hunter's investigation ran into the same blank wall:

Rosalynde Hagen had not been registered as a prostitute with the police of France for over a year. A check through the postal system failed to turn up any address for her. The Sécurité Sociale had never had any registration for her. The vast archives in the cellars under the Préfecture de Police on the Île de la Cité held nothing recent on her. The files at the Panthéon offices of the Renseignments Généraux had nothing since her registration as a prostitute had lapsed.

Only one tentative positive came out of all this: There was a record of Rosalynde Hagen's entrance into France, from England; but no record of her having left France.

Hunter considered the two items remaining for him to work from: The girl was from West Germany; and he had her name, hopefully her real name. But getting information from Germany through normal channels presented a time problem. In Germany the bureaucratic red-tape system is more strictly adhered to than in other countries of Europe. Even with a regular officer of the German police making the inquiry for Hunter, working through the various government departments concerned could consume days.

There was, however, a way to slip past all that red tape: via an *ir*regular contact who had methods of bypassing normal channels. Hunter phoned Irmgard Stiller in Nice. It was too early in the day for her husband's nightclub to be open, so he phoned her apartment on Rue Verdi. He spoke to her with care, keeping in mind her justified wariness about possible phone taps. Their conversation was oblique:

Irmgard: "So nice hearing from you, Simon. I've heard absolutely nothing about our friend since we last met. How have you been?"

Hunter: "Not too well, to tell the truth. I've fallen for a German girl. From Düsseldorf. Her name is Rosalynde Hagen. And she's disappeared. I can't find her anywhere."

Irmgard: "You are foolish to become so upset by a girl, Simon. When there are so many girls available in this world."

Hunter: "Not like this one. She's very pretty. Long dark red hair. And young—eighteen or nineteen, but she looks sixteen."

Irmgard: "She sounds much too young for you. That's the trouble when you older men become infatuated with these young things. Sooner or later they run off with boys their own age. What do you expect?"

Hunter: "I'm not infatuated with her. It's love. If I at least had a picture of her to keep me company. But I don't. I'm going to go crazy if I don't locate her soon."

Irmgard: "That is a shame. You met her in Düsseldorf?"

Hunter: "No, she left Germany some years ago. Went to England as an *au pair* girl. But then she came here to France. She's a whore, I admit; but I still want to find her."

Irmgard: "You have my sympathy."

Hunter hung up knowing she would put through the inquiry without delay, via her own intelligence network to the Bfv, the counter-intelligence Office for the Protection of the Constitution, which operated within West Germany. It was then 3:45 P.M.

Five minutes later, at 3:50, the Air France caravelle which Bel

Jahra had boarded at Athens landed at the Côte d'Azur Airport outside Nice.

Young Kosso Shamir felt pleasantly relaxed as he sipped his tea on the terminal observation terrace and watched the landing of the Air France from Athens. He had the early shift today, and it was almost over. In a few minutes his relief would arrive, and Kosso could go home for one of his pregnant wife's gradually improving dinners.

The scream of four huge jet engines suddenly blasting to life assaulted Kosso's eardrums. He glanced toward the source: an SAS jumbo swinging into position at the end of the main runway, its passengers for Copenhagen having finished boarding ten minutes ago. The Air France from Athens swung off the runway to make room for its departure. The screaming of the SAS engines calmed to a throaty sound as the jumbo eased forward and began its takeoff run.

The plane from Athens taxied to a stop. The BP trucks were already on their way to refuel it; but the passengers wouldn't be coming off for at least another five minutes. Kosso leaned back in his chair and admired his view of the calm sea. It was dark from the horizon, then green as it got closer, then white spumes of spray lashing along the edge of the runway. The SAS jumbo was already high overhead, trailing jet streams as it turned heavily above the sea and headed north.

Much lower, a two-engined prop training plane buzzed in over the surface of the sea and made three wild bounces past six little planes parked along the short private runway to the right of the airport. Kosso felt a certain sympathy for the pilot of that trainer. It had been practicing landings and takeoffs for a solid hour. The takeoffs were all right, but the student pilot was having trouble with leveling-in for the landings. The teacher in the plane kept him touching down and taking off, circling over the sea and back for another try. Kosso was watching the trainer take off again when Hayim Cohen sat down across the terrace table from him.

Hayim was a bent, elderly man with a crippled leg; a survivor of a Nazi extermination camp in Poland which his wife, two children, and mother had failed to survive. He had demanded that Israel find a use for the hate still burning within him. They'd assigned Hayim to this job because he had an unusually good memory for faces; though certainly not on a par with Kosso's abnormal one.

"I am here," he announced needlessly. "Anything of interest so far today?"

"Nothing." Kosso was automatically watching the passengers coming from the Air France jet to the terminal as he spoke. He continued to watch them as he stood up and shook each leg to get the blood circulating. "Maybe you'll have better . . ."

He stopped talking when he saw Bel Jahra in the line of arriving passengers, carrying a leather overnight bag with a shoulder strap.

"Hayim," Kosso said quietly without pointing. "The tall man down there with the gray suit and dark blue turtleneck. Ahmed Bel Jahra. The one Uri Ezan and Simon Hunter are so interested in."

With an unsure scowl, Hayim observed the man below until he vanished from sight under the terrace. "Sure?"

"Yes I'm sure," Kosso told him flatly. After a long boring day, the sudden surge of eager excitement made him forget his anticipation of a quiet evening with his young wife. "I'm going to try to follow him, and find out where he goes. Phone control. Tell them I'll call as soon as Bel Jahra stops somewhere long enough to give me a chance to."

Hayim eyed him dubiously. "You have some training in how to follow a man?"

"I said I'll *try*," Kosso growled, and hurried in off the terrace.

Bel Jahra was standing near the baggage department when Kosso came down the stairs to the ground floor. But he wasn't waiting for luggage. He was looking around for someone, and appeared irritated not to see whoever it was he expected. Kosso planted himself behind the Air-Inter counter, and kept Bel Jahra under observation.

He didn't notice Driss Hammou coming through a doorway to his right. But Driss Hammou noticed *him*. He stopped, and looked past Kosso toward Bel Jahra, whose back was to both of them at the moment. Then Hammou returned his attention to Kosso. Hammou had spent a number of years with the secret police in Morocco. It was not difficult to recognize what he was seeing. Turning, Hammou went back out the way he had come; still unnoticed.

When Hammou reappeared, it was through the doorway to the

taxi rank, on the other side of the terminal's reception room. He went straight to Bel Jahra with a broad smile of greeting.

Bel Jahra frowned at him. "Why are you late?"

Hammou didn't explain about the traffic snarl. He said, still smiling: "You are being watched. One man. He's trying to make sure you don't spot him. But he's not good at it. Bad position."

Bel Jahra kept his eyes on Hammou. They narrowed a bit, but otherwise his expression didn't alter much. He extended his hand. "What does he look like?"

Hammou shook his hand. "He looks like nothing. A young man. A boy. Inexperienced. Nervous, and it shows."

Bel Jahra told him what to do. Hammou shook his hand again, grinned again, and walked out leaving Bel Jahra behind.

Kosso watched him vanish outside the terminal. He had never seen a picture of Driss Hammou in the terrorist files, and he couldn't follow both of them at the same time. Bel Jahra was the one everybody was so eager to find. Kosso returned his attention to Bel Jahra, who was now sauntering over to the Hertz counter. Waiting until Bel Jahra began making out the papers to rent a car, Kosso left the terminal building.

Outside, he sprinted across the main driveway into the parking area. His car was a 1967 Volkswagen with a reconditioned engine. Kosso drove it to the parking exit, and stopped there but kept his motor running. From that spot he had a view of the space next to the terminal building where the rental company cars were kept.

Bel Jahra came out with his overnight bag a few minutes later. He strolled to a blue Ford sedan in the rental area, unlocked it, and tossed his bag in the back seat. Then he got in front behind the steering wheel, shut the car door, and wound down the side windows. He did not seem to be in a hurry to get anywhere.

Kosso waited until the blue sedan was on its way out of the airport before turning his Volkswagen into the main driveway and following. Bel Jahra took the short Avenue Lindberg and turned west onto the heavily traveled RN7 heading away from the direction of Nice. Kosso maneuvered into the fast-moving traffic on the national route and went after him. At Cagnes-sur-Mer, Bel Jahra switched to the RN85, cutting inland. Twenty minutes later he turned right at Le Pré-du-Lac and drove onto the narrow, winding D3, a country road that climbs into the high pre-Alpine hills of the Gorges du Loup.

As the road switchbacked its way up steep slopes, the land around it quickly became more rugged and flanked by wild forests. There were long stretches with no habitation in sight; and minutes passed with no other traffic in either direction. Kosso tried to allow more distance between him and the blue Ford he was following. But his main objective was not to lose sight of it. Kosso had no experience at this sort of work. He had to concentrate all his attention on it. At no time did he notice Driss Hammou's gray Peugeot 404 trailing well behind him.

The three cars passed the town of Gourdon and continued to climb above the Gorges du Loup; with Bel Jahra seemingly unaware of Kosso, and Kosso unaware of Hammou.

Where the D3 made a very tight bend through a pine forest high above the Loup River, Bel Jahra turned off into a dirt road. Kosso stopped at the turnoff, and watched heavy dust rise from the woods to the right, churned up by Bel Jahra's tires. After several seconds, the dust stopped rising. The car had stopped.

Kosso pulled his Volkswagen off the D3 and got out. He wished he had some kind of weapon as he began walking warily along the side of the dirt road, into the woods. As soon as he caught a glimpse of the blue Ford sedan ahead through the foliage, he stopped. The car ahead was motionless. Kosso couldn't see if Bel Jahra was in it or not. Leaving the dirt road, he took a few steps into the cover of the trees and bushes. Then he turned again, moving parallel to the dirt road but keeping inside the cover of the woods, moving cautiously and quietly.

He stopped again when he had all of the blue car in sight through the foliage. No one was inside it. Crouching, Kosso moved between concealing bushes for a closer look. Bel Jahra was on the other side of the car, on the crest of a low mound. He was looking the other way, down into the steep-walled gorge below the other side of the mound. He might have been merely enjoying the view of the river far below. But Kosso didn't believe this. He remained crouched in the bushes, watching.

Suddenly, Bel Jahra raised a hand and waved. As though he had spotted someone he was looking for, in the gorge. Kosso watched him start down the other side of the mound. As soon as Bel Jahra disappeared from sight, Kosso rose from his crouch and stepped out of the bushes to follow.

He was going past the car when a voice behind him said in guttural French: "Stand still."

Kosso spun toward the voice. He stopped moving when he saw Hammou standing there holding a snub-nosed .38 revolver aimed at his stomach. Kosso stared at him, numbed by surprise and sudden fear.

Bel Jahra reappeared over the mound. He came down around the car to them. "Who are you?" he asked Kosso. "Who do you work for?"

The voice was quiet, but the pale eyes scared Kosso. His mouth dried up, and his throat became too constricted for speech. He swallowed hard, his prominent Adam's apple bobbing ludicrously.

Hammou smiled viciously and moved closer to Kosso, making a small, threatening gesture with the gun in his fist. "Answer him!"

Kosso had the quick reflexes of youth; and his extensive paratroop training was only a few months behind him. He twisted sharply and kicked Hammou's extended forearm. Hammou gasped with pain as the gun flew from his hand and fell in the dirt thirty feet away. Kosso went after it on the jump.

Hammou sidestepped in front of Kosso and tried to grab him. Kosso ducked under the short, thick arms and rammed an elbow into Hammou's midsection in passing. Hammou doubled up on the ground gagging for air. Kosso dove for the fallen gun, hitting the dirt on his left side and reaching with his right hand. His fingers were closing around the revolver when Bel Jahra reached him. Kosso started to roll on his back bringing the gun up to fire.

Bel Jahra did the only thing he had time for. He raised his right foot and rammed the heel of his shoe down, expertly and very hard, against the back of Kosso's neck just below the base of the skull. Kosso's neck broke with a harsh splintering sound. The side of his face fell in the dirt, his eyes turning up in their sockets. His fingers clawed feebly at the ground and his legs continued to twitch spasmodically for some time. Bel Jahra squatted beside him and watched his dying with distaste, cursing softly through clenched teeth. Now the boy couldn't tell him anything.

The hands had ceased moving, but the legs still shuddered, when Hammou came over, bent forward and clutching his middle with his hands. He looked at Bel Jahra like a dog expecting to be whipped. Bel Jahra picked up the gun and gave it back to him without a word.

Bel Jahra did not go through Kosso's pockets until the last vestige of life had ended. He found an international driver's license issued to Kosso Shamir, an Israeli. And a temporary French residence card identifying Kosso Shamir as a student from Israel. That was all he found. It didn't give Bel Jahra everything he wanted to know. But it told him a great deal.

It told him that Israel's secret agents knew of him, and were interested in knowing more. This meant they had somehow found out he was involved with Arab guerrillas. The most likely way this could have happened would be that he'd been seen meeting with Bashir Mawdri in Geneva.

It was almost impossible for them to know anything of what he was now up to. But they did know his face, and had recognized him arriving at the airport. The death of this boy who had tried to shadow him broke their line of contact to Bel Jahra. The vital thing now was not to let them re-establish it. No one must be able to trace his movements, from this moment until the accomplishment of his objective at Valasi's birthday party.

Bel Jahra pondered the methods of handling this problem as he rose to his feet and got back into the rented car.

On returning to Nice, Bel Jahra turned in the blue Ford sedan at the main Hertz office inside the city. Then Hammou drove him out of Nice in the Peugeot 404. Halfway to Monte Carlo, they stopped beside a country lane and Bel Jahra burned the papers he had used to enter France and rent the car at the airport. In Monte Carlo, he used an alternate set of identity papers, passport and visa, to rent another car.

It was getting dark when he drove it up through the hills toward Roquebrune, with Hammou following in the Peugeot. By the time Bel Jahra entered his apartment there and snapped on the lights, he knew what steps he intended to take.

He was not overly worried about being recognized again. When he was traveling anyplace where Israeli agents might be watching, a simple disguise would do. A false moustache, sunglasses, or a wig. Any of these would suffice, as long as he didn't have to leave France and show his papers to border guards. Bel Jahra knew from experience how little was required to alter a man's appearance, enough to pass a superficial observer. Unless someone looked closely at you—*expecting* you to be the one looked for—no elaborate

disguise was needed. Observers planted at airports and other transport centers had to look at too many people to give each one that
kind of suspicious scrutiny.

Bel Jahra's first concern, at this moment, was the fact that the
airport outside Nice had been selected as a means of entry into
France for two of his guerrillas. Both had taken part in previous
commando operations. If Israeli agents planted at the airport had
recognized Bel Jahra, they were more likely to recognize these two
known terrorists.

He placed a call to the Libyan Mission in Geneva. And identified himself as "the manager of the Double Eagle Company."
Project Double Eagle was the code name that had been given, by
the Libyans, to the execution of Bel Jahra's plan.

A man came on the phone and identified himself as an undersecretary for the Information Department. He told Bel Jahra that
Bashir Mawdri was out of Switzerland—but was on his way back;
his return was expected sometime this night. Bel Jahra left his
number, and an urgent request that Mawdri phone it whenever
he returned. No matter how late.

It was not until after midnight that Bashir Mawdri phoned. Bel
Jahra told him: "The salesmen we instructed to come to Nice—
conditions have changed. I've been looking over the business situation here. It is not the right place. I'm sure you can find another
potential sales area that would be better. It is important to do so,
immediately. I will hold the final sales conference in the same place
we discussed."

"I understand," Bashir Mawdri told him. "I'll take care of it."

"Good." Bel Jahra hung up the phone, considering the problems
caused by Mawdri returning his call so late. It meant that Juliet
Shale would have to be taken care of tomorrow, instead of today
as planned. Which meant postponing his meeting with al-Omared,
in Paris.

Bel Jahra phoned the house on the Parc Monceau. Al-Omared
never went to sleep before three in the morning. When he came
on the phone, Bel Jahra told him: "There has been a small delay
here in the South. No problems now, but I may not be able to see
you until late tomorrow evening."

"I'm afraid that won't do, for me," al-Omared said. "I have to be
out of Paris tomorrow evening, and all night. Call me the day
after. I should be back by late morning."

Bel Jahra agreed to this. It would work out well. It left him all of tomorrow, to find time in which Juliet Shale could get away from the Valasi estate to be with him here. He would arrive in Paris late in the evening, and not see al-Omared until the following morning. That still left a full night with Rosalynde Hagen.

FIFTEEN

The next morning there was an eight-by-ten manila envelope wait-ing for Hunter the embassy. He picked it up at the information desk inside the main entrance as he came in with Shansky. It con-tained a black-and-white photograph of a young, pretty, snub-nosed girl with long dark hair. She was grinning into the camera, showing small, irregular teeth.

There was nothing else in the envelope. Hunter turned over the photograph. On the back someone had neatly printed a name with a ball-point pen: "Rosalynde Hagen." And the German words: "*Adresse Unbekannt*"—address not known.

Shansky whistled softly. "Your friend in Nice gives nice, quick service."

Hunter glanced at his watch. It was 9:28 A.M. The meeting he had scheduled for this morning was due to begin in two minutes.

Shansky took the picture from him. "I can be getting the copies while you're up there making your sales pitch. Unless you need me along to back you up."

"I'm used to holding my own hand," Hunter told him dryly. "Try USIS, around the corner. They're the most likely to have a copying machine free."

Shansky nodded and went out of the main embassy building, heading for the annex on the side street. Hunter climbed the em-bassy steps to the third-floor conference room he'd requested for his morning meeting. It is a large, dark-paneled room with dark blue carpeting. The tall windows overlook the trees that separate Avenue Gabriel from the end of the Champs-Élysées. All six of the men Hunter had asked to attend this meeting were already inside waiting for him, seated informally in black-padded chairs around the long oval of the glass-topped table.

In addition to Mort Crown from the embassy's security office, two of the other men present had the right to use green license plates bearing the prefix number 6-CD; which meant they were attached to the embassy staff. One was a liaison officer in France for the Bureau of Intelligence and Research, which is responsible for integrating "hard" information throughout all branches of the State Department. The other was the embassy's civil air attaché, concerned with all matters having to do with international cargo and passenger air traffic; except for those involving military planes.

The fourth man in the conference room was also permanently stationed in Paris, but not directly connected with the embassy: a major from the Personnel Security Division of the Army Intelligence Organization. His job was to try to give advance warning of any brewing threat to the safety—or reliability—of American military personnel in Western Europe.

The other two men present were "rovers"—for whom Paris was only one stopover in a tour of duty around Europe. These were the two Hunter was most interested in at the moment.

One he knew well from the past: Colonel James MacInnes. They had been students together at Army Intelligence Command's advanced school for branch officers, at Fort Holabird, Maryland. Mac-Innes was presently European rover for the Defense Department's Ultra Sensitive Positions Program. This is the agency charged with conducting follow-up security checks on any highly placed person with access to secret national defense materials or information. MacInnes' assignment was to co-ordinate the findings of the various USPP agents in Europe; reporting his own conclusions directly to the office of the Secretary of Defense, in Room 3E880 at the Pentagon.

The last man was Fred Rivers, a special agent for the Executive Protective Service. This is a branch of America's secret service agency. It is entrusted with protecting the lives of foreign diplomats in the United States. Rivers kept tabs on the European movements of members of terrorist groups: the Rengo Sekigun group from Japan, the German Baader-Meinhof gang, Uruguayan Tupamaros, Ireland's UDA, IRA, and Red-Hand Commandos, Spain's ETA, Italy's Red Brigade, the French Canadian Front de Libération du Québec, "Red Army" guerrillas from Turkey, and the Swiss anarchist "Baendlistrasse" group—in addition to the multiplying number of Arab terrorist organizations. His job was to alert the Executive Protective Service when he detected indications one of these groups was trying to infiltrate members for an operation in the United States.

Hunter passed out to these six men copies of Bel Jahra's picture and vital statistics. He then proceeded to explain what he knew about Bel Jahra, what he suspected, and what he needed.

"Each of you has his own network of contacts," Hunter told them. "I'm asking you to spread copies of Bel Jahra's picture to all of them. And the word: Whoever turns up anything on him—*any-thing*—I want to get it, fast. If I'm not here at the embassy, my secretary will know where I am, and pass it on to me. That's all I asked you here today for. Nothing complicated."

Jim MacInnes laughed. "*That* all? Hell, Simon, I'm so snowed under with my own work I'm just about managing five hours' sleep a day. Sometimes not that much. I reckon it's the same for all of us. I can pass on what you want to the people I meet—*as I meet them*. Not before. Beyond that—I got my own eggs to suck."

Hunter nodded amiably; but his eyes were stubborn. "I know that, Jim. Just do the best you can for me, okay? That's all I'm asking, from any of you."

He looked at the others. Their mirror images reflected unevenly on the glass top of the oval conference table. "It's this simple: The more people there are scattered around that know about Bel Jahra —the more chance one of them'll happen to know, or find out, something I could use concerning him. Sooner or later."

Fred Rivers had been studying Bel Jahra's picture. He looked up slowly, frowning. "That sooner-or-later business—there's your rub, Hunter. Sure I'll pass it on to my contacts. And I got some that're really good. Remember about the trip made to Korea back in 1971 by an Arab guerrilla courier? His code name is Bassam, which means "He Who Laughs." He had a meeting over there with some people from Japan. Members of the Rengo Sekigun group. *I'm* the one that found out about that meeting, through one of my contacts in Switzerland. You know *when* I found out? Two days *after* they pulled off the operation the meeting was all about: the massacre of all those Puerto Ricans at Lod Airport. Bassam's probably still laughing. I'm sure not."

Hunter made a loose fist, and rapped his knuckles on the polished wood of a table leg. "I'm looking for luck," he admitted evenly.

The Personnel Security major from Army Intelligence was leaning back in his chair, observing Hunter critically. "I have the feeling," he said slowly, "that you're looking for your luck in the wrong direction. You say yourself that this Bel Jahra is fairly new to the terrorist game. If you're right about him being the controller for that attempt in Rome, I'd say it was a onetime thing. Knowing what I do about the Arab outfits, he isn't likely to be given another opportunity for some time. Concentrate on the established guerrillas, Hunter." He tapped the picture of Bel Jahra on the table before him. "With this guy, I think you're taking a long run up a blind alley."

Hunter was silent for a moment, regarding him deliberately. Then he spoke, with equal deliberation: "I think you're mistaken."

"Would you mind explaining why?"

The air attaché shot an impatient look at the major. "Hunter's *already* explained his reasons for concentrating on Bel Jahra."

"Uh-huh. And I happen to disagree with them."

Hunter said, through his teeth: "I can't *force* you to co-operate, if you don't want to."

"Oh, I'll *co-operate*. As much as I can. But I just don't believe you're tackling the right end of things."

Hunter's smile was bland, almost pleasant. "If I get your co-operation, I guess I can learn to live with your disapproval."

The major gave a sulky shrug and began drumming his fingers impatiently on the table. The civil air attaché turned from him to Hunter. "Explain one thing to *me*. Suppose someone does locate this Bel Jahra. What do you propose doing then? You don't have enough hard evidence for any police force to arrest him. If you do get proof he's planning something, the French would probably merely expel him politely from the country. He could then return —here or elsewhere—under another identity. And start over again."

Rivers heaved a gloomy sigh. "That's been the big problem all along, in trying to do something about terrorists."

"Preventative surveillance is what I have in mind," Hunter said. He was not sure it was the whole truth. The cold hate stirred by Bel Jahra's face looking out of all those pictures on the table wouldn't subside. But neither his expression nor his voice revealed this: "If we can locate him, we can sew him up. Stay on top of every move he makes, and play it as it comes. At the least, we make it impossible for him to go on with whatever he's planning. At best, we get so much on him we can put him out of business."

MacInnes looked at him sardonically. "Thinking of driving him to suicide, maybe?"

Mort Crown drawled: "If he was to run into a hard rock on a dark night, *that'd* close him down pretty good."

The man from the State Department's Bureau of Intelligence and Research had been looking upset but biding his time. Now he spoke up: "I don't like any of this. I'll tell you what's been worrying *me*. You're talking about hurting this guy, or anyway making a lot of trouble for him. Right? And you say he's probably backed by the Libyans. So for a starter, we get Libya sore at us. . . ."

"They hate us anyway," Mort Crown pointed out.

"Exactly my point. This'll make it worse. On top of that, suppose Bel Jahra takes a prominent part in another coup in Morocco? One that succeeds. Then he'll be a big wheel in the new Moroccan government. Able to make trouble for *us*. So we'll have made America's relations with both Libya and Morocco that much more difficult. I've seen things like that happen before."

"You may remember," Hunter told him thinly, "that we're talking about a criminal responsible for a bomb that killed four adults and a baby. Now, I have a crazy theory. It's not popular with some I know. But I kinda like it. It goes like this: What stops the wholesale murder of innocent people is automatically good for the U.S.A. Okay?"

Fred Rivers was shaking his head bitterly. "That's a noble sentiment, Hunter. I admit it's the one *I* operate on, too. But you won't find many others who agree with us."

"I know that."

"Sure you know it. In your head. But do you know it in your guts?" Rivers sighed wearily. "You're a cop, and an ex-soldier. Both of those professions are very unpopular these days. It's the *terrorist* everybody likes. Everybody."

Rivers held up a stiff finger. "First, he's a hero to every kind of revolutionary—no matter how many innocents he kills."

Rivers held up a second finger. "The biggest businesses in the world back him, to the limit. With their money, and their power. Because the international oil companies want to keep the Arabs co-operative, and almost every other kind of industry runs on oil or oil by-products."

The third finger shot up. "And because of big business, and big politics, most of the governments of the world back the terrorist. Or at least protect and excuse him. Including some people in our own government. So the terrorist has it all, now. He's popular, and he's got most of the authorities on his side; the powers that be. What've *you* got? You're all by yourself, pal. Doing a lonely, unpopular job."

Hunter's expression was wooden. "It's still my job. And I'm still going to do it. The big business interests, the fanatics that like terror tactics, the governments that look the other way—they can all go *screw* themselves."

The BIR man from State asked him softly: "May I quote you?"

Hunter looked at him with bleak humor. "I expect you will, as fast as you can."

When the conference broke up, half an hour later, Hunter was discounting any help from State's BIR man and the Personnel Security major. The others, he knew, would do what they could. Even there, however, MacInnes' point was valid: Their assistance would only be marginal. If one of their contacts came up with something on Bel Jahra, it would be gravy. But the meat-and-potatoes digging would still have to be done by Hunter and Shansky.

Shansky was waiting in his office, sitting in Hunter's chair with his legs up on Hunter's desk. "How'd it go?"

"Four to two, our favor."

"That's something, I guess. I don't know exactly what."

"It gives us that many more people who know about Bel Jahra. The girl's pictures ready?"

Shansky swung his legs off the desk and took some small copies of Rosalynde Hagen's photograph from the right-hand pocket of his jacket. "These're for you." He tapped his left pocket. "Suppose I take the high road with mine? I've been on the low one long enough, for real. For you, it'll be slumming."

"Fair enough." Hunter pocketed his copies and led the way out, and down the stairs. They parted outside the embassy. Shansky

ambled off in search of the prosperous whores along the Champs-
Élysées. Hunter headed for Les Halles.

The Halles is no longer what it represented for so long: the
stomach of Paris—a vast, bustling conglomeration of huge meat,
produce, and flea markets; full of cheerful din and thousands of
tradition-proud, independent-minded working people. The Gaullist
government decided to cut out the city's stomach, in the interests
of a more modern-looking France. A high-rise office complex and
a very deep parking garage are supposed to take its place, eventually.

When Hunter arrived at the Halles that overcast spring day, all
there was to be seen was a monster-sized hole in the ground: six
blocks long by five blocks wide. So deep that the huge red-and-
yellow steam shovels and bulldozers working the bottom looked like
moving matchboxes. The hole was already eighteen stories down,
and they were still digging; surging through lakes of brown mud
left by a rain the night before.

The only vestige Hunter could see of the old markets was a
gutted iron skeleton teetering at one edge of the hole, near the
church of Saint-Eustache. Around all the other edges rose the
blocks of tall, narrow seventeenth- and eighteenth-century houses,
their curved, slate-gray roofs shiny under a low blanket of dingy
cloud. Many of them had been abandoned; as though their inhabitants had been the first to flee in fear that all of Paris was soon
doomed to fall into that hole. Hunter's ears were pounded by the
racket of wrecker's steam hammers at work demolishing them;
hurriedly destroying the evidence of the government's insanity.

He left the monstrous open grave behind, and walked into the
warren of crooked streets behind the buildings around the edge.
A wreckage-littered passage led between a half-demolished house
and an abandoned bistro, its windows smashed and the zinc-and-
copper bar inside covered with plaster and dust. At the other end
of the passage Hunter entered a crowded area where the old
teeming life still bustled noisily; where the myriad little bistros and
smaller markets carried on as before, though now with a sprinkling
of boutiques and antique shops among them. An area never abandoned by the inexpensive whores who were so integral a part of
the traditional Halles ambience; big hole or no big hole.

Les Halles has the youngest and often prettiest whores in Paris

—and also some of the oldest. This is where most of the new girls come to learn their trade. Having acquired the experience, and the expertise with male frailties that is more coveted by Frenchmen than youth or looks, most of them move up to the more expensive hooker areas of Pigalle—and possibly even the Champs-Élysées. And then, when the passing years make them less obviously alluring to higher-income transient customers, many return home to Les Halles to finish their careers in familiar, friendly surroundings. Some of the old ones, however, started there young and never left. They remain, forming lasting relationships with steady clients who come to treasure their particular charms, and grow old along with them.

But the whores don't start working Les Halles until lunchtime. So Hunter began by showing Rosalynde Hagen's picture around the bistros, shops, and markets. Especially to "the strong ones" of Les Halles, when he spotted them; powerful porters famed for their ability to carry a huge barrel of wine or half a steer on their backs. Most of these men now work outside Paris, where the big markets have been moved. But they come back here, some once each week, to visit the same whores they always patronized.

Two of them, and a bistro owner, knew Rosalynde from the past. But not where she could be found now.

It began to drizzle shortly after noon. But Hunter's hands told him it wouldn't last long. He went through the narrow Rue Pierre Lescot and entered the Guillaume Tell, a bistro of old-fashioned dignity near the Étienne Marcel metro station. The old couple who ran the place didn't recognize the girl in Hunter's photograph. But a hefty truck driver having a *pastis* at the zinc-top bar did.

"I'm sure I went with this one a few times, perhaps two years back." He studied Rosalynde's picture and scratched his bristly jaw with a thick, cracked thumbnail. "I don't remember what she called herself. But she was a good girl. Intelligent. Understanding."

"Seen her around lately?" Hunter asked him.

"No. If I had, I would have gone with her again."

"Who was she friendly with?"

"I don't know. Some of the other girls, certainly. They'll be coming to work soon." The truck driver smiled happily. "That's what I'm waiting for, too."

Hunter ordered an omelet, and ate it at a black wooden table with a white marble top, in the dry warmth of the Guillaume Tell's back room. By the time he'd finished his lunch, the rain had ended and the overcast was breaking open to reveal incredibly pure blue patches. Hunter went out to talk to the whores.

The whores of the Champs-Élysées area refer to themselves as call girls or models. Their clothes are elegant, they own good cars, and they charge enough to be able to afford both. With calm patience, they sit for hours in the big tourist cafés, the posh side-street bars, and their own parked cars; waiting for well-to-do foreigners who make up the greatest percentage of their customers. With the prices they charge, they can afford to wait. Three or four customers a day are enough for a comfortable income.

By two that afternoon, Shansky had completed his search through the blocks along one side of the Champs-Élysées. He crossed to the other side at the Étoile end and began working his way back down in the direction of Concorde. So far he'd found no one who remembered Rosalynde Hagen from her picture. It was possible she had neven risen to the top income bracket of this area. Shansky decided to give it another hour. If he didn't connect by then, he would switch to the middle-bracket area between the Madeleine and the Opéra.

Glancing into the Rue Balzac, Shansky saw three cars double-parked in a line behind each other. Each with a lovely lady waiting behind the wheel. The girl in the first car cocked her head and smiled faintly as he strolled over. The prostitutes of this area are conscious of the obligations of superior status. They don't beckon imperiously, like those of Les Halles. Neither do they grab you physically, like the ones in Pigalle. A small smile, a hint that it might be possible; this is sufficient. Shansky ducked his head in the open side window and showed a picture of Rosalynde Hagen.

"I'm trying to find this one."

The girl in the car glanced at the picture. "She is very pretty. But I think I am just as pretty. You don't agree?"

She had deep dimples when she smiled. Shansky pushed aside the temptation. "This is business. If you can help me locate her, I'll pay you for it. *Do* you know her?"

The girl studied the picture and thought about it. "Perhaps . . ."

Shansky read the way she was thinking about it. "You won't get paid until whatever you tell me turns out true."

She laughed softly. "In that case, no—I'm afraid I don't know her."

Shansky tried the girls in the other two cars. The last one thought she'd seen the girl in the picture before, in a bar on Rue Lord Byron.

It was a plush, discreetly lighted place, with a vaguely tropical motif and curved high-backed booths affording privacy. It had just opened for the day. There was no one behind the bar when Shansky entered; and no customers yet. Only a blue-jowled man working on a business ledger in a front booth; and a girl who looked and dressed like a Dior model perched haughtily on a padded barstool, gazing at last night's dreams.

She dropped the haughty look as soon as Shansky perched beside her. Her smile was warm without being aggressive. Her voice was quiet: "Shall we have a drink?"

Shansky put the picture on the bar. "Know her?"

The bar girl glanced at the picture and nodded. "Rosalynde. She doesn't work here anymore."

"Where does she work now? And live."

She shook her head. "We were never that close. Try the boss." She nodded at the man with the ledger.

Shansky went over and showed him the picture.

"She used to come around," the man admitted warily. "But not for the last year."

"Where'd she live when she did work here?"

"I wouldn't know. She didn't *work* for me. Just hung around, sometimes. I don't even know her last name." He was obviously worried about the Sécurité Sociale, which he wouldn't have paid out for a bar girl, though he was supposed to by law.

"I'm not a cop, for Christ's sake," Shansky told him. "I'll pay for the information."

But the man stuck obstinately to his lack of any pertinent information. In the end Shansky believed him. The girl didn't have anything further, either. Shansky left the bar and went into the *tabac* next door. He bought an excellent Havana cigar and phoned Hunter's extension at the embassy. There was no message from Hunter. Shansky went out and continued his search.

The girls of Les Halles don't solicit in the bars. Some lean against corners on the tiny side streets between Saint-Denis and Pierre

Lescot. But more are to be found just inside every narrow doorway with the word "Hotel" painted over it. Just that; no name.

The men of Les Halles gather in tight bunches in front of each of these doorways. From time to time, one goes in and strikes a bargain. Others pause for a few seconds, and then move on. But some stand there for as much as fifteen minutes; admiring, desiring, wrestling with the problem of whether they can really afford a few minutes in a room upstairs.

The whores inside the doorways grin at them, unabashed. They don't mind being on display, like diamonds in a jeweler's window. Some of the men are foreign tourists, of course; Germans who leer, Americans struggling with their own embarrassment, Englishmen who appear to be making scientific studies of native life. But most are French workers, staring with open admiration and respect.

There were three girls behind the glass door of the "hotel" entrance on Rue Saint-Denis, across from the Saint-Leu church. One sat partway up the dingy inner stairs, elbows on knees, chin cupped in her hands, gazing thoughtfully out at the street. The other two leaned against the flaking walls just inside the glass door, chatting casually with each other as they automatically beckoned at any new passerby who paused. All three looked fresh and healthy, with firm, ripe young bodies in low-cut blouses and differently colored miniskirts.

They waved and smiled saucily when Hunter paused to look at them. The two against the walls were in their teens. The one on the stairs was in her early twenties. She had carroty red hair and freckles, reminding him of Odile Lamarck. The notion amused him. She saw she had his interest, stood up and braced her hands on rounded hips, cocking her head at him challengingly.

Hunter walked inside and opened the glass door. "How much?" he asked the red-haired one. The other two leaned against their walls in businesslike silence. He had made his choice; now there was a bargain to be struck.

The girl on the stairs considered his accent. "Only a hundred francs," she told him sweetly, for openers.

Hunter got out the picture of Rosalynde Hagen. "I'll give you fifty, if you can tell me where to find this girl."

The three of them looked at the picture in his hand. The red-haired one asked: "Why? You used to go with her?"

"Fifty," Hunter repeated firmly.

The girl on his right said, "That's Rosalynde. Remember?"

The one on the steps nodded. "The German bitch. I never got along with her. Too full of herself." She looked to Hunter again. "Anyway, she hasn't been around here in over a year."

"Where *has* she been?"

"Who knows?"

Hunter got out a fifty-franc note. He dangled it between thumb and forefinger, letting them look at it. They delved into their memories, but couldn't find much.

"She used to go with Whisper Charlie," the girl on his right remembered. "At least I saw her with him, a few months ago."

"Where?"

"The bird market. She was buying him a canary."

"Has he got a last name?"

"I don't know it. Only Whisper Charlie. They call him that because he can't talk loud. He got hit in the throat. In a fight."

"Ring fight? Or street?"

"Street. He doesn't box professionally. He's just a tough boy. Girls like him."

Hunter had the feeling *she* liked him; or had. "Where does he live?"

The girl shrugged. "I don't know anymore. He moves around a lot. But he works at the Hello Club in Pigalle sometimes, as a doorman."

Doormen for the tourist traps in Pigalle serve two functions: They drag in passing suckers, and throw them out if they don't walk out when their money is gone. Hunter tried a few more questions. The girl guessed, obliquely, that when Whisper Charlie was not working as a tourist trap doorman, he handled strong-arm jobs for any petty gang with the cash to pay for it. That was all she knew.

Hunter gave her the fifty and went to Pigalle.

The Moulin Rouge, where Toulouse Lautrec used to draw his cancan dancers, still stands there on the Boulevard de Clichy in Pigalle's honky-tonk heart. And the whores that were another favorite Lautrec subject, and passion, still abound in the side streets around it. But the types of whores, and bars, are sharply divided by the wide boulevard; as though the shooting galleries in the middle are there to prevent passage across a border between two countries.

On one side of the boulevard the bars are sleazy; and the whores rough, middle-aging, and aggressive in their sales approach. A favorite approach, on the streets or in the bars, is to seize the penis and testicles of a prospective customer through the material of his trousers. This can also serve another purpose: riveting the man's attention on one part of him, while a hand more gently removes the wallet from another part of him.

On the other side of Boulevard de Clichy the bars have a brassy Las Vegas look. And the whores are young and soft; with a startling percentage as pretty as movie starlets. The Hello Club was on this side, near the triangle formed by Rue Pigalle and Rue Frochot.

Each of the pretty young girls lining the right sidewalk of Rue Pigalle spoke to Hunter in turn as he came down past them from the boulevard; each asking softly if he would not care to go home with her for an hour of love. Doormen tried to snatch at his arm and warn him these girls were of low quality; the really talented whores being inside their particular traps. At the corner Hunter turned off Pigalle into the Rue de Douai. There was no doorman on duty yet at the Hello Club. Hunter went inside.

A very lovely blonde in a very low cut black evening gown slid off the first barstool and blocked his way with a friendly smile. She didn't go in for the crotch-grabbing indulged in on the other side of the boulevard. She only cushioned her soft breasts against him and looked in his eyes. "A little wine and love?" she asked demurely.

Hunter said: "I'm looking for Whisper Charlie."

The bosom was withdrawn. "He doesn't work here anymore."

"Where would I find him?"

"Don't ask me. He's not my onions. I don't like them that tough."

"Who *would* know about him?"

"Babette, for sure. She owns this dump. Whisper Charlie's her cousin."

"Is she here?"

"Not now. She's out in the country somewhere, for the day. Some fresh air for her kids."

"When'll she be back?"

"She usually gets here by nine at night."

Hunter glanced at his watch. It was 4:30 P.M.

The blonde gave him a speculative look. "What about that wine and love, while you're waiting?" Suddenly, she laughed good-naturedly. "Or at least a beer and some friendly conversation?"

Hunter ordered two beers and went in the back. He phoned the embassy and left word for Shansky. When he returned to the bar there were two tall beers on it and the blonde in the low-cut gown was waiting with them. She took a long swallow of hers as he settled on the stool beside her and asked the bartender if he knew where Whisper Charlie could be found. He didn't. Neither did the other two bar girls.

"Don't worry," the blonde reassured him. "I told you, Babette will know."

"When she gets here," Hunter pointed out irritably.

"That's right." The blonde took another long swallow of her beer.

"Don't hurry it," Hunter warned her. "You won't get another. Unless you say something interesting."

"Try me. Sex, politics, or sports?"

Hunter put Rosalynde Hagen's picture on the bar. "Know her?"

There was no hesitation: "Whisper Charlie's girl. She's German, I think."

"Know where *she* lives?"

"No. I've just seen them together. He still comes around sometimes. Sometimes with her."

"Recently?"

"Last night."

Hunter ordered her another beer.

It was 5 P.M. when Juliet Shale left Bel Jahra's apartment in Roquebrune. She had stolen three hours from her work for Valasi, including the party preparations, to achieve that short afternoon of pleasure in Bel Jahra's bed. But as she understood it, he had done much more than she to get those brief hours together: His business in Paris would continue for at least two more days. He had flown down for the day only to be with her.

She was deeply touched—and Bel Jahra now had an official engraved invitation to Dezso Valasi's party.

An hour after she left, he was on his way to the airport. He wore a light brown moustache, lightly tinted sunglasses, and an excellent brown wig a shade darker than the moustache. If you had known him well for some time, and looked closely to see if it was him, you would penetrate the disguise. But not if he was only one in a long line of passing possibles you were scanning; after doing the same with previous lines, and anticipating doing so again with more.

No one recognized him boarding the plane at the Côte d'Azur Airport, nor during the flight, nor when he got off at Paris-Orly at 8 P.M.

It was shortly after 10 P.M. when Hunter and Shansky arrived at Whisper Charlie Moinier's address. It was in a dark and dismal back street near the Bastille. The building, blackened by centuries of grime, had once been a royal château. Now the main section was a plywood factory, the right wing a storage warehouse, and the left wing had been cut up into cheap one-room apartments. They entered the left wing.

Shansky lit their way up three flights of creaky, dark stairs with a pocket flashlight. There was no light showing under Whisper Charlie's door or through the keyhole. They knocked. No response; no sounds from inside. Hunter got a wire lock-pick out. There were two locks on the door, different types. Shansky watched admiringly as Hunter unlocked both.

They went in and shut the door behind them. Hunter relocked both locks from inside while Shansky flashed his light around, careful not to let it point at the single dusty window. The room was large, cluttered, and untidy. A huge unmade bed, a big sofa with clothes dumped on it, two bureaus with male and female toiletries piled on their tops, a number of chairs, and a wide table with dirty dishes, opened cans, and a canary in a cage.

Most of the wallpaper had long since peeled away. Whisper Charlie had covered the big bare patches with pictures cut from magazines and newspapers: sports figures, combat photographs, scenes from Western and gangster movies, and naked girls. There was an open side alcove with a toilet, a double hotplate on a shelf, and a sink filled with more dirty dishes. But no Whisper Charlie.

They settled down to wait for him. A wait that stretched through a long night, with them taking turns sleeping. But they were both awake when he finally unlocked his door and walked in—a few minutes before eight in the morning.

SIXTEEN

He was about twenty-five, of average height but with the heft of a weight lifter. Short thick legs in tight faded dungarees; burly torso stretching the dirt-stained material of his black pullover. There was scar tissue across the punching knuckles of his wide fists, and more of it slightly distorting the left side of his upper lip. A nose that had been broken and never set properly gave exactly the right touch to a reckless, hard-ugly face of the kind attractive to women with a masochistic streak in them.

Shansky was sitting on the sofa and Hunter stood against the wall next to the door when he stepped into his apartment. He was about to shut the door when he saw them. Until then he'd had the groggy look of someone who'd gone an entire night without sleep. But his reaction was instant: He twisted to dodge back out through the still-open door.

Hunter took a long side step, caught his wrist with one hand, and spun him across the room. His legs tangled and he sprawled across the unmade bed. Hunter kicked the door shut and put his back to it. Shansky stayed on the sofa, watching interestedly.

Charlie did a fast roll across the bed and landed nimbly on his feet on the other side of it, whipping something from his back pocket. There was a tiny snicking sound, and a long, sharp blade flashed into the open from the push-button knife in his fist. He shot a glance toward Shansky, saw he was still just sitting, and started around the bed toward Hunter. He held the knife expertly: low and forward, the point aiming up and out. He advanced slowly in a slight crouch, well balanced.

Hunter stayed where he was, watching him come. "I don't want to hurt you," he said with quiet concern.

The tone of it made Charlie pause. He took in Hunter's size; and thought about the careless ease with which he'd been flung across the room.

Shansky decided the fun was over. He drew out a five-hundred-franc note—a bit more than a hundred dollars then—and dangled it before him at eye level. "We're here to give you money, Charlie, not trouble. Relax. We're not the cops."

Charlie looked at the money, then shot his attention back to Hunter leaning against the door. "I can *hear* you're not French," he sneered in a thin, strained voice. French cops were the only ones he worried about; he didn't deal in anything big enough to interest any others.

"That's right," Hunter told him soothingly. "We're American businessmen. With a business proposition for you."

"So why break in here?" The voice was still strained thin, an impairment of the vocal cords.

Hunter shrugged a shoulder. "You weren't home, so we had to wait."

"Where were you?" Shansky asked casually. "With your girl friend Rosalynde?"

Charlie blinked. "No . . ." he said cautiously. "I . . . had a night job." He was still poised with the knife.

Hunter said, "Put away the knife, Charlie. It's a money proposition we're offering you. You do work for money?"

Charlie lowered the knife, but did not close it or put it aside. "What kind of job?"

"Information." Shansky rustled the five-hundred note.

Charlie shook his head angrily. "I'm not a pigeon."

"And we're not cops," Hunter reminded him. "It's a business matter. You get that *first* five hundred if your girl Rosalynde's got another boyfriend, too. A tall, handsome Moroccan. In his thirties."

"I thought he was Tunisian," Charlie said.

Hunter felt warm pleasure flowing through him. He got a picture of Bel Jahra and stepped away from the door. The knife instantly jerked up protectively. Hunter stopped and looked at Charlie disapprovingly. "If you don't put that away, I'll have to take it away."

Charlie considered the measured tone and the matter-of-fact expression. He backed to a bureau and put the knife on it. But stayed near it.

Hunter shook his head. "No. Close it. We can't talk business if you don't trust us."

"If we wanted to hurt you," Shansky pointed out sensibly, "we'd have been waiting for you with guns." He rustled the money again.

Charlie closed the knife and stuck it back in his pocket. His grin was almost sheepish. "So, okay—tell me the proposition."

Hunter showed him Bel Jahra's picture. "This Rosalynde's other boyfriend?"

Charlie looked at it. "Hamid Adir, yeah. He's from Tunisia. A businessman, travels around a lot. He keeps Rosalynde to screw when he's in Paris."

Shansky nodded happily. "And you screw her when he's not."

Charlie shrugged a burly shoulder. "Sometimes. I screw other girls, too. She's not the only one on my string. What the hell, I'm young and healthy."

Hunter flicked the picture of Bel Jahra. "Is he in Paris now?"

"He wasn't, yesterday. I don't know about last night. Like I said, I was working." Charlie got a worried look. "You still haven't told me the proposition. He's a business rival, and you want him beat up a little? I don't do any *killing*."

"We don't even want him beat up," Hunter told him. "Just found, so we can talk to him."

Charlie looked at the money in Shansky's fingers. "You can find him easy, if he's in Paris. It's his apartment Rosalynde lives in, up in Montmartre."

"What's the address?"

Charlie went on looking at the money.

"Give it to him," Hunter told Shansky.

The money changed hands, and vanished into Charlie's pocket. He told them the address.

Hunter opened the door. "You come show us," he told Charlie. "There could be another five hundred for you."

They went out together. It was fifteen minutes before nine in the morning.

At nine o'clock Bel Jahra was fully dressed and finishing his coffee with a croissant in the main room of the apartment in Montmartre. Rosalynde was sipping her coffee on the couch, sitting cross-legged without a stitch on her provocative little body. Her nakedness didn't stir Bel Jahra this morning. He'd had a full night of her. Now he wanted to be off on his own. He never took walks with her, or even ate out in restaurants with her. Except in bed, he found her boring.

Besides, there was his meeting this morning with al-Omared. He'd phoned the house on Parc Monceau and learned that al-Omared would not be in until eleven. But he wanted to use the next two hours walking by himself, and thinking.

He took a last sip of coffee, finished off the croissant, and pushed back his chair. Rising, he got some money from his pocket and put it on the table. "The rent, and enough to take care of yourself for a couple weeks."

That he was leaving again after only one night did not surprise Rosalynde Hagen. By now she was used to him coming and going without explanation or warning. She didn't know anything about his business, connections, or where he went and returned from. Nor was she overly curious. All that interested her was that he paid her bills and didn't take up too much of her time.

"When will I see you again?" she asked, uncurling from the couch as he picked up his overnight bag.

Bel Jahra watched her stand up and stretch, yawning sleepily. "I may call you in about ten days. Not before that, certainly." He wasn't sure he would see her even then. It was unlikely that he'd be able to re-enter Europe for some time after the slaughter at Valasi's party. If that was a success, he might not want to. He'd be busy preparing the coup he dreamed of. But he knew from experience that he might begin wanting another taste of Rosalynde, no matter how occupied he became. In which case he could phone and have her meet him someplace both safe and enjoyable. Beirut, probably.

"I'll miss you," she told him with a pretty pout. It was true enough. She enjoyed variety in her life. He gave her a special kind of sexual excitement; just as Charlie gave her another kind; and occasional one-night flings with some new man or woman gave her still others. She was genuinely fond of the man she knew as Hamid Adir, and she stood on tiptoes to wrap her slim bare arms around his neck and give him a passionate farewell kiss.

Bel Jahra's mind—and emotions—were already totally engaged in what lay ahead. He gave her a light slap on her saucy buttocks, disengaged himself, and went out.

Hunter, Shansky, and Whisper Charlie arrived fifteen minutes later. From across the street, Charlie nodded at the building on Rue Duratin. "That's it. Top floor, Apartment Nine."

Hunter looked up at the top-floor windows hungrily. "Take him to that *tabac* on the corner," he told Shansky. "Call her and find out if our man's in there with her."

Shansky and Charlie went off to the corner of Duratin and Lepic. Hunter stayed where he was, watching the windows up there. Their panes of glass reflected the morning sunlight, revealing nothing inside.

Shansky returned with Charlie five minutes later. Hunter took one look at his face and guessed the answer before he asked the question: "What happened?"

"We missed him," Shansky snarled. "*Just* missed him. He was up there with her *all night*. And now he's gone."

Hunter looked back to the house across the street, his face savage. "Sweet Jesus . . ." He fought to make his facial muscles relax.

"She asked me to come up," Charlie said. "So that means he's on his way out of Paris again. She never lets me in if he's around. Too much chance he'll walk in and surprise us."

"I already called Mort Crown," Shansky told Hunter. "He'll get some men out to Orly fast; and the likeliest train stations. But if he goes out by car or bus . . ." He shrugged.

"Probably will," Hunter said bleakly, "the way our luck's running." He rubbed a hand hard across knotted muscles along his jaw.

"I had Charlie here tell her to meet him at the Dôme, in Montparnasse. I figure I'll go with him, and see what she knows. If anything. And it'll give you plenty of time to pop in for a look around."

Hunter nodded gloomily. Bel Jahra was somewhere around them, here in Paris. But Paris was an awfully big city. And if he was on his way out, there was no time to spread any kind of dragnet that would be worth the effort.

He got a five-hundred-franc note from his pocket and turned to Charlie. "You don't tell her about our interest in the guy that keeps her. Shansky's just a new friend of yours. You help him pump her, but carefully. And after that you stick with her and try to pick up more."

Charlie grinned at the money. "Don't worry. I'll help any way you want."

Hunter gave him the five hundred. "You get another one of these, every time you come through with something we like."

Ten minutes after they'd gone off to Montparnasse, Hunter saw Rosalynde Hagen come out of the house across the street and hurry around the corner in the direction of the Blanche metro station. He recognized her with no trouble. She looked exactly like her picture, but even younger: about fifteen, and a whore. Hunter entered a little deeper into the mind of Bel Jahra.

After she was out of sight around the corner, he crossed the street and entered the building. Climbing to the top landing, he picked her lock and went in. Shutting the door, he stood inside for a moment looking grimly at the two recently used coffee cups on the table. Then he began a systematic shakedown of the place.

It took him over ten minutes to search every inch of the main room. There was not a single item in it that revealed anything about Bel Jahra. He went in the bedroom.

There were some men's clothes in the closet and bureau. No labels, nothing traceable, nothing in the pockets. Nothing useful anywhere else, either; not behind the drawers, nor under the mattress or rug; and nothing tucked in any little hiding place in the bathroom. A blank.

It disappointed him, but didn't surprise him. He was reaching for a miracle. And miracles were in short supply these days. Hunter went to the phone in the main room and copied down the number. Then he let himself out, relocking the door.

He found a taxi at Place Clichy and had it take him to the embassy. To arrange with Mort Crown for a round-the-clock tap on Rosalynde Hagen's phone—and round-the-clock stake-out on her place. He didn't really expect Bel Jahra to call her and say where he was. That would be another miracle. He was just doing another cop routine: spreading glue every place he could think of. If you spread enough of it around, sooner or later your fly had to step in it, somewhere.

Sooner or later. As Fred Rivers had said, there was the rub.

Al-Omared sat behind the long Louis XV desk with his back to the library windows of his house on the Parc Monceau. In this position the thin sunlight filtering through the day curtains left his face shadowed, while revealing every nuance of expression on the face of Bel Jahra, who was seated on the other side of the desk facing the windows. Al-Omared was as interested in gauging the Moroccan's inner emotions as he was in judging what Bel Jahra was telling him of the practical steps he had taken toward their mutual goal since they'd last met.

On both counts, emotional and practical, al-Omared found the man across from him as solid as when he had first revealed his plan for the double assassination. When he was sure of this, al-Omared nodded approvingly and leaned back in his Voltaire armchair, permitting himself a benign smile. "You are a thorough man," he pronounced. "I can find no fault or lack in any of this. You have been able to obtain the name of the company which insures the Valasi estate?"

Bel Jahra nodded. "This I learned yesterday from Valasi's social secretary. The fire and theft coverage for the place on Cap Martin is handled by the Assurances Générales de France."

"Excellent. The AGF is part of the Phenix international insurance group. It will not be difficult for me to acquire the bonding documents you need through channels which cannot later be traced back. You have the pictures of the men to be attached to these documents?"

Bel Jahra slid a small envelope across the desk. Al-Omared took from it five formal full-face portrait photographs. These were the five commandos Bel Jahra planned to infiltrate into the party as part of the catering staff. Al-Omared spread the photographs out and studied each face in turn. Again he nodded approvingly. "Each seems to me a good man."

"They *are* good men," Bel Jahra said flatly. "They will arrive over the next three days, separately, through various routes—Belgium, Germany, Switzerland, and Italy. They will proceed separately to Nice, where my aide Hammou has booked them into separate houses. So the sudden gathering of five men there will not be noticeable."

"And the other five men? Your second commando group?"

"Will arrive in the same boat that brings the arms and explosives from Libya. The transfer to the yacht Bashir Mawdri has waiting will take place at sea, by night. If, at the time of the transfer, I feel certain this second group will not be needed, they will stay aboard the first boat and return with it to Tripoli."

Al-Omared put the five photographs back in the envelope. "It will require perhaps two or three days to obtain the insurance bonds for these five. When they are ready, one of my people will deliver them to you personally at your apartment in Roquebrune. I assume you already have the other documents these men will need: the work and residence cards, passports, et cetera."

"These were all prepared by the government printing plant in Tripoli before I left. I brought them with me."

"And the name of the chief security man the insurance company will have at the Valasi party?"

"This, too, I learned yesterday. His name is Gilbert Soumagnac." Bel Jahra had found this out from Juliet Shale, along with the name of the insurance company, by expressing concern for the safety of Valasi's valuable paintings, with such a large catering staff wandering about the place. "Soumagnac will have four security men with him."

"You *are* thorough," al-Omared repeated. "You overlook no detail, and attend to each efficiently. I believe, even more now than at our first meeting, that your plan will succeed."

Bel Jahra looked at him with a quiet smile. "With luck, as you pointed out."

"Luck is most likely to operate in favor of a man who gives it every opportunity. This you do, Ahmed. My faith in your future continues to grow."

Bel Jahra left the house on the Parc Monceau considering with deep satisfaction what the faith of a man like al-Omared could mean to that future. Carrying his overnight bag, he got into a taxi on Avenue Hoche and had it take him across the Seine to the Luxembourg Gardens. For some time he strolled through the gardens, seeming to be merely enjoying the trees and statues, turning to admire them from various angles. Reaching the large circular pool behind the Palais du Luxembourg, Bel Jahra walked around it slowly, watching the children sailing their boats across it. Then he turned without warning and retraced his steps, circling the pool in the opposite direction.

When he was entirely assured that no one had followed him from the area around al-Omared's house, Bel Jahra left the gardens. He walked quickly down the Rue Tournon, past the houses where John Paul Jones and Casanova had lived, and turned right on Sulpice toward the Odéon Métro. Going into one of the big bistros facing the metro station, he went down the steps to a basement men's room. It was unoccupied. Bel Jahra went in, locked the door, and opened his overnight bag.

When he came out he was a different man: moustache, sunglasses, and wig; plus a different jacket. He got into one of the taxis lined up beside the metro, and had it take him out to Orly, where he purchased a seat on the next plane to Nice. He was seen by both of the men Mort Crown had planted at the airport. Neither recognized him from the photograph that had been given to them. Observers at the Côte d'Azur Airport also failed to recognize him getting off the plane. No one bothered to note down the license of his rented car; and no one tried to tail it as he drove away from the airport to check with Hammou and Mawdri's Nice agent on the preparations for the arrival of his first commando group.

There was a phone message waiting for Hunter at the American Embassy in Paris. The caller had left no name; only a phone number in Nice. Hunter recognized it as the number Uri Ezan had given him for contacting Mossad on the Riviera.

A man whose voice Hunter did not recognize answered in French at the other end: "Good day— Hôtel Lédru."

"My name is Simon Hunter," he told the man. "I have a message to call this number."

"Just a moment, Mr. Hunter. . . ."

The next voice on the phone was a woman: "Mr. Hunter, Uri Ezan wants to talk to you. If you'll let me know where you will be for the next hour, I'm sure I can find him quickly."

Hunter gave her his number at the embassy. Twenty minutes later, Uri phoned his office: "Simon?"

"Yes. What're you doing in Nice?"

"Kosso Shamir has disappeared." Uri's voice was quietly serious, tightly restrained. "Yesterday he saw Bel Jahra get off a plane from Athens. Kosso left word, and followed him. There has been no word from him since. Nothing. This can mean only one thing."

Hunter said slowly: "I'm sorry, Uri. He was a nice boy." But his mind was already dealing with what it meant.

As though reading his mind, Uri said heavily: "One thing is certain now. Bel Jahra is here, somewhere along the Riviera. And that is why I am here."

"He was in Paris last night," Hunter told him. "But he's on his way out again." He explained, briefly, how he knew it. "This gives me another reason to think he's heading back in your direction. How long will you be there?"

The hot rage that Hunter knew Uri Ezan to be capable of simmered just under the surface of his controlled tone: "I lived for many years across the street from Kosso's family. I know him since he was born. I will stay," he finished deliberately, "until this Bel Jahra is found."

"I'll be down there this evening," Hunter told him. He hung up and strolled to his office windows, gazing down at the Place de la Concorde as he methodically considered each of a number of points apparent from Uri's call:

Since the bomb explosion at Leonardo da Vinci, Bel Jahra had been in the Côte d'Azur area at least two separate times. His presence in that area was no longer an educated hunch. The circumstances around Kosso's disappearance made it fact.

Which increased the likelihood that Hunter's original instinct had been correct: Bel Jahra was now involved in something somewhere along the Riviera.

Kosso's disappearance almost certainly meant he was dead. Which in turn meant that from now on, for the duration, Hunter could expect the total, determined help of Mossad in tracking down Bel Jahra.

But Kosso's disappearance created a new problem. And a question. Bel Jahra had caught Kosso trying to tail him. Had there been time, before killing Kosso, to question him under torture? If so, Bel Jahra now knew all about who was searching for him; and why. Even if Kosso had died without talking, Bel Jahra knew that *somebody* was on to him, trying to track him down. So from now on Bel Jahra would be taking precautions to insure that no one could spot him again.

Hunter was deep inside Bel Jahra's mind, working out what to do about this last problem, when Shansky came in looking none too happy.

"Whisper Charlie's gonna stick with the girl," he told Hunter as he flopped into a chair. "We can depend on him to give us anything of interest that turns up. He likes the dough. But I don't think she knows a goddamned thing about Bel Jahra that'll be of use. I did get *one* thing out of her, though: When he left her this morning, he said she definitely wouldn't hear from him again for at least ten days." Shansky fell silent, watching for Hunter's reaction.

Hunter didn't say anything for a time. He took the three Byzantine coins from his pocket and jingled them in his fist, scowling at Shansky as though looking beyond him at something not in that room. Then he opened his fist and looked down at the coins. He examined them as if he had never seen them before, his dark eyes narrow and the lines getting deeper down the sides of his face.

"Sounds to me," he said finally, "like that's our time limit."

Shansky nodded. "I agree. Whatever it is Bel Jahra's planning, he's gonna pull it by then. So that tells us when. What we still don't know is where."

Hunter told him about Uri Ezan's phone call.

Shansky grimaced. "That stupid goddamned kid! Doesn't that outfit teach them how to tail a guy without getting spotted?"

"How many times've *you* been spotted on a tail job?"

"A few," Shansky acknowledged. "But at least I was armed for trouble. But that poor stupid kid . . ." He angrily dropped the subject and got out a cigar. "I want to go down there with you, Hunter. Nothing for me to do in Paris. I talked to Mort Crown on my way in. He'll have the stake-out on Rosalynde Hagen operating by this evening; and the phone tap. And Mort can stay in touch with Whisper Charlie for me."

Hunter nodded. "That's what I figured." His voice seemed coolly detached. He used the phone, asking his temporary secretary to book two seats on a late afternoon plane to Nice.

Shansky had his cigar burning. "One thing," he said as he flicked out the match, "about Mossad being in it this deep. It takes care of just what the hell to do with Bel Jahra if we do find him. *They'll* put him out of business for us."

Hunter thought about Uri's voice on the phone. "Uh-huh," he said. "Permanently." He smiled. It was a singularly unpleasant smile.

SEVENTEEN

The five members of Bel Jahra's first commando unit arrived in Nice over the next two days. They settled into small furnished rooms which Driss Hammou had rented for them; each in a different part of the Old Town. This is the original Nice; a colorful, congested section of close-packed houses and narrow streets between the harbor and Boulevard Jean Jaurés. A large part of its population is North African. The five guerrillas had no trouble blending into the general atmosphere.

On the third day Hammou went through the Old Town collecting the five guerrillas from their separate furnished rooms. He took them to a garage where a white Simca 1100 was waiting; lent to Hammou by Bashir Mawdri's Nice connection, an antiques dealer named Ayad Sirfet. Driving out of Nice in the Simca, Hammou and the five guerrillas met with Bel Jahra at a prearranged rendezvous in the mountains some twenty miles inland.

There, in an isolated valley surrounded by pine-forested slopes, Bel Jahra gave each of the five guerrillas the bonding guarantee required from AGF, the company that insured the Valasi estate. These documents had been delivered to Bel Jahra, the previous night, by a messenger from al-Omared.

Next, Bel Jahra watched critically as the five guerrillas tried on their waiters' uniforms. These had been obtained by Sirfet, Mawdri's contact in Nice, from the same uniform-rental company which supplied the Giovanetti Catering Service. Bel Jahra had given the guerrillas' measurements to Hammou on his return from Libya. The uniforms fitted perfectly.

The five real waiters, whom the guerrillas were to replace at the

Valasi party, were already under continuing surveillance. To obtain men for this job, Bel Jahra had traveled the previous day to Marseilles. For while there were hundreds of Arabs in Nice with some connections to the terrorists, in Marseilles there were thousands—and a very efficient Rasd cell. It was this Rasd cell that had supplied what Bel Jahra needed: two men to keep tabs on each of the five waiters. And to snatch and kill them, on their way to the Valasi party. Plus two more men for the woman who was secretary to the director of the Giovanetti Catering Service. These two would keep track of her until the night of the party; when they would force her to make the vital phone call, before disposing of her.

That night was still four days off, when Bel Jahra began rebriefing Hammou and the five guerrillas in the mountains twenty miles from Nice. For three straight hours he hammered questions at each of them in turn—making certain that each knew every step of his individual job, and had a detailed mental image of the place in which he would have to accomplish it.

Bel Jahra intended to repeat these three-hour briefing sessions during some part of every day that followed—right up until the night on which they would execute what he had taught them.

Hunter and Shansky had flown from Paris to Nice late on the day that Bel Jahra had made the same trip. In the three days since then—while Bel Jahra's preparations had proceeded on schedule—Hunter's impromptu but far-spread network of informants had not turned up a single clue to these preparations.

Late on the third afternoon, shortly after Bel Jahra wound up his first briefing session in the mountains, Hunter arrived at the American Consulate in Nice. The consulate for this area is a cozy affair: a pleasant and modest two-story white house dwarfed by large trees on the corner of Rue Docteur Baréty and Rue Maréchal Joffre. A little high-hedged garden conceals the side of the house from Joffre. The front entrance is on Baréty. Hunter pushed open the tall gray door under the white eagle-medallion and climbed the marble steps inside to the waiting room. The clerk at the Consular Services desk, across the room from the American and blue-and-white consular flags, had a message for him.

He consulted his desk pad. "A Mr. Uri phoned. He'll be in to see you by five P.M."

Hunter glanced at his watch. It was four forty-six. "No other messages?"

"No, sir."

Hunter grimaced, and then thanked him. The consular clerk didn't have to handle his messages; he was doing it as a special favor. The Nice consulate had no personnel to spare. No spare facilities, either. That Hunter had been able to get partial use of a file room to operate from meant that State hadn't cut off his clout yet. His other operational center, in the evenings after the consulate closed, was Lamarck's house just outside Nice. Odile had agreed to stay by the phone there every night, for the duration.

"Is Shansky upstairs?" Hunter asked.

"Yes, sir. Also Premier Commissaire Lamarck." In spite of his perfect English, the consular clerk was French, and automatically gave Lamarck the title he'd held on retirement.

Hunter glanced at the stairs leading to the second floor, hesitating. He'd been moving around out there in the hot sun all day, and his face felt dried out. Going around the desk, he went into the corridor behind it. The washroom was across from the consul's office. But the small sign hanging on a brass chain beside it read: "Women—Dames."

The Nice consulate is too small for more than one washroom, with a reversible sign. Hunter leaned against the wall next to the mimeograph room and waited, deliberately keeping his mind a blank. It had become cluttered through that day with a frustrating assortment of non-facts and blind leads. He wanted to clear it for another assessment of the efforts being made, against the failure to achieve any progress at all.

A pretty passport-applications clerk came out of the washroom, and gave him a slightly embarrassed smile. She turned the sign so it now read "Men—Messieurs," and hurried into the visas office to the left. Hunter entered the white-tiled washroom and turned on the cold-water tap of the single sink beside the wooden toilet-booth. He bent and cupped his big hands under the water until they felt cool; then sloshed more cool water on his face and head.

When he straightened, dripping, he felt fresher. He dried himself with one of the blue-and-white towels with "Property U. S. Government" printed on it. Then he headed for the second floor.

The room Hunter had the use of was mostly file cabinets packed with old visa and citizenship applications. There was just room for a half-sized desk with a phone on it, and two wooden chairs. Shansky was waiting in the one behind the desk; Lamarck in the other. The hopeful looks they gave him as he came in told Hunter what they had for him. "Nothing?"

They shook their heads. "Same for you?" Shansky asked dispiritedly.

Hunter shrugged a shoulder, and leaned it against a file cabinet, gazing out the window without expression. None of them found anything to say for a time, as they contemplated the blank wall their investigation had so far failed to breach.

From Marseilles to the Italian border, Hunter had tapped every contact he knew. Shansky had all his spook connections alerted. Lamarck had spoken to every police and customs officer he was sure he could trust. Frank Lucci had passed the word to French narcotics agents and American undercover narcs. Uri Ezan had his Mossad people digging, and had also rung in some of Iran's SAVAK agents. With Arab activists determined to change the name of the Persian Gulf to the Arabian Gulf, Iran's secret police had their own reasons for keeping tabs on terrorists.

And after three days of all this: nothing. Hunter told himself it couldn't continue like that. They had the entire Riviera covered. Mort Crown was on top of the Paris situation. MacInnes and Fred Rivers would be tapping everybody they met on their tours around Europe. Something had to give.

Rivers' gloomy words mocked him: sooner . . . or later.

Hunter stared out angrily at the red roses climbing the trunk of the tall palm tree in the center of the consulate garden. "We're doing everything we can," he decided aloud, finally. "It's impossible to lay down as much coverage as we have, and not get *some* feedback. Impossible."

"If," Lamarck pointed out, "we are covering the correct area."

"We are." Hunter said it without emphasis, but also without doubt. He looked at the large map of the Riviera they'd tacked on the wall above the brown cabinets. There were red pins in it for the most likely targets; blue for possibles. "It's here—somewhere along the Côte d'Azur."

"That's still a lot of territory to blanket," Shansky mused. "There's too many places they could hit. Just look at all those lousy pins. And too many things going on, over the next five, six days."

That was the *maximum* amount of time left before Bel Jahra

pulled whatever he had in mind, according to the timetable indicated by what he'd told Rosalynde. Hunter had already alerted
the most obvious places for a terrorist attack: the airport of Nice,
and the smaller one in Marseilles. He had also warned security
people concerned with certain scheduled events in the next week
that would be natural targets:

The Monte Carlo tennis matches were starting in four days, and
the American team was a possible target. The Nice Book Fair was
another. So was an international medical conference in Cannes; a
fashion show at Saint-Tropez which would include official entries
from Israel; a new display of ancient Persian art from Iranian
museums at the Maeght Foundation outside Saint-Paul-de-Vence,
a cruise ship from England making a stop at Marseilles on its way
to Haifa. And many more.

Too many, as Shansky had said, to cover them all.

Behind Hunter, a voice said, "I have something."

Hunter turned and looked at Uri Ezan standing in the doorway.
Uri got out a damp handkerchief and mopped perspiration from
his dark face. Hunter hadn't seen a trace of a smile on Uri's face in
the three days since getting down here. He wasn't smiling now;
but there was something in his eyes.

"One of the SAVAK people under cover in Marseilles just passed
us an interesting piece of information," Uri told them. "A group of
Arab activists—the SAVAK man *thinks* they're part of a Black
September setup—left Marseilles last night. About ten of them, from
what he heard. Heading for Nice. Here. That's *all* he heard. So it's
limited—but definite."

Olivier Lamarck rose from his chair with a tight smile. "I think I
will go pass on this information. And make some inquiries." He
looked at Hunter. "It seems *something* is about to boil here.
Whether it is anything to do with our Ahmed Bel Jahra is another
matter."

"It's him," Hunter said quietly, with absolute certainty.

Within the hour, they were out passing the word and tapping
their contacts again. But this time with total concentration on Nice.
They kept at it well into the night. Without managing to turn up
another clue to fit together with the one from the SAVAK agent
in Marseilles.

Late the next morning, Shansky met with two old and dear friends: Count Basil Malinov and Natasha Krechevsky.

They were both in their late seventies, and had been exiles on the Riviera ever since the fall of Imperial Russia during the revolution at the end of World War I. Basil had been forced to flee without any of his considerable family fortune. But they had managed to get by ever since, by selling, piece by piece, the jewelry he'd given Natasha back when he'd been a titled rakehell. Many people assumed they were married. Shansky, who'd known them a long time, knew better. Natasha had been Count Basil's mistress; and still was. Though she'd had children by him, she would have considered it highly unromantic to change that.

Shansky was enormously fond of them. There was no professional reason behind seeing them that morning; only nostalgia and a need to relax his nerves for a bit. The rotunda café of the Negresco Hotel was the perfect place: 1890s decorations, old gypsy music and Viennese waltzes from muted loudspeakers, waitresses in nineteenth-century costumes with bustles, the food and drinks quasi-American.

The old Russian couple fitted well into this mixture. Natasha was a tall, wide, grandmotherly woman in an aging sable stole and black-velvet gown, with three diamond rings winking on her wrinkled fingers. She handled herself with a coy warmth that never changed; and claimed to be sixty. Malicious acquaintances pointed out that this would make her daughter two years older than she. Natasha insisted that this was her daughter's problem, not hers. *She* was sixty.

Basil had always been short, and had shrunk still more with age. His head was barely higher than Natasha's shoulder, even with a jaunty Tyrolean hat perched on it. And his skinny figure seemed extremely fragile beside her formidable bulk. But Basil was unquestionably still her master—a mastery based entirely on his undiminished passion for her.

Basil and Natasha ordered *capucinos*. Shansky, feeling vaguely homesick for an America he hadn't seen in eleven years, asked for a chocolate milkshake with vanilla ice cream. He sipped it and thought about his childhood while Basil admired Natasha's nail polish.

"And the way they've done your hair," Basil enthused. "Absolutely perfect for the party." He looked to Shansky for confirmation. "Don't you agree?"

Shansky looked dutifully at Natasha's wavy hair, which was dyed pitch black, and nodded. "Very nice."

"Her perfume is new, also." Basil half closed his eyes and breathed it in deep.

Natasha smiled at him with arch affection.

Shansky sipped more of his milkshake through the straw and asked idly, "What party?"

"Dezso Valasi's eightieth birthday party," Basil told him.

The faint stirring of professional interest in Shansky faded away completely. The Valasi party was one of the many coming events along the Riviera that he, Hunter, and Lamarck had learned about, and considered. And then dropped from consideration; because although there would be celebrities at the party, none were of a kind political fanatics would be interested in.

Valasi himself had been something of a political figure, in his time. During World War II the Germans had burned his paintings because he was a communist sympathizer. After the war, the communists had burned his new paintings, because they'd considered his work decadent. But the time when anyone had considered him as a *political* figure was long past.

So it was only personal interest that prompted Shansky: "I didn't realize you knew Valasi that well."

Natasha beamed proudly. "We saved his life, in the last war."

Basil nodded gravely. "We hid him, for several months. When the Nazis were searching for him."

"Nice of him to remember," Shansky said. And, because he knew nothing of the two very special guests whose invitation to the Valasi party was secret, he dropped the subject and finished his milkshake.

Later, when they were talking of other matters, Shansky asked them, just for the hell of it: "Ever seen this guy?"

He took out a picture of Bel Jahra, and showed it to them. Basil studied it a long time and shook his head. "No . . . I don't think so."

"I'm certain *I* haven't," Natasha said, with a slightly naughty smile. "He's so handsome. I always remember good-looking men."

Basil frowned at her. She patted his cheek, blew him a kiss, and asked Shansky, "Who is he?"

Shansky shrugged. "Just somebody I'm trying to locate."

"An old friend you've lost touch with?"

Shansky laughed softly. "Something like that." He put away the picture of Bel Jahra, and they returned to speaking of other matters. By the time he left them, Shansky felt relaxed and ready to return to work.

Later that same day, a junior inspector of the Brigade Criminelle in Nice left the *préfecture* wearing his usual civilian outfit: faded jeans, sneakers, and a dark sports shirt. Since he was off duty, young, and had recently broken with his fiancée, he decided to spend the afternoon looking at girls. With this in mind, the junior inspector—whose name was Christophe Raffalli, and who was a darkly handsome Corsican—went to the nearest logical place.

A sidewalk table at the snack bar across from the Galeries Lafayette on Rue Gioffredo is one of the best spots in Nice for girl-watching. Christophe Raffalli ordered a beer and sat down to watch the girls.

He got the rear view as they went into the department store across the street; and the front view as they came out carrying their purchases in plastic bags. Personally, Raffalli had a preference for the rear view. A large percentage of French girls, in his experience, had cuter *po-pos* than bosoms. So as he sipped his beer it was the *po-pos* he watched—wiggling their way into the store in skirts, slacks, and dungarees. The skintight jeans were best; they really showed what you were looking at. But there was one *po-po* in tight orange pants that made his mouth water most of all.

So fifteen minutes later, when those same tight orange pants came out of the Galeries Lafayette, Raffalli looked to see if the front view was anywhere near as good. It was. And she knew it, in a nice way. She came across Rue Gioffredo with a young girl's half-shy pride in her blooming figure, and the new power it gave her. Raffalli nerved himself to try to pick her up. Then he realized there was a man with her.

Disappointed, he examined the man critically to see why he deserved this juicy beauty. The man was about twenty-four, stocky and strong-looking, with coal-black eyes and a dark moustache. Ugly, Raffalli decided enviously; but in a virile way . . .

Suddenly, Raffalli recognized him.

He tried not to stare as the guy turned past him with the girl. The memory was vivid, even after almost two years. Because of what the guy had done. He'd been part of a gang extorting funds for an Arab guerrilla organization, from well-off Arabs living in the South of France. It was common enough. Arabs all over the world were subject to such extortion. Some found themselves having to contribute money to as many as four different guerrilla groups at the same time.

If they failed to pay, they were not killed; because dead men can't contribute. They were "taught a lesson," by thugs like the one Raffalli had just recognized with the girl in tight orange pants. This one's speciality had been kneecaps. He'd shot them off. Teaching a terror lesson no one ever forgot. The police had gone after him in earnest after he'd gotten carried away with himself on one job. A Lebanese shopkeeper had balked at paying out more than he already was to two Arab groups. The guy Raffalli had just recognized had dragged the man's fourteen-year-old daughter into an alley, and shot off *both* her kneecaps. The girl would be a cripple the rest of her life; she would never walk again, without crutches.

Raffalli had not been in on the capture and arrest. But he'd seen him, when he was brought in to the Palais de Justice. Hate had etched that face in Raffalli's memory he acid. Hate made worse by the results of the trial. Even back then, the reluctance of French officials to mete out tough justice to Arab terrorists had been in effect. The guy had merely been expelled from France. He wasn't supposed to come back. But he *was* back.

Raffalli put three francs on the table beside his beer glass. He got up and began following the girl in the orange pants, and the young Arab whose name he couldn't remember. He thought of him as "Knee Cap."

French officialdom's unwritten warnings against annoying Arab guerrillas were much more potent these days. Nobody was supposed to push them around, unless they were caught red-handed doing something so horrible it was impossible to ignore. Even then, it could wreck a policeman's career. Raffalli knew better than to bother Knee Cap. He was merely following him, cautiously. His boss, Commissaire Yvan Sbraggia, was, like Raffalli, a Corse. Corsicans have no love for Arabs. Corsican cops care even less for Arab criminals. Commissaire Sbraggia liked to be kept current on Arab activities in his area.

Orange Pants turned right off Rue Gioffredo with Knee Cap—one of Bel Jahra's imported commandos.

Raffalli turned after them into Rue Alberti. He was good at shadowing people; beginning to acquire a reputation in the Police Judiciare of the Alpes-Maritimes for seldom being spotted at it or losing his quarry. These two were continuing up the right pavement ahead of him. Raffalli strolled across to the left pavement, taking his time. He could afford to let them get well ahead of him, with plenty of other people in between. Those orange pants were easy to keep track of, even a full block distant.

Ambling along, Raffalli trailed them across Avenue Félix Faure. They strolled into the lush greenery of General Leclerc Square, the girl's arm around Knee Cap's waist, his hand on her buttocks. Raffalli was no longer enamored of that *po-po*. He kept remembering the sadistic crippling of a girl much younger than her, by the guy she was with. Picking up his pace sharply as they vanished among the trees, Raffalli strode around the square and across Boulevard Jean Jaurés.

The street markets of the Old Town begin on the other side of the boulevard. Raffalli lounged past a fruit-and-vegetable stand, and turned slightly to admire the assortment of open cheeses spread out for sale on an egg-and-dairy stand. A spot of orange winked in the greenery of the square on the other side. Then the girl wearing the color emerged from the trees with Knee Cap. They dodged the traffic across the boulevard in Raffalli's direction, holding hands and laughing. Knee Cap's laughter curdled in Raffalli's stomach.

They turned past him along the right side of the boulevard, going in the direction of Place Garibaldi. Raffalli waited until they disappeared into the Old Town by way of the Porte Fausse. Then he went after them. Most of the Old Town is lower than the rest of Nice. You descend into it by way of inclined streets or time-worn stone steps. Raffalli went down the twenty-three steps of the Porte Fausse, and spotted his couple pushing through the crowds of shoppers and strollers between the open markets lining both sides of narrow Rue Boucherie.

Raffalli tailed them away from the main markets, into a complex of short, crooked streets and tall, narrow houses jammed against each other. Few of these streets were wide enough for cars, none had sidewalks, all were congested with slow-moving crowds. As they went deeper into the Old Town the streets became narrower, the people in them predominantly Arabic, and the music from the shuttered windows overhead Middle Eastern. Raffalli's dark features enabled him to blend easily into this area.

He followed them down a descending alley, made dim by the balconies and hanging laundry cutting off the daylight above. They vanished around a corner into a small square. When Raffalli went around the corner he found them standing there right in front of him, kissing. He strolled off at an angle past them, and stopped to look in the window of a music shop. There were racks of North African records inside; one rack each for Egyptian, Moroccan, and Tunisian records, two racks of Algerian records. The window itself held the vague reflections of Orange Pants and Knee Cap.

They were separating. Raffalli watched the girl go off in the direction of Rue Rossetti. She turned once, to call good-by to Knee Cap. She called him Kamal. Raffalli continued to think of him as Knee Cap, as he followed him in the direction of the hill that rises between the Old Town and the harbor. He tailed him, at a wary distance, up an alley that climbed along the base of the hill. It climbed by way of age-grooved, dirty steps; turning left, right, then left again. Slogans in Arabic were scrawled with white paint on the flaking orange walls on either side of bright blue doors. The music from the green-shuttered windows was entirely Arab now; and there was a lot of it, loud.

Up ahead, Knee Cap entered a small square. Raffalli got there in time to see him vanish into the darkness of a narrow open doorway between a private Arab nightclub called the Oran, and a cinema showing a rerun of Cecil B. De Mille's *Ten Commandments*. A small sign over the dark doorway advertised furnished rooms for rent to tourists up on the third floor.

There was an open bistro on the other side of the square, between a butcher shop and a fish stand. The men at the little iron tables (there were no women) were all North African. Raffalli settled himself at a free table. The men around him were drinking either mint tea or soft drinks. Raffalli ordered a Coke and looked at the third-floor windows across the square.

Like all the others, they had faded green shutters and little iron balconies. An old woman in a black hooded gown sat in a wooden chair on one balcony, staring at life moving past in the square below her. There was a small white dog in her lap, and potted geraniums hung on the opened shutters behind her. She turned her head as the shutters behind the balcony next to hers suddenly banged wide open. Knee Cap appeared up there, stripped to the waist; his arms, shoulders, and torso thick with rippling muscles. Raffalli bent his head and sipped his Coke.

When he glanced up again, the old woman in black was still there, but not Knee Cap. Raffalli sipped, and waited. He reminded himself that he had to get some sleep before going back on duty that night; and that he already had enough to report to Commissaire Sbraggia. Then he thought again about a fourteen-year-old girl without kneecaps. And continued to wait.

Driss Hammou entered the square. He went into the doorway under the sign advertising rooms for rent. There was nothing special about him, in that North African setting, to attract Raffalli's attention. But there was when he came out again a short time later: Knee Cap was with him.

Raffalli put money on the table for his Coke. He didn't get up until Knee Cap and Hammou were out of the square, hurrying away through a twisting, alley-like street. Then he rose and went after them.

EIGHTEEN

Driss Hammou and Knee Cap—an Egyptian from the Cairo slums named Kamal Ghyat—made four more stops within the Old Town of Nice. Always it was at a place with a *Meublé—Chambres Touristes* sign. As was usual with cheap rooms for rent by the day, they were always on the second or third floor of an old building. At each stop Hammou went up inside to get another man, while the others waited outside and looked around to see if they were being followed.

They never caught Raffalli at it. He was too skilled at this kind of job, and knew the Old Town too well. Many times he was able to anticipate their route, and make a fast detour that wound up with him walking ahead of them, instead of behind. Each time they stopped to pick up another man, he circled the place to approach them from a different angle. He never allowed himself to get close enough to be distinguished from other people in the always crowded streets.

Each of the men they picked up was of a distinct type Raffalli had come to recognize in the past few years: a young Arab with an intense expression, and with a way of moving that revealed serious military physical training. The furnished rooms they had taken were as far apart from each other as it is possible to get within the Old Town: over a judo club on the Rue de Jésus; at the top of a flaking yellow house on the steps of Rue de L'Ancien Sénat; inside a dark courtyard off Rue de Collet; and above the Joker Bar on Rue du Four.

That was the last of them. The men with Hammou now numbered five. Walking swiftly, Hammou led them out of the Old

Town and into the stadium-sized Place Masséna by way of the palm garden around the Fountain of the Sun. They hurried down the length of the *place* under the red arcades of the big eighteenth-century buildings flanking one side. Raffalli moved parallel to them through the arcades on the other side, watching them through the hundreds of cars parked in the middle. When they turned left at the other end of the *place*, he dodged across after them.

They were a full block ahead of him on the Rue de France when they vanished into an alley. Raffalli strolled past on the other side of the street. Hammou was standing watch just inside the mouth of the alley. The other five were entering a door in the deep end of the alley. Raffalli busied himself studying the newspapers and magazines at a corner kiosk.

It was not until Hammou suddenly turned and went in after the other five that Raffalli remembered where the door inside the alley led. Cursing, he sprinted across the street and circled the block on the run. A white Simca 1100 came out of the garage on Rue Buffa just as Raffalli got to the corner of Buffa and Meyerbeer. He stood panting as it cruised toward him.

Knee Cap was driving. Hammou was beside him with one of the men they'd picked up. The other three were in the back seat. The Simca turned into Meyerbeer and headed away in the direction of the train station, and the hills behind Nice. Raffalli watched it go. There was no taxi around; no way to follow the Simca. He memorized its license number before it became lost to sight in the heavy traffic.

After the car was gone, sudden weariness reminded Raffalli that he should have started getting his day's sleep almost two hours ago. But he was angry at the way they'd lost him, by using such a rudimentary anti-surveillance technique. Retracing his steps to Place Masséna, he angled off it through Rue Saint François de Paule, heading back to the Préfecture de Police which he had left on going off duty.

He strode through the open flower market between the seafood restaurants and fish shops of the Cours Saleya, and made a left turn into Place Gautier. The *préfecture* for the Alpes-Maritimes is in a magnificent palace built three hundred years ago by the Duke of Savoy. Its facade, with four floors of huge deep-set windows, bulks imposingly across one entire side of the *place*, with tall palms out front and a great radio antenna sprouting from the roof. Raffalli nodded at the uniformed police guard on duty at the wooden booth beside the gate, went in past the palms and up under the wide arch of the entrance. The marble reception salon inside is wide and high enough to hold three normal-sized houses. Raffalli hurried across it under the enormous crystal chandeliers, and opened a thick oak door in the back.

Beyond that, the great rooms of the palace have been for the part divided into small cubicles by wooden and plasterboard partitions. Raffalli threaded through the maze this created to the rear of the palace, where the Police Nationale Corps Urbain has its garage and headquarters. There he put in a request for information about the owner of a Simca 1100 bearing the license number he had memorized.

The name of the owner brought a small smile to Raffalli's dark face. He noted it down, together with the address, and went back through the palace, up narrow paneled stairways to Commissaire Sbraggia's third-floor office in the Brigade Criminelle of the Police Judiciare: Georges Sorel, the aging police detective who functioned as the commissaire's secretary, told him that Sbraggia had gone out to lunch.

Raffalli knew where to find him. Trudging back down the stairs, he left the palace by a rear door opening onto Rue de la Préfecture. This leads along one side of the adjoining nineteenth-century Palace of Justice to the Place du Palais. Yvan Sbraggia was at one of the sidewalk tables of the Café du Palais, under a sun-faded striped umbrella, having an herb omelet with a demi-carafe of Provençal wine.

The commissaire was fifty; a solid man with a heavy pock-marked face, receding curly black hair, a small moustache, and a restrained manner. He eyed the approaching Raffalli with mild surprise, saying nothing as Raffalli sat down opposite him with a sleepy grin. He sipped his wine and listened without any sign of awakening interest as Raffalli told him all he had done since going off duty that morning.

Raffalli didn't tell his boss that his attention had first been drawn to Knee Cap by a marvelous *po-po* in orange pants; but everything else he gave in detail. He read off the addresses where Hammou had picked up each of the five guerrillas. Tearing this page from his small notebook, Raffalli put it on the table beside the carafe. Then he read off the name and address of the Simca's owner. This page, too, he tore out and put on the table. Then he leaned back looking pleased with himself.

The white Simca Hammou and the other five had gone off in was owned by Ayad Sirfet. This was a name known to both of them. Sirfet operated as a front man for at least two Arab guerrilla organizations. The police had turned up positive proof of this two years ago. A year ago Sirfet's lawyer had gone to the Ministry of the Interior to lodge a protest about detectives following Sirfet everywhere, interfering with his privacy and freedom. Wrists had been slapped in the Police Judiciare of the Alpes-Maritimes. Commissaire Yvan Sbraggia's wrist still stung from it.

He reminded Raffalli of this. "You know that Ayad Sirfet is a respectable businessman, residing legally in our country, and has as much right to his privacy as anyone else. You come to tell me he lent his car to some fellow Arabs. A generous thing for him to do. Is there anything illegal in his generosity?"

"No, but . . ."

"And these fellow Arabs," Sbraggia cut in caustically, "also have a right to their privacy. Unless they break certain laws. Not all laws; but certain ones. You interfered with their privacy by following them about for several hours. Did you observe them breaking any laws?"

Raffalli was looking at him unhappily. "No, sir. But I thought you would find it of interest."

Commissaire Sbraggia shrugged daintily. "Gossip about strangers in my district does have a certain curiosity value, perhaps. Nothing more. On the basis of what you have told me, there is absolutely no excuse for taking any official interest. I think you should go home now and get some sleep. You look as though you need it."

Raffalli stood up slowly, crestfallen. Commissaire Sbraggia picked up his two pages of notes, folded them neatly without changing his bored expression, and slipped them in the breast pocket of his dark jacket. The grin came back to Raffalli's dark face. He gave his chief the wink of a co-conspirator, turned, and went off jauntily to catch up on his sleep.

Commissaire Sbraggia ate a last forkful of his herb omelet, washed it down with the delicious wine, and gazed thoughtfully at the Palace of Justice on the other side of the small *place*. Six Arabs—one of whom had been expelled from France and was not supposed to return—had gathered today in Nice and gone off somewhere together, for some purpose. At least five of them were recent and temporary visitors to Nice, judging by their accommodations. They were using a car that belonged to a known contact for Arab terrorist organizations. And there was nothing Sbraggia could do about any of this information Raffalli had given him, under existing French policy.

But it *was* of interest to him. Especially when put together with the rumor passed on to him the other day by Olivier Lamarck, concerning a group of Arab guerrillas leaving Marseilles for Nice—purpose unknown. This group that Raffalli had tailed might be part of that same group; or a group with no connection to the first one, acting for some purpose of its own; or an allied group, co-operating for a common purpose. Still nothing Sbraggia could do about it, in his capacity as a police official. Olivier Lamarck, however, was no longer a police official.

Lamarck had been his premier commissaire, back when Sbraggia had been a chief inspector. There was a mutual respect and friendship between them. Sbraggia was one of the men Lamarck had trusted enough to confide in, after he had begun helping Hunter. Lamarck was interested in any new Arab activities in the area. And Lamarck was retired; as a private citizen, he could perhaps do what Sbraggia could not, concerning Raffalli's information.

Paying his bill, Commissaire Sbraggia left the café table, crossed the *place,* and climbed the wide steps of the Palace of Justice. There were three big polished-oak doors at the top. One under the gilt-lettered word *Liberté;* the second under *Égalité;* the third under *Fraternité.* Sbraggia had for some time considered with amused interest the fact that Liberty and Fraternity no longer worked; while Equality, for some reason, did. He pushed it open and went in past the concierge in the glass booth on the left, and climbed one of the twin stairways to the third floor.

Going down a long corridor to the rear of the Palace of Justice, where it was joined to the side of the *préfecture* palace, he went through a connecting door to the partitioned halls leading to his office. Georges Sorel, at the metal desk outside it, had a number of slips with phone messages on it for him. Commissaire Sbraggia took these with him around the low wooden partition into his office, and sat down behind his own desk, which was of solid dark wood.

He took Inspector Raffali's notes from his breast pocket, smoothed them out on the top of his desk, and gazed at them for a moment. Then he picked up his phone and dialed the home of Olivier Lamarck. Lamarck's daughter, Odile, answered. After exchanging casual pleasantries, she put her father on.

Sbraggia told his former chief about Raffalli's late morning, in detail. "It seemed to me," he said without emphasis, "that this just might fit in, somehow, with the matters that interest you."

"It is possible," Lamarck agreed. "Hold on a moment. I'll get a pencil and paper. . . ." After a short silence, Lamarck came on again: "Go ahead, Yvan."

Commissaire Sbraggia gave him the name and address of Ayad Sirfet, and the address of the garage the Simca had been driven out of. Then, slowly enough for Lamarck to copy, he gave him the addresses where Hammou had picked up Knee Cap and the other four guerrillas in the Old Town.

On the other side of the partition, Georges Sorel listened attentively. Sorel's wife was in a private mental asylum, where proper care cost a great deal, which had to be paid promptly at the beginning of each week. He had no sons to help him with this. His only daughter was married to a loafer who was always losing his jobs and whining for help. Sorel's police pay was too small to carry the burdens required of him. And would soon become much smaller, when he was forced to retire on a pension. Because of his wife, he had no savings from his regular income.

It had become essential for Sorel to find extra sources of income. For the past few years, his main extra source had been Arab guerrilla organizations, which paid generously for any information of use to them. Sorel didn't know who his chief was speaking to on the phone, because Sbraggia had not addressed Lamarck by name. But everything else he heard quite clearly.

Sorel was far too nervous to risk making a secret phone call from the *préfecture*. He had already had his lunch, and there was no excuse for leaving the building for the rest of that day. It would have to wait until he went off duty that evening. Then he could make the call to Ayad Sirfet.

It was after 5 P.M. when the white Simca returned to the parking garage on Rue Buffa. The five-man commando team was in it; but not Driss Hammou, who had returned to Roquebrune with Bel Jahra after the long briefing session. Hunter, dawdling over a *pastis* in a bistro across the street, with Uri and Lamarck, watched the Simca vanish inside the garage with its five occupants. Uri left the bistro immediately, crossing the street at an angle and striding swiftly around the block. Hunter and Lamarck remained behind, on the off-chance that the five Arab guerrillas might leave the garage in this direction, instead of by the same way they'd gone in.

On Rue de France, Uri sat down at a sidewalk table in front of a *tabac* next to the alley exit from the rear of the garage. A young man and a middle-aged woman were nursing beers at that table. They exchanged casual greetings with Uri. Four men at the next table paid no attention to his arrival, seeming absorbed in their own conversation. The five Arabs emerged from the alley, and went past the *tabac* in the direction of Place Masséna.

Uri said softly, "That's them."

The woman at his table dropped her cigarette lighter. The four men at the next table appeared to remain absorbed in their conversation. The five Arabs split up at the corner; two continuing straight, one turning to the right, the other two going left. When they were gone, Uri and the four men at the next table got up. They went to the corner and split up in the same way; each taking on the tailing of a single Arab. If they had to lose the Arabs to prevent being spotted, they were to go to the Old Town, and wait at the addresses supplied by Raffalli.

The woman at the table Uri had left remained where she was. The young man got up and walked around the block. Hunter and Lamarck came out of the bistro when they saw him.

"They've gone," he told them. "Chana will remain on watch by the alley. I'll take over here." He strolled off and got into a car parked near the corner, lighting a cigarette and settling back to wait, watching the garage. Lamarck went off to get a taxi and return home, where Odile had been staying by the phone as co-ordinator all day, and needed a few hours' relief. Hunter headed for the shop owned by Ayad Sirfet.

It was on the Avenue Verdun, one of the most elegant shopping streets in Nice. Set between the Italian Tourist Bureau and a posh store selling prestige-label women's clothes, Sirfet's shop specialized in expensive antiques imported from the Orient and Middle East. Hunter joined Shansky on a park bench in the Jardin Albert I, across the street.

"He's still in there," Shansky told him, and got an expensive Havana cigar from his breast pocket, lighting it lovingly.

"Better not get too used to those," Hunter said absently. "This job won't last forever."

Shansky gave a philosophic shrug. "Nothing lasts forever, pal. That's one thing I've finally gotten through my head. The other thing's to enjoy what I can, while I can." He took a slow pull at the cigar, savoring the delicate flavor.

The two of them continued to sit on the park bench, watching Sirfet's antique shop across the street.

It was almost 7 P.M. when Sirfet closed the shop for the night, drawing a steel grille across the door and display window, and locking it before going hurrying off along Avenue Verdun. Lamarck had described him to Hunter and Shansky. Sirfet's extremely fat bulk, and a dark mole on the left cheek of his plump, pale face, made it easy. Hunter and Shansky got up and followed him, going down opposite sides of the street, to the Quai des États-Unis.

Sirfet's penthouse apartment was in the opposite direction, atop a modern apartment house on Boulevard Victor Hugo. He had an upsetting phone call to make before going home; and for calls like this one he didn't like to use the phones in his shop or apartment. Though the police had been taught to leave him alone, and a Rasd expert regularly checked his phones, there was always a chance they'd been bugged again, between times. He hurried along the quay, and entered the Hôtel Beau Rivage, facing the sea and beach. At no time did he look back to see if he was being followed. He assumed that he was.

Inside the hotel lobby, Sirfet went to a single phone booth in the rear. It was a solid wooden booth, with a small window of thick glass in the door. Hunter entered the lobby while Sirfet was in the booth, dialing. Strolling past the booth, Hunter turned back as soon as he was on its blind side. Going quietly to the side of the booth, he put his ear to it. But the wood proved too thick; almost soundproof. Hunter could hear a muffled voice inside the booth; but not the words or even what language Sirfet was speaking.

Shansky had come into the lobby and was buying a newspaper at the desk beside the entrance. Hunter shook his head at him, and went to sit down in a wing chair near the men's room. Shansky settled into a lobby chair with his paper.

Inside the phone booth, Sirfet was passing on to Bel Jahra the alarming news that Sorel, Commissaire Sbraggia's secretary, had phoned to him just before he'd closed his shop. When he finished, there was a long silence at the other end of the line, in Roquebrune. The silence gnawed at Sirfet's raddled nerves. "Ahmed . . . ?"

"What number are you calling from?" Bel Jahra's voice asked in his ear. He sounded calm. Sirfet found that incredible, under the circumstances. He read off the number of the booth phone.

"Go for a walk," Bel Jahra told him in the same controlled tone. "Come back to this number in exactly half an hour." There was a click at the other end. Sirfet checked his watch, and left the hotel to take a nervous half-hour stroll.

Hunter didn't like the way Sirfet never bothered to check on whether anyone was tailing him.

In the apartment in Roquebrune, Bel Jahra remained standing beside his phone, one hand still resting on it, his mouth thin and hard.

Hammou studied the dulled look in the pale eyes, and asked anxiously, "What is wrong?"

Bel Jahra slowly removed his hand from the phone. "Stay here and take any calls," he told Hammou shortly. That was all he told him. He left the apartment and walked quickly down through the tunneled passages of the town to the car park. Getting into his car, he drove away in the direction of Carnoles, a new working-class suburb between Menton and Cap Martin.

As he drove, he went over again everything Ayad Sirfet had told him. He was still shocked by it. He knew he faced yet another disaster. But he didn't allow this to interfere with his logic. There were ways to prevent this disaster, since he had been warned in time. Valasi's party was still forty-eight hours away. Almost exactly forty-eight hours. That was close enough to make the problem acute. But it still left scope for dealing with the problem. With forced coolness, Bel Jahra considered alternative methods.

He didn't know who Commissaire Sbraggia had phoned with

his information. It had to be assumed he was speaking to another police official; perhaps one of higher authority. Nor did Bel Jahra know how the police had come by their information.

Bel Jahra could feel unknown forces closing in around him. First there'd been the fact that Israeli agents had known about him, and tried to follow him. Now the plice knew about his first team of commandos, exactly where each was staying, and the fact that they were using Sirfet's car. Perhaps they knew even more. How *much* more? Where was the leak? And why were certain police officers so interested?

Whatever the reason, Bel Jahra had to find a way to put an end to their being this close on top of his operation. Not knowing the answers to those questions made that especially difficult. One factor was certain: They had a lead to his operation through their interest in the commando team, and Sirfet. If they were being watched, and followed, it might be possible to lose the followers. But not easily; not with five men, plus Sirfet, being tailed.

And if it could be accomplished—if his first commando team *could* be shifted to another location without being followed— that might still not be enough safety. There was a leak to that team, somewhere; and to Sirfet. And whoever had found out about them might also know about the guerrillas brought in from Marseilles, and be on top of *them.*

Someone was just too close to the angle of the operation Bel Jahra had planned for his first commando team. There was only one way to be *certain* this connection was cut off, with the time element getting so tight. It was for some such eventuality, after all, that he had insisted on having a *second* commando group prepared.

By the time Bel Jahra entered Carnoles, his mind was made up. There was an outdoor phone booth on Avenue Foch, across from St. Joseph's church. His watch indicated a bit more than a minute left of the half hour he had given Ayad Sirfet. Getting out of the car, Bel Jahra lit a cigarette. He strolled into the booth and shut the door, took a deep drag at the cigarette, and let the smoke trickle through his teeth. Then he dropped the cigarette and crushed it with a twist of his heel.

Dropping a fifty-centime piece in the phone's coin slot, he dialed

the number Sirfet had given him. Sirfet answered on the first
ring. With cold precision, Bel Jahra told him what he must do.

Every Mossad agent Uri could get hold of, and some narcs
that Frank Lucci managed to pull temporarily off other jobs,
were rung into the surveillance net that Hunter had set up. At
midnight, two narcs took over the stake-out on Sirfet, who was
by then back in his apartment. At eight-thirty the next morning,
when Sirfet left his apartment building, Hunter and Shansky
were back on him. Again, he didn't bother to look around for anyone
watching him. And again it bothered Hunter.

Sirfet didn't go to his antique shop. Instead, he entered the Old
Town. When he left it, he had the five guerrillas with him. Hunter
sent Uri circling ahead to the garage area with three of his men;
and continued following the six Arabs with Shansky and the remaining Mossad agent.

On Rue de France, the Arabs entered the alley leading to the
rear of the garage. Leaving the Mossad man outside the alley,
Hunter and Shansky hurried around the block to a waiting car
with one of Uri's men ready behind the wheel. Uri was in
another car farther up the block. When the white Simca left
the garage, it was loosely bracketed by the two surveillance cars.

No one in the Simca seemed to notice. The Simca traveled
west along Route 7, without attempting any evasion tactics, and
swung into the airport. It was left in the parking area. Ayad
Sirfet led the five young Arabs into the terminal building. At the
Mid-East Airlines counter they picked up six tickets that were
waiting for them.

Half an hour later all six were airborne in a 707 jet on its way
to Beirut. There was nothing anyone could do to stop them.

NINETEEN

The situation conference was held on the upper terrace of Lamarck's home, shortly before noon: Lamarck, Hunter, Shansky, Uri, and Frank Lucci. The question: Why the abrupt pullout of Ayad Sirfet and the five guerrillas? They played with different answers, none quite satisfactory. The one answer that would explain it most logically was delicately avoided as long as possible.

The phone in the house rang. Odile came out, and told Uri it was for him. Uri went inside. When he came out, he didn't sit down again. He stood there with his short strong legs planted firmly, scowling down at Hunter. "One of my people just got word from the SAVAK man in Marseilles. That bunch of guerrillas that left there for Nice—they're back in Marseilles."

After that, the logical answer had to be put in the open. "Sounds to me," Lucci said judiciously, "like your boy's quit. Whatever it was he was building to, somehow he tumbled that somebody was too close. And gave it up."

Shansky didn't want it to be that way. That way, there was nothing left—and he wasn't needed any longer. "I just don't believe that's so." His face was miserable. Old again. Older than Olivier Lamarck's.

Hunter thought about it—from deep inside the mind of Bel Jahra. "I don't believe it, either. If he was quitting, he'd get out. There wouldn't be anything left for him in Europe. Not after *two* failures. He'd have gotten on that plane to Beirut, with the others."

"Maybe he's slipping out another way," Odile suggested, without conviction. "So he wouldn't be spotted."

"No reason for that to worry him," her father pointed out. "No one can arrest him for anything. He knows that. And if he had turned up at the airport, there would have been no time for anyone to snatch him illegally, before he boarded the plane."

Uri nodded. "But it's also possible Sirfet and the five he took off with are part of something else—not connected with Bel Jahra. There is no shortage of Arab activity in the South of France."

"That is for *damn* sure," Lucci agreed.

Hunter shook his head. "The timing fits too well," he said slowly, thinking it through as he spoke. "There's the other possibility: Bel Jahra found out somebody was getting too close. He doesn't know who we are—or how much we know. He *wanted* us to figure his operation's been dropped, whatever it is. That's why he sent the others out—in a way we couldn't miss."

The notion appealed to Lamarck's devious mind: "He *could* bring them right back. Tomorrow. Through a different point of entry. Belgium, Switzerland, Italy, Germany. They return here by car, with new papers. And Bel Jahra has them back in operation by tomorrow night or the next day."

Lucci looked dubious. But Shansky had some of his color back. He stood up and snapped: "So—let's go find him."

They began recombing Nice all over again. But Bel Jahra had no intention of coming anywhere near Nice for the thirty-one hours left to Valasi's party.

Hunter's earlier prediction turned out to be correct: It was impossible to spread so much coverage over one subject without *some* information beginning to leak back.

A French narcotics agent recognized Bel Jahra's picture, and his information was passed back to Frank Lucci: The agent remembered seeing Bel Jahra in Morocco several years ago—several times in the company of a beautiful European woman. The woman turned out to be Helena Reggiani. End of lead.

MacInnes phoned Hunter from Munich, where he had showed the Bel Jahra picture to an investigator for the Ultra Sensitive Positions Program. The USPP man was certain he'd seen Bel Jahra around Munich about a year ago, shortly before the Olympics massacre. On the strength of that slim possibility, MacInnes said he'd check deeper around Munich and try to dig up something more substantial. Hunter didn't think much of it; but he was grateful for the try.

One of Shansky's contacts definitely identified Bel Jahra as a man who'd been around Cap Ferrat and Monte Carlo about a year and a half earlier. Again, with Helena Reggiani. The contact agreed to check around both places for a lead to something more recent. Good enough—but the deadline was closing in very fast.

A customs officer who lived in Carnoles told Lamarck that he was fairly sure the picture of Bel Jahra matched a man he'd seen making a phone call from an outdoor booth near St. Joseph's church last night, while he'd been out walking his dog. That was a lot better, if only because it was so recent. Uri put some Mossad people to work combing Carnoles for Bel Jahra. But Carnoles was another place Bel Jahra had no intention of returning to.

Fred Rivers phoned hunter from Cannes, here he'd just finished lunching with an old girl friend who did work for the film festival held there every year. Rivers had showed her the picture of Bel Jahra. She'd recognized him.

"This is a gal with an eye for good-looking guys," Rivers told Hunter caustically. "So she's *sure* she remembers seeing him here during the festival two years ago. He was having drinks with a half-assed Hollywood movie producer she knew. Guy named Murray Norman. They were having drinks out on the terrace of the Hotel Carlton bar. She got one look, and dug your boy so much she went over and said hello to this Murray Norman, just so she could get introduced. She doesn't remember Bel Jahra's name, but she does remember the bastard's face."

Rivers hesitated, before adding: "Trouble is . . . she never got to see him again. And she's got no idea what happened to him after that. Didn't even find out where he was staying in Cannes."

"That's some lead," Hunter told him without pleasure. "Two years old—and going absolutely no place."

"I know, I know . . . but it's what I got, so I'm passing on."

Hunter asked: "Okay, where do I find this Murray Norman character?"

"That's another trouble. My gal here's got no idea. Seems he was trying to do a movie on the Riviera, and ran out of money. Never got to finish it. He was in Cannes trying to talk people around the festival into advancing him some more dough. Couldn't get any. He finally did a runout with a bunch of creditors after him. Hasn't been heard of since."

"Beautiful," Hunter muttered disgustedly. After hanging up the phone, he gave some irritable thought to the fact that a shoestring movie producer had once been seen with Bel Jahra. It was still two years old; and he still didn't think much of it. But until he had something better, he couldn't pass up the remotest possibility. So although he regretted the waste of time and effort, he put through a call to a California contact: Commander Joseph Bianco of the Los Angeles police.

Bianco phoned him back an hour later. He had pretty much the same story that Rivers had gotten from his girl friend in Cannes: Murray Norman had returned to America, for a time. And then skipped the country with a pack of creditors after him, including Internal Revenue. As a special favor, Commander Bianco agreed to put through a location-requested inquiry through Interpol for the man, as a tax dodger. Hunter himself put a similar request through the State Department, to embassies and consulates all over the world.

Hunter still didn't think much of it.

Just routine.

Gilbert Soumagnac, the insurance company's security man, spent two hours that afternoon checking around the Valasi estate, in preparation for handling everything properly at the party the following night. He was thirty-five, with a massive build and the calm expression of a man who does not expect other men to pick quarrels with him. Most security men are former policemen. Soumagnac was not. He had begun as a private bodyguard; from that he had worked and educated himself up to his present position with AGF. He was a thorough man, and had never yet failed to live up to the responsibilities of the position.

Soumagnac began by taking a slow stroll around the grounds with Valasi's personal secretary, Juliet Shale. When they reached the seaward edge of the estate, he looked down the cliff to the rocks and surf with the eye of a skilled burglar. He noted that while the sea cliff was practically sheer, it was not terribly high. He made a mental note to station one of his four men here during the party the following night.

It did not occur to Gilbert Soumagnac that this might not be sufficient security there at the sea cliff. He had no reason to think in terms of a paramilitary assault by trained assassins. One armed security guard was quite sufficient to discourage jewelry or art thieves.

As he turned away from the cliff edge, he glimpsed Dezso Valasi in the half circle of the collapsed tower among the abbey ruins. The old artist sat behind his easel: a tall lanky figure, the burly shoulders bowed with age, the long horsey face with its sharp-humored mouth deeply seamed and weathered, a black seaman's cap perched on his tanned bald head. Juliet Shale shot Soumagnac a warning look, and put a finger to her lips. Soumagnac didn't need such a warning. He was quite used to respecting the privacy of the distinguished persons among whom he performed his function.

He did not tramp through the abbey ruins, but circled around them quietly. By doing so he failed to see the partially choked and covered entrance to the crypt under the ruins. Whether he would have given any special consideration to it if he had seen it is impossible to know. At any rate, he did not notice, because he was being careful not to disturb the painter at his work. He did not speak to Juliet Shale until they were well beyond Valasi's hearing.

But Dezso Valasi, though he appeared to be totally concentrating on the huge blank square of canvas before him, was well aware of their presence. Ordinarily, anyone coming near while he worked, even silently, would have infuriated him. The reason was simple: With all the fame that had finally come to him, he still feared that each painting he worked on might prove to be horrible. This oppressive anxiety lifted once the work was completed. But until then, he didn't want anyone to see him at work on a potential failure.

In the case of Gilbert Soumagnac, however, Valasi didn't mind the near-intrusion. The presence of the insurance company's security man eased an irrational fear that was always with him. Valasi didn't care if someone stole all the jewelry and money of his guests tomorrow night. He could even stand it if someone found and removed the gold coins he hid under the house, like any sensible Hungarian peasant who'd seen paper money turn worthless.

But he had nightmares about someone stealing or destroying

his paintings. The terror was irrational, but it grew out of what had happened to him in the past. He had been painting for seven years in Paris when the German blitzkrieg swept into France. Valasi was a known Communist, and had done posters for a number of Party causes. He was forced to flee Paris to save his life, leaving all his work behind in his studio. Even in the South of France the Nazis had sought him. He had been hidden by Basil Malinov and Natasha Krechevsky, saving his life. But the paintings left in his Paris studio, the work of seven long years, had been found, and burned. In those days Dezso Valasi was just beginning to make a name for himself; the Germans hadn't thought his work might be worth a great deal of money to them someday.

After the war ended, Valasi had gone to Moscow and started over again, in the more congenial atmosphere of the communist regime. Two years later that regime had turned less congenial, when some people denounced him as a counterrevolutionary, for making what he'd considered good-humored criticisms of certain government officials. His paintings had been reviewed with less good-humored criticism; and Valasi had been officially declared a polluter of youth, a corrupt carrier of the germs of Western decadence. Again he had been forced to flee, leaving all his paintings behind. He had no idea of what had happened to them; whether they, too, had been burned, or were rotting in some damp cellar.

Dezso Valasi's fame as an artist came from the work he had done in the South of France, after his escape from the Soviet Union. He lived in fear that these paintings, too, would somehow vanish—as though he had never done the work at all. But the presence of the security man eased, for the moment, that ever-present nightmare.

Valasi shook away the thought, and chuckled at himself. You are becoming senile at last, he warned himself. He picked up a tube of French vermilion, and squeezed a large gob of it in the middle of one of the clean squares of glass laid out on the table beside him. Then, on a corner of the glass square, he squeezed out just a small point of burnt umber. Taking a Number 20 brush, he touched the burnt umber with it delicately and then dipped the brush in the gob of French vermilion, swirling to mix.

When he had what he wanted, Dezso Valasi turned from the table and made one clean, sure slash down the center of the canvas with the brush. The wide line of livid color that sprang at him from the white of the canvas gave him a shock of pure delight.

Valasi smiled. Vivid color, rich food, and old friends—these passions he could still enjoy.

While Valasi continued his work among the sun-drenched abbey ruins overlooking the sea, Gilbert Soumagnac finished his tour of the grounds and returned to the house with Juliet Shale. He listened attentively, taking in the area behind the house with quick observant glances, while she explained the seating, entertainment, and catering arrangements. He already had his own list of the catering staff, and knew each man's name and background.

Now Juliet Shale gave him a list of the guests. He sat on the veranda and went through the list with her. Many of the names he knew. But there were obscure people, old friends of Valasi's, whom he did not know. Juliet told him briefly about these.

When they came to the name André Courtois, she explained that he was a businessman she had known a long time—another old friend. She did not make it clear to Soumagnac that Bel Jahra—André Courtois—was *her* old friend, not Valasi's, because she did not consider her personal life any of his business.

Nor, since Valasi's two special guests of honor were supposed to be kept quite secret until the last moment, did she tell him about the King of Jordan or the Secretary of State.

Günther Dietrich began worrying about the weather at four that afternoon. Until three it had been sunny and clear, with the sea gentle and the wind light, about force one. But then a very low pressure area had begun to move in on Côte d'Azur; the kind of dense atmosphere that started people's nerves crawling. There were still no clouds, and the wind died out entirely; the sea becoming flat as glass in the dead calm. But the heat of the sun kept sucking up moisture from the land and water; and now that moisture had nowhere to go. By four o'clock the mixture of mountain mist and sea fog was spreading out low and thick.

Dietrich worried because even on a clear night, with the aid of surface radar, two small vessels finding each other beyond sight of land could be tricky. Fog made it much more difficult. If it got worse—and he sensed that it would—the transfer at sea that Bel Jahra required could be delayed for hours.

Dietrich didn't know the operation Bel Jahra had planned—only his own part in it: the transfer and landing tonight, the pickup the following night. But he did know it was something important. Bashir Mawdri had made that very clear. And Dietrich couldn't afford to fail in anything important. Not with these kind of Arabs. It could result in his losing what was even more important to him than the money. So Dietrich paced the outermost quay of Beaulieu anxiously watching the steadily worsening visibility.

Beaulieu is the last place along the Riviera that one would look for a vessel involved with gun running and terrorist smuggling. Sheltered from cold winds by an amphitheater of high hills and cliffs, Beaulieu has a quiet flavor of genteel wealth created by generations of upper-class British families that have built their winter villas there. Though relatively tiny, the town has three four-star hotels, a large variety of fashionable boutiques and expensive restaurants, and the greatest concentration of yacht brokers on the Côte d'Azur.

That was why Günther Dietrich had chosen to moor his boat in Beaulieu's modern marina. He knew that there he would not be subjected to suspicious interest by the customs and port officials of the harbor's *capitainerie*. Beaulieu treats its yachtsmen with respect. Most of these yachtsmen pay a very great deal to purchase permanent ownership of their docking space. Dietrich was docked at the Quai du Levant, inside the long, connected seawall protecting the marina. His space was owned by an oil tycoon who had given him written permission to use it—after being requested to do so by Bashir Mawdri.

Armed with this permission, Dietrich had experienced no problems at all with Beaulieu's port officers. The prestige of the man who'd lent him his space inclined them to be extremely polite. Even if they'd had reason for suspicion, they would have been inclined to curb it. And they had no reason. Dietrich's boat, named the *Shalimar,* had a Panama registration, which indicated that it belonged to some international corporation. Its falsified logbooks showed that it had been pleasure-cruising the northern Mediterranean for the past two years, having last docked for four months in Cannes. And the *Shalimar* looked like it belonged in Beaulieu.

Most of the marina's docking space was taken by motor vessels ranging from sleek cabin cruisers to enormous oceangoing yachts. International home-ports were lettered on their transoms: London, Jersey, Gibraltar, Panama, Hong Kong, San Francisco, Palermo, Colon, Hamburg. The *Shalimar* was at home among them: a forty-two-foot sports cruiser with teak decks and bronze fittings; a spacious and luxurious main stateroom, two smaller cabins and galley; a wheelhouse equipped with the latest navigational aides including surface radar, echo sounder, radio direction finder, and autopilot. The engines were powerful twin Perkins diesels, there was a high flying bridge with complete alternative steering and engine controls, and the big open cockpit had two blue-padded swivel fishing chairs bolted in place. And all of this had that special spotless sheen that only money can buy.

It was Libyan money that had bought this dream of a lifetime for Dietrich. For a number of years before that, he had been down on his luck; and beginning to think he was too old for another upswing. He was a long, bony man of fifty-nine with a weather-ravaged face and the bearing of a naval officer. He'd been second-in-command of a U-boat in World War II. The fall of Hitler's Germany had ended his career, for several years. Then a Lebanese smuggling syndicate had hired him to skipper a converted patrol boat.

Four years of that had earned him plenty. Then an Italian customs patrol had captured the boat and sent him to jail. Most of his savings had gone into buying his way out after two years. He'd invested what he had left in a small smuggling vessel of his own. But he'd been barely earning eating money with it when the Libyans had come along with their proposition.

Dietrich had never regretted going along with it. There'd been a spot of trouble four months ago, when a German cop had somehow gotten evidence that he was moving guerrillas and arms from Hamburg to England. But Bashir Mawdri had paid off the cop, squashed the evidence, and transferred Dietrich to the Med. That was the only time there'd been trouble; and the last three months along the Riviera had been practically a vacation. He owned the *Shalimar* now, though it had originally been bought by the Libyans. And there would soon be enough in a Swiss bank for him to really retire on.

But failure to carry out an important job properly could bring an abrupt end to this good fortune. So Dietrich's anxiety grew as the weather got steadily worse.

By six that evening, there were occasional long, slow swells on the gray surface of the sea; like nervous ripples under an oily skin. But the dense mist hung motionless, with no breeze to stir it. Dietrich could see the nearest headland of Cap Roux off to the left only indistinctly; and Pointe Saint-Hospice farther to his right not at all. The whole scene had a mirage quality to it. The town behind the marina seemed to be smoking and the mountains vanished upward into the murk. The yellowish cliffs dropping to the new beach across the Quai Nord looked transparent; and a number of small boats coming in toward the breakwater outside the marina seemed suspended in the white mist above the gray water.

Scowling apprehensively, Dietrich abruptly stopped pacing and walked quickly around the quays to the shore-side docking area. Going past the long lineup of smart shops, restaurants, and yacht brokerages of the marina's commercial gallery, he went into the *capitainerie* for an official weather forecast. The prediction wasn't bad: The low-pressure area was supposed to lift, sometime in the night. Exactly when was not certain.

Dietrich walked back out to the Quai du Levant, studying the mist and not quite believing it. But around sunset, as the mist began to acquire black patches, it did lift. Not much. It rose until the bottom of the mist was about five feet above the darkening surface of the sea, and then stopped. But that was enough. Dietrich boarded his boat and began warming up the engines.

He had made a point of taking the *Shalimar* out several times for night fishing, staying away all night each time. No one in the Beaulieu marina would wonder about his doing it again this night. The lights of the marina went on as full darkness closed in. No moonlight penetrated the dark overhang of mist. The red and white lights of the Total fuel dock at the end of the quay reflected a long way against the bottom of the mist and the surface of the sea, creating a horizontal corridor with a seemingly solid ceiling and floor. Dietrich looked at his watch and flicked on his binnacle and navigation lights. It was almost time.

Five minutes later a car swung down from the Boulevard d'Alsace-Lorraine, into the marina. It parked among the other cars on the Quai Nord, and two men got out. Bel Jahra was dressed for fishing, including a long-peaked fisherman's cap that completely shadowed most of his face. Since he wasn't going to have anybody looking at him closely in a strong light, that was all he needed. Dietrich had only met him once before, and wouldn't have recognized him; except for the build and the fact that he was expecting him. And the fact that Hammou was with him.

Dietrich left the wheelhouse and went out in the cockpit. Bel Jahra and Hammou had turned onto the shadowed Quai du Levant and were coming toward the *Shalimar*. They came on board without speaking; Bel Jahra merely giving him a short nod as he ducked inside. Dietrich cast off the lines and went up the ladder onto the open flying bridge. The visibility was better there for close maneuvering inside the marina. Standing at the controls, he eased the *Shalimar* away from the quay, heading for the open end and keeping below the marina's maximum limit of three knots.

He had installed special mufflers for the engines upon acquiring the boat from the Libyans, so the boat would be safer for the kind of work they'd wanted. When they were going slow like this, the engines were very quiet, their sound hardly carrying. Making a U-turn around the end of the quay, he took the *Shalimar* out through the main channel between the quay's outside seawall and the breakwater. When the boat was well clear of the red signal lamp on the end of the breakwater, Dietrich took it on a wide swing to starboard and steered south, leaving Beaulieu behind and increasing speed.

In a few minutes Pointe Saint-Hospice emerged from the dark mists off the starboard bow. Going past it, he waited until he could just make out the hilltop crowned by the marine semaphore on Cap Ferrat. Then he put the controls on autopilot and went down into the wheelhouse. In the dim light inside, Driss Hammou looked very short and thick sitting on the settee across from the helmsman's chair. Bel Jahra stood leaning against the forward bulkhead, peering ahead into the misted night through the long, low front windows.

Dietrich turned on the wheelhouse radar. "Even with this," he warned Bel Jahra, "it may take some time to find the other boat with so much fog."

Bel Jahra turned his head and looked at Dietrich, not saying anything. Something in the set of his shadowed features made Dietrich nervous. He disconnected the autopilot and busied himself with the controls, kicking the speed up to twenty knots. The engines responded with an instant surge of fierce power, hurling the boat across the black water with a smooth, dull roar. Dietrich glanced at the main compass in its illuminated binnacle, and angled southwest.

It was 9 P.M. There was almost exactly twenty-four hours to go, before the operation went into execution.

It was 10 P.M. when the combing of the Carnoles area was abandoned. Lamarck stayed for dinner with his friends from customs, who still insisted he'd seen Bel Jahra there the previous night. Uri went off to get a night's sleep. Shansky drove to Monte Carlo to see if he could dig anything of interest out of his old contact, Hammelring. Hunter dropped into Lamarck's home on the way into Nice, to bring Odile up to date and check for messages.

She had a veal stew cooking on the stove when he came in. "If you're hungry, there's more than enough. I was expecting Olivier back."

"Thanks. Smells good." Hunter sat heavily and leaned his forearms on the table, watching Odile move in the kitchenette. Even at that time of night she radiated health and vigor, making him unreasonably irritable. It had been a frustrating day.

"Any calls?" he asked her.

"A couple. Mort Crown phoned from Paris. Bel Jahra's girl there told her other friend he took her to St. Tropez late last summer. The Paradis Hotel. Bel Jahra seemed to know people there. If that's any use to you."

"It could be. . . ." At any rate, it couldn't be ignored. Hunter only hoped it didn't turn out like Carnoles.

Odile studied Hunter, frowning. "You look tired."

"I am."

Odile nodded at the alcove off the main room. "Why don't you get some sleep after we eat?"

"It's not lack of sleep. Just nerves. What's the other message?"

"Your consulate phoned, before they closed for the night. Said to tell you a man named Murray Norman was living in Italy when last heard of. Somewhere around Rome, probably. No definite address."

Hunter picked up the phone and put a call through long-distance to Major Diego Bandini's apartment in Rome.

He didn't expect anything to come of it.

But he did it, anyway.

TWENTY

Through the mists of the moonless night, the two vessels circled in search of each other.

The seventy-foot cutter had come a long way for its rendezvous with the *Shalimar:* from the port of Zuara, on the Libyan coast west of Tripoli; north and then west around Tunisia; north past the west coasts of Sardinia and Corsica. It looked like nothing more than what it had been for twenty years: a commercial fishing vessel. What didn't show were the new engines that took up most of the aft fish hold—and could push the cutter along at twenty knots. And the sophisticated radar antennae which were disguised when not in use.

It was after midnight when its radar screen picked up the blip of a smaller vessel circling slowly to the north. Thirteen miles away, according to the screen's grid.

There wouldn't be many vessels that size out that far from land at night—especially a night with such poor visibility. The Libyan cutter altered course and closed on it.

The *Shalimar*'s radar picked up the larger vessel as it changed course. Bel Jahra watched the blip moving in a straight line toward them on the screen. When it was seven miles away, and still coming, he spoke briefly and went up onto the flying bridge with a flashlight. Hammou got a high-powered rifle with a night scope from behind a false back in the oilskin locker, and climbed up after him. Bel Jahra spread his feet to the gentle roll and pitch of the *Shalimar,* standing in the open with the flash ready. Hammou went down on one knee beside him with the rifle. Just in case.

Dietrich kept the *Shalimar* throttled down, circling slowly;

but ready to feed all her power into an abrupt escape surge if the big blip turned out to be the wrong kind of vessel.

Sound carries farther in damp air. Bel Jahra heard the powerful engines of the cutter while the vessel was still invisible. But it was impossible to tell where the sound came from; it echoed off the heaviest banks of fog and reached Bel Jahra from different directions. Then he saw a patch of white off the port quarter: the bow wave of the oncoming vessel. A moment later the dark length of the cutter materialized out of the mists a couple hundred yards away. Its bow wave diminished as it slowed on spotting the *Shalimar*.

Bel Jahra aimed the flashlight in the cutter's direction. He thumbed it: on, off; on, off. Down inside the wheelhouse, Dietrich had one hand on the throttles, the other on the wheel—poised to swerve away and slam on full speed if the correct answering signal did not come quickly.

It did: four quick blinks from the dark cutter. Bel Jahra lowered the flashlight and smiled. A powerful searchlight stabbed out from the top of the cutter's deckhouse. Its beam found Bel Jahra and held on him. Bel Jahra slitted his eyes against the glare as he faced it, remaining standing and removing the fishing cap so he could be identified through night binoculars. The searchlight went off, and the cutter heaved to, barely drifting.

Bel Jahra called down to Dietrich. The *Shalimar* swung toward the waiting cutter. Climbing down to the starboard deck, Bel Jahra and Hammou hung the big rubber fenders over the side. Seconds later the fenders touched as Dietrich eased his boat alongside the cutter. With the sea and air dead calm, it was a simple maneuver without risk. Dietrich throttled back as Bel Jahra and Hammou grabbed hold of the Jacob's ladder hanging down the cutter's side.

One by one the five guerrillas of Bel Jahra's second commando group came down the ladder, going quickly into the *Shalimar*'s big cockpit. Each had a canvas pack strapped on his back; containing weapons, ammunition, grenades, a twenty-four-hour supply of dry food rations and water. Plus quick-energy pills to be taken before the moment of the assault, the following night. When all five guerrillas were in the cockpit, Bel Jahra pushed against the flaking metal hull of the cutter. The *Shalimar* drifted away from the Libyan vessel. Dietrich fed power into his engines and swung the bow to port. A wide, curving wake churned the black surface of the sea astern of the *Shalimar* as it pointed its bow north, the throbbing engines revving up to full speed.

Hammou followed Bel Jahra into the cockpit. Bel Jahra silently gripped each guerrilla's hand in turn, looking into their faces. In each he saw an eager, nervous excitement. Bel Jahra settled himself in one of the fishing seats. Hammou took the other. The five guerrillas unstrapped their packs and settled in a tight semi-circle on the cockpit desk, facing them. Without preliminary, Bel Jahra began hammering questions at them; testing each for his detailed knowledge of his special task, and the layout of the Valasi estate. None of them failed to answer a single question correctly. Their Syrian instructor had rebriefed them repeatedly, following Bel Jahra's minutely detailed orders to the letter.

Bel Jahra continued his own briefing of the group, hitting one and then another with tricky, unexpected problems. Every move of their separate tasks was already ingrained in their brains. Bel Jahra concentrated on embedding all of it in their guts as well. He was leaving absolutely nothing to chance.

There were only two unknown factors at this point: the exact position of Valasi's main table; and the exact places at that table where the two main targets would be seated. During the party the following night, Bel Jahra would wait until he knew both of these factors. Until then Hammou and the five guerrillas would remain hidden under the ruins on the Valasi estate. When Bel Jahra was able to give them the final two points which must be known, the execution of the operation would instantly begin.

The smallest member of the commando group was code-named Khdanni. He had proved himself one of the best marksmen with a pistol in the Tocra camp. Khdanni and Bel Jahra would concentrate on the two main targets; nothing else. They would get in as close as possible—Khdanni to Hussein, Bel Jahra to the American—before anyone around them sensed any danger. At very close range they would bring out their .45 caliber revolvers, and fire as many shots as possible into the heads of their separate victims.

Their first shots would be the signal for the others to instantly join in the slaughter. Rasul and Abu, the two who would be using submachine guns, would have already approached to one side of the main table. As soon as Bel Jahra and Khdanni whipped out their revolvers and placed the first head-shots into their targets,

Rasul and Abu would sweep the entire table with long, low machine-gun bursts. These would accomplish a number of objectives: The two main targets would almost certainly be among the people at the main table struck by the slashing bursts, making their deaths doubly certain. The general slaughter at the main table would create panic and confusion. The bodyguards closest to the main targets were likely to be slaughtered along with the others, before they could get their own guns out.

At the same time Samoud, the commando team's demolition expert, would start lobbing in his special grenades. Two on top of the table, two rolled under the table. Again, three objectives: more confusion and terror among the enemy; the certain blasting of any close bodyguards who managed to survive the flailing machine-gun fire; and the final insurance that the two primary targets were left dead, not merely wounded.

The fifth guerrilla, code-named Kurfi, had the emotional makeup required for his own special task—as proven by his diligence as a torturer for a Fatah extortion team. Armed with pistols, it would be the job of Kurfi and Driss Hammou to seize the children to be used as hostages for their escape. Bel Jahra's instructions were to grab the smallest children; because these would be the easiest to control. The instant there was a lull in the first assault on the main table, before security guards not killed in the general slaughter there could move in to attack, Hammou would shoot one of the children. This should make the advancing security guards fall back and hold their fire. If any of them failed to immediately heed the warning, Kurfi would shoot another child to make the warning absolutely clear to all of them.

For two hours Bel Jahra continued to drill them relentlessly. Dietrich turning off his navigation lights signaled the end to it. The boat was off Cap Martin.

Darkness and mist made the cliffs below the seaward edge of Valasi's estate indistinct; and the great ripped boulders in the surf at their base invisible. But inside his wheelhouse, Dietrich was now using the echo sounder to give him the depths, and there was a sharp outline of the coast on his small radar screen. He throttled down to two knots, angling the boat toward the precise spot Bel Jahra had showed him on his chart of the Cap Martin shoreline.

Bel Jahra rose to his feet and watched the nearing bulk of the cliff through the dark mists. The guerrillas began strapping the packs on their backs. The sounds of surf sloshing lazily in and out of the rocks at the cliff's base reached them. Dietrich cut the engines entirely. The boat continued to glide forward through the water, slowing gradually. It came to a slow-swinging stop as Dietrich quietly paid out the anchor. The cliff ahead was now a black mass that shut off everything else, the top disappearing into the mist above.

Bel Jahra gazed at it, and wondered at his complete lack of emotion. Until now a driving excitement had sustained him. Now that he was so close, it was gone; leaving nothing. He *thought* about a number of things: the faint possibility there'd be someone on top of that cliff, waiting to spoil it; the time elements involved in getting up there, and getting away. But he *felt nothing.*

If bothered him, though he remembered similar times, and understood the reason for it. The driving excitement had been necessary to force his project along this far. That was no longer needed, now that the project was in the actual initial stage of fulfillment. What was necessary from here on was clear, calm, quick thinking; without the impingement of distracting emotions. And his brain *was* functioning with almost abnormal clarity. But he was still bothered by the temporary loss of feeling.

There was a large rubber raft secured to the bow deck. Bel Jahra and Hammou removed the fastenings. Kurfi and Rasul helped them lower it over the side, into the water. The commandos went down into it, quickly and quietly. They had been well trained, in every aspect. No further spoken instructions were necessary.

Bel Jahra and Hammou went down last. As they settled in the raft, Khdanni and Abu began paddling it away from the *Shalimar,* working carefully with a minimum of splashing.

Dietrich had gotten the boat quite close. It took only ten seconds for the rubber raft to reach the rocks. As it bumped quietly, Kurfi and Hammou climbed onto the rocks and secured a mooring line to a stone projection. Bel Jahra moved past them toward the cliff base on his rubber-soled shoes, moving cautiously over the jagged, storm-torn rock surfaces.

Samoud followed him. In addition to being a demolition expert, Samoud was the member of the group with rock-climbing experience. He had brought pitons in his pack, to help him make the climb. But as he moved his hands over the dark cliff base, and studied what he could see of the rest of it above him, he decided these would not be needed. What had seemed to Bel Jahra a sheer, difficult wall was to the more experienced Samoud a basic hand and toehold climb.

He whispered this in Bel Jahra's ear. Bel Jahra's hand gripped his shoulder, briefly; then gestured upward. Samoud removed his pack and opened it. He got out a rolled-up nylon-cord ladder; its strands thin but enormously strong. To the last strand was knotted one end of a ball of fishing line. Samoud tied the other end of the line to his belt, and began the climb.

The others came in around Bel Jahra as he stood there watching Samoud go up the dark cliff wall; pausing occasionally to grope for another toe or hand hold, then inching upward again. Khdanni, the pistol sharpshooter, knelt and got one of a pair of .45 caliber revolvers from his pack. He loaded it quickly and silently, by feel. He stood up and gave the gun, and a flat box of spare cartridges, to Bel Jahra. Samoud was by then halfway up the cliff. Bel Jahra watched the dark mists up there absorb him. He tucked the revolver in his belt, and the spare ammunition in his pocket. Samoud could no longer be seen up there.

Minutes later, Samoud hauled himself over the top of the cliff, onto the edge of Valasi's dark, silent estate. For a time he lay there flat to the ground, getting his breath back as he looked around. As far as he could see in the darkness, he was alone. There was only the black loom of high trees, and the nearer jut of some of the ruins. When his breathing was under control he continued to lie there, listening. But there were no alarming sounds.

Getting to his feet, Samoud moved crouched along the edge of the cliff top. He located the tree stump where Bel Jahra had said it would be. Kneeling, he began pulling up the fishing line. When one end of the nylon ladder came up to him, Samoud attached it securely to the stump.

Down on the surf rocks below, the other end of the nylon ladder was at Bel Jahra's chest level. He had judged the height of the cliff perfectly. Grasping the vertical strands of the ladder to hold them wide apart, he began climbing the rungs. Hammou hung

Samoud's pack on his shoulder, and waited until Bel Jahra's weight was off the ladder before following him up.

At the top of the cliff, Bel Jahra crouched beside Samoud with the revolver held ready in his hand as he squinted inland through the night. He couldn't make out Valasi's house through the hills and trees; nor even lights from that direction. He couldn't see or or hear anyone around them; but that had to be made certain. Leaving the edge of the cliff, Bel Jahra vanished silently into the darkness, for a search of the area around the abbey ruins.

All the men, arms, and supplies were on the top of the cliff when Bel Jahra returned, having found no sign of danger anywhere. Motioning, Bel Jahra led them back across the dark terrain, into the ruins. There, behind the half-collapsed cloister wall, he knelt beside the dark, partially covered hole leading down to the crypt. He had already gone down into it, during his search a few minutes ago. What was left of the interior of the crypt was small. But enough space to hide them all—though not in comfort.

Khdanni lowered himself in first, the pitch-blackness below ground swallowing him. His hands appeared darkly as he reached up out of the hole, pulling in the packs that were handed to him one by one.

Bel Jahra leaned close to the other men and whispered: "There is a low tunnel at the bottom, to the left. It doesn't go anywhere, but it's just large enough for all of you to crowd inside, when it is daylight. There is a part of a broken stone stair. Pull it across the end of the tunnel when you're inside. That way, if someone looks down in this hole during the day, you won't be seen. It won't be comfortable, but it's not something you can't endure. And there is no other way."

They nodded tightly, and disappeared into the black hole in turn. All except Hammou, who went back to the cliff edge with Bel Jahra. Taking his revolver and ammunition box, Bel Jahra gave them to Hammou to keep in the crypt for him. He couldn't risk walking into the party with a gun tomorrow night; even as an invited guest. There was always the chance of an electronic detector hidden by the security men near the entrance door.

Bel Jahra went quickly down the ladder to the rocks. As soon as his weight was off it, Hammou hauled up the ladder and carried it with him to the crypt under the ruins. Bel Jahra got in the rubber raft, detached the mooring line, and paddled back to the *Shalimar*.

Dietrich was waiting on the bow deck. Bel Jahra climbed up beside him. Together, they hauled up the raft and attached it. Bel Jahra stood for a moment staring back at the black cliff rising out of the dark sea into the overhead mists. Thinking of his men hidden inside the ruins at the top. Suddenly, a touch of the old excitement ran swiftly through his veins.

It was no longer necessary. But he enjoyed the feeling. Quietly, he told Dietrich to get them back to Beaulieu. It would soon be dawn.

There was still an hour to go before dawn when the *Shalimar* rounded the deep end of the Beaulieu breakwater, and entered the marina.

Dov Tohar's rented cabin cruiser was temporarily moored out at the end of Beaulieu marina's central pier; to a public dock where visiting boats were allowed short-term privileges. He was falling asleep sitting up inside his main cabin, when a powerful light glaring briefly against his drooping eyelids shocked him awake. The light had passed on when his eyes snapped open. He looked through the windows on the wheelhouse side of the cabin, and saw he'd been wakened by the searchlight from the *capitainerie*, sweeping past to help a yacht find its way in between the breakwater and the end of the seawall. Dov saw that the incoming boat was the *Shalimar*, and sat up straighter.

Some months ago, a Mossad agent in Germany had reported evidence that the *Shalimar*, run by Günther Dietrich, was operating out of Hamburg smuggling arms and terrorists for the Arab guerrilla organizations. Before close surveillance could be clamped on Dietrich, he'd sailed his *Shalimar* out of Hamburg and failed to return. Word had gone out through Mossad to keep an eye open for it at the other ports of Europe.

After months with no further word on the *Shalimar*, it had finally been located here in Beaulieu, four days ago. Dov Tohar had been working in Haifa at the time. He did not belong to Mossad. For most of his twenty-four years he'd been a seaman. During five of those years he skippered a patrol boat for the tiny Israeli coast guard. For the past year his job had been marine security, working for Shin Beth, Israel's internal counterespionage service.

But it had been decided that Dov was the best available man for this particular need: keeping track of *Shalimar's* movements whenever Dietrich got around to leaving Beaulieu. Flown to Nice two days ago, he'd rented the cabin cruiser, sailed to Beaulieu, and managed to get temporary mooring rights at the public dock.

Two days of keeping an eye on the *Shalimar* had netted him nothing but boredom. At six the previous evening, with Dietrich showing no sign of departing, and the fog making it unlikely, Dov had taken a nap so he'd be fresh for night surveillance. He'd overslept. When he'd wakened, the *Shalimar* was gone.

Dov didn't feel guilty about it. He was only one man, and couldn't mount a round-the-clock stake-out all by himself. But the bad luck of his nap-timing did upset him. His boat was equipped with excellent radar, for the purpose of keeping tabs on the *Shalimar* at sea. But without any indication of the direction Dietrich had taken, the odds were that Dov would wind up locating the wrong blip, and following it all night before learning his error.

He checked at the *capitainerie*. There he learned that Dietrich had made no arrangements for permanent departure; and that he sometimes went out for a night of fishing. The odds were in favor of his returning. Dov settled down to wait for him.

He waited first over an extravagantly priced pizza at a terrace table of the marina's African Queen restaurant. Then he shifted next door to an outside table at the Clipper Bar, where he primed himself for a long night with heavily sugared black coffees, and flirted with the pretty girls off the biggest yachts, most of them English, German, or Italian. When the bar closed at one-thirty in the morning, he returned to his boat and settled down to play double-deck solitaire in the saloon half of the main cabin. By the hour before dawn, when the *Shalimar* finally returned, Dov was exhausted. But he reacted quickly, snapping out the cabin lamp and picking up a pair of binoculars.

He didn't go out of the cabin for a better view, because at that hour it would have drawn Dietrich's attention to him. All the boats in the marina were dark, and there was no one in sight anywhere around the marina. Remaining seated on the saloon settee, Dov trained the binoculars through his side window. The *Shalimar* backed into its usual docking space. Dietrich came out on deck and began securing the mooring lines. Another man appeared in the *Shalimar*'s cockpit. The first visitor Dietrich had had in the two days Dov had been watching.

Dov adjusted the focus a hair as the visitor left the *Shalimar* and stode off along the quay. He was a tall man, with a lean, powerful figure; dressed for sports fishing. That was all Dov could tell about him in the night shadows under the seawall. His long-peaked fishing cap made a black blur of the man's face. Dov continued to follow him with the binoculars, waiting patiently.

When the man strode past one of the low quay lamps, the light reflected up against his face. Dov had an instant feeling he knew that face. But before he could figure out where he knew it from, the man's next stride took him out of the light and the face became darkly shadowed again.

Dov kept the binoculars on the moving figure, waiting for it to pass another quay light. But when it did, the superstructure of a moored yacht was between the man and Dov's point of view. A moment later the man was among the parked cars on the Quai Nord, and Dov couldn't catch another look at his face.

The man got into one of the cars. Dov tried for the license number with his binoculars. But other cars were in the way. Dov kept trying as the man drove away. But parked vehicles and docked boats concealed the moving car almost entirely the whole way around the marina and up onto the boulevard exit.

When it was gone, Dov lowered the binoculars and rubbed his eyes, thinking about that briefly glimpsed face. He still had the feeling of knowing it from somewhere. But his glimpse of it had been too short, and the features were already becoming indistinct in his mind.

Dov decided, finally, that the familiar feeling had come from the man reminding him of a commander he'd once known in the coast guard. He returned his attention to the *Shalimar*, where Dietrich seemed to be setting in for a morning's sleep.

It was ten in the morning when Diego Bandini learned where Murray Norman could be found. Getting the information had not been difficult: a phone call to the Rome office of CMA, an international talent agency handling film actors and directors. It seemed that everyone in the movie business in Rome knew of

Murray Norman. His reputation as a producer was low; but as a man who left bad debts behind him it was widespread.

Bandini personally drove out of Rome to see him. He could have sent a subordinate, or waited until Norman's return to the city. Hunter's request had not been urgent. But this was Bandini's day off, his wife was visiting her family for the week, and he enjoyed the idea of a few hours of fresh country air.

The villa where Murray Norman was shooting his first picture in three years was in the hills north of Rome, overlooking Lake Bracciano near Bagni di Vicarello. It was a large, dilapidated building wrapped around a decaying courtyard and surrounded by walled grounds that hadn't been tended for decades. It had been built in the Middle Ages, on the foundations of an emperor's villa destroyed thirty years after the death of Christ. The family that still owned it hadn't been near it for fifty years. The rundown and overgrown condition of the place, and the fact that the owners were willing to wait for payment for its use, made it perfect for filming Norman's picture, which concerned vampires.

Bandini found Norman, who was acting as his own director, inside the courtyard. He was setting up a scene in which a male vampire and a female vampire were to fight to the death in the huge basin of a silted-up fountain. Since the camera crew spoke only Italian, while the male vampire was French and the female vampire was German, it was a difficult process. Bandini advanced across tiled paving that broke beneath his weight, and introduced himself.

Murray Norman appeared to be about thirty; a short, compact man with a pugnacious face and long yellow hair. He took one look at Bandini's police I.D., and closed his hyperthyroid eyes in deep pain. "Oh my God . . ." he whispered, and forced his eyes to open. "Look, Major," he pleaded, "I swear to you . . . everybody's gonna get paid. Everybody. I *know* I still owe Marghera for that last batch of film, and—"

"I didn't come about that, Mr. Norman," Bandini interrupted, touched by the man's agony. "I'm trying to locate someone, and you may be able to help. That's all."

Norman closed his eyes again, and gave a deep sigh of relief. When his eyes snapped open, he was smiling. "Okay, glad to help in any way, Major." He yelled at the crew and actors: "Take a break. But stay close where I can find you." He repeated it in Italian, French, and German, took Bandini by the arm, and led him through a cracking arcade into a much smaller courtyard.

A card table and several canvas chairs had been set up there. A makeup man was painting blood on the face and throat of a pretty actress. Norman shooed them away, and gestured Bandini into one of the chairs. He sat in another, mopping his perspiring face. "This goddamn heat in this part of Italy . . ." He pulled off his yellow wig and mopped his bald head, transformed abruptly into a man of fifty. "Who's the guy you want to know about, Major? Or is it a girl?"

Bandini got a picture of Bel Jahra from his pocket and handed it to Norman. "This man." He watched Norman frown at the picture without recognition. "Someone in Cannes," Bandini prompted, "saw you having drinks with this man on the terrace of the Carlton bar at the film festival two years ago."

Norman took another look at Bel Jahra's picture. "Yeah . . ." he said slowly. "Now I remember. . . ." He snapped his fingers several times to aid his memory. "André . . . André Courtois . . . that's his name."

Bandini hunched forward a bit. "That is the only name you know him by?"

"Yeah." Norman grinned suddenly. "You mean it was a phony? I should've known. And there I was, trying to con him into lending me some dough to finish a picture. He was *supposed* to be loaded. Big business in Morocco or someplace like that. According to my secretary. *That's* the way it always goes at those film festivals: guys without dough trying to con other guys without dough." He laughed, mostly at himself.

"Anything you know about him," Bandini said, "might help us locate him."

Norman shook his head. "I don't know *anything* more'n I just told you. Just saw him that once, two years ago. The girl who was my secretary then might know more. She's the one introduced him to me. I'm pretty sure he was screwing her, so she should know *something.*"

"And where can I find your secretary?"

"Search me. Ain't seen *her* in almost two years. Guess she went back to England. That's where she's from."

"Do you have her address?"

Norman shrugged. "Nope. I couldn't pay her anymore, so she split. Haven't heard from her since, so what can I tell you? Except she's English, and her name's Juliet Shale."

Hunter was at the consulate in Nice at two that afternoon, when Bandini phoned this information to him from Rome. Hunter thanked him for taking the trouble.

At the other end of the line, Bandini laughed quietly. "You don't have to be polite, Simon. It is a two-year-old lead, which doesn't make it very interesting for your purposes."

"Not very," Hunter had to admit.

But he did call Inspector Klar in London and pass it on. "Her name's Juliet Shale and she's English. That's all we've got. If you can find her and speak to her about it for me, she just *might* have something on Bel Jahra a little more recent."

"It's a fairly busy day for me," Klar told him, with what was obviously massive understatement. "I don't know when I can get to it."

"No rush," Hunter told him. "Whenever you have the time."

He hung up and decided to go to St. Tropez. It was the most resent lead they had, and there was nothing else left to work from. Shansky was already there; but two men could cover the ground a lot faster and more thoroughly. He was getting his jacket off the back of his chair when the phone rang. Hunter snatched it up with a momentary surge of hope; which died when he heard the voice at the other end.

It was from Washington; a switchboard operator at the State Department. Hunter sat on the edge of his desk and waited for his caller to be put on, bracing himself.

Chavez came on the line with the kindly voice one uses visiting a sick friend one does not expect to recover: "'Lo, Simon. How's it coming?"

"Not bad," Hunter lied. "We're covering it like a blanket."

That, at least, was the truth. "Whatever Bel Jahra's trying to pull off, it's going to happen inside the next couple days. That, I'm sure of." Hunter hesitated, and then gave Chavez the whole truth: "If we're not on top of him by then, we've had it."

There was a pause at the other end. Then Chavez told him quietly: "I'm afraid you've already had it. I promised I'd let you run with it as long as I could. Until I started getting kicked in the ass over you. Well, I'm getting kicked. They're not getting the reports at this end they expected from you. People over there're complaining you're not meeting with them like you were supposed to. And now on top of that, the word's in that you're some kind of anarchist revolutionary nut. Don't like big business-men, the government, or anybody that counts."

Hunter thought about the conference he'd arranged in Paris, and what he'd said to State's BIR man during it. That had been a mistake. "Sorry," he told Chavez stiffly. "I'm not much of a diplo-mat."

"No," Chavez agreed, "you're not. You *are* a damn good cop." That was the glass of brandy for the condemned man before the kill: "But this job does call for a diplomat. I should have realized, when I picked you. *My* fault." There was another slight pause. "Listen, Simon, *maybe* I'm making this more definite than it really is. There could still be a way: You get over here. On the next plane. And start talking—real fast and real good. Maybe you can make them understand, what you're doing and why. Pull *that* off, and you've got a new lease on life."

"I'd like to make the try," Hunter said slowly. "But it'll have to wait. Like I said, the next couple days are going to do it here. One way or the other."

"It can't wait two days," Chavez told him flatly. "You'd have to get over here now. Right away."

"I can't," Hunter told him, just as flatly.

There was a long pause at the other end. "That's it, then." Chavez's voice had no emotion left in it at all.

Hunter looked through the window at the roses climbing the palm tree in the consulate garden. "That's how it goes sometimes. See you around." He hung up the phone and sat there for a time, surprised to find that he was not depressed.

His stubbornness had its own reasons, deep inside him. It was worth it. Even if he was finished at State. Even if, in spite of his re-fusal to rush back to save it, he failed to nail Bel Jahra. It had ab-sorbed him totally. And it had put a wall between him and the past. Because of it, he was functioning again. All of him.

He got off the desk and went out of the consulate, to drive to St. Tropez and join Shansky.

He was still gone at 6 P.M., when Inspector Klar phoned for him at the consulate in Nice. By then everybody was gone except the consular clerk, who was getting ready to leave for a family gathering, for which he was already late. He took down Klar's message carefully, left it on his desk so he'd remember to give it to Hunter first thing in the morning, and locked up the consulate on the way out.

At 7 P.M., Bel Jahra prepared to leave the apartment in Roquebrune and drive down to Valasi's birthday party. He stuck the engraved invitation in his pocket and surveyed himself critically in the full-length mirror of the bedroom. There was to be no formal attire at the party; Valasi insisted on that, Juliet Shale had told him. Bel Jahra was wearing gray slacks and pullover, with a dark sports jacket. It seemed to him that his reflection in the mirror looked entirely relaxed; his features coolly controlled, actually calm.

He continued to study his reflection as he got a cigarette and lit it. He took one drag, and then snatched it from his lips and dropped it on the carpet. He ground it under his heel as he turned and walked out.

Win or lose, he would not be coming back.

TWENTY-ONE

At seven-thirty, half an hour before the sun set, Günther Dietrich left the *Shalimar* and walked around the quays toward the Beaulieu marina's commercial galleries. He walked with the measured step of a man with a purpose; but not hurrying.

Dov Tohar, washing down the deck of his cabin cruiser at the end of the central pier, watched the way Dietrich was moving. Turning off the hose, Dov left his boat and sauntered down the pier. Since this was a much shorter route, he reached the galleries well before Dietrich. Sleepily, he examined the display of expensive pullovers in a sports shop window while he waited.

He had been up all of the previous night, and most of this day, and he was dog-weary. And resentful. This was actually a Mossad job he was doing here. They couldn't really expect him to maintain a twenty-four-hour watch on Dietrich, all by himself. But that was pretty much what he was doing; and if Dietrich gave him the slip they wouldn't like it. Yet they wouldn't lend him a single Mossad agent to help. It seemed that all of them in the area were involved in Uri Ezan's hunt for that Moroccan—whose named escaped him.

Dov frowned at his blurred reflection in the shop window, vaguely annoyed with himself. He prodded his sleepy memory. They'd told him the Moroccan's name, when they'd showed him the photograph. . . .

Bel Jahra—that was the name.

And with the name, Dov suddenly saw again the picture they'd showed him.

Dov became very still as it hit him: The face in the picture was the face he'd glimpsed briefly just before dawn, when the tall man had left the *Shalimar*.

Dov turned slowly from the shop window, looking around with eyes no longer sleepy. He saw that Dietrich had already passed him, and was entering the *capitainerie*. Still absorbing the significance of his discovery, Dov strolled to the *capitainerie* and paused by the opened door, lighting a cigarette as he listened to the voices inside.

Dietrich was settling his docking facilities bills, in preparation for a permanent departure from the Beaulieu marina.

Dov turned and walked quickly to the nearest public phone booth.

The night was pleasantly warm, and cloudy without menace. The clouds were in high, stately movement across the sea, with open patches of black sky cluttered with stars. The awnings and braziers that Juliet Shale had arranged as precautions against rain and cold proved unnecessary. The benign night seemed to have been ordered especially for Dezso Valasi's eightieth birthday party. There was nothing to spoil the jovial mood of the guests assembled around the wide lawn behind the house—over seventy so far, with more still arriving. But Gilbert Soumagnac, the insurance company's chief security man, did not share in the general festive spirit.

Soumagnac was furious. The case of his fury was the unexpected arrival of the King of Jordan, a few minutes ago. He was shocked by the stupidity of Juliet Shale's failure to inform him earlier, so he could have made the proper arrangements for increased security.

He tried to keep his anger under control and his opinion of her intelligence to himself, as he led Juliet aside for a private talk. But some of what he felt came through. Juliet was unimpressed. She considered that she had acted properly in keeping the secret, and explained this to Soumagnac. The security man gritted his teeth and asked her, with some pain, if she had any further surprises in store for him.

It was then that she told him about the one still to come. Not because she was intimidated; but because she judged that the time for secrecy was past. Soumagnac made a low growling sound, deep inside his massive chest. He turned away from her abruptly, and went off across the crowded lawn to rearrange the positioning of his small security force.

Bel Jahra, having his glass refilled at the bar the catering staff had set up on the right side of the lawn, watched Soumagnac go about it—noting precisely the changed positions of Soumagnac's three plainclothes guards. He knew about the fourth, stationed somewhere close to the sea cliff beyond the trees. Soumagnac did not go off to bring in that one, but left him where he was. This did not worry Bel Jahra. He had already taken into consideration the unseen presence of that fourth guard, so close to the ruins where his guerrillas were hidden.

Bel Jahra had had ample time to himself, since arriving for the party, for a complete final reconnaissance of the actual situation in which the operation must be executed. He and Juliet had their assigned seats at one of the smaller tables fanning out across the lawn from the main table on the rear patio. But Juliet had been far too busy since his arrival to exchange more than a few hurried words with him. Which left Bel Jahra to do pretty much as he wished: to drift around among the other guests and reconnoiter, fixing each vital element in his mind.

The most important elements, of course, were the two targets of the operation, and their positions. One had now arrived: Jordan's King Hussein ibn Talal. He sat at the main table on Valasi's right, a short, muscular, youthful-looking man dressed casually in a sports jacket and slacks, smiling easily as he chatted with the old artist.

Though the second target had not yet arrived, it was obvious where he would be seated when he did. There was only one unoccupied seat remaining at the main table, on Valasi's left. This brought Bel Jahra's planning down to the last-details stage. But the execution must continue to wait, until that last seat was occupied. Bel Jahra had no way of knowing how long that wait would have to be dragged out: another few minutes, or an hour.

He kept his nerves under tight control as he left the improvised bar with his drink, strolling with apparent aimlessness among the other guests. Pausing occasionally to sip his drink, or exchange pleasantries about the weather with other strolling guests. Establishing his presence. Giving everyone—especially the security men—a chance to grow used to him as part of the normal, general ambience of the party.

The security men were the elements of second importance to be taken into consideration. Two burly, blank-faced men had arrived with Hussein. They wore gray silk business suits, the jackets very loose on them so the bulge of the guns they wore in shoulder holsters were not too obvious. They sat at one of the three tables between the main table and the lawn, almost directly behind their King. One sat facing the table and house; the other sat across from him, facing the lawn and the bulk of the party guests.

Bel Jahra was certain more bodyguards would have come with Hussein. One had probably remained outside the estate, with his limousine; out along the dark road where several local uniformed policemen were also stationed. Perhaps another bodyguard was stationed just inside the entrance to the estate, where one of Valasi's tough-faced nephews leaned against the gatehouse eyeing new arrivals with stolid silence.

On arriving, Bel Jahra had noticed a slight irregularity in the shadows along the gatehouse wall beside this man. Bel Jahra had paused and bent to retie his shoelace there, giving himself time to see what the irregularity was: a short-barreled shotgun.

Also stationed at the entrance was one of the catering staff. As each new car drove up to park, this man used the gatehouse phone to alert the main house. Then Gilbert Soumagnac, sometimes accompanied by Juliet Shale, went out to receive the guests, identify them, and bring them into the estate.

The guards at the entrance, and outside it, did not interest Bel Jahra much. Once the attack began, they could not possibly get from the estate entrance to the scene of the assault in time to affect its execution in any way. The guards of most interest were the ones protecting the main table on the patio:

There were the two Jordanese bodyguards. At the small table next to theirs were two empty chairs. These were obviously reserved for the pair of bodyguards who would arrive with the American Secretary of State. And Soumagnac had just stationed one of his security men at the third small table. That made *five* armed men between the targets and the lawn.

On the other side of the main table was the rear of the house. It was into the house that Soumagnac had just sent his other two security guards. Bel Jahra had glanced in a side window earlier, and seen another of Valasi's male relatives in the big sun-room near the open doors to the patio; seated on a couch under which the stock of a rifle or shotgun protruded a bit. With the addition of the two insurance company men, that made three armed guards on the house side of the main table. Plus the five in the open, on the other side of the table.

The approach was going to be very difficult. Bel Jahra continued to stroll about, sipping at his drink, smiling at other guests, and reassessing the approach situation from different angles. At the deep end of the lawn, near the dark profusion of trees and hedges that concealed the area of the sea cliff and ruins, a three-piece orchestra was playing waltzes. A few couples were dancing on the grass there. But most of the guests were at the tables that took up most of the rear lawn, or standing in small clusters chatting. The catering staff had set up its serving center on the right side of the lawn. Across the lawn, on the opposite side, were the tables for the children of guests, the puppet show to keep them amused, and two female members of the catering staff with nursemaid experience to oversee them.

The approach to the children would be the easiest part of the operation. There were hedges and flowering bushes flanking this area. Using these as cover, Hammou and Kurfi could be among the children before anyone was aware of them. Bel Jahra counted sixteen children in all. The smallest were four or five years old. Bel Jahra noted their table. These were the ones to be seized, as hostages.

Rasul, Abu, and Samoud would have to make their approach through the trees on the other side, behind the catering center. There was no way for them to get near enough to the main table without being seen during the last stage of the approach. They would have to remain hidden just inside the shadows among the trees—waiting for the signal of the first shots before springing into the open and charging the main table with machine-gun fire and grenades.

Those first shots would be Bel Jahra's and Khdanni's, fired at point-blank range into the heads of the two targets. *They* would *have* to be able to get close to the main table, in plain sight of the bodyguards and security men.

It was time for Bel Jahra to establish his *right* to approach that close, without arousing suspicion.

Juliet Shale was out on the lawn with a recently arrived couple, leading them toward a group of four guests standing in conversation near the three-piece orchestra at the deep end of the lawn. Bel

Jahra watched her and waited. Juliet introduced the new couple to the other guests, lingered for a short while to be sure they jelled, and then turned and started back up the lawn, pausing to exchange pleasantries with guests at the tables she passed. Bel Jahra put his glass on a nearby table and crossed the lawn to intercept her.

He caught her by both hands, halting her progress toward the house and smiling down at her. "Praise Allah! A friendly face . . . just when I need one."

Her laugh was harassed and halfhearted. She shook her head guiltily. "I'm sorry, André. I know I've been neglecting you, but there's *so* much for me to tend to. . . ."

"I know," he assured her. "It's all right. I'm enjoying just being here. We'll have plenty of time for each other, after tonight, when you've finished this chore."

She looked at him gratefully, relieved. "I appreciate your being so understanding, André. I did warn you what it would be like."

He nodded, still smiling and holding both her hands. "Yes, you did. But you also promised me something. I hope you haven't forgotten."

She frowned uncertainly, looking toward the main table on the patio. What she had promised was that she would introduce him to Dezso Valasi. Bel Jahra had made her understand how much he admired the old painter; and how much it would mean to him to have met him. Against this, and her own desire to please Bel Jahra, was ranged Valasi's reluctance to meet strangers. And that Valasi was at that moment absorbed in telling a story to King Hussein; apparently concerning Count Basil Malinov and Natasha Krechevsky, who sat on Hussein's other side.

"He's so involved right now. . . ." Juliet said hesitantly. "Perhaps later. . . ."

Bel Jahra's hands tightened around hers, just a bit. "You did promise."

His smile was still there; but it was on the verge of being a hurt smile. She suddenly felt guilty again. Up at the main table, Valasi was laughing at something Natasha had said. He was in a good mood. . . .

Juliet nodded. "All right," she said bravely, "let's get on with it." Holding one of his hands, she led him up the lawn to the patio.

Bel Jahra was careful not to look directly at any of the security men as they passed them on the way to the main table. But he was sharply aware of their appraising stares, sizing him up—and taking in the fact that Juliet Shale was leading him by the hand.

She hesitated at the head of the table, nerving herself to make the introduction. Valasi surprised her. He looked up, suddenly smiled, and rose to his feet. "Is this the young man you've been telling me about?"

She stared at him in deep gratitude. "Yes . . . this is André. André, Dezso Valasi."

Bel Jahra held out his hand. "I'm honored, sir."

Valasi shook his hand, with surprising strength. "*My* pleasure."

They looked in each other's eyes. Valasi started to frown, slightly; then the smile came back. "I hope you are not going to give me trouble, young man."

"Trouble?" Bel Jahra was hyperconscious of the eyes of the security men on him. At no time did he look at Hussein; or anyone else except Valasi.

"Miss Shale is extremely valuable to me," Valasi growled, the eyes still smiling. "From what I hear, you may be taking her away from me, soon."

Juliet Shale colored in embarrassment, almost closing her eyes. Bel Jahra forced an embarrassed shrug. "Well . . ."

Valasi relented, and laughed. "Well, if you do—treat her well. She is a marvelous girl." He patted Bel Jahra on the shoulder. "Good to meet you." And with that he sat down, shooting Juliet a faintly mocking grin. Like a child who has just surprised his mother, and amused himself, by unexpectedly behaving in front of guests.

Bel Jahra took Juliet's hand and turned away. He still did not look at the armed guards. But they knew him now—as a friend of Juliet's, and Valasi's. They would not be wary the next time he approached, with an arm around Khdanni, as though bringing him over for an introduction to Valasi. They would be able to get as near as they wished to the main table, before drawing their revolvers and commencing to blast apart the heads of their targets. But not *too* near—because of the machine-gun bursts and exploding grenades that would strike at the guards and everyone else around that table, an instant later. . . .

Thoughtfully, Natasha Krechevsky watched Bel Jahra move away with Juliet. "Basil," she murmured, "isn't that the friend whose picture George Shansky showed us, the other morning? The one he was trying to find?"

Basil Malinov thought about it, studying the man leaving the patio. "I'm not sure, dear. . . ."

Natasha nodded suddenly, "I am sure. Handsome devil. Quite sure."

"In that case, we should tell him George is looking for him. Give him George's number."

Natasha patted Basil's scrawny, wrinkled hand. "Oh, it can wait. Later, when the party's ending. . . ." She turned back to the King beside her, and began to recount an amusing story about the time when Valasi was hiding from the Nazis in their house, and her daughter tried to seduce him.

Valasi laughed as he remembered that time. But he was only half listening. The painting he had begun the previous day had been troubling him. Something did not feel right about it. Now, suddenly and for no reason, he understood what was wrong with it, and how to correct it. Though he continued to seem interested in what was going on around him, Valasi drifted into an excited anticipation of the following morning, when he could resume work on the picture.

St. Tropez had been a bust. There were still people there who remembered Bel Jahra, as an occasional vacation visitor. But no one had a semblance of a recent lead to him. It was late when Hunter drove back to Nice, trailed by Shansky's car. He still hadn't had the heart to tell Shansky the job was over.

In Nice, Hunter drove to the consulate and parked out front. Shansky pulled up behind his car, as Hunter climbed out. "You can wait," Hunter told him. "Just checking for messages. You never know."

Getting the spare key the consul had given him, Hunter unlocked the entrance door and stepped inside. In the darkness, he couldn't remember where the light switch was. He slid a hand down one wall beside the door, then the other side, before locating the switch and flicking it on. Squinting against the sudden glare of electric light, he climbed the marble stairs to the lobby. Before going up to his office, he checked on the consular clerk's desk.

There was an interoffice memo addressed to him, under a glass paperweight beside the phone. Hunter removed the paperweight and picked up the square of paper.

The message was from Inspector Ivor Klar: "Juliet Shale is in *your* neck of the woods. She works for Dezso Valasi, at his residence on Cap Martin."

Bel Jahra strolled down to the deep end of the garden. There were eleven couples there now, waltzing to the music of the three-piece orchestra. Bel Jahra strolled around them. When he stopped, the musicians were between him and the dancers. The thickly wooded area that led to the sea cliff was at his back. He stood there with his hands thrust in his pockets, seeming to be idly enjoying the musicians and dancers—but looking past them, up the sloping, crowded lawn toward the rear of Valasi's house. More guests had arrived to swell the partying crowd. There were over a hundred of them now. And one of them was Bel Jahra's final target.

He had just been seated where Bel Jahra had anticipated: at the chair on Valasi's left. The two secret service bodyguards who'd arrived with him had taken chairs close to the main table; between the Jordanese pair and Soumagnac's security man. The waiting was over. The time had come for Bel Jahra to trigger the operation into the execution stage.

A constriction in his chest belied his casual stance as the pale gray eyes scanned all the people on the lawn and patio, picking out certain ones for brief observation. Soumagnac's back was to the lawn as he bent to whisper briefly to his man near the main table. Juliet Shale was near the bar, introducing an elderly local potter to a young sculptress. No one who would have any interest in him was looking his way. Bel Jahra turned slightly, and sauntered toward the edge of the wooded area.

Juliet finished making her introductions, and turned in time to see Bel Jahra enter the shadows among the trees. She felt another stab of guilt for having had to neglect him so much. He was probably bored with the party, and going for a stroll to be alone. On a sudden eager impulse, Juliet started to go after him. She was intercepted by the mayor of a local village. He began to discuss with her, at length, the possibility of Valasi attending a showing the following week of the work of young local artists, at his village church.

When he was completely hidden in the darkness under the close-set trees, Bel Jahra quickened his pace. He drew his hands from his pockets as he moved. In his right hand was a flat blackjack—two lengths of thin, spring leather sewed together, with a quantity of steel pellets packed in one end. A simple weapon. But it could sting, stun, or kill, depending on the skill and intention of the man wielding it.

Letting it dangle from his hand so the shadow of his leg concealed it, Bel Jahra turned sharply left and found the path he remembered. He followed it into the total blackness of the tunnel formed by bushes whose upper branches entwined overhead. Feeling his way through with his free left hand, he emerged into the labyrinth of high hedges. There was starlight here; and his eyes were becoming adjusted to the dark. He found his way through the hedges without difficulty, went down the stone staircase between the double rows of cypress trees, and crossed the miniature bridge at the bottom.

The ruins of the abbey rose ahead of him. Murky, tormented shapes outlined in the starlight, casting black, broken shadows. Bel Jahra angled away from the ruins, toward the top of the sea cliff, once more strolling idly. He reached the edge of the cliff and stopped, both hands hanging down beside his shadowed legs, gazing out at the sea.

Great patches of darkness and starlight moved slowly across the calm surface of the water. There was a long cabin cruiser anchored some distance out. Its navigation lights were on. Another light—a yellowish one—glowed up on its flying bridge. As Dietrich had been instructed. As the clouds moved, starlight enveloped the boat in silvery outline. It *was* Dietrich's *Shalimar*.

The insurance company security guard that Soumagnac had positioned between the ruins and the cliff emerged from the shadow of a tree and came toward Bel Jahra. Turning slightly to face him, Bel Jahra smiled and said, "Hello—again."

The man's slow approach ceased being wary as he recognized Bel Jahra. "Oh, it's you, sir. The party—it is still dull?"

During one of the two visits Gilbert Soumagnac had made out here to check on his man, Bel Jahra had followed. He had acted faintly surprised to find them here; and had explained he was having a stroll to relieve his boredom. Because Soumagnac had admitted Bel Jahra to the party, and been introduced to him by Juliet Shale, the security chief had accepted his presence without suspicion. Which established Bel Jahra's right to be there, for Soumagnac's man.

"It is not dull," Bel Jahra told him offhandedly, "but I always become restless at these large cocktail parties, I'm afraid. Far too many people. Too much noise."

"The music sounds nice, from here." It could be heard faintly, muffled through the trees.

Bel Jahra looked out to sea again. "There is a boat out there."

The security man nodded and looked in the same direction. "It's been there for almost an hour. I had a look through binoculars. A man is fishing from it. He won't catch much out there. Not without a net. The fish left are much too small—"

Bel Jahra whipped the flat blackjack at his head, with a full swing of his right arm and all of his twisting strength behind it. The steel-weighted end thudded across the man's temple. He toppled sideways with a thin cry. A cry that would not carry past the nearest grove of trees. He sprawled on his back and rolled slowly on his side, his arms and legs moving awkwardly, with no co-ordination.

Bel Jahra bent and struck him again, full-force squarely in the middle of his forehead. The small sound the man made in his throat was like a sigh. He rolled face-down in the dirt and lay still, a few inches from the edge of the cliff top. Bel Jahra put a heel to the man's hip and shoved, rolling him limply over the edge. The sloshing of the surf almost drowned the impact of the body striking the jagged rocks below.

Folding the blackjack and slipping it back in his pocket, Bel Jahra turned away from the cliff abruptly and strode into the shadows of the ruins. He squatted beside the hole in the ground near the cloister wall, and called down softly into the remains of the crypt.

One by one they crawled out into the open: Hammou first; then Khdanni, Rasul, Abu, Samoud, and Kurfi. They were slow and stiff from the long, cramped wait. But they did what they'd been briefed to do, with no need for words from Bel Jahra. Khdanni gave him one of the loaded revolvers and a spare box of ammunition. Bel Jahra stuck the gun in his belt, buttoned his jacket to hide it, and slipped the spare cartridges in a side pocket. Hammou gave him the rolled-up nylon ladder, and Kurfi gave him a flashlight.

Bel Jahra carried these back toward the cliff. The others remained in the ruins, immediately beginning a series of limbering-up exercises to get the kinks out of their muscles and their blood circulation back to normal.

At the edge of the cliff, Bel Jahra aimed the flashlight out to sea, at the anchored *Shalimar*. He signaled it: two long blinks, three short ones. Then he moved along the edge of the cliff to the tree stump. Putting the flashlight down, he fastened one end of the nylon ladder to the stump. When it was secured, he pushed the rest of the ladder over the edge, letting it unroll to dangle down the cliff. When he straightened, he saw that the *Shalimar*'s lights were out. The dark shape of the boat was already on the move, gliding slowly in to get as close as it could to the shore rocks.

Bel Jahra picked up the flashlight and returned to the ruins. Hammou and the other five were waiting for him, armed. Rasul and Abu held their submachine guns ready, the ammo clips already attached and the change-levers set for full-automatic fire. Samoud had a grenade in each hand, and two more hung from his belt. Hammou and Kurfi had their pistols out. Khdanni, like Bel Jahra, had his revolver tucked in his belt, out of sight inside his buttoned jacket.

Hammou gave Bel Jahra the folded sketches. Squatting, Bel Jahra flattened both sketches on the ground. He snapped on the flashlight as the others hunched down close around him. Shining the light first on his sketch of the main table, he showed Khdanni which of the small circles around it represented the positions of their two targets: the two on either side of Valasi's position.

Khdanni touched a fingertip to one of the circles. "This one is mine, the other yours."

Bel Jahra nodded. "Remember, keep firing at the head of your man; nothing else."

Khdanni smiled. "After the first three shots," he whispered, "there will be no head left to shoot at."

Bel Jahra did not smile back. He shifted the light to the other sketch: the layout of the patio and lawn behind Valasi's house. He showed them exactly where the main table was, and the tables with the five armed guards; explaining about the others inside the house. To Hammou and Kurfi he pointed out the children's area; the placement of the puppet show and the table containing the smallest of the children. Then his finger moved across the lawn area, to the catering center.

"You will have to remain hidden *here*," he told Samoud, Rasul, and Abu. "Just inside the edge of the trees. Until you hear our first shots. Then, instantly, you break into the open and do your work."

Bel Jahra estimated that their "work," with machine-gun bursts and grenades, would wipe out the armed guards—and everyone else at the main table and close to it—within the first few seconds. He showed Khdanni the exact point to which he would lead him toward the main table. A point close enough for them to make sure of killing their targets; but far enough so they wouldn't be caught by the machine-gun bursts and grenade explosions. The instant the shooting began, Hammou and Kurfi would seize one child each. The instant there was a lull in the firing, Hammou would kill a child they weren't holding, and Bel Jahra would shout his warning.

There was no more to be said. Bel Jahra's blood was racing as he snapped out the flashlight, put it down, and rose to his feet. He started through the ruins in the direction of the lawn area behind the catering center. He was followed by Khdanni, Rasul, Abu, and Samoud. Hammou and Kurfi angled off together to circle toward the other side of the lawn area.

Something moved in the shadows ahead of Bel Jahra, next to the ruins of the tower. He froze, his hand slipping under his jacket to the gun in his belt. A figure emerged from beside the tower, coming toward him uncertainly out of the shadows. It was Juliet Shale.

She stopped, staring in confusion at the men behind Bel Jahra. "André? What . . ."

Hammou suddenly appeared behind her, one hand clamping across her mouth and the other bringing up a knife. She began to struggle, but became still when the cold point of the knife touched her throat. Hammou looked past her head to Bel Jahra.

Bel Jahra drew a breath—and nodded. Hammou drove the knife in and sidewise, severing vocal cords and jugular vein with one hard twist. Juliet Shale's blood gushed out blackly as her entire body spasmed, wrenching loose from Hammou's grasp. She fell to the ground, writhing like a hooked fish, her life pouring from the savage wound. Hammou bent and delicately wiped his knife blade clean on the grass.

With an angry grimace, Bel Jahra led the way around her still-quivering figure and out of the ruins.

Because Shansky knew the area better, his car led the way out into Cap Martin. Hunter drove after him along the dark, curving road. As they neared the Valasi estate, the road became lined on both sides with cars parked bumper to bumper. There were a number of men around the more ostentatious cars who were obviously waiting chauffeurs. There were other men, close to the entrance to the estate, who were obviously not.

Shansky double-parked near these men. Two of them converged on him as he climbed out. Hunter, stopping behind Shansky's car, recognized one of them: Don Yates, a veteran secret service bodyguard. He rammed his car door open and got out fast.

Yates turned and looked at him, startled. "What're you doing here?"

"Which one have you got in there?" Hunter demanded. His voice was unnaturally controlled.

"Woodcutter," Yates said, his eyes narrowing. Woodcutter is the secret service code for the Secretary of State.

Hunter brushed past Yates toward the entrance gate.

The look on his face had Yates automatically reaching for the gun holstered on his hip under his jacket, as he turned to go after him. "What is it?" he growled.

Shansky, striding alongside, told him what it was.

Bel Jahra, with Khdanni beside him, came to a halt behind a dense cluster of high bushes. Samoud was on one side of them with his grenades. Rasul and Abu, with their submachine guns, were on the other side. They were near the edge of the lawn, behind the catering service area. But they could not see the lawn or house, without moving out into the open where they could be seen in turn.

They waited there, allowing more time to be certain Hammou and Kurfi were in position behind the children's area on the other side of the lawn. Then, motioning the other three to wait where they were, Bel Jahra linked an arm with Khdanni's, and led him out of the bushes.

They emerged into the open between one end of the catering center and the rear of the house. Bel Jahra strolled out onto the lawn with Khdanni. And then he stopped.

What he registered first was the beginning of confusion and alarm among the people around the guest tables. Then he saw the cause: several men spreading out swiftly down the lawn, quickly scanning the faces around them—and Soumagnac almost running down the other side of the lawn, with a revolver in one hand.

Bel Jahra snapped his head around to look toward the patio. The people who had been at the main table were on their feet, being moved inside the house. The two Jordanese bodyguards, and the pair of secret service agents, stood with guns drawn facing the lawn, their bodies shielding the patio area. The insurance security man who'd been stationed near them was hurrying toward the catering side of the lawn. He, also, had his gun out. So did the three men who ran out of the side of the house, circling into the wooded area behind the catering center: two with pistols, one with a short-barreled shotgun.

Bel Jahra dropped his arm from Khdanni's, his brain swirling dizzily. He understood with cold clarity what was happening. What he couldn't grasp was *why* it was happening.

In that moment one of the men spreading out across the lawn saw Bel Jahra. It was Shansky. He yelled to Hunter: "There he is!" And started to charge at Bel Jahra.

Halfway to him, Shansky remembered he was unarmed, and began to slow his charge. By then it was too late.

Bel Jahra broke out of his shock, and his reaction was to whirl around to get away. Khdanni was quicker; but not as intelligent. He saw Shansky coming at them, and reacted on instinct, snatching out his revolver and squeezing off two shots so rapidly their explosions blended together. The large-caliber bullets rammed into Shansky's chest, spinning him around and dropping him like a smashed puppet.

The insurance security guard who'd been advancing on the catering area went down on one knee, raised his pistol with both hands, and shot Khdanni in the side of the head.

After that, a number of things happened almost simultaneously:

Bel Jahra drew his own revolver as he sprinted away; but only to be used as a last resort. He plunged into the cover of the wooded area. Not back to where he'd left his other three men. That was too close to the house. He angled off toward the deeper end of the estate, circling in the direction of the sea. It was a sensible decision.

Rasul, Abu, and Samoud reacted to the roar of the gunshots as the signal to begin their part of the operation. They charged out of the bushes, toward the patio area. As they came out into the open, they found a number of men with raised pistols off to their right.

Abu twisted toward them with his submachine gun. Three bullets ripped him off his feet before he could complete the turn.

Rasul threw down his submachine gun, and raised both arms high, standing very still. Samoud looked at the guns aimed at him, and let the grenades fall harmlessly from his hands. . . .

Hunter reached Shansky and went to one knee beside him. Shansky lay sprawled on his back, his chest darkly wet, unmoving. His eyes stared up at Hunter, seeing nothing. He looked surprised. Hunter drew one large, scarred hand gently down over George L. Shansky's face, closing the eyes. Then he rose and went into the wooded area after Bel Jahra.

He was out of sight of the lawn area, deep among the shadowed bushes under a grove of old olive trees, when a single revolver shot sounded off to his right. Going into a crouch, Hunter began circling to the right, keeping to the darkest of the night shadows. He went very cautiously, because he was unarmed. But he went.

A man lay in a heap beside the base of a gnarled olive trunk. One of Valasi's nephews. Bel Jahra's bullet had caught him in the side of his forehead. The shotgun he had tried to swing on Bel Jahra lay beside his crossed hands. Hunter picked it up and moved deeper through the olive grove, searching.

Bel Jahra didn't hear Hunter's movements some distance behind him. But he did hear men moving ahead of him; between him and the sea. He shifted direction and went to the ground, crawling under a heavy growth of bushes. Everything had collapsed on him too abruptly; without reason. He needed time to think. . . .

On the other side of the lawn, Hammou and Kurfi had also taken the first shots as their signal to move in. They emerged from the trees behind the puppet booth and angled quickly around it with their guns held ready, charging at the last children's table to their left.

Gilbert Soumagnac, hurrying down the side of the lawn, saw them—and their guns. He whirled toward them and fired the instant his sights lined up on a head. The bullet smashed Kurfi's face, throwing him against Hammou and knocking them both to the ground. The children around them began screaming, scrambling to get away. Hammou threw Kurfi's limp weight off him, and his left hand shot out, closing around the thin ankle of a five-year-old boy.

He yanked savagely, bringing the boy down on top of him, partially covering him. Soumagnac had swung his pistol to fire down at Hammou. His finger froze, just touching the trigger. Hammou wrapped his left arm tightly around the whimpering child and put his gun to the side of the child's head. He rose on one knee, the child clamped across his chest in the powerful grip of his arm, the muzzle of the gun against the child's head.

Hammou's lips were drawn back from his teeth, like a panting animal. "I'll kill him!" he screamed at the insurance security chief. "Even if you kill me, I'll kill *him*, too!"

Soumagnac remained half-crouched, aiming his pistol at Hammou but not firing, his face a blend of fury and terror. Glancing past him, Hammou saw what was happening on the other side of the lawn, and knew it was over. His eyes snapped back to Soumagnac, who stayed positioned exactly as before, afraid to move because of the child. Other men with guns were closing in from both sides. But they, too, stopped as Hammou rose to his feet and they saw the gun pressed to the crying child's head.

"You have to let me go!" Hammou shouted. "Or I kill the child! If you shoot me I'll kill him as I fall! You can't stop me!" He began slowly backing toward the deep end of the lawn, keeping the gun to the head of the boy clamped to his chest.

That presented Hammou's back to armed men behind him. But none of them were willing to chance it. A shot that hit Hammou might also hit his captive. Even if it didn't, there was too much chance of Hammou squeezing the trigger as he went down. Reflex action could do it, even if Hammou died instantly. The men behind him gave way as he continued to back up, fanning to either side of him. They moved as Soumagnac did, following Hammou and the captive child, but not getting any closer.

When he was certain that none of them were going to make the try, Hammou turned and walked straight ahead into the wooded area at the bottom of the sloping garden, carrying the child and keeping the gun at his head. Soumagnac and the others followed him all the way, past the hedge area and down the stone steps, across the small bridge and past the ruins. But keeping their distance. Afraid of alarming him into shooting his small hostage.

Reaching the edge of the cliff, Hammou stopped and turned again, looking down at the sea. What he saw sent a surge of relief through him. The *Shalimar* was anchored just off the rocks below. The rubber raft was waiting against the rocks as it was supposed to be. With a figure sitting bent forward in it, holding it to the rocks with both hands. A figure that had to be Dietrich, because that was where Dietrich was supposed to be at this point, waiting to paddle them out to the *Shalimar*.

Hammou carried his hostage along the edge of the cliff to the secured top end of the ladder. "Keep back!" he warned Soumagnac and the other armed men, loudly.

They kept back, watching anxiously.

Hammou spoke to his hostage sharply, enunciating each word so the child would understand him: "Wrap your arms around my neck. Tight. We go down the cliff. If you let go of me, you will fall—and die. Understand me?"

Choking back sobs, the little boy put his arms around Hammou's neck, clinging as tightly as he could. Hammou lowered one foot over the edge of the cliff, planting it on the first rung of the ladder. "Don't come any closer as I go down!" he warned the watching men. "If I see any of you along the top of this cliff, the boy dies!"

They stayed where they were. He knew they would continue to obey. He took the gun from the child's head as he used both hands to start down the ladder. They could not risk shooting him now that he was on the ladder. Because he would fall—and so would the boy. Hammou looked up as he carefully continued his downward climb with the boy hanging from his neck. None of the armed men showed themselves at the top of the cliff. They *were* heeding his warning, for the child. Hammou felt relieved, exultant laughter rising in him. He controlled it, going down the ladder rungs carefully, one by one.

He reached the bottom of the ladder. Holding on to its vertical strands with both hands, the gun hanging by its trigger guard from his thumb, Hammou lowered his left leg the rest of the way. As his foot touched the rocks below, he looked up again. The cliff top above was still empty. Hammou seized one of the boy's wrists with his left hand, pulled him away from his neck, and lowered him to the rocks.

Until that instant, Uri had remained pressed flat against the dark base of the cliff, part of its shadow. The second Hammou lowered the child, Uri launched himself away from the cliff wall. He dove at the boy, both arms spreading wide. His right shoulder struck the child, tearing him from Hammou's grasp.

Uri's arms snapped shut around the boy as his driving momentum carried him off the rocks. They plunged into the water locked together, sinking from sight as Hammou spun around bringing his gun into firing position.

Dov Tohar straightened from his bent-over position in the rubber raft, bringing up a stubby Uzi submachine gun. The brief thunder of its stuttering burst echoed off the cliff wall. Five bullets slashed across Hammou's chest, driving him backward and nailing him to the base of the cliff. Then the thunder ceased. Hammou sank in an inert heap on the rocks.

Up on the top of the cliff, Soumagnac and the other men, rushing to find out what had happened, looked down as Uri rose to the surface with the choking, sputtering child. Treading water, Uri handed the boy up to Dov, and then hauled himself up onto the rubber raft with them.

Some distance from Soumagnac, Bel Jahra lay in deep shadow near the edge of another part of the cliff top. He, too, saw what had happened below. And read what it meant for him. There was no escape for him down that way.

It might still be possible to escape from the Valasi estate in another direction. But it was more possible that he would be spotted, and killed in the attempt. And, in spite of his failure, Bel Jahra did not want to die. He was too sensible to think that death would solve anything. Too sensible to believe that life could hold nothing further for him.

Time, he knew, changed everything. In time, change could come to his country through other means; other men's plots. And he could still be part of it—if he lived. With enough time, this failure would be forgotten. Other opportunities would present themselves. If he lived. And to live, he must now surrender himself to the authorities of the law.

There was little to fear, once he had surrendered. It was more than possible that the French government would consider that there was not enough real evidence of his complicity in this plot, to bring him to trial. If they did try him, it was more than likely he would not be found guilty. Even if he was, he would soon be released. Along with his other surviving guerrillas, as a goodwill gesture to the Arab nations. Or as part of a freeing of all Arab prisoners, the next time a guerrilla group seized a planeload of hostages.

Bel Jahra was as aware as anyone that no Arab terrorist had ever spent more than eight months in a European prison. So he reasoned; and did the sensible thing: He put the revolver on the ground and got to his feet without it. Spreading both arms above his head, his fingers open to show that his hands were empty, he walked slowly along the edge of the cliff toward Soumagnac and the group around him.

They turned, staring, as they saw him calmly approaching them, his hands in the air.

"I am not armed," he announced firmly. "I place myself in the custody and protection of any officer of the law who has the proper authority."

Hunter stepped out of the shadows with the shotgun and squeezed the trigger. The gun boomed like a small cannon. The concentrated load of steel shot smashed into Bel Jahra's stomach and broke him in half as it flung him off the cliff.

Hunter didn't wait to watch him fall. He put down the shotgun, turned, and walked away.

TWENTY-TWO

At nine the following morning, Odile Lamarck left the house and went down to Villefranche to get fresh vegetables and meat at the morning markets. It was almost noon when she returned to the house. Her father was on the upper terrace, pruning rosebushes. He looked at her, and then told her what had happened the night before. All of it.

She listened gravely. When he was finished she said, "Shansky's death isn't his fault. He knows that. None of it is."

"He knows," Lamarck agreed. "But . . ." He finished with a slight shrug. Some things, he decided wearily, he was getting too old for.

"Where did he call from?" his daughter asked.

"He's here." When she looked toward the main room he said: "Down in the bedroom. He's exhausted. Emotionally, more than otherwise, I think. But he didn't want to be alone."

Odile considered that as she went into the house and deposited her shopping baskets on the table. She stood there for several moments, gazing out the windows at the sea far below. Then she took her pack of Gauloises and some matches, and went out.

Lamarck had shifted to the far end of the upper terrace. He watched Odile go down the steps to the second terrace.

Quietly, she pushed open the door and stepped into the small bedroom. The shutters were closed, and the room was dim. But she could make out the man sprawled out under the bedsheet in deep sleep. When her eyes adjusted to the dimness, she could see him better.

Picking up a clay ashtray, Odile sat down in the low wicker

chair beside the bed and lit a cigarette. The scratch of the match didn't waken Hunter. She drew her bare feet out of their sandals, and put them on the edge of the mattress. That didn't wake him, either.

Odile placed the ashtray on her lap and leaned back in the wicker chair, smoking and watching Hunter sleep.